FRANKLIN HOBBS AND THE QUAGMIRE OF DARKNESS

D. HUDSON HALLOW

For information, or to order additional copies, please contact:

Beacon Publishing Group
P.O. Box 41573 Charleston, S.C. 29423
800.817.8480| beaconpublishinggroup.com

Publisher's catalog available by request.

ISBN-13: 978-1-949472-89-9

ISBN-10: 1-949472-89-2

Published in 2019. New York, NY 10001.

First Edition. Printed in the USA.

www.dhudsonhallow.com

Illustrations and cover art designed and drawn by Matthew Allan

*Dedicated to
my wife, Jennifer,
for being a constant
source of encouragement,
ideas, feedback,
and above all, patience!*

PROLOGUE
TOGETHER TIME & A TOUGH QUESTION

From his perch behind the bushes, he could see clearly through the open shutters and into the house, although they couldn't detect him. The woman and boy were there. He could barely keep from trembling as he thought about the upcoming events of the night. His hunger would be quieted… and it would be so gratifying to put an end to this human boy once and for all.

Now he would just have to wait until the house was dark. He sunk down into the weeds.

Nearby, flies buzzed.

****

In the middle of the dreary room was a lime green sofa. It had once merely been a fashion nightmare, but now its wool fabric was tattered and timeworn as well. It was a couch most people would cast off as rubbish. Nevertheless, Franklin Hobbs lounged on it, snuggling close to his mom. Several of the rusted cushion springs had forced their way up through the fabric, poking him in the back, but it didn't bother him, there was nowhere else in the world he would rather be.

In front of them was an undersized television on a card table that looked like it might collapse at any time. Every few seconds, when the show they were watching switched scenes, the level and hue of light coming from the television screen changed with it, delivering new pulses of balefire intensity on the walls and ceiling. This caused the poorly lit room to blaze brightly for a split second before falling back into darkness. The fantastic shadows that flickered and flared against the wall made it seem as if a miniature lightning storm had found its way into the house and was now suspended above the couch where they sat.

It was a nature show that was playing on the television; one in which the King of the Jungle, a tremendous lion with a thick, blonde mane, was about to win a death race with a spindly-legged gazelle.

When the beast had finally snared the gazelle in its unforgiving jaws and had begun to feast, Franklin scrunched up his face and asked, "Mom, why should that lion get to live, and the gazelle has to get eaten?"

His mom paused, "Good question, kiddo," she said.

These were the moments his mom, Angel, lived for; lounging in pajamas with her son, watching nothing in particular. It was Sunday night, and she had been working all weekend at the store, barely getting to spend any time with Franklin at all since he had gotten off the bus Friday. He had been by himself all day and now wanted to stay up late with his mom, who was happy to oblige. She figured that maybe he could sleep in late in the morning and make it to school by lunch. After all, tomorrow was his birthday.

"That's pretty tough to answer, honey," Angel finally replied, looking down at Franklin. Her fragile boy lay on the couch, resting his head on her lap.

"I'm not sure I can give you a good reason, except that in this world there are predators and then there are the prey. That's just the way things are I guess; the strong get to eat the weak." As she talked, her own confusion about nature's unjust selection process became evident to her.

On the screen, other lions from the pride had come to join in the savanna picnic. "But... it sure is hard not to feel sorry for the poor gazelle," Angel said, thinking out loud.

"Which are we, predator or prey, mom?" the boy asked drowsily, turning away from the gory documentary, his eyes heavy with sleep.

As she tousled his blond hair around in her fingers, Angel pondered the question. How could she tell him how she really felt? They, mother and son, were the underprivileged, the down-and-outers. They were the prey.

When she heard the steady sound of snoring coming from below, she knew that she would not have to answer his question. At least not now. She carefully lifted his head off her leg and laid it back on the cushion. Slowly, she stood up, her muscles ached from a long day of being on her feet at the store, helping check out customers. After turning the television off, she went back to the couch to pick up her son. She looked at the rusted wheelchair that sat next to the couch and decided against putting him back in it. Not wanting to wake him, she scooped him up in both arms and carried him carefully to his bedroom. There, she laid him down in the racecar-shaped bed, which earlier that day she had salvaged from the end of a driveway.

It had been garbage.

But someone's junk was now her boy's treasure.

Angel quickly got the wheelchair from where she had left it in the other room and rolled it next to his bed. She wanted it to be there in the morning for him when he woke up.

Pulling the shabby covers up to his chin, the way he liked it, she kissed him on his forehead. His feathery hair clung to her sweater for a brief second, static electricity creating a link between them, before letting go and falling back to his forehead. Angel walked out the door, took one last glance at her precious son, and pulled it shut behind her.

Not much later, Angel let sleep overcome her as well, and the house fell silent. Midnight came and went. A few minutes past one in the morning, as Franklin dreamed of racing his new bed up and down the streets, something slipped ever so silently into the boy's room.

CHAPTER ONE
PREDATOR & PREY

It was March 18th, 2015, the eve of his tenth birthday, and Franklin Hobbs was visited by Darkness. It didn't make a sound as it slithered along the worn laminate floor and quietly snaked its way up the headboard of his bed. It certainly knew what it was doing, undoubtedly had done this before, as it surged upwards into the stale air and hovered within inches of his nose, the dark edges of its mass rippling like the dorsal fin of an eel in a slow current.

Out of the inky core of this threatening presence extended a single black appendage, which seemed to pause and study the boy before moving with guarded deliberation towards his face.

Then, like a bowl of jello in the epicenter of an earthquake, the floating mass began to violently shake and quiver, stretching this way and that, making way for something resembling a human head, which now began to protrude up from its top. Another appendage sprouted from its side and developed into an arm, followed by a second on the opposite side. From these blossoming arms shot little stubs that expanded into hands and fingers. At the same time, legs and feet materialized from the bottom of the black sludge, extending all the way down to the floor beside the bed.

A StyJeen, prowler of the dark, stood next to nine-year-old Franklin. It now wore a black sweatshirt, along with a pair of worn out blue jeans. A dark hood concealed its head for only a moment until it lifted a hand to lower it, revealing black hair that flopped down on its scalp like a mop of grungy yarn. This creature was an impersonator of human beings, and every human feature had now emerged from within it.

With one exception.

The smooth, white skin beneath its hair had not yet sprouted any facial features. No eyes, nose, or mouth. Not even a set of ears appeared on the side of its head. A StyJeen had no need for a face.

He (for it appeared to be a male) turned his head down toward the sleeping boy; then, above the creature's chin, the tight skin split open, leaving an exposed hole. Apparently, it did have one facial feature after all; a mouth, from which a wicked cackle arose and echoed out through this newly formed crater. His hand reached menacingly towards Franklin's parted lips, but before he could touch him, the boy began to stir in his sleep.

For such an ominous fiend, the creature surely didn't linger in the small bedroom very long when Franklin, thinking he was lost in a nightmare, cried out, "Mommy!" The faceless apparition, not wanting to be discovered just then or exposed to light, quickly ingested its appendages. Its legs and arms both shrank back into its mass, the head simply melted down into the black sweatshirt, and soon the whole thing had regained its previous form as a pulsating, pitch-dark globule.

The globule fell to the floor with a dull splat, and again it began to shake like it was demonstrating a popular 1950s style dance. But this time the gyrations created an eruption from within it, accompanied by a silent explosion that shot thousands of black flies into the air like lava from a volcano, their wings beating wildly against each other. The insects operated together in perfect sync, with equal energy and dexterity, the same subtle directional changes, like one brain was controlling their movements.

A housefly can beat its wings up to two hundred times per second, and when a great many of these tiny wings are acting together, as they were now, it created a haunting drone, which filled the room.

In its retreat, the horde of black flies darted as one to the window, departed through a crack in the rotted frame and disappeared into the night air.

Beyond the bedroom door, another sound broke the silence. It was the tender voice of his mother. "Franklin!" she called. "Franklin, what's wrong?" Jolted from her sleep, she had come running upon hearing her son call for her. The foreboding clamor of the beating fly wings only added to her set-in panic. The door flung open, and Angel burst into the room just as the Darkness had slipped away. The buzzing had stopped.

She looked down to see her son sleeping soundly in his bed; he had seemingly yelled out in his deep slumber.

Hopefully, she thought, *it was a dream of recreation, like running, riding bikes, and jumping, rather than the other possibility…a nightmare.*

Her little boy had already lived through a real-life nightmare when he was two, and it had taken away his ability to ever walk again.

But here he was, safe, lying in the bright orange racecar bed.

Angel had wanted to wait and give him the bed on his birthday, which was the next day, but the thought of him sleeping on the floor one more night was more than she could bear. So she had driven to the nearest furniture store while Franklin was in school and begged the owner until he agreed to give her one of the used mattresses that had been tagged for recycling.

The bed itself was sitting at the curb of the street with a sign that said 'Free' next to it. She knew right away it was perfect. But, in order to make the bed fit in her car, Angel had to take it apart right there at the end of someone's driveway, and so it had been in pieces in the backseat. She had brought it in, part by part, up the front porch stairs and into their meager two-bedroom house. There she reassembled it in Franklin's room.

The mattress, which had only two or three moderate-sized stains on either side, did not go up the front porch stairs with ease. Once, when she lost her balance, the mattress fell, knocking her backward onto the ground. Determined, though, she finally managed to get it inside and position it on the racecar frame.

When he came home from school that day, his eyes grew as big as saucers upon seeing the orange racecar in his room where the pile of old sleeping bags usually lay. His tears flowed. Joyous tears.

"Happy early birthday, Franklin!" she told him.

He had crawled from his wheelchair to the bed, managed to pull himself up onto it and then lay with his arms above him, stretched out in glee; he would have jumped up and down on it right then if he were able to.

"Mom, this is unbelievable! But how did you... Thank you so much! I love it!" he had been able to say, despite his onset of emotion.

And he truly did love it. In fact, the peeling orange paint and the rusty screws, which held the frame together, hadn't even remotely bothered him. If it hadn't been for the fact that his mom told him they could stay up and watch television, even though it was Sunday, he would have gone to bed early simply to be with his new bed. But he did not want to miss out on spending time with her.

Angel had to smile, thinking about her little boy, how he had insisted that he cook dinner for her that evening. He had made their favorite Italian dish, Chicken Risotto, and his attention to detail, using the precise amounts of rosemary, thyme, and garlic had made her proud. Yesterday, she had mentioned that they hadn't had apple crisp for dessert in a while, so he made it for her. Although Franklin had to do everything from his wheelchair, his limited reaching ability had never deterred him from preparing a meal. His mom had to help him get some of the ingredients, which were higher up in the cabinets, but everything was put on the kitchen table, where he was able to work.

Now Franklin slept soundly again, the only disturbance Angel could see was a house fly fidgeting on the corner of the bed. Angel swatted at it, and it zigzagged away into the darkness.

Relieved and a bit apprehensive, she left the room with the door ajar so that a stream of light cascaded in and landed on Franklin's face, highlighting his blissful countenance.

Angel had decided there was no danger to her son and chalked the ominous sound that she had heard up to a car or motorcycle tearing through the streets of their neighborhood. An event that happened far too frequently where she lived.

As Franklin lay there in the cozy glow of the hall light, something else emerged, this time coming from a vent that brought in fresh air from the outside. The new intruder casually glided across the floor towards the treasured racecar bed and the sleeping boy.

CHAPTER TWO
A MISERY & A MIRACLE

The modest room, previously lit only by the crevasse between the open door and the molding, now began to take on a new radiance. A radiance that arose from the latest trespasser in the bedroom. It started with the dazzle of distant starlight, and then, as the glowing advanced closer to the bed, it grew even more blazing and brilliant. The source of the light slowly rose above the floor and suspended itself so that it was level with the boy's face. Its lavender luster burst forth with such profound intensity that the room seemed to be ablaze with a purple, torrid flame. As he slept on his side, the light approached Franklin's face and made a quick movement towards his exposed ear, disappearing down the canal and into the depths of the boy's head. The room was dark once again, and Franklin only adjusted his sleeping position so that he lay now on his back. No cry for Mommy or even a slight sign of alarm on his face.

But then his eyes opened. Wide. He did not move or even blink and had not woken up. The light, which previously had been radiant enough to engulf the entire room, now stabbed again at the darkness, escaping from within the boy's face. His eyes shone brightly from the inside, beaming like a powerful flashlight. The pale skin on his face, which had always made him appear sickly, now was bright and balmy. Each strand of his blonde hair seemed to act as a vessel for the light, giving his hair a violet hue. The light escaped through his ears and nostrils, casting wild shadows on the walls of his room.

A tranquil smile spread across Franklin's face, and in this dream-like backdrop, one might have mistaken him for a heavenly cherub.

In an instant, however, the jubilation was over. The unusual light was gone, as if flipped off by a switch. Once again, Franklin turned over on his side and continued his steadfast sleep.

Just as it had entered, the source of the light used the ventilation to exit the house, and nothing else disturbed Franklin that night.

When the sun rose only hours later, Franklin woke. He bound into his mom's room and jumped onto the comforter that lay spread on the floor. Beneath this blanket, on the carpet, was where his mother slept each night. Angel, still slumbering, pulled her son next to her and held him tight, even in her sleep.

"Mom, wake up!" Franklin yelled, tenderly shaking her arm. "Something amazing has happened!"

Angel had little trouble waking up, she had been in the midst of her own recurring nightmare, and her relief to see Franklin next to her was evident; almost as if she had been given a reprieve from torture. The nightmare she had been experiencing that morning, and for the last eight years, was not just an unconscious hysteria. It wasn't a prophetic-type dream about something bad that was coming for her. The dreams pursued her because the awful events they depicted had already happened. When Franklin was only two, he had tumbled out the door of her moving car.

****

Angel was sure she had buckled his car seat in that morning, almost eight years ago now. Positive. She would never do something as careless as leaving the seat unbuckled. Her son unprotected.

True, she had been frantically trying to make it to her work on time after waking up late, but she *always* had a mental list of safety precautions that she would check off, one by one, as she accomplished them. Stove off. Check. Toaster unplugged. Check. Door locked. Check. Both car seat and Franklin safely buckled into the backseat of her red, compact 1986 Volkswagen Rabbit.

Check and Check.

'Compact' actually made her car sound larger than it was. This was practically a tin can on wheels.

After finally leaving her apartment and traveling for a few minutes through the awakening neighborhood, she took a quick glance into the back at Franklin. She breathed a sigh of relief. Her son was smiling back at her, his bright blue eyes twinkling from the reflection of the car's overhead dome light.

Despite her husband's quick exit from her life only months before Franklin's birth, she and her toddler were surviving. They still had each other, and up to this point, they still had their health.

Daylight had not yet reached Abundant Lakes, Minnesota, and as she turned her eyes back to the road, the person had suddenly appeared out of the dark, only ten feet in front of the car. The woman, for Angel surmised from the long hair that it was most likely a woman, lurched backward, almost as if it were the gleam of the headlights that frightened her more than the vehicle itself. She made no attempt to get out of the

Volkswagen's path, and Angel swerved the car sharply to avoid hitting her.

Angel whispered to herself, "Oh, no," then screamed out, "Franklin, hold on!"

She knew her two-year-old couldn't comprehend what was happening, but the warning came from her lips, regardless. When she veered left, Angel had thought the swerve was severe enough to miss the mysterious woman, but the car still struck her. The woman rolled up onto the hood and wracked the windshield. For a split second, Angel could see the lady up close and personal as she struck the glass. A black hoodie, jeans, long jet-black hair, and…something else.

To Angel's puzzlement, even though the front of the woman's head was right there on the other side of her cracked windshield, she had no memory, no recollection, of what the stranger's face looked like. Almost as if she had no features on her face at all.

What happened next was a detail that Angel's unconscious memories always made sure to include when they haunted her at night. As quickly as the woman's body had battered against the windshield, it burst apart like some sort of awful fireworks display into a myriad of black fragments which scattered all over the road. Angel's confusion at this bizarre phenomenon was only made more severe by the high-pitched scream that came from her car's brakes as the vehicle continued to skid in a circular pattern, finally colliding into an ancient oak tree along the boulevard.

She yelled out something incoherent as one of the thick, lower-hanging branches smashed through the rear window on the side where Franklin was strapped in, causing glass to shatter into the car's interior. Angel felt the glass hit the back of her head and wedge into her hair. The Volkswagen came to an abrupt halt; its front end stuck out from the ditch, and the tree branch had become lodged into the rear window like a giant hand reaching in to take Franklin from her. Almost as fast as it had happened, everything was quiet again. Not a sound came from the backseat, and the jungle of leaves and branches blocked her view of her little boy.

Panic set in. She needed to get back there and try to open his door.

Now!

As she frantically grabbed the handle to throw open her own door, something that appeared in the car's side mirror caught her eye. Behind her.

There was an object on the street, in the area where she had first struck the woman. She catapulted herself out of the car and began sprinting to see what it was, but after a few steps, she knew. It was Franklin's blue car seat; somehow it had fallen out of the car... and it wasn't empty.

At thirty-five miles an hour through a residential area, Franklin had tumbled three or four times on the blacktop after plummeting out of the car door. He lay there now. Perfectly still. Only occasional muted cries rose from him. Events became a slow-motion sequence to Angel as she ran toward him. It seemed to her as if she would never reach her injured son. Memories of Franklin flooded her mind: his first teetering steps, the contagious giggling he would erupt with when she tickled him, his tightly clasped hands as he prayed with her at night.

She began sobbing as she ran. Red-hot tears raced down her face. When she finally reached her boy, she carefully unstrapped him and picked him up; her salty tears smudged the dirt and dust that covered his body. Angel turned him over in her arms, examining his wounds. Franklin looked up at her, whimpering softly, confused at what was happening. Her heart broke as she realized that in his two-year-old mind, he probably thought that she had tried to do this to him; that she had betrayed him.

The only thing she was able to say to him, again and again, was, "I'm so sorry, baby. So sorry."

But, after looking him over thoroughly, she saw that he didn't seem to have sustained any life-threatening injuries. A gash in his head that would need stitches, along with several scrapes and bloody scratches, seemed to be the worst of it. She thanked God and held him tightly to her chest as she rushed to the nearest house; she had no cell phone to call an ambulance.

Then, carrying him back to the car, Angel noticed that Franklin's legs were limp, drooping lifelessly, merely bouncing to the rhythm of her step. She found out later at the Children's Hospital that her worst fear was true, her beautiful boy, her perfect little miracle, was paralyzed from the waist down.

After that, Angel had to quit her job, and they were forced to move to a homeless shelter for women, where she devoted every moment of her time to care for Franklin.

Angel never did see an injured woman anywhere in the vicinity of the accident as she carried Franklin to the closest house. Also, she firmly believed that it had only been her imagination that the victim, after hitting her windshield, had shattered into small black shards, which had been thrown in all directions. Being under extreme duress, she decided that her mind must have played tricks on her.

The police had later come back to the scene of the accident and found no sign of an injured woman either. Not even a drop of blood.

Angel remained certain that she had only been imagining things…until later that same day, after the accident, when she caught sight of the woman again at the hospital.

****

In her room now, reclining on the thin carpet, Angel's eyes fluttered open to see her son staring down at her, an eager smile on his face.

"Happy Birthday, honey! You're ten today!" she said, wiping the sleep from her eyes. Then, glancing around her bedroom, she asked, "Where's your wheelchair? You didn't crawl in here on the dirty floor, did you?"

Still smiling, he playfully shook his head no, not yet alluding to his surprise.

Her voice cracked, "Well then, how did you—?"

Angel didn't have time to finish the question before Franklin stood up, jumped off the comforter, and ran around the small room as best he could without crashing into the walls.

At first Angel's eyes grew wide, and her face gave off a deep, pink blush, but soon the pink blush modified into a pale sheen as she gasped and then promptly passed out.

CHAPTER THREE
A CELEBRATION & A SURPRISE

"Here Mom, this will help." Franklin held his mother's head in his lap, her long dark hair fell onto his legs and to the floor around him. He gently applied a cool washcloth to her forehead, rubbing the washcloth over her temple and eyes, mimicking what she had done so many times before to him when he was ill. He then lifted a glass of ice water to her mouth, which she accepted eagerly.

"I guess you were probably pretty shocked to see me run around like that, huh?" Franklin asked, smiling, though he knew the answer. "I guess I should've maybe told you first, to prepare you, but I was just so excited."

For the second time that morning Angel's eyes fluttered open to see Franklin looking at her.

Angel Hobbs was a stunning woman, whose beauty, even at thirty-six, had not yet peaked. Life had been hard on her;

she had to struggle for anything she had ever had, yet not one wrinkle or scar appeared on her delicate face. Her emerald eyes stared back up at her son.

"Fr…Franklin? I saw you... running... and jumping…" she managed to sit up, "How did this happen? When did this happen?"

Franklin thought hard, "I'm not sure, Mom. I had a really terrifying dream last night and —"

Angel interrupted, "Yes, I heard you scream out for me. I came in to check on you, but you had already gone back to sleep."

"I don't remember what I was scared of…but then…then I had the most wonderful dream," Franklin said, recalling the range of emotions he had experienced during the night.

"What happened in your wonderful dream?" Angel asked, pushing him to recall.

"All I remember is the feeling it gave me. Like being outside, the sun beaming down on me... holding your hand. Safe and warm. When I woke up this morning, I felt tingly. I felt…my legs! At first, I thought it was just one of those weird, creepy feelings I get sometimes, like when my leg itches, but it's just my brain doing something weird because when I go to scratch it, it's still numb…"

"But it was different?"

"But," Franklin continued, "when I reached for my wheelchair and pulled myself near it, I could *feel* my legs moving along the bed! I stood up, really slowly and started walking, then running, to your room. You know the rest…" he trailed off. "What do you think happened, Mom?"

Up until this point, Angel had remained calm while Franklin told his miraculous story. Almost like she was a detective conducting an interview. But now the tears flowed easily, as they had when she had picked his limp body off the street eight years ago; only this time they were tears of joy. She sat up and in between sobs, said, "Franklin, a miracle happened! Stand up and let me see you. Let me see you walk! Let me see you jump!"

Doing what his mom asked, Franklin began dashing and dancing around the room, skipping over the pile of bed covers, and hopping on top of the threadbare armchair in the corner. Shouts of exuberance and hilarity filled the room, from both boy and mother.

How many times had they looked outside to see other children scampering around playing games and going on adventures, not bound by the clumsiness of an aging wheelchair? How often had Franklin wept in his mother's arms, while she tried to remain strong for him?

Angel had never let Franklin see her cry for him; she never wanted him to think that there was a reason to cry. But now…now!

In a way, the bad hand that life had dealt Angel and Franklin had been the primary reason they were able to develop a bond that most parents and their ten year old could not claim to have. *She* was all he had, and *he* was her treasure, her life.

He came to a halt in front of her now and laughing, asked, "Do you want to see me do it again?"

It went on like this for a while, both of them soaking in the wonderment of last night's miracle.

The rambler-style house they lived in was an eyesore in a neighborhood already full of decrepit homes. Much of the stucco siding had fallen off, and the parts that hadn't fallen had turned from white to a dismal yellow. The window shutters, once an attractive feature of the home, now were in need of nails to hold them up and some paint to bring them back to life. Angel did not have the time to care for the lawn, and so long weeds and overgrown grass gave the house an abandoned, ramshackle look.

Two large weeping willows in the front yard, at one point majestic, were now close to pathetic; their leaves dwindling because of parasites. The condition of the yard, along with the peeling paint, crumbling brick, and swaying roof would be enough cause for most people to demolish the house and start over.

Angel and her husband had been married for three years before he had tragically died of heart failure, something that the doctors had said was genetic in his family. They had accumulated only a few possessions in the small apartment where they used to live in downtown Abundant Lakes. Angel had received the eviction notice from the manager of the building only a few weeks after Franklin had become paralyzed. Rent was four months overdue, and she and Franklin had just weeks to get out. They would be moving to a shelter, and any furniture they had could not come with them. She would have to start all over again.

The home they now occupied had belonged to Angel's aunt. This eighty-something-year-old woman was Angel's only family member, besides Franklin, who lived in Minnesota. That was, until she had passed away two years ago. Her Aunt Addie, for some reason, had decided to leave the house to Angel in her final will. Angel had always assumed it was probably out of a sense of guilt.

Aunt Addie had never really helped Angel when she was alive. In proof, after Franklin was born and Angel had to leave her apartment, her aunt had offered no assistance at all and seemed to be all right with Angel and her toddler living at the local shelter.

Upon Aunt Addie's passing, Angel and Franklin had attended her funeral; in fact, they had made up one-third of the six people that were there. One of those was Aunt Addie's estate lawyer. When the lawyer had approached Angel and told her that the house was hers, she had laughed in his face and then promptly apologized when she realized he was serious.

Now it *was* hers. No more living in a shelter with thirty other women and children, although some of the ladies had become her close friends. Tiny and dilapidated as this house was, it was more than she had ever had.

They lived off the small paycheck that Angel received for cashiering at the local grocery store. She had gotten the job the day before they moved out of the shelter. It didn't give them enough to buy new furniture, nice clothes, or the latest toys, but it covered the necessities: electricity, heat, water; those sorts of things.

Food wasn't an issue. Once a week, Angel was able to bring food home that had passed its expiration date. All sorts of food. Her boss, not really trying to be a generous man, didn't care what happened to the expired food as long as he did not have to deal with it. So Angel took what she needed and brought the rest over to the shelter that had been so kind to her and Franklin. She had become quite the cook and had taught Franklin many of her recipes as well. French and Italian cuisines were their favorite, but both enjoyed the greasy hamburgers and pizzas that made it on their menu once or twice a week.

Angel's cashier job allowed her to be home by the time Franklin's bus dropped him off. Since they didn't have a ramp for the wheelchair, she would carry him up the stairs and then go retrieve the chair. Inside the house, there were two bedrooms and a living room, which also served as a kitchen. All in all, it wasn't even as big as most apartments. They did have a kitchen table, which was another throwaway Angel had rescued. It had been dumped in the ditch on the side of a county road. For kitchen chairs, they used milk crates, ones that were left behind by his aunt. Everything else of Aunt Addie's had been pillaged or vandalized by local hooligans before they moved in.

It was on these milk crates where they sat now, after leaving Angel's room, and ate a breakfast of toast and jam with kool-aid to wash it down.

"So, I was thinking," Franklin started, "this has got to be the two best birthday gifts ever. First of all, my legs work! And second, that racecar bed you got me!" He wiped away grape jam from under his mouth.

His mom laughed, "Franklin, having working legs will be the best present you'll ever get, and even though the bed is definitely nice, it doesn't really compare to walking!"

He pondered that for a second, then, "I guess you're right, but sleeping in a racecar is incredible! Where did you get it from, Mom?"

"I, uh…" Angel didn't want to make the present any less special for him by telling him it was someone's garbage, "Don't worry about where I got it, just know that it was meant for you."

The half-answer seemed to suffice for Franklin, and he happily continued munching on his toast. Angel studied her son as he ate. Not only could he walk again, but he looked so healthy and full of life this morning. His normally pale skin was flush, and his blonde hair seemed to shine. He was a handsome boy; he always had been, especially with his twinkling blue eyes.

That's when Angel noticed one other change that almost made her choke on her toast; Franklin's eyes were no longer blue.

CHAPTER FOUR
A NEW SKILL & TWO SPECTERS

Franklin Hobbs' light blonde hair hung below his ears, and in the front it fell to his eyebrows. He had a natural curl so that his locks gently waved over his eyes. Many times he would arrive at school and his hair would look exactly like it had when he woke up that morning, even though he had spent time combing it. Being told he had a 'hockey haircut' by other kids only caused him to laugh and point to his wheelchair, saying, "Have you ever seen a pair of hockey skates big enough to fit on this thing?"

He looked like a child out of a clothes catalog, with his bright, blue eyes and tough, handsome face. A local modeling company had once contacted Angel asking if she had any interest in having Franklin come in for a casting call. It seemed that a talent scout had come across his picture in a school yearbook and thought he would be a great fit. When his mom mentioned her son's wheelchair to the agent on the phone, he immediately made up some excuse about legalities and insurance; blah blah blah. That was the end of that.

"Franklin Hobbs, look at me!" Angel said.

Franklin looked at her, a bit rattled; she usually used his full name when something was wrong. He met her eyes only briefly, though, before turning his focus back to where it had just been. "Mom, check out all those flies there on the glass." He pointed to the window.

Not quite seven in the morning yet, it was still dark outside. She turned to the kitchen window, and through the smudged glass, with the help of the single light bulb above the table, she was able to make out what looked like twenty to twenty-five house flies moving agitatedly around on the pane.

Disgusted, she said, "Must be something dead out there. I'll check when it's light outside."

Franklin glanced back at her and noticed the anxious vigor with which his mom now studied him. "What? What's wrong?" he asked.

"I can't believe I didn't notice this before. It was too dark in my room, I guess. Your eyes. They're different... not blue anymore."

She leaned over the table, looked right into his eyes, and saw that they were, in fact, a shade of purple. A beautiful, light purple. Some would call it 'amethyst', like the lavender-colored jewel. She didn't look away, so he didn't either, and as she continued to stare into his eyes even more deeply, she detected a luminous quality, a light behind the shade of amethyst. She had a hunch, call it a mother's instinct, that this light, this purple glow, was responsible for the changes, the new strength her son seemed to possess.

Finally breaking the stare, Franklin leaned back and said, "I can see better now, clearer. I guess my eyes were healed, too." He had never worn glasses, mainly because his mom couldn't afford them, but his eyesight had been giving him problems recently, causing headaches at school.

Angel stood up and walked down the hall past her bedroom, about fifteen feet away. She put her hand in the air in front of her. "How many fingers am I holding up?" she asked, a fun quality in her voice, though Franklin knew she was nervous about his eyes.

"Four," Franklin answered.

"No, three. This one's a thumb," she replied, wiggling her thumb and grinning at him as she came back to the kitchen table. "You really can see better, can't you?"

"Yeah, and now I can see even *more,* too," Franklin said, holding his hand up and making a large circle in the air, gesturing towards his mother. "Like all around you, I see colors; magenta, pink, yellow, blue… you know, pretty pastel colors. Somehow I know that it means you have a kind spirit, you're a very good person."

Angel tried to conceal the concern she had over her son's new ability, "Hmmmm. Well, I guess that's true," she kidded. "But you already knew that."

He laughed, "But now I can see it and feel it, too! Your shine of colors, they're showing me what I already knew about you."

She grabbed her son and hugged him, wondering as she held him what exactly had transpired last night. Why did he suddenly have the ability to see colors…auras, around her? Then she reminded herself that her little boy had been healed. He could walk! But whatever benign force had caused such dramatic physical changes in her son had also left him with this peculiar ability.

Despite her name, Angel was never really a religious person. She had always believed in God, and when the accident first happened, she prayed every day for Him to heal Franklin. After the first year, though, her prayers for her son's healing had been much more inconsistent, so had any prayers at all for that matter. At times her requests would only consist of the words, "Dear God, ditto from last night."

She had started to ask herself what the point of praying was, anyway.

Now, though, she wondered if her prayers had finally been answered.

Should she schedule a checkup with the doctor just to make certain Franklin was all right? Out of the question, she decided, unless she saw his health somehow failing. A doctor may want to use Franklin as a lab rat, trying to figure out how his legs could have possibly been healed; why his eyes were different than they had been, trying to use science to explain something that was undoubtedly supernatural.

Then there was the media. They would have a hay day with this, and if she took Franklin to a medical clinic, there was no doubt in her mind the media would be tipped off; probably by some greedy receptionist who was looking for a nice payout in exchange for the medical story of the decade. As a single woman, and mother, Angel had been accustomed to people trying to take advantage of her.

Franklin's voice broke her thoughts, "Mom, my bus is going to be here pretty soon, so I should get ready. Geez, I can hardly wait to go to school! No more having to struggle to get my wheelchair through the halls or going to a special gym class with only me in it. I can be in the regular class! And recess... I can play football with the other guys and—"

He stopped in mid-sentence; as he had been sharing his frenzy of thoughts out loud, an obscure, shady figure had appeared out of the corner of his eye…something, or someone was leaning on the glass where the flies had just gathered. Remembering the nightmare that he had only hours ago, the hairs on the back of his neck stood on end; he turned to look slowly, not sure he was ready for what it might be. In the pre-dawn morning, with only the moon providing any ambient light, he could clearly see the silhouette of someone tall peering in at them. From his position, the angle of the ceiling light cast a harsh glare on the pane of window glass, which made it even more difficult to see what the gangly figure looked like.

"Whoa, Franklin, wait a minute," his mom said. "I don't know that school is such a good idea today. What's everybody going to think? That you have been faking being a paraplegic since kindergarten? What will you tell them? 'I woke up and I was all better, I can even see colors around you now'? That might not go over too well for everyone. We need to think this through for a day or two before you go back to school."

Franklin heard his mom's voice but didn't *hear* his mom, sort of like she was trapped in some other realm trying to communicate with him. He was too busy concentrating on the dark figure in the window. The visitor appeared to be aware that Franklin could see it, but didn't care. Franklin had the sense that it was studying him, looking him over; almost as if it were trying to decide if he might be a worthy adversary. Surrounding its form, Franklin was able to see an aura, as he had with his mom earlier. A 'shine', as he had begun to think of it. But the outlining aura surrounding whoever, or whatever, he saw outside was pitch black; black enough that it still stood out in contrast to the dark background.

As the lurking figure turned away, for a fleeting moment the moon allowed Franklin to discern that it was a man. A man dressed in something like a hooded sweatshirt. But even when the thin beams of remaining moonlight peeled back the darkness, Franklin found that he still couldn't see any features of the man's face. Only pale skin.

As the dark stranger slipped out of view, Franklin ran to the window and looked in the direction he had departed.

Nothing.

He tried to remain calm, not wanting to frighten his mother. Try as he might, however, he was not able to hold back his horror, and so he blurted out, "Did you see that? Where did he go? The man that was there?"

His mom stared at him, not exactly sure how to respond.

Seeing his mom's bewilderment, he said excitedly, "That guy in the window! Didn't you see him, Mom?"

Angel had not been paying any attention to the window and had noticed nothing unusual since seeing the flies several minutes ago. They were gone now.

Franklin continued, almost thinking out loud, "I thought he was staring at me…but I think he was… was missing his face."

Angel's own panic now welled up inside her, and it was her turn to try and keep her young son from being frightened. She casually said, "Uh, no, sorry buddy. Are you sure it wasn't just a shadow from the willow tree?"

"Yeah, I am sure," he paused, "but… he actually did look like a shadow, just not from a tree. More like a…a living shadow. And he wanted something from me. I could feel it."

It was the detail… the detail Franklin had given... 'missing his face'... that had caught her attention immediately, and made her start to go numb with fright. This was far too familiar to her. In her mind's eye, she replayed the awful scene of the woman rolling up on the hood of her car and smashing her windshield eight years earlier.

She had seen that woman again, later the same day. It was in the hospital after it had been determined that Franklin was, indeed, paralyzed; he had been sleeping peacefully in a recovery room, and Angel had used the opportunity to talk to the doctors in the hallway, leaving Franklin alone. No one had entered in the ten minutes she had been standing outside his door.

But when she walked back into his darkened room, a nurse was leaning down over the bed peering closely at her son; stringy black hair hung below her shoulders, some falling near to Franklin's face. Hearing Angel walk in, she turned. In the dark room, with only a spray of outside light coming through the blinds, Angel was able to see that underneath her lime-colored nurse scrubs was a black sweatshirt. The nurse hurriedly yanked at a floppy hood that had been tucked away under her uniform, against her back, and easily slipped it up over her head. This made it even more difficult for Angel to discern her face; especially since the woman had only looked her way for a split second. But in that moment of scrutiny, Angel was positive. Positive that there was no face *to* discern.

That's when the specter flashed a grin with a mouth that had not previously been there. It opened wide. Wide enough to reveal the sharp teeth on both upper and lower jaws that ran the length of the mouth.

Panicking, Angel yelled, "Who are you? Get away from my son now!"

Before she could flip the lights on, though, the woman had just melted away; at least that's what it looked like. The other nurses and doctors, close enough to hear her yelling, came rushing in to find Angel standing by Franklin, who, having been woken from his sound sleep, was wide-eyed with confusion.

The woman had vanished.

Angel thought she had gone crazy that day. Seeing this phantom woman not once, but twice. The police had agreed with her, that she was crazy, although they did not quite phrase it in those words.

A faceless woman eight years ago…and now a faceless man? She blinked hard, trying to rescue herself from this troublesome memory.

Change of plans.

"Honey, I think you're right. You need to go to school. It would be good for you. Go get dressed," she said, trying to hold a smile.

Franklin's face lit up when he heard this and he said, "Really mom? Awesome!" and he took off around the corner.

Angel sat in the kitchen and contemplated her decision. It was better if Franklin was not here right now. What if he really did just see what he thought he saw? It couldn't be a coincidence that on both the morning her son was crippled and the morning he was healed, each of them had thought they'd seen a faceless person.

Could it?

Not likely.

Moving towards the window and peering out into the darkness, Angel saw nothing peculiar. Still, she had an eerie feeling that something was looking back at her. She closed the blinds.

Even though she had already called into work earlier to let her boss know she wouldn't be coming in today, she decided to call him back. Work sounded better than being here alone right now.

After hanging up the phone, Angel considered the idea of packing up what they needed and being ready to leave when Franklin came home from school. They could leave here and go somewhere far away.

That was definitely overreacting. How would they survive if they left? Another shelter? Here they had their own house and she had a job that provided for them, just barely, but they were getting by.

No, they would stay here. At least for now, anyway. For all she knew, they *were* both seeing things. Most likely, the apparition Franklin thought he saw was just a result of his bad dream the night before. Maybe both she and Franklin had an over-active imagination. Like mother, like son.

She tried to console herself and forced another smile. Thank goodness for morning light. The sun was just thinking about poking up over the horizon, and the first song of the morning doves helped soothe her ominous thoughts.

Besides, after hearing Franklin talk about what a blast school was going to be, Angel really had changed her mind about him going. How could she possibly deny him from having the time of his life? Walking and running in the places where he could only wheel around before!

But the students and teachers… what would he tell them? How would he handle the questions that would come his way about his legs? They would be impossible questions for him to answer, at least in a way that would make any sense. All the logic in the world couldn't explain a miracle. What would he say?

Angel reminded herself what a fantastic problem this was for her son to have!

As Franklin hastily brushed his teeth, he thought about what today would be like; he imagined walking off the bus with the other students and then running up the stairs and into the building. The idea was mind-blowing to him. Although he hadn't forgotten the specter in the window, his excitement over the anticipation of what the school day would now bring had, for the moment at least, overshadowed his terror. Later, he could ponder what he might have possibly seen.

Using his newly restored legs, he ran to his room to put on some school clothes. He only had three shirts that were respectable enough to wear to school, and he chose his favorite red one. His jeans, which usually hung loosely on his previously scrawny legs, now fit like they were meant to.

He knew it would be a day that came with a lot of questions, and in his mind, he tried to role-play how he would answer them.

"Play dumb," Angel told him as he put his backpack on, "let them wonder."

He thought about that, then said, "Yeah, which might work for the kids, but what about the teachers and principal? They're going to want answers. I've been in a wheelchair since I started there in kindergarten, Mom. What should I tell them?"

"You tell them you were miraculously healed, and if that doesn't satisfy their inquiring minds, then you tell them to call me. I'll think of something by that time."

Moderately satisfied with this solution, Franklin smiled, hugged his mother, said, "I love you so much Mom!" and walked out the door. Angel started to follow him; he had never boarded the bus without her help before.

Franklin turned back, "Mom, I got this. Now you can watch me get on the bus from the door like the other moms do."

She yelled after him, "I'm proud of you Franklin! Oh, and I love you, too!"

As she watched him walk away, she felt tears welling in her eyes once again. "Thank you, thank you…" She wasn't exactly sure whom to thank for this miracle, but she knew the words needed to be spoken.

Behind her, the buzzer on the stove went off. Franklin's cake was ready. She was baking his favorite flavor, marble with chocolate frosting. Angel closed the front door and went to rescue the cake before it burned. The thought of any danger still lurking in the yard had slipped from her mind almost as rapidly as the StyJeen had slipped away from the window.

CHAPTER FIVE
A SWARM & A SPRINT

It was going to be a splendid day. Minnesota spring was in full-force; Franklin looked at the sun, which had just climbed above the horizon now. Melodies of robins and chickadees splashed the air with notes of revival; nature had begun to take back what it had lost when the long, bitter winter had invaded back in November. That morning, Franklin felt a kinship with nature like he never had before.

He passed under the two towering willow trees that made up most of his front yard. Many times he had gazed out the window at these trees, watching their long branches whistle and whirl in the gentle breeze. He often would imagine what they might say to him if they could talk, the stories they would tell. Their name, "Weeping Willow", was appropriate, for their drooping branches almost seemed to be hanging in despair.

Lately, both trees were looking a bit under the weather as well as mournful. Their leaves were discolored and sparse due to the tent worms that had been using them as a home. These parasites actually gave them something *to* weep about. Now maybe he could help the willows fight back. He decided that when he got home from school that day he would climb his first tree ever and perhaps also fall from his first tree ever, but with him, he would bring a rake or broom to knock down some of the netted homes that the dastardly little worms had dotted the trees with.

In the overgrown grass, right under one of the trees, he noticed something on the ground. Clothing. He dared another step and saw that it was a crumpled black sweatshirt.

Above him, he heard movement.

It was still very early, and the shadows he saw up in the canopy of the trees appeared normal in the dim light. As he stared intently, trying to see what had made the branches move, something began to come down, lowering itself from the shadows. What he saw could only be described as animated blackness... thicker and darker than the mere shadows it had been hiding in. With it was a sinister quality that immediately reminded Franklin of the man he had seen through the kitchen window. It hovered over the lowest branch, appearing to him like a floating oil spill.

He stepped backward, ready to dash if necessary, but his powerful sense of curiosity wouldn't let him leave quite yet. Ripples ran through the black mass like waves in a turbulent ocean. It puffed out and then shrank again; doing this several times before Franklin noticed that it began to separate into thousands of individual pieces. These pieces hoarded together, so they still moved as one, and a steady murmur, like the sound of a mosquito in his ear, came from within them.

The chorus of buzzing grew louder as it came closer to the ground and closer to Franklin, who was still mesmerized by the strange scene. As it finally descended to his eye level, he saw that it had become a great swarm of black flies. He saw the sweatshirt on the ground also began to shed these devilish insects, leeching them off little by little, until there was nothing left of the fabric. The smaller swarm then merged into the larger one and the buzzing became so powerful that Franklin had to cover his ears.

When a section of the swarm molded itself into the shape of a human arm with a hand and reached out in his direction, he wasted no time in sprinting towards the sidewalk where the bus had always met him. Although terror-stricken as he ran, Franklin noticed the thrill that the fresh morning air brought him as it streamed against his face. Something he had never experienced before.

A jab of ice-cold pain sliced into his leg, and he forgot all about his delight in running. It was searing pain, harsh and raw, and it caused him to stumble forward. Even though he had never used his legs until that morning, Franklin was as agile as any other ten-year-old and was able to catch himself with his hands before his face met the grass.

So utterly frigid was his leg, that it muddled his brain and gave him the opposite physical sensation; it felt like his skin was on fire. As he stood up, he glanced down at the source of the pain and shuddered in terror at what he saw. At least fifteen of the jet black flies were attached to his skin and digging into his flesh. But only for a brief moment did they remain as flies. In the next instant, they came together as one and merged into a squid-like tendril of blackened goo, which coiled itself entirely around his lower calf.

He sprinted again. The bus was rounding the corner of his block.

He could hear the supernatural drone of wings beating together, pursuing him, gliding atop the grass. A spidery voice whispered from behind him, "Franklin Hobbssss, where are you going? You have sssomething I…"

He didn't hear the rest or chose not to listen. The lower half of his body, where the goo circumnavigated his leg, began to go numb.

No way! Not now. He had experienced enough numbness in his legs over the past eight years.

The only way to do this was to stop running, which he did. He reached down and ripped the band of slime from his leg, hearing an audible pop as it came off, like a suction cup being released from its surface. Again he shot forward, his strength returning.

Ahead of him, he saw the long, yellow safe haven; only ten more feet. The bus was parked in front of his driveway and the driver had lowered the wheelchair platform. This had been the routine for the last five years, ever since kindergarten, to allow Franklin access. The bus driver had also opened the main door, as he always had done, so that Angel could get on the bus to help Franklin with his straps.

For the first time ever, Franklin flew to the open door, and with the last few breaths that his lungs could muster, he bolted up the three short stairs and down the aisle. It was then that he noticed that the mouths of not only the bus driver but also every student on board had dropped in astonishment as they saw him in full sprint.

He could understand the looks of wide-eyed bewilderment on all of their faces; he knew they were used to witnessing the same, tedious procedure every morning; the motorized platform lifting him up to the ground floor of the bus, his mom coming to help him, and so on. Seeing him like this must be a bit of a surprise for all of them.

Oh well.

Franklin took a seat by himself in the back, gulped in a gallon of air, closed his eyes, and put his head down. He rubbed his leg where first the flies and then the black sludge had covered it. His skin was still icy cold, and a band of raw, red flesh circled his leg, but the pain seemed to be subsiding. The palm of his hand, which he had used to wipe the gunk away, was also stinging.

After a few moments, he found the nerve to put his head up and peek out the window before the bus pulled away. Looking out at the place where he had almost tumbled to the ground, between the weeping willows and the street curb, Franklin could see him. Standing coolly in the prickly weeds and dandelions that had taken over the yard, arms crossed over his sweatshirt, and his pitch-black hair plastered flat to his forehead, was the man whose face was not there. And somehow... somehow he seemed to be glaring back at Franklin.

As the faceless man watched the bus roll away, he opened the only feature he had below his hairline and above his neck, a dark mouth full of bladed teeth, and laughed with all the intensity of a maniac. Then fluidly, almost gliding, he moved towards the street and stood right above the storm drain, which lead to the sewer.

Without eyes, walking should be difficult, but for the StyJeen, eyes were not needed for sight. They were merely a weakness, an invitation for an enemy to enter into the body and cause harm. The facial features which humans needed to hear and detect smell were equally as dangerous. Openings of any kind on the head suggested frailness and fragility, and, if present, might allow penetration into its dark soul. Only to speak, eat, or occasionally cackle, will a StyJeen open its concealed mouth. In their humanoid form, a StyJeen's three main senses; sight, sound, and smell, were absorbed through the pores of its rubbery flesh, which had nerve cells that were constantly shifting and moving and ultimately sending messages to its brain.

Since his kind needed to remain in darkness, humans were not apt to notice this glaring facial abnormality (or *non-facial abnormality*, to be more precise) which they had when disguised in human form. A person would have to get extremely close in a dark area in order to realize that they had no face, and getting close to a StyJeen most likely meant dying; this is how his kind had kept their existence fairly unknown. They rarely let people see them in their human-like form, and when they did, the unlucky person who caught a glimpse of them was destined to be destroyed and consumed, perhaps parts of them were to be gathered for their master, the Lord of Dark Earth.

Occasionally, a human was able to spot a StyJeen and see their disfigurement without being eliminated, but the creatures knew that other humans would not believe one or two of these isolated stories. For that reason, they did not always bother to extinguish the life of everyone who saw their hideous countenance, although they would like to. They certainly found pure joy in eradicating humans. However, Lord Bramfasa, ruler of Dark Earth, had warned them that too many missing humans wasn't in their best interest and would eventually make it more difficult to remain unnoticed.

This particular StyJeen, Nefari, as the creature had been called for thousands of years, was a Gatherer. This was his designation among the others of his kind. It was his job to collect any items that had been gifted to humans by the Luminos, and many times he would be tasked to collect their souls as well.

The job of dealing with this irritating boy named Franklin Hobbs should have been over years ago. One of Nefari's kind, a female StyJeen named Askew, had caused the toddler to become crippled in a car accident. Askew's title among the StyJeen, at that point in time, had officially been 'Guardian and Finisher', and as the Finisher part of that title suggests, she should have ended him then, murdered him, consumed him if she wanted to, but it should have been over. Askew, however, had wrongly figured that the Luminos (which is the name of those uptight henchmen who work for The Suveran) would have no use for a boy who could barely move his body; a boy with legs that didn't work.

Lord Bramfasa had actually agreed with her and had taken her off the assignment, assuming Franklin could never be a threat again. Neither of them could have guessed that the

Luminos would wait until eight years later to heal the boy's broken body, as well as bestow upon him powers from The Suveran.

Now Nefari had to finish the job. The boy Franklin, heir to the throne of Dark Earth, had to die.

In the original plan, Franklin Hobbs was supposed to have been perfect evil like Bramfasa himself. But Askew (it's always that witless Askew!) somehow lost track of him at the hospital when he was born. It took two more years before she found him again, and well, by that time Bramfasa just wanted him dead.

Angel, a human of absolute honor and virtue, had raised the boy, and instead of Franklin experiencing the wonderfully *awful* first two years of his life that Bramfasa had planned for him, the woman had tainted him. She had treated him with that corrupt emotion called 'love'. He was no good anymore at that point. According to Bramfasa, the first two years are the most crucial years when trying to turn a child's soul black. The boy was better off dead.

But that's when Askew failed in the murder attempt and instead put the child in a wheelchair. Why Bramfasa hadn't thrown that good-for-nothing StyJeen into the Void right then was beyond Nefari's understanding.

Now Angel Hobbs had ruined Franklin for *ten* years, and Bramfasa hated her for what she had made the boy into; and yes, she would have to be dealt with eventually. The boy, now that he was a threat again, must obviously die, and Nefari planned on ingesting him whole, if possible, so that his new powers would never be used against Dark Earth and Bramfasa. If he did swallow him whole, he first needed to scoop out those awful eyes, given to the boy by the Luminos only the night before. Along with the child's soul, these two orbs were to be taken back to Bramfasa.

Nefari had his chance last night before Franklin had been given these gifts. After receiving word that the Luminos had been detected moving towards the boy, he had gone to Franklin's home to murder and consume him before they got there. But when the boy hollered out in his sleep, Nefari didn't want to get caught in the possibly fatal light of the overhead lamp (if his mother came in and flipped the light on, which she had).

Awful woman.

And now Franklin had gotten away, made it to the bus. Nefari had not been entirely sure what he would have done if he had caught the boy a few minutes ago, with all of the humans on the bus watching him in the yard. Would he have taken the boy's eyes out, while they all looked on in horror? The thought made him smile.

The sun was coming up now, and Nefari could feel himself growing weak. A StyJeen will wither, shed pieces of its mass, and eventually die in under a minute of exposure to any light from Mortal Earth. Even the current dim light of dawn was hard on him. He needed to rest in the serenity of darkness, for he would require energy in the coming days if he were to eradicate Franklin Hobbs, especially now that the boy had been given some powerful gifts from the Luminos.

Time to go then.

Like last night in Franklin's bedroom, Nefari's whole exterior again started to tremble and quake; within seconds his arms and legs shrank down into his body, his head disappeared into his neck, and the clothes he wore were consumed by the Darkness underneath them. Then he was a black mass, oozing over the pavement. He could bathe in darkness now and maybe find a few big rats to eat.

He slithered and slipped until he disappeared down the rusted grate leading to the sewer tunnels below.

CHAPTER SIX
A MEMENTO & A MEMORY

Out of habit, Angel fiddled with the silver necklace that hung from her neck, running her fingers over the smooth surface of the mother and child at the end of it. She had received this keepsake from a special nurse at the hospital after Franklin's accident, and the shiny cast of a mother holding her boy always reminded her of the day she had carried Franklin in her arms after finding him in the street. It reminded her of how blessed she was that he had lived.

She was looking out her front window now, only seconds after Nefari had taken shelter in the darkness of the city's sewer system.

Shoot! The bus had picked Franklin up already, and she had missed it! Down the road, she heard the shrill complaint of the brake pads as the bus came to a halt at the next stop. It made her grin to think Franklin would be sitting, for the first time, in one of the regular green seats.

Work. She had to get ready for work, but the wonderment of his healing kept creeping into her thoughts. *Amazing. Crazy amazing. My little boy can walk again!*

Her mind drifted back to the day Franklin was born. Ten years ago to the day. From the moment she took him into her arms for the first time, she knew that this boy would be her whole life, the rest of her life. She knew she would do anything for him.

Bringing Franklin into this world had taken all of her strength. She had only been able to hold her brand new baby boy for a little while before feeling like she might pass out. The nurse had taken him from her and brought him to the nursery so she could sleep.

She remembered how she had woken up sometime later, confused, and had become frantic when she realized Franklin was nowhere around. In her groggy state, she had not remembered that he was being cared for in the nursery and so was about to scream for help when she saw *them* in front of her. An elderly man and woman were sitting in two chairs facing her bed. They were a winsome looking old couple, with the warmest of smiles on their faces. In response to Angel's perplexed look, the old man raised his eyebrows; the woman just nodded her head gently.

A deep, soothing voice came from the man, and in a cryptic answer to her silent wonderment, he said, "You are a good person, Angel."

She could see the man's eyes, twinkling deep green as he spoke, "and you will be a great mother." Normally, praise of this magnitude, coming from someone she just met, would not mean a whole lot. But for some reason, this compliment seemed more genuine than any she had ever received.

The elderly woman only continued to engage Angel with her smile until finally speaking herself, "Franklin is sleeping soundly in the nursery dear, we just now came from watching over him." She paused, "He is a very special boy."

She began humming a slow tune that Angel could have sworn she had heard before. So familiar. But that's how she felt about the two strangers as well; they were familiar. An overwhelming peace massaged her thoughts; she nodded weakly in agreement, closed her eyes, and fell back into a deep, undisturbed sleep.

Now, standing there in her house, staring out the window, Angel realized that this was the first time she had remembered the enchanting old couple since Franklin had been born.

CHAPTER SEVEN
A HILLTOP & A NEW HOME

It was March 16th, 2017. A Thursday. Three days before his twelfth birthday and almost *two years* since the night his body was healed. Franklin, his eyes now a brilliant shade of sparkling violet, stared at the seventy-foot-high mound of stone and dirt looming ahead of him.

In the midst of a small cluster of other children who lived at the Open Arms Orphanage with him, Franklin sat motionless on his bike, silently contemplating, but ready to tangle with this natural rocky wonder. The red mountain bike, which the orphanage had given him just last year on his eleventh birthday, made him feel unstoppable, as if he was riding on the back of an eagle ready to take flight. By now, his legs had become muscular from the constant use that he put them through. With this new confidence in his abilities, he had developed into quite a daredevil, not afraid to put his body at risk.

The gigantic hill of rock had become a gathering place for kids in the town of Abundant Lakes, Minnesota. The mass had been left behind thousands of years ago by a glacier, the same glacier that had formed many of the lakes in the area. Only a handful of people, Franklin soon to be one of them, dared to attempt its descent on bike. The rest merely came to ride around at the base of its great incline, finding enough of a thrill in just trying to avoid the boulders that lay scattered there.

It had been dubbed "Cast-Maker Canyon" by the locals, due to those adrenaline junkies that had tried, but failed, to maneuver down it; they had ultimately ended up with multiple fractured bones held together by fiberglass casts.

There were city signs posted all around the area pleading with children to stay away from the hill, warnings such as "Dangerous Hill, Stay Off" or threats in big, red letters saying "Trespassers will be Prosecuted". True, Cast-Maker Canyon wasn't exactly a canyon, but the name had stuck because it was catchy. In the last ten years, only one person had made the bottomward flight unscathed; he was now twenty-nine and a professional dirt bike racer.

Franklin was almost twelve, and he could go down in Abundant Lakes' folklore if he made a successful run.

And that sounded pretty good to him.

He rode his bike far enough away from the others so that they couldn't hear him as he said out loud, "Mom, I'm going to do this for you."

His mother, his precious mother, had been gone for a year and a half now. The tears came as he thought about her. Anger and sorrow now spurred his determination to conquer the Cast-Maker, and he began pedaling slowly towards the tumultuous incline…

A kind man at the shelter where they moved after the accident had given a wheelchair to Franklin when he was three. The man had seen Angel struggle as she carried her son all around, and he knew where he could find a used chair. Franklin was slow at first, but eventually, his arms became strong from wheeling everywhere, and both his agility and speed maneuvering it around were something to see. When he was older, the state of Minnesota had provided him with a larger chair.

He had always been a fairly competitive boy, even when he was bound to a wheelchair. His mom would actually have to run to keep pace with him as they went for a 'leisurely' stroll outside. It had made him laugh to see his mom huffing and puffing behind him, trying to keep up with his rigorous, rolling pace. Franklin remembered the pride which veiled her face. Pride in him. He longed to see that look from her now.

After the miracle that night, his mother always made a point to sit on the couch in the evening, listening to Franklin recount the stories from his day at school. Stories about his newfound strength and ability, along with the feats he had accomplished that day. Feats that in the past would have only been a misguided hope passing through his mind.

Now, to him, being able-bodied and fearless was one way of continuing to honor his mother. Like a prospector guarding his gold, Franklin's desire to keep his mother's memory alive grew more intense with each passing day. He didn't turn down a challenge. Ever.

The healing of his body had been Angel's own restoration, too. The miracle had inspired her to go back to school and work to fulfill her dream of becoming a nurse. It seemed after several months of night school that she might be able to earn her degree in another year. She could finally get a decent paying job at a hospital, one that could help them live like normal people who didn't have to scrounge for every dime.

His life, however, had come apart just as quickly as his body had been healed. He had gotten off the bus one day last year, and, as usual, the willow trees had been the first things that caught his attention. They still had those parasitic tent worms, which he had yet to kill. But then his eyes caught another much more sinister and disturbing sight. The front door of his house was wide open, and he could see inside. Their belongings were scattered everywhere, even the kitchen table had been overturned; no doubt signs that a struggle had taken place. He had run through the door, crying for his mom, desperately trying to find her.

He never did.

****

"C'mon Frankie Hobbs, you can do it!" One of his screaming friends below brought him back to the present for just a moment.

Someone else yelled, "Franklin, be very, very careful. Please? I don't want my only basketball rival at the orphanage to end up in a body cast for the next year!"

He recognized the voice of Sami, his best friend at the home. She had been the only thing that kept him from going crazy after the social worker had dropped him off at Open Arms Orphanage on that oh-so-lonely day last year. He had noticed her right away playing in the yard; the colors that were emanating from around her, her shine which only he was able to see, were like his mother's. Beautiful pastels, delicately toned. Very few people he knew had this type of aura about them, some had darker shines, most had a little color, but nothing like Sami or his mom.

As he had sat alone at dinner later that night, dejected and crying, wondering what he might have done differently to help his mother, Sami had tossed her dinner tray right down next to him on the table and proclaimed, "Hey there. I'm Sami. I know you're sad about something and I want to help. What's your name?"

Franklin looked at the girl perched in front of him. Her curly, dark hair was tied in a ponytail, which fell to her shoulder blades. She wore blue high-top sneakers and white socks pulled inches from her knees. A shirt that was too large for her hung past her waist and had a picture of a basketball swishing through a hoop with the words "Game On" underneath it.

"It's Franklin," he said.

"Well 'It's Franklin', I am Sami Watkins, and as reigning basketball champ of all the Open Arms Orphies, I challenge you to a game of one-on-one!"

Wiping away some tears, figuring he needed a distraction from his grief, Franklin decided to play along with her, "Are you sure you want to do that? You don't know who you're going up against!"

"I think I can handle a kid who has been crying all night," Sami laughed, then paused, "…sorry, that was a little harsh."

"Apology accepted. Now, where is that hoop?"

His tears had stopped flowing for a while, and they had played basketball for three hours that night. From that point on, they were all but inseparable friends. Her honesty and humor reminded him of his mom, and Sami had turned out to be a true companion. Not only that, she was actually the only one in the last two years that had ever come close to catching him in a foot race, and she had beaten him in basketball more than he liked to admit.

Many of the kids at the orphanage had become Franklin's comrades. This had probably been the biggest surprise for him. Socially, he had never been Mr. Popular among the other kids at school, in fact, quite the opposite. Often, before he lived at the orphanage, he had gone whole days without talking to another person, except his homeroom teacher Mrs. Dwight, who had always greeted him with a kind smile in the morning.

No one knew how he had been healed that night, not even Sami. Most kids felt too awkward to ask him how he could suddenly go from being paralyzed from the waist down to being able to walk. So, in the two years since his miracle, he had not told a soul. His mother had informed the principal to tell all of the teachers and staff not to bring it up and that it was a very emotional subject. In reality, he would have been happy to talk about how his legs were healed, but he understood that it was not a story that would be easily accepted.

Some of the kids at school were always trying to build their egos up by putting others down, and they would often remind Franklin about how he had once been a paraplegic. One older boy in seventh grade, named Brad, liked to explain to Franklin and others around him, that only a mutant could be crippled one day and then walk the next day. Brad especially liked to do this after Franklin would embarrass him in basketball or track. One day after school, Brad had even become physical and pushed Franklin down in the dirt after being beaten by him in the 50-meter dash. Up to this point, Franklin had not attempted to stick up for himself. What could he do? Brad was almost twenty pounds heavier and five inches taller than him.

Having extraordinary eyes the shade of violet had not proven to be a friend-magnate at school either. Most boys thought it was too bizarre to be cool, and girls often giggled when he passed them in the hall. Franklin never knew if it was because they thought he was cute or strange looking.

Sami had told him she thought his eyes made him look mysterious and said that people were actually intimidated by him. She also told him that she personally loved them and couldn't imagine him any other way. They were "uniquely stunning."

Her words.

She really did remind him of his mom.

CHAPTER EiGHT
MATH BOOKS & MONSTERS

Franklin's bike had reached the hill and his wheels skidded a bit before the knobby tread caught and began to climb the dry earth, higher with each anxious second. His legs pedaled hard as he slowly worked his way to the top. The fear of great bodily harm began creeping into him; he didn't want to be confined to a wheelchair ever again. Fear, however, was nothing new to him. It had been a part of his life ever since he had first run across that ghoul two years ago.

Although Franklin had only seen the man, or presence, which he now knew as Nefari, one more time since that miraculously horrible day, the memory of him was unfading. Franklin dreamed of him every night. He dreamed, too, of the massive swarm of black insects that he had seen in the shade of the willow tree, how they had attacked his leg as he ran away and then changed into a tendril of slime that stung him with an icy chill. This fear would prove to be inescapable for years. It haunted him, and he was beyond certain that it was this fiend who was responsible for abducting his mother.

The police were not so fast to call it a kidnapping. They were suspicious of a single mom who allowed herself and her son to live in such poor conditions. They had heard of it, or some variance of it, happening before; the woman makes it look like a struggle, throws some furniture, dishes, towels, and other things around. Then she runs away and starts a new life, leaving her past, including her son, behind. Gone without a trace.

Franklin knew his mom was not capable of such a thing.

He had made the decision to never show the police the note she left for him either. They would think she was crazy.

If he were ever to find his mom, it seemed as if he would have to do it alone.

****

The second, and only other encounter to this point, with the Darkness that called itself Nefari, had happened at school, of all places, two weeks ago…and the heinous creature had brought some sidekicks with him this time, too.

It had started in his homeroom class.

"Franklin dear, could you please run downstairs into the storage area and get some additional textbooks for our new math unit?" Mrs. Dwight had asked him after he had settled into his desk that morning.

Mrs. Dwight, his homeroom teacher, also taught his third-period math class. Grey-haired and in her fifties, she was more like a grandmother to Franklin than a teacher, and he enjoyed helping her any way he could. Her shine was bright, too. All shades of pink surrounded her presence, and he had concluded long ago that this unique aura was why she displayed such warmth and soft-heartedness to all her students.

Setting his backpack down on the floor, Franklin replied, "No problem, Mrs. Dwight." He had helped her before and knew where the storage room was, but the thought of going down there now frightened him beyond words.

He didn't want Mrs. Dwight to pick up on this hesitation. "Anything else you need down there?" he asked. And he heard his own voice, the overly confident tone it carried.

Looking around the brightly lit classroom, where there hung myriads of posters showing off geometry formulas and rules of algebra, Mrs. Dwight paused, trying to spark her memory of something she might need in her lessons for the day. Finally, she said, "No, I think the unit two textbooks are all we need. A class set please, dear."

Franklin nodded. He jogged out the door and down the hallway to the staircase that could take him either up to the second level or down to the basement. Stopping to avoid a group of giggling, pig-tailed girls who came from the story above, Franklin inhaled deeply and looked fixedly down the flight of stairs. He gathered his nerve and cautiously descended into the bowels of the school, second-guessing his own willingness to do it with each step. Places like this, where light was an afterthought, were not his cup of tea. Not anymore. It was pitch black as he stepped off the last stair and onto the ceramic tiles covering the basement's concrete floor.

He struggled to find the light switch, and as he ran his hand up and down on the wall where he remembered it being, he heard what sounded like faint but hysterical laughter. Chances are that this wasn't another student; for good reason, the kids never came down here. Maybe it was Gus, the custodian with the lazy eye and only a half nose? Franklin smiled at the thought of the friendly old jokester, who rarely did his job but loved talking with the students when he could.

Just as he thought he heard the shrill cackle again, his hand hit the switch, and the lights flickered on to reveal a narrow and dingy hallway. Franklin decided the sound he had heard had been air hissing as it passed through the heating ducts or possibly a chair being dragged across a floor in a classroom above him.

The lights hanging from the ceiling must have been the original light fixtures from the 1960s, when the school was built. They flickered for a few moments, deciding whether to stay on or not, as if they, too, had heard the eerie laughter and weren't sure they wanted to see its source. Finally, the ancient bulbs flashed one last time, and to Franklin's relief, stayed on. He breathed a great sigh.

As he made his way down the hallway, he whispered to himself, "just like a dungeon...," half expecting that at any moment he would see a skeleton with its hands and feet in shackles, chained to the wall. Maybe even with a snake halfway into the skull's mouth and coming out an ear. He had watched too many pirate movies, for sure.

Up ahead, he could see the door to the storage closet. He sprinted to it, wanting to get this increasingly difficult task over with. The aged, wooden door to the storage room was already cracked open an inch, and Franklin pulled it, causing its rusty hinges to groan as he swung it open just far enough so that he could slip in.

This time he was able to find the light switch right away. The lights crackled on, and he could see the small square room that had been designated to hold the school's math supplies. Boxes were stacked as high as the ceiling on three of the four walls, and he searched for the one that told him with permanent black marker that it was the sixth grade, unit two textbooks.

After a few seconds of tense investigation, he almost did a fist pump when his eyes fell on one that had the correct label. "Yes! There you are!" he declared. He knew that talking to himself was strange, but who would ever know? Besides, it made him feel better.

Scooting the box out from the middle of the stack without causing them all to tumble was like playing a giant game of Jenga, he thought. When he had finally liberated the cardboard behemoth, he heaved it up and cradled it with all his might; thirty algebra books were not exactly for the weak or weak-hearted to lift. He was glad he could help Mrs. Dwight; it would be dangerous for her to attempt to carry these by herself. But shouldn't Gus, the custodian, be doing this? They couldn't expect an elderly teacher—

Just then Franklin heard a click behind him. He turned to see that the storage room door had shut. Then, as if the door closing also triggered a temperature change, the room became frigid, causing a shiver to run down his spine, then back up again. He dropped the box.

Flickering once, then again, the lights went out.

"What next?" he whispered, with a slight chuckle, but didn't really think this situation was humorous at all, in fact.

Almost in an answer to his question, from behind him, he heard the laughter that had spooked him earlier, no longer faint, but intense.

It was a metallic, discordant, *evil* laughter that ushered Franklin's mind back into his nightmares of the last two years. This ghostly chortling could only be coming from something as sinister as the creature he had seen watching him through his kitchen window almost two years ago, and then later, staring at his bus as it drove away.

At once, Franklin turned towards the sound; he pushed the glow-light button on his digital watch and held it in front of him. Although the watch was not meant to be a flashlight, when combined with the narrow sliver of light coming from underneath the door, he was able to get a look around the room. The laughter had stopped for the moment, and he waved the light to his left, then his right, desperately trying to locate his enemy.

His wrist smacked into something icy cold, and when he pulled back and aimed the small light over into the corner of the room, he had to catch his breath. Less than two feet away, leaning against a stack of boxes, the faint glow of his watch revealed a lean, angular body. In the fraction of a moment that

Franklin had, he confirmed his belief that it was the faceless man. No eyes, no nose, and where the creature's mouth should have been, only a slight crease ran horizontally. His black hair, which appeared shiny and wet in the light, had adhered itself to his upper forehead, and black specks of stubble congregated on the lower half of his smooth face, where the beard on a normal man would have grown.

He wore a black baggy sweatshirt, and one hand rested informally in a pocket of his blue jeans.

Although he had no facial features to give away his immediate emotion, Franklin sensed that the creature was enjoying the terror he was causing. Even as this thought ran through his mind, the crease running across the bogeyman's face parted, opened wide, and then broadened into a horrendous smile. The wicked cackle arose from the hole, reverberating off the walls of the small room. Razor sharp teeth appeared in the opening, four pointing up and four pointing down; when he finally closed his mouth, they fell into the opposite-facing gaps, like a vile jigsaw puzzle.

Franklin's watch light was growing dimmer.

The faceless man decided to break the quiet. In a serpentine whisper, he said, "You are a coward, aren't you, Franklin Hobbssss? A ssscared rabbit. How you can be hissss boy, I do not underssssstand," the creature's voice was as chilling as its laugh, "but the fact remainsss that you are blood of hiss blood, flesh of his flesh. However, you have been a great disssappointment to him."

"Disappointment to who?" Franklin shouted into the chilly darkness. "Who are you talking about? And *what are you* anyway?" He managed to sound bold.

In the silence that followed, Franklin thought he heard a sickly, slobbering sound coming from either side of the room.

"I am Nefari. I am a Gatherer," it answered.

Now the slobbering gave way to panting, then slurping. It sounded closer to him than before.

Franklin always knew this day would come. A day when he would have to confront this faceless creature, the creature that had ruined his life... had taken his mom from him. He had been preparing himself, and although scared stiff, he remained calm, trying as hard as he could to turn his fear into an appearance of self-confidence, even annoyance. He needed to get this thing to talk, get any information about his mom from it that he could.

"Gatherer? I suppose you are here to gather me away? Well, I guess you can call me Franklin the Finder. I'm trying to find some math books. Actually, I found them. See?" He pointed in the general direction of the box he had dropped.

He surprised even himself, and he hoped his mocking sarcasm would not cause Nefari to take action sooner than he had planned.

"So, Nerfy," Franklin continued, "if you could just let me grab this box here and go back to my homeroom class, that would be fantastic."

Nefari the Gatherer was apparently speechless, possibly surprised at the apparent lack of fear in Franklin.

Rabid snarling now sounded in the darkness, this time almost at Franklin's feet. Really? Dogs in the basement? It was time to move.

Franklin ducked low and made a bolt for the door. Too late. As he made his move, a hand wrapped around the front of his face, scrunching both of his cheeks into his nose, and lifting him off the floor.

"Nefari isss my name child! Do you realizzze what you are dealing with? I am a SssstyJeen! I do not enjoy your attempts at humor." The icy hands squeezed Franklin's cheeks harder, forcing his mouth to open. The cold spread across his skin, down his throat, and into his lungs. Breathing became more difficult with each inhalation of chilled air.

He grabbed the arm of Nefari; it was ice cold. Freezing! He slid his own hand up the monster's wrist and twisted the polished fingers that squeezed his face, but with the tight grip that the creature had on either side of his cheekbones, it was hopeless.

Then something strange happened. Franklin felt a sudden tingling inside his head. The odd sensation was coming from the back... no, it came from the front of his head, by his eyes... directly behind both eye sockets. Not painful really. More of a tickle near his eyeballs.

He decided that this wasn't really a great time to be diagnosing the health of his eyes right now.

But in another instant, the tingling became a powerful throbbing, and energy flowed freely behind both eyes, causing a blazing light to radiate out from Franklin in all directions. At first, the light thrust itself from his open mouth and nostrils, but then, like two brilliant stars, his eyes burst forth with such illumination and ferocious, intense heat that Nefari became momentarily dazed and loosened his grip.

Franklin saw his chance. He gave a last, hard twist of the hand holding him up, causing Nefari not only to release the grasp he had on his aching cheeks, but also snapping the hand right off his arm. Light was still beaming from Franklin's eyes, but diminishing somewhat, when he heard the bloodthirsty growling and snapping coming from both sides of him once more. The heavy stench of animal breath surrounded him.

Wasting no time, he made a move to the door and turned the handle. It refused to budge. Twisting it the other way, the archaic mechanism finally released. He heaved his body against the door with such force that he sent it crashing open, slamming against the cement wall in the hallway. He was close behind, dashing into the welcoming light beyond. Once in the hall, Franklin threw the door closed behind him with all his might and immediately regretted doing this. The vibrations from the slamming door caused the hallway lights to twinkle, as they had earlier, but this time they flickered once, twice, and then went out. No longer energized with the mysterious light from within him that had saved him seconds ago, Franklin was again in complete darkness.

One good thing; at least a thick wood door now separated him from the abominations he had just escaped in the storage room.

A single floodlight, halfway to the stairs, came on. The light was battery powered and designed to take over when the other lights malfunctioned. It cast only enough light so that a person would not smack into the wall when exiting the basement.

It was something anyway.

From inside the storage room, over the cacophony of the scratching, slurping, and savage barking, came the laughter once again. Then, his voice, "That issssss an impressssive talent you have there, Franklin Hobbsss. And, I am sure there are more which you have not disscovered yet. I am ssso sssorry you will never get to experienccce the wondersss of thosse talentssss. Frankie, Frankie, Frankie…I am not here to gather *you*. You are worthlessss to ussss. I am here to gather the sssource of your ssstrength."

The barking stopped.

The StyJeen was quiet, too, then he spoke again, "Your eyesss. I am here to gather your eyesss, Franklin. To rip them from your sssskull and take them with me, along with your missssserable sssssoul."

Beneath Franklin rose a soft whisper of muffled voices from what seemed like a great number of restless spirits. They spoke quietly at first but then became increasingly louder. When Franklin bent down to listen to what they were saying, he discovered that the noise was not the sound of lingering souls, but rather thousands of flies fighting and scraping to get underneath the door and into the hallway. They brushed against his face and some became tangled in his hair, but their ultimate goal was not to land on him; he could see they were gathering together in a large cluster, inches from the door. He scooted away from the swarming insects but remained where he stood, in a fascinated stupor, to witness what sort of evil was transpiring in front of him.

Even in the dull light, he was able to see the ever-growing number of flies divide themselves into two distinct groups, and then he watched as the miniature demons, in each of the two smaller clusters, somehow fused with one another, becoming a solid mass. And finally, to his bewilderment, the solid masses contorted and stretched themselves until they manifested into what looked like two dogs the color of perfect midnight. Although it was much like seeing a pair of shadows on a wall, Franklin surmised that these were two of the largest dogs he had ever come across.

Deciding that staying to watch this bizarre scene had been a poor choice and that it was way past time for him to make an exit, he jolted for the staircase down the hall. Because of the bad lighting, he wasn't able to tell when he reached the first stair, and when his foot caught the step he was catapulted forward.

From down the hallway, the murderous barking had started up again. He looked back and discovered that what he had thought were dogs, were, in fact, a pair of enormous wolves bounding towards him, drooling profusely and ready for dinner to be served. As fast as he could, he pulled himself off the floor and started taking the stairs two at a time, but stopped when he heard a familiar voice.

"Franklin dear, are you down here?"

It was Mrs. Dwight.

"You are taking such an awfully long time that I was afraid something had happened to you, so I thought I would check." She came into Franklin's view.

From his teacher's vantage point on the stairs, she was not able to see the two monsters that were closing in upon them. Her line of sight was blocked by the corner of the wall. Franklin was right at the corner, where the staircase turned, allowing him to see both his teacher and the approaching canines.

He froze. He didn't want the wolves to follow him up the stairs so that Mrs. Dwight would become dessert.

"Did those old lights go out down there again in that hallway? I am so sorry, Franklin! You must have been scared to death! Let me at least turn on these stairwell lights for you."

She reached over and flipped on a light switch, one that Franklin didn't even know existed. How could he? The stairwell was dark every time he had come down!

"That makes sense," he heard himself saying.

And with that, bright lights flooded the stairs, overflowing into the basement hallway, showering the wolves with rays of acidic light.

Acidic to them, at least.

An unusually high-pitched whimper came from both of them, but they didn't seem to slow down.

Still worried for Mrs. Dwight's safety, Franklin almost yelled at her to run, but before he could get a word out, fur and flesh on the wolves began to unravel and then shred away, even as the savages bore down on him. These small pieces of a wolf, before ever hitting the ground, disassembled back into the parasitic flies from which they had started.

In three more steps, both of the wolves' bodies had completely wasted away. Franklin had to choke back a joyous yelp as the remaining horde of black flies hovered for a moment, then scuttled down the hallway, away from the light, and made their way back underneath the storage room door.

Waves of sweat poured down his forehead, as if a water main had just exploded under his scalp. He realized he had not breathed in a while, so he took in a gulp of air and blew it out rapidly, trying to calm himself. Mrs. Dwight eyed him suspiciously as she continued down the stairs towards him. He stepped back, behind the corner and out of her view, wanting to regain his composure.

That's when he felt something like a dead fish in his palm. He looked down. In all of the chaos, he had never dropped

Nefari's hand, which he had twisted off during his quick escape. Somehow, he had ripped it from the Gatherer's arm.

The skin of the hand had a milky white tint to it, and the fingernails had been neatly trimmed. Surprisingly, coming from such a gruesome creature, the hand was smooth to the touch, even the knuckles had no texture. There was no blood either, it was almost a clean tear.

He wasn't sure what to do with a severed hand, it wasn't really a situation that most people prepare for, although he thought it might be fun to see Mrs. Dwight's reaction.

No, not a good idea.

He had only another fraction of a second before she turned the corner, so he stuck it in his back pocket.

"What was that barking sound, Franklin?" she asked with furrowed eyebrows.

It was an odd sound to hear in a school basement, he thought, but he didn't know how to explain the appearance of ravenous wolves without sounding crazy. Then an idea struck him, and so he barked like one of the wolves himself. Repeatedly. Trying to imitate the sound they had made.

"Sorry, Mrs. Dwight, I have this nasty barking cough, you're not the first to tell me I sound like a dog!" He lifted his arm and hacked into it, this time embellishing it with a bit of a growl.

"You poor boy…but the books, Franklin. What happened to the books?" She had been looking intently down the hall; now she turned her gaze towards him. "My dear, you look dreadfully pale! And that cough! You must really have caught some bug! I think I might have a cough drop in my purse!" She grabbed his arm, "Come on, mister."

"What about all those unit two math books?" Franklin asked, feigning concern, but knowing he was off the hook. "Won't we need them later today?"

Mrs. Dwight laughed, "Don't worry about them, dear. I'll send Gus down after them. You know, the sweet old custodian who lost part of his nose to frostbite? He'll be happy to do it. I guess it really is his job, after all."

Franklin nodded as he casually untucked his tee shirt, hiding the fingers that protruded from his right back pocket.

CHAPTER NINE
A KIDNAPPING & A CLUE

"Frank-lin…Frank-lin…Frank-lin…" The loud, emphatic chanting came from below, like the chants that once went out for any of a hundred doomed warriors in the Roman Coliseum, warriors who had lived their whole life only to become nourishment for a lion.

Cast-Maker Canyon had a more gradual incline going up on the north side, otherwise, getting to the top would have been impossible on bike, even a bike being walked up. But once at the top, facing south, the slope was just short of a sheer drop off.

It was at the top of this precipice where Franklin would start his journey down Cast-Maker. Now, as he reached the apex of the hill, his mind once again wandered back to that fateful day.

Upon searching his house and not finding his mom, Franklin had slumped down in the middle of the kitchen and sobbed. Glancing up at the chaos of broken dishes and food on the floor, he noticed something sticking out from under one of the wooden crates used for a chair. His heart skipped. Had she left him a note? He picked it up.

Just old math homework.

He walked down the short hallway to the bedrooms and went into his mom's room. Nothing seemed out of place. The struggle must have been contained in the kitchen and front room. He traveled across the hallway to his own room. It was just as he left it that morning; bed unmade, dirty clothes on the floor, and random papers spread out on the flimsy table he used as a desk.

The table. Something was just a little off about it. Then his eyes picked up on the orange and green cover of the book that his mom had read to him ever since he could remember. It was the picture book, *Goodnight Moon,* and it was sitting on the table.

Strange, he had always kept this book on the little plastic shelf in the corner of his room, stacked with an ensemble of others. Franklin took the beloved storybook into his hand and opened it. On the inside cover was the familiar note in tiny handwriting:

'To Franklin, my dear son. May this book always put you right to sleep and bring you miraculous dreams! I love you, Mom."

He flipped through the pages and had been startled when a folded piece of lined paper slipped out from the middle of the book and fell to the floor. He bent over, picked it up and began opening it. Immediately he recognized his mom's loopy, yet precise handwriting before he even finished unfolding it. It was the same handwriting as the note that was inscribed inside the book's cover.

The letter was dated July 20th, 2015. Two months ago. Fearful of what he might discover, he had read it:

'My Beloved Franklin, My Joy and Inspiration,

I hope you know how much I love you and how proud I am of you!

I also hope you never have to lay eyes on this letter. I pray it's not real. I want to be imagining everything, but something seems very off. I didn't want to tell you for fear that I am wrong. You have been through enough. So I wrote you this, in case you ever needed to know. In case something was to prevent me from telling you.

Strange things are happening. I can't exactly put my finger on it, but darkness follows me. Colors change into black and white, shadows appear around me when there is nothing to cast them. I see things out of the corner of my eyes, but when I turn my head, there is nothing there.

Franklin, I can't help but think that your miracle is connected to this. You are at the center of something. Something important. I think someone is very unhappy that you were healed, and whoever or whatever that may be is now keeping a close watch on us. Waiting.

On the day you were healed, you said you saw a faceless man in the window. I have seen a woman, more than once, who had no facial features either. The first time I saw her was on the night of the car accident. She caused it. She appeared in front of my car from out of nowhere.

The second time I saw her was at the hospital later that same night...

This means that it has always been you, sweetheart; probably from the day I had you. Not just since your legs were healed. I think you were selected before you were even born, and now powers are competing over you. The dark powers are trying to stop you from something. I don't know who, and I don't know why.

Franklin, you need to know that the police told me if you had not fallen out of the car that day, the branch that went through the window would have crushed you. I know this is strange, because that fall to the pavement crippled you, but something else was right there protecting you. I am sure I buckled the car seat in and put the safety lock on the door. There is no way it could have just happened. Not without some help."

Franklin had stopped to wipe the tears streaming down his cheeks. How could this be? His mom had seen a woman without a face, just like the man he had seen in his yard? Eight years ago? Has something been stalking him for this long?

If it was him they wanted, why had they taken his mom?

He wondered why he never said anything to her about the dark shadow coming down from the tree, those flies that had chased him, and then that man again... the man standing in the yard staring at him as the bus drove away.

After he had told her about the figure in the window earlier that same morning, she had acted like she didn't believe him; just brushed it off. Maybe that's why he never mentioned the other things.

If only he had told her, they could have fought it together.

They might have prevented this from happening. He might have prevented his mom from... from what? He had no idea if she was alive or dead.

Furious with himself, Franklin kicked the side of his bed. He was so stupid! This was his fault!

The tears came again, and he wiped them away before looking back down at the letter. He kept reading.

'Franklin, you need to be very careful. I suspect that there are people in your life who are not what they seem, some want to hurt you, some may want to help you. Be aware of this. Be aware of the Darkness. I have come to believe that the evil cannot hurt you if you stay in the light. This is why I have been leaving the lights on in the house all day and night. We can't take any chances."

Franklin thought about this. For the last month, the lights had not gone off. Even in their bedrooms, she left two or three night-lights running while they slept. In the rest of the house, the lights had burned bright twenty-four hours a day. On one occasion, he remembered trying to switch the hallway light off before going to bed, and without telling him why, his mom had immediately turned it back on. He knew something was going on because his mom was usually very stubborn about turning the lights *off* in order to keep the electricity bill low.

'I will always love you, Franklin. I hope the reason you have found this letter is not because something has happened to me. The thought of being separated from you is more than heartbreaking. If this is the case, know that nothing can stop me from being with you again someday.

Love Forever, Mom"

He folded the note up and put it in his back pocket.

His mom must have put the letter inside the book so that who or whatever took her, did not see it. She had probably then rushed to set the book on his desk when she had known something was coming, or possibly, already in the house.

Only he would know that the book was out of place.

He would find his mom. He would get her back somehow. Deciding to take one last look around before calling the police, Franklin walked the length of the cramped house, looking for anything else out of place; inspecting the two bedrooms, the small hallway, and finally one last search of the living room, which shared space with the kitchen. Nothing else looked out of the ordinary.

Time to call the police then. His mom never could afford monthly payments for a cell phone, so all they had was the landline. He walked to the phone hanging on the wall, perched above the tattered green couch he and his mom had spent countless hours on together. As he reached for it, he saw something scrawled in pencil on the wall right above the couch. It said, "Baby Box."

That had not been on the wall this morning. He had used the phone to call school, letting them know he would be tardy today because he had missed his bus. Of course, he would have noticed it then.

The writing was his mom's. But the loops were not precise and the letters were not in uniformed size; his mom must have had to write this in a hurry, at the last second.

Baby box.

She was referring to the brick red box that contained many pictures and trinkets from when he was an infant. Only five months ago, he and his mom had looked through it, but after his birthday, she had moved it back under the bed so that it would be out of the way. He ran back to his bedroom, stooped down to the ground, and looked underneath his bed.

Never had he known how much dust could collect here! After sneezing twice, he poked his head back down, this time holding his breath. He was relieved when he saw it there, the small cardboard box. It had been pushed as far back as possible against the wall.

Still holding his breath, Franklin scooted all but his legs underneath the racecar until he was able to hook it with his index finger and wiggle it close enough to him so that he could grab it. He held it like a precious treasure before going back to the phone and calling the police. When he hung up, he erased the words on the wall, sat down on the couch with the box in his lap and waited for the officers to arrive. After glancing inside it and seeing all of the usual contents, he decided he better wait and go through it later. Finding whatever it was that his mom wanted him to see would take time. Somewhere else.

He had a feeling an orphanage was probably in his near future.

****

And Franklin had been correct about that.

"C'mon Hobby!" one boy yelled from seventy feet down at the bottom of the hill, "It's almost dinner! Are you going to do this or are you going to chicken out? Bawk Bawk Bawk!"

Franklin could make out Rufus, one of the orphans, walking around flapping his arms like a chicken.

Oh right, I'm the chicken, Franklin thought.

He heard a few other voices rumbling in agreement. Again, he heard Sami's voice, "Shut up, Rufus, or you're going to be in too much pain to swallow dinner anyway." Good ol' faithful Sami, she always had his back.

Cold sweat cascaded down his brow into his eyes, and he wiped it away with his sleeve. Under his breath, he muttered, "All right, mom, here it goes."

Bringing his bike to the edge, he peered down the steep incline. He thought about turning around; this might not end well. A pebble was jostled over the edge by his front tire, and Franklin watched as it ricocheted and bounced its way out of his sight. Large rocks and overhanging crags blocked his view of the very bottom, but he was able to discern a path that would get him at least halfway down without any huge boulders to stop him. He would have to improvise at that point and do some lightning-quick maneuvers. Pushing off with his toes, then putting his feet on the pedals, Franklin started down Cast Maker Canyon.

CHAPTER TEN
A FALL & A FRIGHT

The moment his front tire left the security of the hilltop, several loose rocks shifted position; he skidded and almost fell right then. But upon regaining his balance, he was able to follow the path he had mapped out in his mind. It wasn't quite a drop-off like it appeared to be, and he was not bombing the hill and going straight down, yet he still was gaining a significant amount of speed. His fear began to subside, and his spirits lifted when he saw that he was already halfway to the bottom of the hill. He looked down to see if he could see Sami cheering for him, but instead caught a glimpse of an empty field. Empty, except for a lone figure in black, far in the distance.

Something was very wrong; the world around him seemed to be wrapped in a thin layer of haze, almost like he was wandering inside of someone's nightmare.

Then his bike struck something… hard. His front wheel had finally found one of those boulders that he had seen close to the bottom of the hill. He had known this was the most dangerous section of the hill, so why had he taken his eyes off the terrain beneath him? Franklin felt himself soaring through the air to the left, the direction in which his bike had rebounded off the boulder. He was still on the bike, but not upright. With rocks of all sizes around him, he knew the chances of landing the bike on both wheels, without breaking any bones, was slim.

In the fleeting moments, while he was airborne, Franklin again saw a vision of his mom, the pride she had in him, the glorious smile on her face—

She wouldn't be proud now. She would be terrified. Terrified that Franklin had jeopardized his life while attempting to prove how brave he was to the other kids.

His leg struck the rocks first and he heard something snap. The rest of him followed and slammed hard into the packed earth between the boulders. Knifing pain seared through his whole body. Then he could taste the blood. His face had taken the brunt of the blow and there was something in his mouth. Teeth. He had knocked at least two teeth out. Franklin struggled to turn his body over, trying to see how far from the bottom of the hill he was. There was his bike, twisted over a rock, five feet further down.

He checked his injury. The bone in his upper leg was broken and partially visible, coming up out of his skin. He needed medical help right away. Why hadn't they come up to help him yet? Raising his hand in the air, a motion for help, he scanned the base of the hill, the rocks, and field beyond.

Then he remembered what he had seen before crashing; no one. There were no screaming children at the bottom of the hill, no Sami, and now as he looked in all directions, it wasn't just the kids that were missing. The bikes and the "No Trespassing" signs were gone as well. And the long prairie grass, once a bright, spring green and blowing gently in the breeze, was now yellow and crushed to the ground. There was no breeze, anyway; the world was eerily still.

"What's happening?" Franklin thought out loud. "Am I going crazy?"

He put his head back, the pain was excruciating now. Looking up at the sky, he saw that it was not blue like it had been. And no cotton ball clouds floated by; no bright yellow sun hung high in the western sky. In their place was a foreign, coral-stained sky and a deviant sun, larger and blood orange, which beat down on him with an intense heat that Franklin had never experienced before. And…and…it was in the eastern part of the sky.

He looked over past his bike and discovered that the forest beyond Cast Maker Canyon, the one he and Sami would go to when they needed a good tree to climb, which once had been filled with massive pines, elms, oaks, and maples, had been transformed into a dead zone. Skeletons of ancient trees reached up to the sky, desperately grasping for help from something unseen. Twisted, warped, and void of any life, this forest had perished long ago.

A sense of dread welled up inside his chest. He remembered seeing *something* in the seconds before his collision with the boulder. Franklin turned his attention back to the desolate field stretched out in front of him. Before his accident, he had seen a figure, far out in the grass, coming towards him. He squinted his eyes from the alien sunlight and scanned the outer edge of the prairie. It was there that he saw something that couldn't have been more bizarre, more out of place. In one distant corner of the field, where a county road was supposed to be running through, he saw what appeared to be thousands of people wandering aimlessly about. All around the area they stepped were great heaps of earth piled high.

What in the world was going on? Where had these people come from, and what were they doing? It seemed to Franklin like they might be carrying something. Shovels? That would explain the mounds of dirt.

Then his eyes found something much closer to focus on. The figure in black. He didn't have to look twice to know that it was the faceless man, Nefari, who was making his way steadily towards Franklin. Walking… no, hovering, right off the ground, through the field of decay, a black shine surrounding the space around him. He was near the area where Franklin's friends had been standing, close enough now for Franklin to see his grotesque mouth split open and deliver the same demented cackling that he had heard in the school's basement only a few weeks ago. The black hooded sweatshirt made him appear like any ordinary man, just out for a stroll in this abnormal world, but with the hideous smile that decorated his otherwise formless face, he reminded Franklin more of a fallen angel soaring across the river Styx.

As Nefari started up the hill, Franklin saw that angling in from both sides of him, further out but running like cheetahs, were the two large wolves that had pursued him down the basement hallway. They were making their way at such a speed that they soon would be side by side with their master.

He tried to move, to get up, or even just drag himself into hiding behind the nearest boulder which was only a few feet away, but his injury would not allow him; when he put any weight on it, his leg would fold in at the point where the fracture had occurred. So there was no getting up, no running from the faceless creature this time, his leg was too far gone for that; and the closest crag of stone was not nearly big enough to conceal his entire body, even if he could move. Besides, he was pretty certain Nefari had already spotted him.

With nothing to do but wait for the inevitable, Franklin watched as all three phantoms, Nefari and his two wolves, closed in on him. As the wretched trio approached each other, they did not slow their pace so as to avoid a collision, but did just the opposite; they seemed to accelerate right before simultaneously hammering into one another. But instead of bouncing off each other, as the laws of physics would suggest, there was an explosion of gooey flesh, which very suddenly, like a movie playing in reverse motion, snapped back together. Body parts fused, and the three became one.

One; as in *one creature*.

The majority of the wolves' mass was consumed by the body of the faceless man so that they disappeared into him. Only their savage jaws, along with the rest of their mongrel heads, were now fused on top of Nefari's shoulders, on either side of his own head. They both snarled, foam spewing from the razor-sharp knives inside their black mouths.

Twenty-five feet downhill from Franklin came the most horrible, ungodly thing he had ever seen; a three-headed monstrosity.

The head in the middle, Nefari's, opened its mouth.

A chilling voice rang out, "Franklin Hobbsssss, it issss time to gather what I have come for. Will you give yoursssself over easssily or make thisss ssavagely painful?"

Franklin pretended to look around, "Oh, you're talking to me? Yeah, I'm not planning on making this easy for you."

He cringed at the psychotic laughter which his gallant response had provoked from the faceless demon. It said, "That trick you did in the bassssement with the light wassss quite ssssimple, yet it caught me off guard. Not again, that little gimmick will not work here."

Franklin *could not* stand letting this monster that abducted his mother, who may have already murdered her, have the satisfaction of seeing weakness in him. Not wanting to show the fear that coursed through him, he continued to use reckless humor to diffuse his own terror. He said, "Nefari, your name is Nefari right? Looking at those ugly mugs next to you, I am guessing you have some major doggy breath, soooo, I would appreciate you not coming any closer."

The hounds both snapped their jaws in the air, practicing for the flesh-tearing they would be doing in a moment.

Franklin's splintered bones continued to send cannonballs of torment throughout his body. The ghoul was making its way quickly and was now only six or seven feet from where he lay, helpless. Hovering above, but not actually needing to touch the ground, its ascent to his position on the hill had been much faster than Franklin had expected.

He could now see clearly his adversary's greasy black hair, which sat atop his head in a permanent, yet fluid, wave.

A new hairstyle.

"You make a really ugly Elvis, you know?" he taunted.

The StyJeen stopped short of him and spoke, "You are trying to be ssso brave, young Franklin Hobbsssss, but I can ssssee the fear you bathe in. You have come into my realm! Tell me, how do you like it?"

Nefari stood in front of him now, and it seemed to Franklin like the creature's vacant stare was capable of piercing his soul.

"Really beautiful," Franklin responded, with as much sarcasm as he could muster.

And then, needing to ask, but not wanting to know, he shouted, "Did you take my mom you halfwit monster? Is she dead? Did you kill her?" Franklin glared at the trio of heads, two of which were looking hungrier by the minute.

The psychotic cackle came once again. Then, "Monsssster? I am not a monsssster Franklin Hobbsss. Monsssters don't exissst. And I mossst cccertainly do exissst." He bared his barbed teeth as a grin spread wide across his featureless face, "And your dear mom wassss ssssusssspicious, she wassss going to take you. We couldn't let you go into hiding again."

What did he mean by 'again'? Franklin wondered.

"Is she dead?" Franklin asked, trying to prevent the welling tears from overflowing and spilling down his face.

Nefari, ignoring his question, said, "You have usssed your gift of future-sssssight I sssssee. That isss why you are here now in my beautiful Dark Earth. A very ill-advisssssed move on your part."

Franklin looked at the dreary landscape around him and frowned, "I didn't decide to be here in this god-forsaken place," he yelled.

He wasn't sure why he was trying to find any truth from this cursed being in front of him. But he needed answers, and however detestable he was, this creature seemed to have some.

"What in the name of Sam Hill do you mean by future-sight?" he demanded.

Nefari laughed again.

"What is future-sight, you faceless mutation?" Franklin shouted.

The creature answered with a sinister hiss, "It will be my pleasssure to tell you of the powerssss you possesssss right before I gather their ssssource from your sssskull... and then leave the ressst of you for my faithful friendssss here."

The two wolf heads on either side turned inward to look at him, black drool dripping from both their lower jowls. They seemed to be wondering why they had not yet eaten this fresh meat in front of them.

Nefari continued, "You have no idea the giftssss you have been given, do you boy? You are assss ignorant asssss any fool human I have ever met. The reasssson you are here right now isss becausssse you have willed yourssself to sssee your future fate; thisss created a Gateway to my realm, which you and your bike fell right through. Now you find yourssssself crippled and helplessss again, as you have been mossst your life. A rather fitting way for you to die."

They took a step closer to him.

Franklin tried scooting backwards, using only his hands to push against the dirt and rocks. He knew this was probably the end for him, but he couldn't give up yet. Stalling for more time, he said, "So I have future-sight? Then this is only a vision of what *would* happen if I rode my bike down this hill? That means that you're not really here, then."

"Oh, I am right in front of you, Franklin. I can ssssmell your human ssstench. No, your future-sssight is not jussst a visssion. What you are experiencccing is very real. You are on Dark Earth now becaussse the power of future-sssight you possess originated from this realm."

Nefari paused and from somewhere deep inside his throat slithered up a long, black tongue, which he ran across his front fangs before sucking it back down to the depths of darkness inside him. Both wolves followed his lead, licking the slobber from their jowls with an equally long tongue.

"If you can't call yourssself back to the pressent," Nefari continued, "then thisss issss your new present. Your new reality. You do not know how to control these talentssss, Franklin Hobbssss, or you would already be gone."

He was right, Franklin had no idea how to deliver himself back to the present, on top of Cast Maker Canyon, on *his* Earth. So this place was now his reality.

Frantically, he yelled at the top of his voice, "I want to go back! Do you hear me? I want to go back to the top of that hill!" He was not directing his command at Nefari, he knew this fiend would never grant his request, he was hollering at whatever force had allowed him to see this bleak future and had brought him into this foul realm.

Nefari opened his mouth once more, "No one issss lissstening to you, Hobbsssss. I want to tell you that when my houndsss and I are through here, I will have plucked thosssse purple eyessss from your head and you will be a sssoullesss heap of bonessss. Thessse houndsss have not eaten sssince the lassst time I had to go and gather. And I cccertainly won't deny my own appetite, either."

This time, when he finished speaking, Nefari's mouth did not close but continued to stretch wider and wider. It expanded far enough out so that it could easily slide over

Franklin's entire head and then shoulders, consuming him whole. He could hear the faint, but familiar drone of buzzing insects arising from the gaping cavern of Nefari's mouth, buried somewhere in his body.

The snarling of the wolves became even more savage as their heads advanced closer. Black saliva pooled on the ground around them.

The fabric of the sweatshirt Nefari wore began to contort and twist, then sprouted squirming tentacles, like the legs on an octopus, only the color of coal. They reached out toward Franklin, and as the tentacles wrapped around his neck, they scorched his skin with an icy cold touch that made him forget about the pain from his torn leg.

Another tentacle came from one of the foaming mouths of the hounds, and it wound around Franklin's arm and began pulling him towards it. The movement of his broken body triggered screams from Franklin, although his mind, in its present state, could not pinpoint the source of the stabbing pain.

He tried to stop his forward progress; his hand grabbed at rocks, his fingernails scratched through the dirt. His one good leg, out in front of him, found a rock to push back against. Nothing he tried worked; like a boa constrictor squeezing the life from a rabbit, the pull of these tentacles was relentless.

His crippled leg was the first to reach Nefari, whose mouth was still open, waiting. Franklin's leg went knee-deep into the slippery cavity of his throat, and he watched as a great swarm of flies emerged from the faceless man's mouth, coming up from inside him. They flew around Franklin, taunting him, landing on him. The harsh, buzzing din they produced felt like a drill digging into his ears.

One of the wolves, in a frenzy, ripped into his other leg; a surge of pain bulleted through his body and he went numb. His legs were lost, and the rest of his body was about to meet the same fate. He realized that his own screaming had stopped as shock took over his senses.

Thoughts stopped making sense.

With one last grasp at an idea before he went unconscious, Franklin forced his mind to create images of himself at the top of the hill, not having left the edge yet. He pictured himself still looking down at Sami and the other kids waiting for him at the bottom.

Just then a little tickle ran through his head. In an instant, it was a sharp tingling right behind his eyes. He recognized the feeling.

He imagined changing his mind about taking the treacherous ride down the hill on his bike. Instead, he pictured himself turning his bike around and walking it back down the other side.

That did it. It was like he had slid back the play bar in a YouTube video of his life. There he was, in the sunlight of his own precious Earth again. The searing agony he had been in was gone, only a bad memory. His leg was whole; unbroken. He ran his tongue along his teeth; the two that had been knocked out were still there. His red bike was not twisted and unrideable, but perfectly fine. Franklin was again at the top of the steep hill, looking down at Sami in the green field below. The other kids were still screaming for him, "Hurry up Frankie!" and "Dooooo-it, Doooo-it!"

A concerned Sami shouted up to him, he could barely make out what she was saying from this far away. But he did. She said, "Turn back around if you want to Franklin, don't listen to these idiots."

That was all he needed to hear. Not that he was even thinking about going down the hill after what had just happened, but still, he loved hearing the worry in Sami's voice.

He got off of his bike and turned it around, walking it slowly down the other side of Cast Maker Canyon.

CHAPTER ELEVEN
A FRIEND & A NEW FAMILY

The bike ride back to the orphanage gave Franklin some time to think. From the hill to the steps of their orphanage was only about ten minutes by bike, and Franklin used almost all of it trying to figure out what in the world had just happened to him. These near-death encounters with the creature that called itself Nefari were starting to really wear on him both physically and mentally. It was exhausting to never know who or what would be waiting around the next corner trying to kill you.

Also, he now knew of another ability that he had. Somehow, he was able to live out the future before it happened; he could actually experience the result of a choice he might make. What triggered it though? What was it that allowed him to see the outcome of his perilous trip down the hill before it actually happened? He thought back to the moments before he had gone over the edge; he had hesitated as well as entertained some thoughts about turning back. Also, he remembered that he had been planning his route down the hill, his eyes had been hard at work looking for the path that would take him *around* the boulders instead of *into* them.

His eyes! Something about his eyes. He had already known they were special, not just because they had that inexplicable purplish tint, although he figured that had something to do with it. He knew he had the ability to see a shine, or aura, around individuals, clueing him in on what kind of a person they were. Then he had the gift of light; the strange light that had radiated out from him when Nefari had him pinned in the basement storage room. He knew that his eyes were the source of these unique gifts. Now this new ability too! Not that he could trust the faceless freak, but hadn't Nefari said that this future-sight ability had originated from Dark Earth? He had no idea what that meant, but he figured Dark Earth was the awful place he had just spent the last fifteen minutes of his life.

Was this the only way to use his gift of seeing future outcomes, by somehow being ferried to that other realm? Nefari had said he had fallen through a Gateway. What did this mean? He had a lot of questions... but no one to ask.

This latest encounter with Nefari was disturbing on so many different levels, too. He had thought that he had seen it all in the past two years, but that three-headed beast was definitely going to have the new starring role in his nightmares for a long time. Franklin desperately wanted someone to share all this with, but he knew it would make him appear to be a lunatic who would be better served in the nut house than an orphanage.

Then there was the way he had chickened out at the top of the hill in front of all his fellow orphans and other kids. Although Franklin knew he had made the right decision, and he had the support of his best friend, he still felt like he had let everyone down.

Ahead on her bike, Sami looked back at him and smiled; her smile was one of Franklin's favorite things about her. He smiled back at her. She was a slender girl, with light-brown skin and black hair with extremely tight curls, long enough to be in a ponytail most of the time, like now. As she rode her bike over the rough terrain, it bobbed up and down, almost putting Franklin in a hypnotic trance as he watched it.

He had never learned the circumstances that brought her to Open Arms Orphanage, but he knew she had been at other orphanages around Minnesota most of her life and had only come to live here a few months before him.

On a few occasions, before living here, Franklin had noticed Sami at school, but they had never spoken. On the day he met her before she had introduced herself to him in the dining room and had challenged him to a game of basketball, she had been playing croquet in the orphanage yard with her roommate, Parker. Franklin had just arrived at the house with his social worker only hours after discovering his mom was missing, and the fact that he noticed anything or anyone in such a distressed state was a miracle in itself.

When he looked at her that day, playing in the yard, he had tried to smile, but as sad as he was at the time, it probably looked more like he was trying not to throw up. She had smiled back anyway, and it had warmed his heart, even then. Later, when she had come up to him in the dining room, even though he was crying, his heart had still managed to skip a beat when he saw her. They were best friends now, but Franklin wondered if Sami ever thought of him as more than a friend.

She slowed down on her bike so that they could ride next to each other and said, "I'm glad you came to your senses about that hill. You know you would have killed yourself?"

"Yeah, I'm pretty sure it would have ended up badly," he said, knowing that he couldn't actually tell her that he *knew* for a fact it would have. "But, you know, it has been done before," he finished. He wished he could just tell Sami she was right and not have to pretend to argue.

"By a professional, you dummy! That guy had been traveling on the national BMX circuit. Cast Maker Canyon probably looked like an anthill to him. And if Rufus gives you a hard time about it tonight, ignore him, because he didn't really care if you killed yourself. He just wanted a few seconds of entertainment."

"I know... you're right. I was stupid to even consider going down it. I just thought if all the kids at school found out that I had conquered that hill, maybe they would leave me alone, possibly even respect me. Maybe even Brad would stop being such a jerk."

"I wouldn't count on that. He was born to be a jerk," she said flatly.

They pulled their bikes up to the front porch steps and parked them on the freshly cut lawn. The Open Arms Orphanage was an attractive, two-level home a mile out of the main city of Abundant Lakes. Previously it had been an old battered farmhouse, but the home had been through some major renovations. Now, with green wood siding and gray shingles, a large front porch big enough for three rocking chairs, and a neatly manicured yard, it was one of the nicer orphanages in the area. Counting the basement, it had three levels and fostered twenty-three kids at the moment. The girls lived almost entirely on the first level, the second level was home to the boys, and the basement had several rooms for the older kids who needed more privacy.

"You kiddos need to wash up and get ready for dinner. You look filthy! It's pork and beans tonight, and I made some peach cobbler for dessert!"

It was Gloria Radcliff, or Nonna Glo, as the kids called her, their stern but tender caretaker of the orphanage. She had received this affectionate nickname years ago from a toddler who had moved to Minnesota from his hometown of Genoa,

Italy and had lost both his parents in a fire. He came to Open Arms and had started calling her 'Nonna', which is Italian for 'Mother'. He couldn't pronounce Gloria, so he just shortened it to 'Glo'. She loved it, so it stuck. She'd been Nonna Glo ever since.

Nonna Glo was a large woman, whose thundering laugh and powerful voice could scare the bark off of a tree. Because she did a lot of cooking, she usually wore an apron most of the day over her dress, a specific dress for each day of the week. Her dyed blonde hair was usually kept in a bun on her head, and the gray hair coming in beneath it was almost undetectable. She had a large, jovial face, usually red from working hard at something, and she always referred to the kids as 'Honey', 'Sweetie', 'Darling', and occasionally 'Pumpkin'. She lived there full-time with the kids and loved her job.

Hank Fulsten, or 'Papa Hank', was also a warden at the orphanage, and he stayed there full-time as well. The children had never seen Papa Hank when he wasn't dressed in his blue jean overalls, with some form of a plaid, button-up shirt underneath it. He and Gloria were not married, or even romantic, but had a strong friendship. All the children wished a romance would blossom between the two. Many of the older children had the sense that Nonna Glo was interested in a more serious relationship, but that Hank never wanted one. Both of them had been there since the founding of the orphanage thirteen years ago. Gloria stayed on the main level with the girls, while Papa Hank had a room upstairs to watch over the boys.

Nine children now marched past Gloria, each one in dire need of a shower after riding their bikes through the fields all day. It was Spring Break, a week off from school, and the kids took full advantage of their time away. Today was not unique however, the children were usually filthy at the end of every day, whether it was Spring Break or not. Of course, there were those few kids that would rather spend the days reading or playing games in their bedroom, maybe hanging out on the porch, or under a tree, but Franklin and Sami were not in that group. Those kids tended to stay much cleaner.

Several of the children, including Sami and Franklin, replied, "Okay Nonna Glo" or "On our way, Ma'am" when she told them they needed to shower. The children in the orphanage would never dream of talking back to Gloria or Hank. That is, except for one of them. Not all the orphans at the home were Franklin's friends either. Rufus was the single exception in both cases. Twelve years old and full of anger, Rufus was not friends with anybody and showed very few people respect, including Gloria and Papa Hank.

He was a short and stocky boy, his black skin was covered in scrapes, new and old, from falling off his bike so often, and his hair was cut down to such a short length that he almost appeared bald. Rufus had lived an extremely difficult life, and his behavior in social situations had been strongly affected by it. It was difficult for him to talk to anyone without insulting them.

"Yuck! Peach Cobbler? Can't we have something good?" Rufus asked matter-of-factly, not attempting to hide his disgust. He had quite a way with words.

Gloria, accustomed to this type of behavior from him, said calmly, "I will not force you to eat it Rufus, but you will not have anything else for dessert."

He shot a nasty look in her direction and continued walking up the stairs.

Franklin usually tried to avoid Rufus. He had enough problems with bullies at school, and he didn't need one at the home where he lived as well. Earlier today, though, he had actually made an effort when he invited Rufus to go out and ride bikes. Rufus had scoffed at him, saying, "What makes you think I want to go bike around with you?"

Franklin had given him an insincere smile and walked away without responding. He knew Rufus would end up coming along despite what he said. He was right. Rufus had come along and actually seemed to enjoy himself. Now he was back to being... well, back to being Rufus.

Heading upstairs to clean himself up before dinner, Franklin ran into Papa Hank who stood in front of the basement door. Hank's graying dark hair was kept feathered back against his ears and parted neatly in the middle over his forehead. He had a bushy grey mustache covering his upper lip, which Franklin thought made him look like Albert Einstein, minus the crazy hair. His smile was endearing, and when he did smile, which was often, the fuzzy tips of his mustache came close to touching his eyes. He was fifty-three, but, except for the gray hair, appeared to be much younger.

Now he had a labored smile, "How are you doing buddy?" he asked, his voice dull and lifeless, a stark contrast to the usual amount of contagious energy he offered. Franklin saw that he was pale, without any hint of color to his face.

"Good, Papa Hank," Franklin replied. "Are you feeling okay?"

Papa Hank stared straight ahead for an awkward amount of time, his eyes glossing over.

"Papa Hank?" Franklin asked, concerned with this strange behavior.

Papa Hank shook his head a few times, still staring at the wall, then said, "I woke up with this headache, like something was making a nest in my brain. It won't go away."

"That sounds horrible! Did you take something for it?" Franklin asked.

"Nothing touches it," he said. Then, at last, he looked away from the wall and directly at Franklin. "You coming to listen to my story tonight?"

"Yeah, for sure, but I hope you feel better by then," Franklin answered.

Papa Hanks' expression suddenly changed. He scrunched his face up into a series of wrinkles, and his eyes squinted to a sliver. Spittle came from his lips as he snarled, "I'll bet you do you little…" But he didn't finish, his voice trailed off and instead he glared at Franklin with an unmistakable guise of hatred.

Franklin was at a loss for words, having no idea what he had done or said to offend Hank, who was normally as jovial and friendly as they come.

"I, uhhh. What did you….?" Franklin floundered through his choice of words.

Then, as suddenly as his expression had gone sour, Hank's face forced a smile, and his voice lost its sting. He said, "All right, you better go wash up for dinner now." Opening the door to the basement, he turned and descended the stairs into the dark.

"Whoa, that was really weird," Franklin whispered quietly to himself. He decided, though, that Hank's strange behavior was probably due to his severe headache, and so he tried not to give it another thought as he trotted up the stairs to get ready for dinner.

Franklin shared a room with Shadrack Wence, a shy, quiet boy who had only moved in several months ago. Shadrack had not gone biking today because he spent most days inside, engrossed in his science fiction novels. He was eleven, a year younger than Franklin, and for his age, he was fairly small but more intelligent than many kids in high school or even college. Much of his knowledge had been absorbed from the hundreds of science fiction books he had read. The books had been a way for him to forget his heartbreaking, real-life experiences, which he had faced on a daily basis before coming to the orphanage.

Shad, as the other kids called him, kept his light brown hair cropped short, even though he had ears that stuck out too far. His pale skin was evidence of the severe spring allergies he had, part of the reason he preferred staying inside. The shine Franklin could see emanating out from Shad was a light blue. Franklin took this to mean he was even-tempered and patient, with the capability of being a strong friend. He was not entirely sure of Shad's past, as his roommate was not fond of talking about it, but Franklin had heard that his parents had given him over to Minnesota's Child Protection Agency voluntarily, admitting to the social workers that they were unfit to be parents. When the police came to arrest them the next day after finding signs of physical abuse on Shad, they discovered that the two had left town. They never came back.

After showering and putting on fresh clothes, Franklin looked over at Shad still lying in a prone position, reading on his bed, and asked, "Hey Shad, are you ready to go eat?"

A big box of Kleenex lay on the bed next to Shadrack, along with a pile of used ones on the floor. He reached for another and blew his nose loudly. "Sure, but it seems like I just had lunch. This book, *Surviving Saturn*, is really interesting. The main character Razzelby had to use his knowledge of atomic fission in order to heat Saturn's surface creating an explosion that—"

"Okay, okay. How can you understand that stuff? It makes absolutely no sense to me."

Shadrack sniff-coughed, "It's not tough. Most of the stuff in this book deals with quantum mechanics, my favorite part of physics." He coughed into his hand, examined his palm, and wiped it on his jeans, then continued, "Objects don't follow the same set of formulas for speed based on their size and momentum, which normal science has them following. Probability plays a big factor in predicting the outcomes of events. You know what Einstein's Theory of Relativity is, right?"

"Heard of it, I guess," Franklin said. "But you know what, Shad? It's okay, you just made my brain hurt."

Shad pushed his glasses up to his nose and sneezed, "I just wish I could get the next book in the series. I need to get to the school library, but I have to wait for Spring Break to end."

"You might be the only kid I know who wants Spring Break to hurry up and get over with," Franklin said, patting Shad on the back.

Another barking cough. "Four more days! If you had my allergies, you would too. That pollen outside is making me crazy, I'm better off at school. Uh oh, hold on…"

He sneezed and covered Franklin with a fine layer of saliva and mucus.

Franklin picked up a dirty shirt on his bed and used it to wipe his face, "Hey, Shad, do you think you could cover your mouth next time?"

"Sure, sorry about that. It came from nowhere," his roommate said. "Let's go eat."

CHAPTER TWELVE
A SLIP OF THE TONGUE &
A SECRET TOLD

After dinner, Franklin went with Sami and Shad back to Sami's room. Her roommate, Parker, was still in the dining room finishing up her second helping of peach cobbler, which most children (besides Rufus) had thought was the absolute best Nonna Glo had ever made. Sami sat on the bed, while Franklin and Shadrack found a seat on the floor where they could rest with their backs against the wall.

"Hey Shad, glad you're hanging out with us," Sami said, flashing Shad one of her heartfelt smiles. "It's good for you to get your nose out of those books every once in a while."

"Yeah, I know," Shad acknowledged, "I am beginning to have very real dreams about being lost on some unknown planet. I think I need to take a break from the *Space Survival* series."

Sami looked at Franklin, "You up for some basketball? We could teach Shad how to take a jump shot and show him how I can whup your butt."

"As tempting as that sounds, my allergies are way too bad to step an inch outside right now. You guys want to play monopoly or something?" Shad asked. He had been holding in a sneeze and finally let it go, "Aaaaaachoooo!"

"Easy killer," Franklin kidded, "you're going to get brains all over Sami!"

"That's disgusting, Franklin!" Sami said. "Boys can be so gross! Shad, did you hear how Franklin almost killed himself today trying to impress me?"

Franklin blushed, "Yeah, instead though, I made a fool out of myself."

"What are you two talking about? What happened?" Shadrack asked.

They took turns telling Shad about the events of the day. Sami emphasized how Franklin had made the right decision, which is the reason he was still alive.

Shad looked a little puzzled, "How did you change your mind?" Here he paused and gave Franklin a wry smile, "Usually you are a pretty stubborn roommate. Besides, it sounds like you were dead set on going down that hill. You were at the precipice and everything."

Franklin knew the answer to that, and this was the perfect opportunity to tell them, but he was still hesitant. What should he do? Was there any way that they would ever believe him?

Sami helped him, "It's because you couldn't imagine leaving me here at the orphanage alone, without my best friend. Right, Franklin?"

Then the words came pouring from him before Franklin really thought about what he was saying, "I would have fractured my tibia, you know, my shin bone? For sure. And it would have broken through my skin. The most painful thing ever! I also would have knocked out two teeth. Probably a week at the hospital at least!" When he finished and saw the shocked look on his friends' faces, he realized he had just made a major blunder. Trying to recover, he added, "Umm… that's my best guess anyway…"

Both Sami and Shad had their eyes wide with surprise, staring at Franklin. Sami spoke first, narrowing her eyes into a suspicious glare, "How in the world do you know that? Are you hiding a crystal ball somewhere or something?"

Franklin shrugged his shoulders.

She laughed. "Seriously, why are you so sure about what would've happened to you?"

"Uhh, I was just guessing. You know? I don't think I would have died. Just gotten hurt."

Shad replied, "Yeah, but you sounded pretty sure about what would happen. You distinctly said it would be your tibia that would break, and it would be *two* teeth you would lose. Why would you be so specific about it?"

"When did the two of you decide to become Sherlock and his trusty sidekick Watson? More importantly, which one of you is the sidekick?" Franklin joked.

Sami smiled a little too sweetly at Franklin. He had seen that smile before from her. It was a 'how are you going to get out of this one?' smile.

She said, "It's elementary, my dear Franklin! It's also a little strange, don't you think? I mean, why would you say 'tibia' and not just 'my leg' or something?"

"For dramatic effect I guess. I don't…" He stopped to think things through. He realized if there was ever a chance to get this weight that he carried off of himself, to share not only his burden but also his joy with his friends, this was a pretty good opportunity. "Okay, if I tell you guys something, you promise you won't make fun of me or tell me I should see a psychologist or something?"

Shadrack licked his lips, "No way Franklin. I promise."

"You know I wouldn't, Franklin. I would never make fun of you like that; not about something serious," Sami assured him.

"And, you could never tell anyone else. It has to be only between us." Franklin was already starting to feel the soothing salve of relief as he got closer to revealing his extraordinary secret.

They both nodded their heads, and Sami said, "Go on, tell us. I bet you'll feel better."

She knew him so well.

"Well, you may have heard that at one point my legs–" he started when the door suddenly burst open. In walked Parker Smith. "Whoa, hey guys! Why wasn't I invited to this party? Where's the pop and chips? What movie are we watching? Maybe we should dance? You want me to teach you all some of my mooooooves here on the floor?"

Shad and Franklin laughed at the expression she made when she said, 'mooooooooooves', but Sami looked frustrated. "Hey Park, umm, you know we love you, but any chance you could come back in about thirty minutes?"

Parker, a no-nonsense, outgoing eleven-year-old, was always up for having fun. The previous year, she had been living on the streets with her aunt in downtown Minneapolis, until her aunt was arrested for a series of armed robberies of coffee shops. She picked these stores because, in her aunt's words, "They ain't got any security! Who in their right mind is gonna rob a coffee shop?"

Well, eventually she got caught, arrested, and sent to the Hennepin County Jail, and Parker got sent to the Open Arms Orphanage.

She was a spirited girl; athletic looking with bright eyes, a huge smile, dark hair past her shoulders, and tan skin. Franklin had overheard her say once that she had left her home in Colombia and traveled to America with her aunt when she was four. Parker's time on the street here had turned her into a tough kid with lots of savvy and raw, common sense, yet sprinkled with an occasional soft side as well. Since being at the orphanage, Parker had blossomed as a student, though never having more than a year of formal education before.

Surprisingly quiet when she arrived, her personality and confidence had also grown in leaps and bounds.

As she stood at the door, there was a moment of awkward silence, then Parker said, "Uhhh, sure I can leave if you want. Sorry for interrupting…"

"No, stay, please," Franklin said, looking up at her from his seat on the floor, motioning her to stay with his hand.

He had talked to Parker a few times alone before and could tell she was a person to be trusted. She had been through quite a bit in her short life and knew what it felt like to have somebody betray *her* trust. Besides, the light that surrounded her was white, and he had decided that honesty was one of the characteristics that white light revealed about a person.

"The more the merrier, as they say," Franklin remarked. Then asked, "Are you willing to take a vow of silence, like these two, if I tell you something really, really strange about myself?"

"Yeah, sure!" Parker replied.

"Oh yeah, and no making fun of me or calling me crazy," he added.

"No, sir!" She saluted him.

"All right then, like I was saying, you may or may not have known that my legs, only two years ago, were paralyzed." They looked at Franklin like he had just told them he was actually Superman. So, apparently, they hadn't known about his legs.

For the next two hours, Franklin told them everything that had happened from the miraculous night when he was healed, to his current situation in the orphanage. He didn't leave out a detail. Nothing had ever felt so therapeutic to Franklin as this shedding of information. A long bath in the healing salt waters of the Dead Sea couldn't compare to the amazing feeling he had from telling his stories to these friends. All three of the children were mesmerized during the intense recounting of events, and when he ran upstairs to get the letter his mom had left him, they all seemed relieved to get a short, mental break.

When he finally came to the part of his story that included the events of today and explained to them the gift of future-sight that he had used, Shad yelled, "That makes total sense! Your eyes! Those… those... unique eyes of yours have been given to you from some higher power. You can see the future when you need to!"

"Yeah, I can. Not really far into the future, I don't think; less than an hour I bet."

After telling them about the three-headed beast that had nearly been the end of him if he had not, at the last second, been able to will himself back to the present and to his own Earth, Parker had responded, "Two wolf heads and a faceless dude? That's terrifying, man!"

Franklin nodded his head, "Believe me, it was awful."

Sami just stared at him, enthralled with every word he spoke. And when at last Franklin said, "That's it. That's my story," she walked over, sat down next to him and gave him an insanely tight hug, practically squeezing his marvelous eyes right out of his head.

Still being hugged, Franklin added, "Raise your hand if you think I'm a whacko."

Sami let go of her embrace on Franklin and shouted, "Hey, put your hand down!" to Parker, noticing her roommate had one arm straight in the air. Both girls broke out into laughter.

"Holy buckets of crappy coffee! Wow, Frankfurt. That is one heck of a life," said Parker, dumbfounded. "You got my sad story beat by a mile. My crazy aunt is in jail for robbing coffee shops, but at least she had a face! You're dang brave to stand up to that freak. And those wolves… holy rat crisp!"

Making them all jump, Shad let go a powerful sneeze, "Ahhhhhhchooooo!" then wiped his nose on his sleeve. "We have to protect you from those things!" he said. "From the—"

Parker interrupted him, "We need to protect the sleeve of that shirt from your snot!" she said, exchanging a disgusted face with Sami.

Shad ignored the comment, "From the way you describe it and from what your mom wrote in her letter, it feels like they can't spend much time in the light, so you need to stay out of the dark as much as possible."

"I've been trying to since I moved here, at least kind of trying... sometimes there is no way to avoid the dark," Franklin replied.

"I thought it was a little strange that you needed two nightlights on in your room upstairs. Makes sense now," Sami said.

Parker had been thinking quietly, "Hey Frankfort. If that part's true, about the light, then how come the faceless dude and the dogs could come after you on the hill during the daytime, right when the sun was shining today?"

Before Franklin could answer, Shadrack replied, "Isn't it obvious? I thought it was." He sniffed something up his nose that must have been blocking his airflow, then coughed twice, more of a self-conscious cough as he eyed Parker.

Parker shot back, "You thought *what* was obvious Snotty? Remember, we're not all as smart as you think *you* are."

"Okay, I am sorry for being so blunt. I was just surprised that I am the only one that picked up on this." Shadrack cleared his throat, "The fact that the sun sets in the east in that place, like Franklin said he saw, is a clue that things are very different than they are here. When that thing that calls itself Nefari was able to stay in the daylight today, it was not in our earthly realm, it was in his other world. It is my guess that daylight there does not have the same properties that our white light has here either. I have been turning it over in my mind. You know about *ROYGBIV* ? How Earth's white light is made up of ROYGBIV?"

"Who is Roy G. Biv? And what makes you think he is anywhere near us? You are a strange one Shad." Parker was looking at Shadrack like he had just spoken Chinese. Franklin and Sami both cracked up.

"No, no, no. It's not a person, it's an acronym for Red, Orange, Yellow, Green, Blue, Indigo, and Violet. *ROYGBIV*. The colors that make up white light here on Earth. What if daylight in this other world that Franklin described is different from ours? Maybe it's missing one or two of those color components, and somehow, when he is exposed to these other extra elements of light here, Mr. Faceless can't handle it." Shad was visibly excited; this was the kind of stuff he lived for.

"So he's able to walk freely in the daytime when he's on his own turf?" Sami said, finishing his thought. "Makes a lot of sense."

"I like the way you're thinking, Shad," Franklin said, "the more we know about this thing, the better shot I have against him. You reminded me of something, too. The light coming from the sun in that bizarre world was orange, not so much white or yellow or whatever, like here."

Parker had been quiet for a minute, listening with interest. She finally said, "You know, I'll bet you're right Shad. Sorry to snap like that, Snotty. If the sunlight was orange there, it probably means that red and yellow are two of the major colors in its light spectrum, wherever that place is. You know, red and yellow make orange, right? I'm thinking there might not be as many blue, indigo, green or violet rays of light coming from that nasty sun, you know? Just a guess." Parker seemed to be getting into it now. "So, maybe just ROY? Could be that G. BIV decided to take a vacation," she said, giving Shad a saucy grin.

"Maybe," Franklin replied. "All I know is that it really gives me the creeps when that faceless goon says he needs my eyes. Why would he need them?"

He looked from one friend to the next, and the light of the desk lamp shimmered in both of his deep purple wells as he did. He continued, "I used to have blue eyes. Normal, blue eyes. And now I guess these crazy violet eyes come as part of a package deal along with the new talents I have." He glanced down as if he was embarrassed to show them his eyes.

"Crazy? I wish I had your eyes!" Shad announced. "You should hear what the girls say about you and those violet peepers of yours… I hear them talking sometimes in the dining room after you leave, and they think you are, and I quote, 'like a mystery waiting to be solved.' One girl said you are 'exotically handsome'."

Shad paused and shook his head. His eyes stared into a faraway place, "I'm positive that some of the girls here at the orphanage have big crushes on you, I mean…" he stumbled over his words after noticing Sami giving him a stern look, " I mean no one in this room right now, but some of the nine and ten-year-olds down the hall."

Franklin looked casually over at Sami, who had decided it was her turn to look down and avoid everyone's eyes. Even through the light-brown skin tone of her cheeks, Franklin could tell she was blushing.

CHAPTER THIRTEEN
A BOOK READING & A BABY BOX

From the other side of the closed bedroom door, somewhere in the hallway, came an animated but gruff voice, "All right kids, time for the evening story!"

It was Papa Hank. About twelve years ago, he had started the tradition of reading a book to the kids almost every evening on the weeknights at 8:00 p.m., and he still followed through unless something came up. Papa Hank believed in exposing the children to classic books like *Robinson Crusoe, Treasure Island, Frankenstein,* and *Oliver Twist*; all of these novels, he felt, were ones that kids should read by the time they were out of high school. Tonight he was finishing up *The Call of the Wild*.

"I wish he was reading some Isaac Asimov," Shad whispered to Franklin as they walked to the living room. "Of course, most of these kids would have nightmares."

"Who?"

"Isaac Asimov. One of the first great science fiction authors of our time," Shad answered, a little offended that he had to explain who this obviously remarkable author was.

"Oh…well, I don't need anything else to have nightmares about. Jack London is just fine with me," Franklin whispered back.

He thought for a moment about the book that Hank was reading, *Call of the Wild*. "I wish I had a dog like Buck," he said. "He might give those mega-sized wolves a run for their money."

Franklin and Shad walked over to a brown cushy sofa and sat down. All the other children were either on couches, stuffed chairs or sitting on the floor, gathered around Papa Hank. Most were in their pajamas, as it was going to be lights-out in the orphanage not too long after the story was over.

It was not mandatory for the residents to be at this nightly ritual because some of them had homework to complete on school nights, but not many kids missed the opportunity to be around friends and have a snack afterward. The brick fireplace in the corner of the room housed a few small, dancing flames, although the weather outside was not frightful in the least. Usually, it was Gloria who would get the fire going, thinking it added to the ambiance of Papa Hank's reading.

In an old creaking rocker, Hank rocked back and forth, a smile painted on his face. The whole scene always reminded Franklin of his kindergarten days, right before nap time when the teacher would also read to them from a rocking chair.

Papa Hank was a skinny man, but the kids had no questions about how tough he was. He had been a professional lightweight boxer in his earlier years and still had the muscle tone. Once, after a major storm had blown through Abundant Lakes, causing mayhem around the property, the children had seen him single-handedly clear the yard of large, fallen trees. He had also built the sizable shed in the backyard by himself, unloading at least a hundred cinder blocks, at forty pounds each, from his truck.

"Franklin Hobbs!" Papa Hank spoke loudly above the murmuring voices of the children. "Franklin, I hear you had quite an adventure today on old Rock Hill." The big smile Hank was famous for made an appearance, his mustache twitching at the same time.

The first thing Franklin thought was, *Does Papa Hank really not know its nickname is Cast Maker Canyon, not Rock Hill?*

He noticed some of the girls sitting nearby peek over at him when Papa Hank said this, then turn and giggle at each other, covering their mouths.

Papa Hank was expecting an answer, so Franklin said, "Uh, yeah Papa Hank. Thank goodness it wasn't *more* of an adventure. I think I made a good decision not to go down, though." He spoke loudly so his voice would carry to where Hank sat. Franklin wasn't sure exactly why the man was bringing this up in front of the whole house but recalled his conversation with Hank before dinner and how strange he had acted. At this point, it looked like things hadn't gotten any better.

He studied Hank for a moment. The orphanage steward had always had a greenish-blue shine around him, ever since Franklin had moved into the home. He did now as well. Greenish-blue, Franklin decided, meant that he was a kind man, but had an edge if pushed too far. Not anything dangerous, it usually just meant a bad temper was possible in the right circumstances. Franklin knew some very compassionate teachers at school who had a shine with the same coloration around them, and he had seen them lose their cool with a student every now and then.

Upon closer look, and to his shock, Franklin noticed a blackish tone bordering the rest of the shine; he had not seen this during his earlier conversation with him. It was a very thin black hue, but it was no doubt very dark. Franklin cringed at what this could mean.

"Well Franklin, I'm sure glad you made such a mature decision. We're all so thrilled that you did not die a horrible death on that hill!" His voice was drenched in sarcasm. He began walking towards the couch where Franklin and Shad were sitting and pointed his bony finger towards the middle of Franklin's face. "It was extremely stupid to even consider doing that Franklin! I expect more from such a gifted and talented boy like you!"

Feeling the need to defend himself, Franklin said, "I turned back around, Papa Hank. I didn't go down Cast Maker Canyon."

He had said 'Cast Maker Canyon' a bit brazenly to emphasize the correct nickname. Not quite sassy, but close.

Even so, Papa Hank's face crumpled into a look of disgust, "Do not get mouthy with me, Franklin Hobbs!"

He took the book in his hand and launched it towards Franklin and Shad. It sailed through the air and landed on the couch between them, bounced, and fell to the floor. The whole room grew silent. Not one child dared to look at either Franklin or Papa Hank.

A holler from across the room broke the thickening tension that hung in the air, "Papa Hank, you stop that immediately!" It was Gloria. She had been outside putting away toys left in the yard. Now her large frame was standing at the front door, hands on her hips and exasperation on her face.

Then, as if Gloria had just pushed a button on a remote control, Papa Hank's face melted back into a smile, "April Fools! I'm just yankin' your chain, Frankie boy."

The children in the room, knowing it was still only March, looked puzzled. Hank bent down towards Franklin to pick up the book and said softly, so only Franklin and Shad could hear, "If I had wanted to hit you between the eyes with that book, I would've. Used to be a state champion pitcher, you know? You better be careful, kid."

He turned to the rest of the children and exclaimed, "Let's read, huh?"

A collective sigh of relief was heard from around the room as Papa Hank walked to his rocking chair and sat back down.

"All right kids," he began, "this is chapter seven, it's called 'The Sounding of the Call'. Let's see what kind of trouble Buck gets into."

He cleared his throat and then began reading:
 "When Buck earned sixteen hundred dollars in five minutes for John Thornton, he made it possible for his master to pay off certain debts…"

Hank's deep voice reverberated off the wooden floors and plaster walls, providing a calming pacifier that helped soothe the nerves of the rattled group.

Nonna Glo came over and sat down on the fireplace hearth behind Hank.

Shad asked quietly, "You okay, Franklin?" His nose was dripping mucus, and Franklin instinctively moved his hand away from the area on the couch that would soon be covered in it. He reached into his pocket and handed Shad an old tissue. His friend gladly took it and blew his nose.

"Yeah, I think so. That was a hardcover book. I'm glad he decided to miss!" Franklin said, his heartbeat finally slowing down a bit.

"I'm glad Nonna Glo stepped in," Shad said.

"Yeah, perfect timing."

He looked at Gloria. Surprisingly, the same black hue that was around Hank also outlined the deep blue shine that had consistently emanated from her. The blue aura, he knew, was due to Gloria's faithfulness and love that she had always shown towards the children and anyone in her life whom she cared for.

Now, the black edge went completely around her blue shine. Was Darkness creeping into Gloria, too?

"Franklin," someone whispered to him. He turned around to see Sami kneeling behind the couch. "Let's get out of here. Hank's acting really weird and I had a question for you anyway," she said.

Franklin let Shad know what he was doing, and his roommate nodded. As he tiptoed through the children sitting on the floor like he was in a labyrinth, he could feel Papa Hank's stare, even as he read. This was confirmed when Papa Hank paused his reading in mid-sentence and said, "Be good, Franklin Hobbs."

He shuddered.

Sami led him to the kitchen; far enough away from the group to be sure the two could not be heard.

"Whoa!" she said. "What is going on with Papa Hank? He was acting like a psycho!"

"I don't know. When I talked to him earlier he had a migraine headache, and he acted strangely then, too." He also explained to her about the black shade that was now part of the aura he gave off.

"What do you think that means?" Sami asked.

"It might mean nothing. Maybe he's just having a rough day. I've seen it on other people before who have never shown black in their shine either. Sometimes it just goes away. But Gloria, she also had it. Both of them shadowing at the same time is a little uncanny."

"Shadowing?"

"That's what I call it when someone starts to shine black," he replied. Then remembering that Sami had needed to talk to him about something, he asked, "Hey, is everything all right?"

"Yeah, I just thought of something as Hank was reading," she said. "I remembered that you had mentioned earlier about a baby box of memories that you had taken from your house. Your mom had scribbled something on the wall about it. Did you ever figure out what she meant?"

Franklin thought back to that day, the worst day of his life. He remembered holding the box tight as the police, along with a social worker, had driven him to the orphanage. His tears had discolored the top of the red box so that it was now pink. Later, when he had looked through it, he had found nothing out of the ordinary. Just pictures of him and his mom at the hospital, at the shelter, first steps, first birthday, first cake all over his face, one of him holding a toy that his mom had gotten from the stash of gifts supplied by the shelter. Birth certificate, baby tag and a hospital bracelet, baby shoes, first haircut clippings in a sandwich bag and a few other things that he had seen millions of times. His mom had always made it a special treat to take out the box and have him look through it on his birthday. He had found nothing really new, nothing out of the ordinary in the box, and had no idea what it was that his mom wanted him to see.

Franklin shrugged, "I've looked through that box at least two or three times in the last year and a half. The last time I did was when I turned eleven, a year ago. There was nothing there that was helpful. Just memories in a box. Maybe my mom wasn't really trying to tell me anything. Maybe she just wanted me to remember how much she loved me. I can't figure it out."

"She just happened to write 'baby box' on the wall, Franklin Hobbs, for no apparent reason?" Sami looked frustrated, and she used his full name, which meant she was. "How about you let me take a look at the stuff in the box? Maybe fresh eyes would notice something you missed."

"Sure, why not?"

They walked quietly past the huddled children listening to Papa Hank's story and then up the steps into the boys' section of the house. At the top of the stairs, the wooden floor gave way to worn yellow carpet, which covered the entirety of the second level. The narrow hallway went both left and right; to the right were three bedrooms, and to the left were two. Franklin turned right and went into the first room he came to. Sami followed him in and immediately pinched her nose, crying out, "Franklin, what is that awful smell?"

Franklin looked around. Old, sweaty clothes lay on the bed and remnants of various snacks were crumbling or turning brown on his desk. A piece of moldy cheese that must have fallen out of a lunch bag sat next to the garbage can.

"I really don't know what you're smelling. Everything seems pretty status quo in here to me." The broad smile on his face turned to laughter, and he said, "All right, so Shad and I are a couple of slobs. We're boys without moms or dads to pick up after us. What can I say?"

Sami smiled, "I'll plug my nose while you find the box."

Franklin went straight for his bed, his favorite hiding spot for special things, and got down on the floor, thrusting his arm far underneath it into the darkness. He struggled to get his fingers around the box, but finally got a hold of it and pulled it out.

"You mind if we go out in the hallway and look at this?" Sami asked, still holding her nose.

"Yeah, that's fine, but you need to get your sense of smell checked out." He left the room, but held the door for her, "I wish my mom had given me more of an idea about what I should look for. She must have scrawled that message on the wall after she had seen something coming for her. She probably only had a few seconds after putting the book out on my desk."

"Why do you think she didn't mention the baby box in the letter that she put in the book?"

"Probably because it was a discovery she made after the letter was written. Maybe she just noticed something about the contents of the box in the last few days. That letter was already two months old when I found it, according to the date she wrote."

They sat in the hallway, backs against the painted brown door. The upstairs was empty; almost everyone was down listening to Papa Hank's story. Sami's curly hair swept Franklin's face as she adjusted her position, trying to get comfortable on the thin carpet. It tickled his nose and he almost sneezed in her face but caught himself.

Holding the box, Sami opened it carefully, as if it held precious and ancient relics. Her eyes went wide as she looked at all the contents. Finally, she pulled something out.

"Is this your hair?" she asked, faking disbelief.

"I guess…"

"So adorable Frankie!" she said teasingly, holding up a clipping of his first haircut, which his mom had saved. He didn't mind being teased by her.

Next, Sami pulled out his birth certificate, "Franklin Samuel Hobbs. Born March 19th, 2005 at 4:35 p.m. at St. Marcus Community Hospital. Born to Angel Marie Hobbs and Samuel Broy Hobbs."

She paused, "You never talk about your father."

"He died a few months before I was born; Mom said his heart just got really sick one day."

Sami laid down the paper and picked up a tiny plastic bracelet that had 'Franklin Samuel Hobbs' written on it in cursive handwriting. She ran her fingers along it. "So tiny," she said.

"Do you have one of these, too?" he asked, but immediately wished he could take the words back. "I'm sorry, that was a stupid question."

"No, it's okay. I don't. I haven't been given much as far as my family history or even a birth certificate. They knew my name, but not where I was born. My mom and dad are unknown."

Sami stared without blinking right through the baby I.D. bracelet in her hand. Franklin knew he had brought up a painful topic for her. "One Sunday morning, I guess, when I was about a year old, they tell me I was left at a church nursery while my mom went to the service. There was a name tag pinned to my shirt. She never came back to get me. My first foster parents told me that she was a tall white lady, so I suppose my dad must have been black."

Her glance met his concerned eyes, then she looked back down. "I lived with my first foster parents until I was six, but since then I bounced from home to home; that is until I came here a few years ago, right before you did."

Sami swallowed hard and rubbed her eyes, in case any tears had come yet; but they were dry. She continued, "Most of the families that I thought loved me gave me up at some point. That was tough, but here I am, and hopefully I'll be here for awhile. No more families. I can't handle being rejected anymore." She looked up at Franklin, her chestnut brown eyes had finally welled up with tears, but none had escaped them yet.

"I'm sorry, Sami. I shouldn't have brought it up," Franklin said.

She smiled at him and her face lost any trace of the pain that it had only seconds ago. For the first time, Franklin noticed the slight freckles that dotted her cheeks, barely visible on her brown skin. He thought they were cute.

She said, "Why are you sorry? It feels good to talk about it. Besides, you just told me your whole life story a while ago."

He was quiet for a second. Then, "We just celebrated your twelfth birthday in December. How do they know that was the day you were born?"

"They don't. It was just the day my mom left me at the church, and since I looked close to a year old, December 8th became my official birthday."

She put down the bracelet and picked up some pictures, "That must be you being held by your mom." Sami's eyes went wide again, "She is gorgeous, Franklin! You never told me your mom was so pretty! And look at you. You're a really cute little guy, too."

He looked at the picture and saw a chubby-faced baby with a blue hat on its head looking back at him. And his mom, her beautiful long, brown hair, loving smile, kind eyes, was holding him so tenderly... it hurt to look at her. He missed her so much. The time stamp on the back of the picture showed March 19th, 4:53 p.m., about twenty minutes after he was born.

"She is beautiful, isn't she?" Franklin agreed with Sami. Then, to keep himself from crying, he said, "I've always thought that I look a little like an alien in this picture, with my big eyes and small head."

Something occurred to Franklin for the *first time* as he looked at himself in the picture. In the photo, his legs were both visible. His mom had taken him out of his blanket to cuddle with him. His legs were curled up, resting on her stomach, but both were in plain sight. On the right leg, above the knee, there was no patch of brown on the skin. He looked down at his own knee; he was wearing shorts, so the small birthmark was visible. It had been there as long as he could remember. The shape had always reminded him of a little turtle. Is it possible for birthmarks to form after someone is born? He didn't think it was. That would contradict the word 'birth' in its name.

"C'mon, Franklin, that's how all babies look. Look at the bits of hair sticking up on your head here in this one." Sami handed him another picture where his mom still held him, taken only a minute later than the last one, according to the timestamp. In this photo, his knit cap lay beside him.

"Sami, can I take a look at the bag that you showed me? With my first haircut sample in it?" Again, he thought he might have found something peculiar.

She handed the baggie with the very blonde, almost white, hair clippings inside. Sami peeked over at the picture in his hand and commented, "Your hair isn't really blonde in that picture, is it Franklin?" She was right, his mussed up hair, the little there was, looked fairly dark in the photo.

The baggie had a date written on it in his mom's neat cursive with permanent blue marker; it said 'September 30th, 2005, First Haircut'.

"That's only 6 months after this other picture was taken," he replied. "Is it normal for hair to go from dark to towhead white in six months?"

"Maybe, I don't know. What are you thinking?" she asked him.

"Not quite sure."

Sami rummaged through the box some more, fidgeted with something inside it, then held up two photographs. She began to laugh and held one of the photos closer for Franklin to see.

"Look," she said.

He remembered the photograph that she showed him. It was a classic birthday party photo.

"There's cake all over your face!" she exclaimed.

Franklin laughed with her, "You can barely even see me through the frosting."

"Yeah, but it still looks like you. Pretty much every night after we have dessert," she kidded. "This smaller one here, it was stuck to the back. She handed him a square-shaped photograph and asked, "Who's this lady?"

Franklin took the photo from her. Part of the corner had peeled off where it was attached to the other picture, but most of it was visible. It was a Polaroid, an instant photograph that had the name of the hospital embossed in gold letters on the front. Probably taken by a nurse. Looking at it for only a few seconds, he concluded that he had never seen this particular picture before. He had never noticed it stuck to the cake photo.

Franklin shot Sami a confounded look, "This isn't my mom, that's for sure. No idea who it is."

It was a picture of a woman in her twenties, with unkempt blonde hair. Something about her features struck Franklin as familiar. The woman was also holding a baby. He turned the picture over; on the back was written, 'March 19th, 2005, 5:45 p.m.'.

Franklin shrugged, "Huh. This was taken a little while after I was born. Looks like a brand-spankin' new baby. Same hospital, too."

On the backside of the picture, underneath the timestamp, a note was inked in sloppy handwriting; it said:

'September 2015

To Angel. Look Closely.

Proof so you can understand.

Charles'

"Very odd," he said, "my mom must have received this picture just weeks or days before she was abducted. From someone named Charles."

"Could this be what your mom wanted you to see?" Sami asked him.

"Maybe, just not sure why yet," he answered.

When he turned the worn photograph back over, his eyes went to the infant the blonde woman was holding. This baby also had some hair on its head, but lighter than his own newborn tufts had been in the last photo. He studied the baby's pudgy legs, dangling off of her arm. And there it was. A birthmark. He couldn't tell if it looked like a turtle, but it was in the right spot.

"Okay, I'm not sure what's going on here." He pointed to the infant, "Look at this birthmark on the baby she's holding."

Sami glanced at it, "Yeah, I see it."

He now motioned to his own right leg, where the small birthmark was. Sami looked down.

"Looks like a turtle," she giggled, "but I see what you're getting at. That is kind of a coincidence."

He set the picture down and Sami picked it right back up. She held it closer to her eyes, studying it with more intent. Suddenly, a cry of, "What the…?" erupted from her, causing Franklin to drop the plastic baggie that contained his hair, spilling his little blonde clippings all over the carpet.

"What the heck is that?" she yelled, this time almost loud enough for all the kids gathered downstairs around Papa Hank to hear.

She was pointing to a corner section of the picture.

"I don't see anything... that's just some hospital machinery and monitors that they keep next to the patient," he answered, a little befuddled by her outburst.

"No, not that. Beneath it." Her finger tapped the picture this time.

Now it was Franklin's turn to take the picture near to his face and examine it. He could see the medical equipment on a small table by the bed; he guessed it was a heart monitor and whatever else they use for new babies. Underneath the table was a shadowy, dark space. Seeing anything there was nearly impossible. But.... he saw something!

There was the faintest outline of a head and shoulders lurking ominously in the dark. The shadows hinted at the semblance of long, spindly legs tucked up under the head, coming to a point at the knees.

"Is that Nefari?" He practically choked as he asked the question.

He brought the picture even closer to his eyes. There were no features of a face to see, but on the head, long streaks of a darker color appeared to hang down past the shoulders. Hair.

"I think that's probably a woman, look at the hair!" Franklin said.

Then he remembered what his mom had written in her letter; that it was a faceless woman, not a man, who walked in front of her car, causing the accident that led to his paralysis.

He looked again. "I can't see if she has a face or not. It's too dark, but I'm almost certain this is a creature of the shadows...the Darkness, like Nefari," Franklin said.

And he really couldn't think of any other reason why a normal person would be hiding underneath a table in the shadows.

Still recovering, Sami said, "I believed you before Franklin, about the man without a face, but this makes it so real, so awful." She shivered, then asked, "Do you think your mom saw that thing in the picture? Is that what she wanted you to see?"

He thought for a moment, "My mom's pretty observant. I think she probably noticed both the birthmark and the phantom under the table. Besides, the note this Charles guy wrote makes you want to look at every detail like we just did. I just don't know why she didn't show this to me right away after she got it."

"She must have had her reasons, Franklin. Women like us can be mysterious in our ways sometimes." She leaned into him and let her shoulder bump into his.

He turned to her and smiled, "Yeah, that's true. Girls can act pretty random sometimes... and do things that make absolutely no sense." He bumped her back with his elbow.

"Ha-ha, get used to it, Frankie boy," she chortled but returned his smile.

Sami picked up another photograph from the box, one that had the corners starting to curl up from being held so often by little hands. "It says March 19th, 11:30 p.m. on the back. It was late at night, but still on the day you were born."

"I love that one," Franklin said, looking at it as Sami held it in front of him. "I used to hold it all the time when I was younger and just stare at it."

This particular photograph was of Angel smiling tenderly as she peered down at Franklin, who was lying on a cart table. A pair of hands, probably a nurse's, were in the picture holding a tape measure along his tiny body.

"Taking my measurements," he said, not moving his eyes from it.

He had always cherished this photo because of the gentle way his mom was watching him. Whenever he tried to form a picture of her in his mind now, he always imagined her with this expression.

Just then, Sami poked him in the ribs and asked, "Do you have a magnifying glass?"

He set the photo down, "Yeah, sure. I'll be right back."

A minute later, Sami held a small magnifying glass up to the picture. Franklin laughed at her, "You look like you're about to do your Sherlock Holmes impression again with that thing."

Ignoring him, she exclaimed, "Look! There's that horrible woman again!"

"What?" Franklin asked, positive she was wrong. "No. I've looked at this picture a thousand times—"

Sami interrupted him, "Yeah, but she's in the background. Really tiny. You would have never noticed it."

Franklin held the photo up in front of him and put the magnifying glass an inch away from it, then leaned in.

In the picture, the door to Angel's hospital room was still open. Beyond that, across the hall, he was now able to see that another door was open as well. A different patient's room. It was here that Sami had asked Franklin to look closely. In the dark of the shadows, like the other photo, was the very faint outline of a slim, tall figure, only this time standing. Straight, black hair draped around its shoulders. A nurse or doctor maybe? No, they would probably not be hiding in the dark. Looking again, he saw a slight point on the top of the phantom's head. A hoodie! Like the one Nefari always wore.

Exasperated, he set the photo and magnifying glass down, then threw his hands in the air. "Why is that thing stalking me?" he asked.

Sami tried to help, "I'm not sure she was stalking *you*, Franklin. In both pictures, she's in a different room than you are at the time."

Franklin considered that. He looked back down at the fading picture of the baby being measured on the table. The little guy had a hat on, so his hair color was unknown. But just visible beneath one of the nurse's arms, he was able to see the dark smudge of a birthmark over the baby's right knee.

This was him in the picture, no doubt about it. In the first photograph, though, where his mom held him immediately after he was born, there was no birthmark.

Franklin couldn't make heads or tails of it. It made no logical sense to him. Why was his mom holding a baby that wasn't him in the first picture they looked at? And then how did he end up with her later that same night? What had really happened twelve years ago on his birthday?

"Okay," he declared, "well, I am being stalked *now* for some reason. It looks like Nefari might be this woman's long-lost faceless brother." He laughed despite the grim thought, then said, "Great, a pair of mutant siblings are after me."

For a moment, neither of them said anything, but the silence was okay. Then Franklin said, "My mom told me that Good and Evil are competing for me. I know 'Evil' wants to kill me. What does 'Good' want me for? They haven't even made an appearance yet."

Sami answered, "Your mom also said in that letter that something was helping you when you fell out of the car, or you would have been killed by that tree branch. Somehow your car seat was unbuckled and the door was unlocked and opened. Falling onto the street saved your life."

Franklin picked up the pictures and flipped through them. He stopped when he got to the one he was looking for. It was a photograph of the car, which the police had given his mom a few days after the accident. She hadn't asked for the picture, but the officer in charge thought she might want to have it anyway. The picture showed the small car's front end sticking out of a shallow ditch. Franklin recognized some of the houses in the background; it was a street near his school.

A massive branch, still covered with green leaves and still connected to an enormous tree, had completely smashed out the back window and was jutting into the car's backseat. Franklin knew that he would've been sitting right there if he had not tumbled out the door and onto the street. He would've been right where the branch, with all of its sharp pointed ends, had come to rest.

He sighed, "I know you and my mom are right, Sami. It's just hard for me to believe that being a paraplegic for most of my life was a good thing. I guess I'm super grateful I didn't get killed though."

"Whatever gave you that little push out the car door," Sami replied, "must have known that they would eventually heal you too. It was in their plan from the beginning."

Everything Sami said made sense to Franklin. There wasn't really any other way to explain his life. He was so thankful that he had this incredible friend, who supported him and had these insanely intelligent insights into his life. He only wished he would have told her everything sooner and not waited a year.

A group of boys came clamoring up the stairs; Hank was through reading for the evening and the kids needed to get ready for bed. Franklin put everything back in the box and closed it. They both stood and Sami went back into Franklin's room, with him right behind her. He bent down and slid the box under the bed again as hard as he could and heard it hit the wall.

"Thanks, Sami," Franklin said, "things make more sense when you're around for some reason, and you saw things that I may never have noticed in those pictures."

Sami took a step toward Franklin and wrapped her arms tightly around him. Franklin, several inches taller than her, stood with his arms trapped against the sides of his body for a moment before he wriggled them free and returned her hug.

"I'm always here for you Franklin, you know that," she said.

"Yeah, I know that."

CHAPTER FOURTEEN
A GORILLA & A GANG OF GOBLINS

The Gatherer was in a very unpleasant mood. Because of his recent failures to collect the boy's eyes, Bramfasa, Lord of Dark Earth, wanted to speak with him face to face. No doubt to belittle him like usual. And so he had summoned Nefari to come to Quietus Tumulus, where he sat on the Obsidian Throne. Nefari expected this, so it was no surprise when the Usher, an unintelligent, but nasty creature, tracked him down and relayed the command from Bramfasa.

Earlier, Nefari had decided to spend the night in the human realm, along with his canine companions, to hunt some of the tasty delicacies it offered. There had still been time to partake in the sport, for the slashing and dicing rays of the yellow sun had hours until they would burst forth.

He had traveled in his most true and comfortable form (the shapeless, black sludge) and slithered through one of the many Gateways nearby that led to this middle plane of Earth. Inhabitants of Nefari's realm called it Mortal Earth, for none of its creatures, including humans, would live here forever. That was indeed the part he loved most about it, snuffing out the life of the innocent fauna around him.

He also appreciated the varieties of food on Mortal Earth. So many different critters than where he was from. When in the form of Darkness, almost nothing could outrun him either; his sleek, shapeless body would catch them eventually. And if for some reason his prey was outpacing him, one of his favorite embodiments to become was the swarm of flies, which would allow him to quickly reach his meal and surround it.

Hiding from him was out of the question. The dark was *his* domain. Nothing could hide from him in darkness. So on this night, he had snacked on a few wild rabbits and then on one domesticated pet rabbit, which he had found chewing cabbage in a cage right outside of a human home. He left plenty of blood and fur behind for the humans to find. Imagining the sadness this would bring to the children living there, waking up to see their beloved pet had been something's dinner, helped to cheer him up after his failure of gathering the boy's eyes.

And the cats. They were not even fearful of him when he was in his shapeless dark form. Was it possible because they, too, had some of their own Darkness? Nefari wasn't sure. Whatever it was, it made cats easy to snatch up with one of his quiet, cunning appendages, which he could sprout whenever he felt the need and then maneuver it over to the unsuspecting kitty, dragging it hissing and scratching back into the abyss of his shapeless mass, where his stomach made easy work of it.

The tissue from which he was made could digest these animals almost at once, rarely leaving anything behind, (unless he intended to) except maybe a few small bones.

This night he had allowed the entities of his wolves, which were part of his essence, to emerge from his formless shape and run loose to find their own food. When they had finally come back to him, they had eaten their fill and found a spot to lie near him.

But then that lackey for Bramfasa, the Usher, showed up in the middle of his dinner. How did this thing track him down, especially here on Mortal Earth? Bramfasa must have his little spies everywhere. If Nefari thought he could have gotten away with it, he would have devoured the Usher right then as well. At least as much of him as he could fit into his stomach.

Instead, when the Usher said, in his low, gruff voice, "You must turn into ugly human so I can take you now. I take you to Quietus Tumulus. Bramfasa demands see you. Put this on," Nefari decided to follow the order.

The beast handed Nefari a collar of steel, one which prisoners wear when being transported by an Usher. Nefari, although reluctant, left his shapeless body and became the faceless humanoid, joining with his wolves once again (although this time with only *one* head). He then allowed the moronic creature to fasten an iron leash to the collar. The Usher was a dark being, like him, but was much further down on the chain of command. It was of the species ZiShan, and although an underling, it had been given authority from Bramfasa, and so Nefari had to obey.

This creature was not able to take on human or any other form, like the StyJeens could. A ZiShan had to remain in its own grotesque body throughout the entirety of its life. There were many times when Nefari had scoffed at these low status, unintelligent, and subservient creatures. The Usher was a simple beast of burden, not a trusted, honored StyJeen, who, like himself, was given critical tasks to perform for the good of all Darkness.

A ZiShan was, however, a formidable creature; very large. Nearly two feet taller than Nefari was at present and much wider. The Usher led Nefari back through the darkness, towards the entrance of the Gateway, which would take them back to their own realm. They were currently in a residential area, among smaller, one-story houses. It was not well lit, which is why Nefari had chosen this particular area. The Usher was, for some reason, dragging Nefari towards the only street light around.

"What are you doing you imbecccile?" he shouted incredulously. "I can't be near bright light in thissss realm! There isss a Gateway on the other ssside of thisss human dwelling area, at a farm, where the darknesssss issss thick. Take me there!"

The Usher paid no heed to Nefari's request but kept right on walking into the white light cast by the high-posted lamp. As they approached and the intense rays of light fell upon the StyJeen, he began to itch. He scratched himself furiously all over, so frantically that he ripped into his black jacket and pants, the pieces of falling fabric dissipating into mist on their way to the ground. As his long nails dug into the skin on his head, still trying to suppress the burning itch, pieces of his scalp began to slough off, both hair and skin becoming black vapor as it fell from the rest of his flesh.

"Sssstop! You're going to kill me!" he screamed in vain.

He tried pulling back against the shackles that held him, but the Usher was relentless, it held the chain securely in one hand. The beast reached the metal post and began shimmying up it with its free hand and gorilla-like feet, towards the lamp, dragging Nefari beneath him. Moths and other insects were already there, beating themselves up as they tried to reach the mystical yellow glow of the light; a light that always seemed to elude them. They darted this way and that around the summit of the pole, only to be swatted away by the ascending Usher. Nefari, still molting bits and pieces of himself as the sharp daggers of light burned into him, decided he must defy

Bramfasa; he must escape his captor before there was nothing left of him.

He focused on blackness, and as he did his body began vibrating, trembling, beginning the transformation back into his shapeless entity, which would allow him to slip out and away from the iron neck cuff. But in an instant, before the transformation could be completed, the Usher, having reached the top of the lamp post and already standing atop it, jumped straight up into the air, leaving the pole vibrating like a diving board and dragging Nefari up and along the pole, smashing his head into the bulb's glass casing on the way and finally hurtling him through an unseen, energy-filled passageway, which must have been only a few feet up and over from the top of the light post.

They passed through the Gateway and were deposited into their own realm, Dark Earth; one of the three parallel planes of Earth. Sometimes it was referred to as 'The Realm of Separation' by those humans who theorized of its existence, naming it this due to its eternal breach from any true light.

The pair made their entrance, hammering down onto the ground, and found themselves next to a shriveled river of orange, bubbling water. The river, instead of reflecting the copper rays of light from the sun, absorbed them, giving its water the appearance of ripe apricot juice.

For some reason, Mortal Earth had at least two additional hours of night than here on Dark Earth, where the sun had already risen. Even as early as it was, the heat was absolutely suffocating and felt phenomenal to Nefari. No longer exposed to that horrid white light from Mortal Earth, he had stopped shedding fragments of himself and had momentarily forgotten about the abusive treatment he had endured. He smiled as he saw the familiar black forms of large, winged, reptilian creatures swarming the banks and fighting over the few fish that still remained in the river.

Grey beasts, about the size of a German Shepherd, but closer in relation to a sewer rat, were bathing farther out. Some of them, like great water-striding bugs, used their front and back legs to skim across the water's surface at fast speeds, searching for their next meal. They would only stop occasionally to put their heads under the orange filth when they noticed movement. Other inhabitants, bright red and spider-like, dove down into the muck searching for anything they could find that was edible. Despite their labor, rarely would any of these creatures emerge from the river with something to eat.

All of these sights he took in, and all of these sights caused Nefari to stew in something that was similar to pride; pride at knowing his planet was home to these magnificent, but ordinary creatures. Not as tasty as rabbits and cats, but not nearly as bizarre and hideous looking either.

In the human realm, this was the Pleasant Acres River, which flowed through the middle of Abundant Lakes, Minnesota. Here it had no name, but it was almost anything but pleasant. Further downstream the river had dried up, and soon this section would evaporate as well; these creatures that depended on it would either dry up with it or find another water source, which on Dark Earth was almost as rare as finding a diamond mine.

Nefari returned his glare to the ZiShan who was pulling him along and studied the oaf with disgust. This was a creature that brought no upheavals of pride for Dark Earth from the pits of his gut. The Usher was not a pleasing sight to look at, even with Nefari's standards. The tremendous beast, as well as can be described here, had the face of an old grizzled troll; baggy skin slumped down his cheeks so that the bulge of the cheek-sag hung far below his lower lip. His plump nose, riddled with lumps, also sagged on his face. The ZiShan's ears were large, far too large for his head, and they too, like the rest of his face, drooped down, to the point where they were almost touching his shoulders. His eyes were sizable, mostly white, with only small brown irises. This particular ZiShan must have some sort of disease which brought on deformities, Nefari thought, because apple-sized tumors protruded from its neck and bald head, with smaller ones on his face.

Drool rolled down his chin, and it covered the blood stains and dead tissue left behind from whatever he had for his last meal. From the neck down, this ZiShan resembled a gorilla in appearance. It was obese, but muscular, with thin patches of brown fur covering most its chest and back. Where the fur didn't conceal his flesh, its pale white skin was visible on the bare torso.

Similar to its head, bulges and fleshy knobs also covered the ZiShan's upper body, causing him to appear wonky from one side to the other. Its fur was much thicker from the waist down, and it walked on two legs like gorillas sometimes will do, but when it stopped, it would use its arms and hands to rest on all fours. The Usher lumbered slowly, and the black steel chain around his prisoner's neck hung slack as Nefari walked only a few paces behind.

The sun had been up for two hours now and the sweltering heat waves were visibly scorching the cracked, brown earth. Heat did not affect Nefari, but the ZiShan, with all of his sweat, was beginning to look like a drowning dog. The travelers continued on through dead forests, fields of decay, and canyons of sulfurous gas springs. They descended down into what looked to be at one time the bed of a lake but was now merely a pit for sand and rocks. On Mortal Earth, this was Sunfish Lake, a popular swimming and fishing hole next to Abundant Lakes Junior High School.

"Shortcut," the Usher said to Nefari in his low, raspy voice, not even bothering to turn around when he said it. They walked on through the ancient lake bottom; bones of long-ago fish lay scattered about, some as large as the Usher himself. They came upon a section of the lakebed that had ten or twelve mounds of stones piled high. Nefari knew these to be homes of the creatures that claimed this area. The dwellings were extensive holes which were dug deep into the clay of the lakebed and then hidden from immediate sight by rocks piled up around its edges, so that each dwelling appeared to be nothing more than a stockpile of stones.

Without warning, a green impish creature, no taller than a six-year-old child, appeared from the stones, armed with a wooden club and a dagger fastened to its waist. It had come up from a hole and now stood on top of one of the piles of stone.

Nefari, detached from any emotion, informed the Usher casually, "You brought ussss through a Rock-Goblin village, you halfwit."

The nose of the devilish goblin standing in front of them was long and turned upwards, coming to a pointy end between its eyes. Its ragged ears, resembling those of a pig, protruded directly out from the side of its head and were garnished with golden rings in both lobes. Small yellow eyes were sunk deep into its skull, and it glared at them with menace. The biggest feature on its face was its mouth, which boasted teeth like a surgeon's scalpel. Saliva coated the outer edges of its lips.

Patches of hair stuck out here and there, and a long mullet dangled off the back of its head. It wore no shirt, and through the green skin covering its torso, the outline of its ribcage could be seen. It was obvious this creature hadn't eaten in days. The goblin attempted to thrust out its chest, trying to add to its desired threatening appearance.

On its lower half was an old pair of tattered black pants, held up by a leather belt. It took the dagger of bone from its belt and waved it around its head with one scaly, clawed hand, then smashed the club down on the rocks with the other.

Suddenly, seven or eight more of similar appearance joined the first one and stood on the tops of their homes. Some carried bows around their body and quivers full of crude arrows on their backs; every one of them waved their knives back and forth with sinister snarls on their lips

The ZiShan looked at Nefari for council. It was confused about what the proper protocol was when threatened by an army of nine, made up of much smaller creatures than he.

Nefari would have loved to see them attack and feast upon the Usher, but he figured the goblins were the worse of two evils, for the time being, so he decided to give the ZiShan some advice, "Don't let them all attack you at onccce. They work like a pack of wolvessss and will probably cut you down. They're tougher than they look."

The Usher nodded his understanding.

Yes, Nefari remembered coming to this village before. As a Gatherer, at one point, he had been assigned to reclaim some items from one of the dwellers of this community. One of the greedy little green rats had stolen from Quietus Tumulus, Bramfasa's palace. It had found its way in through a rarely used and little known unguarded door and had taken a small amount, for it can't carry much, of the rubies and diamonds with which Bramfasa adorned his most cherished room, The Hall of Torment. Being the favorite place in his palace to spend time in, Bramfasa had put these jewels in there so that it would be elegant at all times.

Nefari was ordered to come to this wretched community to reclaim what was taken, which he had done. He had found the thief, collected the jewels, and then eaten the goblin. Other goblins witnessed this crime against their own kind but decided that a StyJeen of this strength was not to be messed with.

He looked around now and saw that smaller goblins had emerged. These were the females, and they were holding even smaller ones yet; the offspring of the deplorable imps. They were looking at the Usher and drooling, seemingly ready for a long-awaited meal. The male warriors were not interested in Nefari. They remembered what he was capable of, but they seemed to think they stood a chance against the massive ZiShan, as his reputation of a mindless oaf preceded him. And they were hungry.

"Oh, jussst grab one of the little foolsss and demonssstrate to all of them that you are not to be hassled with!" Nefari screamed.

Four or five of the goblins had been jumping from one rock pile to the next, getting nearer with each leap. The closest one was now within reaching distance, and the Usher, heeding his prisoner's advice, lunged for the goblin, grabbed it around the waist, picked it up, and like a club, used it to batter the next one, which had already closed in on him.

This he was able to repeat five or six times, as more came at him. He sent the other brave goblins flying through the air, until they had finally had enough and retreated into their sandy living quarters, dragging their family with them. The one goblin that remained was still being held tightly in the hand of the ZiShan and had been battered to a pulp.

The Usher spoke, "I not going to waste good food," and with that, he began eating the creature as if it were a large green turkey leg.

The two travelers continued across the dead lake without any more excitement.

"You could have shared a little of your lunch with me," Nefari said to the ZiShan, who was, again, several paces in front of him.

It stopped, turned slowly around, though not all the way, and threw five small ribs, with the tiniest amount of meat left on them, in the dirt right in front of Nefari.

"Eat freaky man. I full," the ZiShan said, a loud belch bubbling up from its throat.

Nefari ignored the insult but did not forget it.

CHAPTER FIFTEEN
A CLASH & A KARATE KICK

The breakfast table seemed crowded the next morning. Franklin sat next to Shad and Parker, the latter of which informed him that Sami was still sleeping. Franklin was finishing his scrambled eggs and toast when Gloria came up behind him and patted him on the shoulder.

With her warm voice, she asked, "How do you like the eggs, honey?" Shad looked at Franklin, silently mouthing the word 'Yummmmm' and rubbing his stomach, trying to signal to Franklin what his reply should be to her. Franklin had mentioned to Shad about how Nonna Glo's shine last night was surrounded in a dark black outline, and Shad was concerned about upsetting her. But Gloria's face looked as pleasant as ever this morning, and she seemed to be in a good mood. Franklin was relieved to see only the blue aura was present around her now; there was no darkness outlining it any longer.

"It was delicious, Nonna Glo. Thank you very much." She stared down at him, but not with any hostility, only with the tenderness that Franklin was used to from her.

"Good, honey. Say, I want to apologize for the way Papa Hank treated you last night. I really don't know what has gotten into him. He has been acting strange since yesterday, but last night with you… I have never seen him like that before. I know how much he cares about you Franklin, so please don't let that ruin your image of him. You know he's usually a very kind man." She stopped talking and looked off into the distance. Franklin knew about the feelings she had for Hank and guessed it was these emotions that caused her to grow quiet.

After a moment Gloria continued, "He and I had such a difficult evening after dinner, with one of the children. I am sure you can guess which one. It put us both into such a horrible way."

Of course, she meant Rufus, Franklin had no doubt about that. Could that be why they both had the black band outlining their aura? Maybe they weren't really shadowing. Maybe it was just a rotten mood they were in. Rufus can do that to people. He had seen others who had gone through miserable experiences, which had left a temporary black outline around their glow as well.

"Thanks, Nonna Glo. I understand. I'm not mad at him."

"I talked to him last night about the way he embarrassed you. If he does anything else like that, you come tell me." She patted him on the head and walked off into the kitchen.

"There was something wrong with that man last night," Parker said quietly, so the other kids around the dining room couldn't hear her. "He had a look in his eye. I saw it when he yelled at you. I was sitting on the floor right in front of him."

"What kind of look?" Franklin asked.

"The kind of look you see when somebody truly hates someone else. A crazy gleam. I have seen that look in some people's eyes on the street right before they do something horrible to someone. Almost evil–like." Parker shook her whole body, "Gives me the absolute creeps."

Shad sneezed loudly. "Bless you, Shad." It was Sami coming into the dining room. She found an empty chair next to Parker and sat down.

"Thanks, Sami. Allergies, you know? Franklin, I have a feeling that Papa Hank's strange behavior has something to do with the other things that are happening to you." Shad looked concerned, "If so, then you are in danger here at the orphanage whether you're in the dark or the bright light."

"He's right Franklin. We all need to help watch your back," Sami said.

The other two nodded in agreement.

"Why would you want to watch his back? Face too ugly?" It was Rufus. He said it as he marched into the dining room with white powder around his entire mouth like it had been painted on by some demented makeup artist. He carried a powdered donut in each hand and had just stuffed his face with a third.

Parker chimed in, "Rufus, you and your donuts better sit down and be quiet, or I'll slap that powder off your face."

"So scared Parker. You guys are lame, the four of you. You think you got a little gang here? Are you better than the rest of us?" Rufus sneered, continuing to stand.

"No, just you," Parker shot back.

"Rufus, you're welcome to hang out with us whenever you want, if you keep your attitude in check," Sami said.

Rufus gave her a look, and just for a split second Franklin didn't see the insolent, unmannerly twelve-year-old, but a little boy who had been hurt his whole life. Was it a hopeful expression Rufus had inadvertently let cross his face?

"Why would I ever want to hang out with you losers?" he blurted out.

"Don't you get tired of being by yourself all the time? I know how that feels. I was left alone most of my life. It really sucks," Shad said, looking at Rufus with something like empathy.

"I like being alone. I prefer being alone. Now leave me alone!" he yelled back, trying to wipe the white-powder smile from his mouth with the back of his hand. The strange thing about Rufus, Franklin had always noticed, was that his shine was not gray, black, or even dark at all. It was orange. Although Franklin didn't know what an orange aura around someone meant, he knew it wasn't as bad as black or gray.

"Hey listen, Rufus. You had fun out there with us on your bike yesterday, didn't you?" Franklin asked.

"Fun? I guess if watching you chicken out at the top of the hill is fun. Yeah. I liked seeing you make a complete fool of yourself," Rufus said, curling his chubby lips into a wicked smile as he spoke. The words dug into Franklin. If Rufus was trying to get at him, that had worked.

"You know what, Rufus? You're a big, fat, jerk!" The voice was Sami's. She had scooted her chair back and stood up as she came to the defense of her friend. Her hands were fixed on her hips as she spoke, which only emphasized the insult she had thrown.

Moving quicker than Franklin had ever seen him, Rufus lunged at Sami. Arms extended, he shoved each of her shoulders with enough force to send her crashing to the floor. She landed with a thud on the hardwood, her head nearly smacking the sharp wooden corner of the edging around the window.

Immediately, Parker ran over to Sami to help her. Franklin wasted no time, either. He got up and charged at Rufus with all the speed and strength he had. He left the ground and flew through the air, slamming into Rufus's solid frame, which, Franklin found out, was like slamming into a rock. He wrapped his arms around him, trying to drag him down to the ground. Getting him to the floor wasn't easy. Rufus was 140 pounds, the biggest kid at the orphanage. Finally grabbing his legs, Franklin got him off balance and they both toppled to the floor, where Rufus was able to roll himself over, gaining the advantage by being on top of Franklin. Rufus landed a few punches before Franklin was able to use his legs to wrap him up and then with a quick flip, twist him back underneath him. He positioned himself on top of the bigger boy, holding his legs down with his own, then reached out and used his hands to pin both of Rufus's flailing arms to the ground.

"You hurt my friend, you chowder head!" Franklin bellowed at him, wanting to hit him. His own mouth was bleeding from where Rufus had gotten off a good shot a few seconds before. It also felt to Franklin like his nose might have taken a fist, too. But he restrained himself from hitting him. Franklin could tell that all the fight was gone from Rufus; his adversary lay limply beneath him, heavy breaths coming at a quick pace.

After Rufus had caught his breath he shouted back at Franklin, "No! No, I didn't try to push her! I slipped and pushed her on accident. Now let me go, or I'll tell Nonna Glo!" Nervous sweat, mixed with his usual perspiration, poured down both sides of Rufus's face.

Franklin laughed. "How are you going to do that? You seem to be pinned down at the moment by a guy that weighs 40 pounds less than you."

"Franklin!" It was Shad. "Hurry up! Get off him, quick." There was some serious urgency in his voice.

Franklin looked up toward Shad, "I'm not done with…."

"Get up now, Franklin!" This time it was Papa Hank barking the order.

He reached down and grabbed Franklin's arm, one strap from his overalls hung loosely, and the buckle rattled against the floor. Wrenching Franklin up, he pulled him off of Rufus.

"Ouch, you're hurting my arm, Papa Hank," Franklin said, wincing.

"It looks like you deserve to be hurt you little trouble-making brat!" Papa Hank jeered. "What do you think you're doing to Rufus here? C'mon Rufus, get up. I got him now. He won't hurt you."

Rufus looked shocked. As he got up, he glanced at Sami, Parker, and Shad, who looked equally as surprised.

Franklin was still in Hank's strong grasp.

The man spoke in a taunting voice, "You all right Rufus? You want to take a swing at Frankie here to get even?"

Sami tried to hold her composure as she said, "Rufus pushed me really hard. I could have cracked my head open on the corner of the window frame. Franklin was only trying to help."

Papa Hank looked at her with obvious irritation. "Is that true Rufus? Did you push Sami down?" Other kids were starting to gather around the room to watch, but still keeping their distance from the mayhem.

"I slipped, Papa Hank," Rufus said. He had never referred to him as 'Papa' Hank before, only Hank. "I slipped and fell into her. I tried catching myself but knocked her down, I guess."

Among other things, Rufus was a great liar.

Hank smiled too sweetly at Rufus, then turned to Franklin, "You hear that Frankie? It was an accident. You tackled this poor boy for absolutely nothing. Come take a punch at him, Rufus. Teach him a lesson."

Sami and Parker had both succumbed to tears at this point. Parker yelled, "Let him go you big monkey's butt! You are supposed to look after us! You're supposed to take care of us! What in the name of all that's bald and fat do you think you're doing?"

"You would be wise to watch your mouth you little street urchin. This is between me and Franklin," Hank hissed back. Then, "Leave us alone. All of you."

Sami scoffed through her tears, "There's no way we're leaving our friend with you. Put him down please!"

Not happy with Hank's insult, Parker retorted, "Who are you calling a street urchin you mustached maniac?" She took a quick step to get around Rufus and then kicked Hank right in the shin, hard, "Who's your mama now?" she yelled.

Hank swore and yelled in pain as he rubbed his leg where Parker had kicked him, dropping Franklin in the process. Shad and Sami grabbed Franklin by each arm to scoot him along, and the four of them made tracks to put distance between themselves and Papa Hank.

CHAPTER SIXTEEN
A CRUEL CAMP & A CHASM

It was almost midday now on Dark Earth, and the orange rays of its sun were heating the atmosphere at the normal, blistering rate. On an average spring day, in this northern point of the planet, the temperature would normally reach about 105 degrees.

The reason for Dark Earth's severe climate was due to an event that, thus far, Mortal Earth has not had the misfortune of experiencing. Thousands upon thousands of years ago, a monstrous comet had struck Dark Earth. The comet was large enough and moving with enough velocity that the force of the impact drove the planet several hundred thousand miles closer to its sun.

This distance, although not far when dealing with astronomical measures, was enough to raise the surface temperature of Dark Earth on average between 25-40 degrees. It did not take long for the polar ice caps to melt in the north and flood the low land around the world. The area called California on Mortal Earth was completely swallowed by the ocean on this parallel Earth; as well as much of the East Coast. Many parts of other continents also suffered large amounts of land loss.

The land that didn't end up under the ocean had widespread destruction caused by the temperature increase. Forests died, lakes dried up, fields were destroyed by fires, and many of the weaker creatures went extinct. Some species were able to find ways to adapt and therefore continued to be a food source for the larger and fiercer beasts, like the ZiShan, allowing them to survive as well.

As for the StyJeen, Nefari's kind, and only a few other species on the planet, as long as they stayed on Dark Earth, they were eternal beings, unable to die. Heat couldn't kill them, nor could lack of food. Yes, most of them did hunt, kill, and eat, but only as a form of entertainment and pleasure, not out of necessity.

The two travelers now came to an area of gradual incline, which brought them up out of the lakebed to what at one point in time was a beach. They followed the sandy terrain until they came to a forest that had somehow survived the intense heat of the planet and actually did so with an abundance of lush greenery. On Mortal Earth, this forest would be on the outskirts of Abundant Lakes.

Their feet slogged through surprisingly wet and marshy soil, which was the reason there was so much life left in this woods. There were still some areas of Dark Earth like this where deep, underground lakes and aquifers, ones that the sun had not yet been able to dry up, supplied enough water to sustain life aboveground. These underground aquifers were also the source of the few streams and rivers still flowing.

Activity was happening all around Nefari and the Usher as they trudged along; furry animals scurried at their feet, while enormous insects, the same size as the furry animals, buzzed around their faces. In front of them, a large, winged creature suddenly dove down and attacked one of the scampering fur balls. At first, Nefari assumed it was one of the Manka Hawks of the area, which had survived in this terrifying world because of their agility and eyesight. Nothing, including small trolls and goblins, were safe from their sharp talons. But, when the predator that had swooped in front of him paused before taking off into the sky again with its fresh meal, Nefari saw that it wasn't as large as a Manka Hawk and was actually another beast called an Enfield.

This curious creature had always intrigued him. With the head and body of a fox, but the wings and back legs of an eagle, it was a formidable predator for almost any size critter, and anything that valued its life needed to be aware of its hovering shadow. Enfields were known to take down giants and then feast on them for days until they had rotted. They would go for the eyes of the giant, poking them out with their talons. Then, while their victim struggled to gain its bearings, the Enfield would use its sharp teeth to puncture the jugular vein in the giant's neck, bleeding it out.

Nefari believed the Enfield to be delightful. Anything with that much enthusiasm for a meal was worthy of his admiration. And the way it tortured its prey before killing it? Absolutely a work of art.

This Enfield, in the brief moment before it flew off, gave Nefari and the Usher a hungry glance. Nefari knew the Enfield was considering having a much bigger feast than just the little furry animal it held in his talons. But, when it decided to leave them and settle for its smaller meal, it unknowingly saved its own life, for Nefari was in no mood to be attacked by anything and would have quickly dispatched of it. If it had gone for the Usher, on the other hand, he might have sat down to watch the show.

Finally, they came to the end of the forest and stepped back into the crusty foliage of the barren fields. As he scanned the great expanse of flat land, a cruel smile spread across Nefari's face. The Usher, happening to look back, noticed his smirk. "Why you smile faceless man?" it asked.

Nefari said nothing, only motioned to the horizon. The ZiShan squinted his eyes and looked in the direction his companion pointed.

"Oh, I see them," it said.

Because of the great distance from them, it looked more like a colony of ants than a slave camp containing scores of humans. This was only one of the two or three hundred thousand camps just like it around the planet of Dark Earth. Nefari could hear the far-off cries of their agony as the humans labored under the whip of the merciless Chenoo and other slave masters; these overseers hated humans and spared no cruelty with them.

The work that the slaves performed all day in the sun's oppressive heat was completely futile as well. They accomplished nothing from their backbreaking labor. These lost souls were forever shoveling dirt and hardened clay, day and night, making mountainous piles, only to eventually fill back in the massive holes with the same dirt. Water was never given to them, and their thirst was never quenched. The sadistic overseers of the camp would not hesitate to use their leather whip across a slave's back, ripping into their flesh, if they paused at all. Sometimes Nefari was jealous of these slave masters; he would be more than willing to lend a hand with this important assignment of bringing eternal suffering to human souls.

The ZiShan smiled. He too enjoyed seeing these arrogant beings get what was coming to them.

The journey to the home of Bramfasa was nearing an end. Ahead of them, Nefari could see Quietus Tumulus towering high above the rest of the land. Nefari knew his lumbering escort was also grateful that their destination was close at hand; the

Usher's pace had slowed considerably as fatigue had set into his mammoth body.

The Usher sat down on the ground and began coughing and heaving loud hacks. His chest thrust outwards in a slow rhythm as he tried to fill his lungs with more oxygen. He pulled a crude, clay container from his belt, which he had filled with muddy river water, and gulped it down.

Nefari was not tired. He was not capable of being tired while on his own plane of Earth; his energy level was eternal here. But he was capable of being annoyed.

"Get up beasssst!" he sneered at the Usher, "there will be time to ressst when we get there."

The ZiShan stood up.

"Take thiss chain off of me now! We're almost there," Nefari demanded.

He was growing exceedingly tired of this simpleton Usher that Bramfasa had sent. Trying to ignore the insult of being his prisoner was aggravating him beyond the scope of self-restraint. An important StyJeen like himself, being led by a low-life ZiShan? The humiliation of this experience had run its course.

Only ten paces in front of them, where, for thousands of years tectonic plates had shifted and torn at each other, was a chasm that dropped miles below the dry, dusty surface of Dark Earth. The ZiShan, not overly agile, but strong enough to clear the fifteen-foot rift, stopped to prepare himself for the leap.

Nefari was infuriated by this plan. "You thick lout! You don't have it in your tiny mind to jump acrosssss that chasssm and drag me behind...with thisss chain around my neck, do you? Show me the resssspect that a creature of my classss dessservesss, you pitiful monkey! Undo the collar now. I order you!"

The ZiShan chortled at Nefari without actually opening its mouth, then from deep in its throat came its gravelly voice, "Can't order me. I have direct command from Bramfasa."

Having made up his mind, Nefari started the process of reconstructing the subatomic particles in his body; enough was enough, and he was going to alter back into shapelessness. He thought of Darkness, concentrated on simplicity, but once again, before he could even begin turning, the enormous primate made a great vault forward, jerking Nefari up into the air, out over the chasm. It felt to Nefari like he was airborne forever, and when the ZiShan finally landed with a thud on his big feet, Nefari followed right behind him and was whipped violently to the ground. This caused him no pain, but the impact was too much for his fragile form to endure.

A StyJeen's body has no real skeletal system to hold it together, even when it is in human-like form. This is why Franklin was able to twist his hand off so easily and why Nefari's body presently shattered into a countless number of black granules, which spread over the ground. The small pieces begin shifting, and like magnets, each began moving inwards towards the others, fusing back into the black mass.

Chain and leash now lay useless on the ground nearby, and the ZiShan, not quite understanding what was happening, looked around, trying to figure out where his prisoner had gone. On all four legs, in the fashion of a gorilla, it ambled over to the deep chasm, where it lifted itself back onto two legs and peered down towards Dark Earth's core. Behind him, the StyJeen had now completed his transformation, the pieces had united back into one, and Nefari had reached the end of his patience.

Within seconds, the mass of blackness behind the Usher again became unsettled, this time fragmenting itself into a cluster of flies, which moved in harmony together, ascending into the air. Three feet off the ground and jellyfish-like in its motion, the swarm moved swiftly toward the unsuspecting ZiShan, who only heard the din of the tiny wings at the last moment. The insects flocked the brute, covering its repugnant head entirely inside of its Darkness. The dimwitted creature swatted and slapped at the flying troops, only to have its hands pass through the swarm, smacking its own face. After a minute, the struggle stopped, and the ZiShan stood still. The dark army glided smoothly away from him. No longer did an unsightly head sit on top of the primate's body. All that remained atop the Usher's shoulders was a fragmented and pitted skull. Nefari, as he had wanted to from the start, had made a meal of this beast after all. Or at least part of it. The ZiShan's lifeless body balanced for a few fleeting moments, then tumbled forward into the gaping chasm.

CHAPTER SEVENTEEN
A PRINCESS & A PATIENT

It was March 19th, 2005, the day Franklin was born. The third-floor maternity ward, where babies were brought into the world, was experiencing a rush of expecting mothers. The St. Marcus Community Hospital was located about twenty-five minutes from Abundant Lakes, and Angel had driven there by herself in the middle of an unforeseen spring snowstorm. She was on the verge of giving birth and had no choice but to speed the whole way there on ice-covered roads. Calling the police and waiting for them to come help her had been out of the question. She did not want to give birth in the back of a squad car.

Upon arriving at the entrance to the hospital, Angel had been immediately helped into a wheelchair and carted to the 3rd floor. She felt lucky to have a room to herself for the moment; the nurse had told her how some of the women coming in to deliver their babies today may have to share a room with another soon-to-be mother, due to the sudden baby boom. Now she was resting in a lumpy bed, experiencing unbearable pain, and wearing an uncomfortable blue hospital gown. But she was so very grateful. None of these other things mattered because soon she would have her newborn baby in her arms. They would meet for the first time.

Marigold Tanner was a patient in the room across the hall from Angel. Marigold was once a pretty girl with blonde hair and a charming smile, but now she was haggard and worn from the hard life she had been living. She had been addicted to drugs since she was fifteen. Now she was twenty-three. Eight years of doing marijuana, meth, cocaine, speed, among other popular methods of getting high, had destroyed her body, her mind, and was working on her spirit. As she lay in the small hospital room, she thought about her life, the mistakes she had made, and about how she had ended up in the hospital ready to have a baby when she could barely take care of herself.

Her parents had been kind and loving to her growing up, and since she was their only child, they had doted on her. She had been a princess her whole childhood and had been given everything she wanted. This constant pampering didn't create a selfish wretch out of her, as it sometimes will in children. On the contrary, she was a compassionate, selfless, young girl. Marigold was also the perfect daughter, never sassing her parents, always obeying their rules, and above all, loving them, spending time with them, and never taking for granted the life she had been given.

At thirteen, however, something changed in her. Her heart began to cloud over, just a little at first, then with an increasing rate, and eventually, her thoughts, ideas, and desires became like a thunderstorm. She never saw it coming, never knew what hit her, but she had been touched by something dark.

Marigold was growing tired of being a princess, tired of being loved to the point of suffocation, and thought it was time to experience the world just a little bit for herself. She had an awful case of thirst for the wrong kind of knowledge and needed relief from this new, dangerous curiosity.

The bad ideas crept in slowly, almost so slow that she didn't even notice they were there until one day she had agreed to stay after school with her new friends and try some pot for the first time. The marijuana was not enough though, as it only led her to bigger and stronger drugs, and before she knew what had happened to her perfect life, she was in too deep.

Addicted.

Of course, her parents tried to do everything they could to help her; programs for drug addicts, counseling, and stricter rules for her to follow.

The new, intense guidelines they instituted ended up to be more than she could bear. Marigold wanted to be free; free to ruin her life however she wanted to. So, at age eighteen, she ran away and took a train to Chicago in the middle of the night. This was only three hours after an emotional apology to her parents, in which she had lied to them and told them she was getting better.

Their hearts were broken the next morning. They hired the best private investigators to track her down, but she had hidden herself and covered her tracks too well in the unsavory life of underground Chicago.

Now Marigold groaned in pain. She knew the baby was going to be with her soon. The thought terrified her. But then she considered again how this might be her chance to turn her life around. Maybe she could go back to her parents, let them meet their new grandchild, and everything would work out just swell.

Marigold knew better, though. Leaving her life in Chicago would be impossible; she needed what Chicago had to offer; the drugs, the freedom, the parties. As she considered all the good times Chicago had given her, she smiled, and her rotting, discolored teeth looked like a yellow crescent moon behind her lips.

Marigold thought about the last party she went to. What a blast it had been! She could hardly wait to get back to her old life. Being pregnant was terrible. She had not completely stopped her raucous lifestyle while she was pregnant, but slowed down a little. Motherly instincts weren't strong in her, but she also knew what having a healthy baby could do for her financially.

The father of her child, Bram Provenzano, was an evil man that one of Marigold's 'friends' had introduced to her. From the moment she met him, everything about him scared her. He was a smooth talking, handsome Italian man with a powerful personality, intoxicating charm, but wicked intentions. His temper was beyond mighty, and his beady, black eyes could intimidate a snake.

The only reason Marigold could figure out why she had started dating him was that he said he loved her. It had sounded very sincere and she had believed him at the time. Marigold hadn't heard those three words since her parents had spoken them to her the night she left.

He was long gone now, and she was glad. Bram had mysteriously left their apartment one night about seven months ago while she was running some errands. She had just told him of her pregnancy earlier that day. Everything he owned was left behind; all of his clothes and personal items, including his wallet full of money. Almost like he didn't care about any of it.

A baby would completely ruin her life, but going through with the pregnancy was never a question. Marigold knew it would be an opportunity to make some desperately needed cash. That's why she had a nice couple, who promised her a lot of money, lined up to take the baby from her the day after it was born.

CHAPTER EiGHTEEN
A SLiMEBALL & A SNEAKTHiEF

"Children, you can come out now." It was Gloria.

"I promise you it's safe. I am so sorry for what you all had to go through. I sent Hank away for a few nights to see if he can figure out where all this anger is coming from."

Franklin, Shad, Sami, and Parker had all locked themselves in Parker and Sami's room after their quick departure from Hank. They had listened through the door as Gloria had come in, shouting something at Hank, and then they had heard some of the braver children tell her exactly what had happened. Gloria had calmly told Hank to get up and wait outside for her on the porch. Franklin knew that Hank, however crazy he had become, was not going to mess with this woman. In addition to being a stern, but tender woman, she was also heavily built, on the big-boned side, with plenty of muscle to go with those bones. Besides that, Shad had peeked under the door and informed all of them that she was carrying a thick rolling pin.

And then there was the fact that Hank probably knew she was on the verge of getting the police involved if he did one more thing, anyway.

"He's gone, children," Gloria said. Sami unlocked the door and opened it. Gloria wrapped her arms around Sami, and Parker came out and joined in the hug. The boys, too, took their turns hugging Gloria after the girls were done. The children in the orphanage loved getting hugs from Nonna Glo. Nothing was better to help you feel safe and secure, and she always smelled so pleasant; like baby powder and skin lotion, with maybe a hint of chocolate chip cookies.

"Are you sure he's gone, Nonna Glo?" Sami asked, her voice cracking as she tried to hold back tears. "Something awful is wrong with Papa Hank. He told Rufus to hit Franklin!"

"Yes, honey, he's gone," Gloria assured Sami. "I saw him get in his truck and drive away. He's going to stay in town with his mom for a night."

"That dude called me a street urchin," Parker said. "I had to open a can of Whoop Butt on him. I hope he has a permanent limp where I got all Kung Fu on his leg."

Nodding, Gloria replied, "I know Hank was in pain when he left, holding his leg, dear."

"Good!" Parker exclaimed.

Pivoting to the boys, she asked, "Franklin, are you all right? Did he hurt you?" She licked her finger and wiped his face with it, then said, "You have a little dried blood on your chin."

Franklin noticed that the shine coming off of her was as pure blue as ever. The black outline had not come back. Thank goodness.

"Yeah, I am. I hope Rufus is all right too. I tackled him pretty hard."

Gloria suddenly grabbed Sami's hand, "Oh, Sami, I am sorry I forgot to ask you if you were okay. Rufus told me he accidentally pushed you down."

Shad scoffed, "Accident, yeah right."

"Don't worry," Gloria said, "I knew better. The other children told me what really happened. How are you feeling, sweetie?"

"I am okay, too. Thanks, Nonna Glo," Sami said sullenly, looking out across the living room and making eye contact with Rufus. He met her gaze and then looked away almost immediately.

Gloria noticed Sami's hard stare and saw who the recipient of it was. "Rufus, you come here right now, please," she yelled. "I need you to apologize to these kids or you'll be cleaning the whole house tomorrow, on a Saturday!"

Rufus gave Gloria a dirty look and walked upstairs.

"He probably needs to cool down a bit more, Nonna Glo. Maybe we'll talk to him later," Franklin offered, but deeply wished he would never have to talk to Rufus again.

****

"Okay, I have something to show you guys," Franklin announced to his friends. It was after supper that night, and things had settled down a bit now that Hank had left. They were down in the basement, Sami and Parker had laundry duty that night, and Franklin and Shad went down to keep them company. "Thanks for believing me about all of the crazy stuff I told you guys. I want to show you something, though; something that I haven't told you about yet."

Parker threw a load of dirty sheets into the rusted yellow machine, poured some soap in, and started the wash cycle. They were standing close together at the base of the staircase, in the cramped room where the washing machine, dryer, furnace, and other necessary household appliances could just fit, leaving only a little room for storage. Besides this utility space, there were a few other rooms in the basement that had been finished when the house was turned into an orphanage.

Franklin took a large bundle wrapped in one of his old white t-shirts out from behind his back. He motioned for them to come closer to where he stood in the shadow of the furnace, and when they did, he peeled away the shirt from around its contents to reveal a family-sized mayonnaise jar beneath it. In the jar was a blob of black goo, two inches thick and big enough to completely cover the jar's base. The blob was slowly flowing, undulating along the glass bottom, and it appeared to be alive. Franklin shook it gently back and forth, causing it to jiggle so that he could show them its gelatinous quality.

"You guys know how I told you about the dark stuff that I saw coming down from the tree branch?" he asked. "Well, this is the material it's made of."

Shad squinted his eyes, focusing on the trembling globule, and without taking his eyes off of it, said, "I remember, but you also said something about a cloud of flies though, right?"

Franklin nodded, then vigorously shook the jar for a few moments like he was playing the maracas, and when he stopped and held it still, they could all see that the ooze had ruptured into scores of black flies, which now buzzed frantically inside the jar.

"Where did you get this sample?" Shad asked, becoming more excited by the second.

"Okay, that day Nefari was in the storage room and grabbed my face... remember?" Franklin asked. He hated recounting this awful memory, especially twice in a period of twenty-four hours, but he continued anyway, "I left out the part in the story where I took a hold of his hand. I jerked it pretty hard to get it off me, but I didn't have a really tight grasp on it."

Here Franklin held out his free hand as he spoke and simulated for them how he jerked Nefari's hand from his face. "It was strange, but his hand actually snapped completely off of his arm; you'd be surprised at how easily, too. When I heard Mrs. Dwight coming down the stairs, I stuck it in my back pocket."

"Like some sort of nasty cell phone!" Parker chimed in.

"Franklin, that's really gross! Your back pocket?" Sami asked.

"It's not like you think. There was no blood, no gross things hanging off from it. When I went back upstairs to the restroom and looked at it, I had to drop it on the floor because it started liquefying into that black ooze you saw in the jar. So, I threw it in the sink, covered it with paper towel, and ran across the hall into Mr. Dillon's science room. Luckily, there was no class or even Mr. Dillon there. I smuggled a pair of rubber gloves and this mayonnaise jar out, went back into the bathroom, put the gloves on, picked up the hand again, saw that only a little of the black junk had gone into the sink, and I let more drip down into the jar here until the hand was small enough to stuff through the top. After a few seconds, the hand was gone, and the jar only had this slime in it. It sounds crazy, but when the goo realized it was trapped, it morphed into the flies, like it has now."

He held up the jar for all to see, "It shifts back and forth between the two forms, the slime, then the flies, and back to the slime again, trying to find a way out, I think."

Sami asked, "Do you think it's dangerous, I mean by itself? Without the rest of its body?"

Franklin lifted up his pant leg, "That day, by the tree, I ran from the swarm, but it reached out and caught my lower leg." Six inches above his ankle, Franklin showed them a thick, white scar that circumscribed his entire calf.

"It was really cold when it grabbed my leg and ended up giving me this scar. But in the school basement, when Nefari was holding my face, it didn't leave any marks. I'm guessing it can burn or freeze or do nothing. He controls that. When it's separated from him, I don't know. But when it becomes a swarm of flies, like this," he shook the jar again, "I'm pretty sure the little suckers have teeth that can devour flesh."

Parker backed away from the jar, "Okay, that stuff needs to go down the nearest drain. Please, Frankie?"

"Wait. Watch this though." Franklin reached up and held the jar close to the bare light bulb on the wood joist above them. The swarm of flies started darting back and forth in a greater frenzy, before finally merging together back into slime. The black slime then continued in its quest for refuge from the bright light, slithering madly around the inner circumference of its prison cell until Franklin brought it back down into the shadow cast by the furnace.

"The Darkness can't stand the light," Shad observed, in amazement.

"Okay, I agree, this is some mind-blowing stuff, but why in the world did you keep it, knowing it's so dang dangerous?" Parker asked. "Why not just hold it in some bright light until it blows up or something?"

"I thought it would be a good idea to get to know a little bit about my enemy. This is the Darkness he's made of. In fact, this used to be a part of him," Franklin answered. "After I got back that day, I hid it in my drawer."

"Franklin, why do you keep calling it *Darkness*?" Sami asked. "It looks like a splash of oil or something to me."

Franklin thought for a second. "If you saw it like I've seen it before, not in this jar, but the way it's able to move, the way it slinks around, even when it's airborne in a swarm; it's almost like a shadow. Very evil, very dark."

"All the better reason to get rid of that crap!" Parker shouted.

Shad went into a coughing fit; deep chest coughs. After a minute, when he was able to settle down, he spoke eagerly, "Franklin, this is incredible! You have an otherworldly substance in that jar which has probably never been seen by other humans before. This is like science fiction, only its non-fiction science fiction!"

"Okay," Franklin said, responding to Shad's emotion with some flatness, "but what do you think I—"

Before he could finish his question, the basement went dark.

The three hanging light bulbs, evenly spaced across the expanse of the ceiling, and the light fixture above the staircase went out.

Utter darkness cloaked the basement, and the monotonous 'clunk-swish' of the washing machine made it impossible to hear footsteps or any other warnings of danger. Franklin set the jar on top of the noisy machine, and acting quickly before it vibrated off the side, he reached out and found the power button.

Then silence.

Franklin hushed his friends. From the dark staircase above, they all heard the groans of the wooden steps as someone, or something, descended into the basement.

"Everyone hide!" Franklin said in a calm, but convincing whisper and he hurriedly led the girls through the dark to several musty cardboard boxes that they were able to crouch behind. By the time Franklin crept back to see if his roommate needed help, Shad had already felt his way to a small pocket behind the furnace

Stale breath suddenly moved the hairs on the back of his neck and he froze in place. "Who's there?" He spoke into the blackness, "Identify yourself! This isn't funny. Someone could get hurt in the dark!"

Deciding not to wait for whatever it was behind him to respond, he made the first move. Swiveling around on his toes, hands up in defense, Franklin took two steps forward and bumped into something that was sliding away from him. Sensing that the intruder had paused for a moment, he clenched his right hand into a fist and took a hard swing into the dark.

He made contact. It was something hard, but also a little mushy. A face maybe?

It made a low, muffled cry, then again started moving, and Franklin could hear heavy footsteps ascending the stairs. As the door opened at the top of the staircase into the dim light of the living room, he saw only a shadowy pair of legs take the last step up before the door slammed shut. Then he listened as the patter of footsteps ran across the floor above them.

No chance this was Nefari; not his style at all. Must have been one of the residents at the orphanage. Hank? Probably not. Nonna Glo had said he was gone. How about Nonna Glo? No way, but he sure hoped he hadn't just hit her! Rufus maybe? Very possible.

Without delay, Franklin ran up the stairs and flipped on the light switch. He opened the door to the main level to look around, but the hallway to the left, which led to the garage, was empty, and to the right, where it opened up to the living room, he saw no one either.

He walked back down the stairs slowly, still listening. As he stepped back onto the concrete floor, Franklin called, "Come on out everyone. Whoever it was ran away. I think someone was playing a joke on us; flipping off the lights while we're in the spooky basement."

"Real funny," Parker said. "If I find out who did that, they're going to find out what the inside of this washing machine looks like when it's on spin cycle!"

Sami and Shad both laughed. "Well, no harm done I guess. Just a prank," said Sami.

"I actually got a good right fist in on someone's face," Franklin said, feeling guilty he had hurt someone if it really was just a prank.

"Well, maybe *a little* harm was done," Shad replied to Sami, a detectable note of dread in his voice. He turned to Franklin, "I thought I heard you set the jar on top of the washing machine when the lights went out."

"Yeah, I did." Franklin looked to the spot where he had set the jar, but it was gone. "Okay, this is a problem," Franklin said, "somebody must have been listening to us and decided they wanted in on the action."

He looked at his friends. Sami was red-faced. "Can't think of anyone who would want to do that, can you?"

CHAPTER NINETEEN
A SNITCH & A SNACK

Nefari knew that just because he had murdered the
ZiShan, it did not change what he must do. He still had to go
report to Bramfasa. Ignoring these orders was not an option. He
also knew Bramfasa would already have heard the pleasant
details about how he had consumed the head of the slow-witted
creature.

The Lord of Dark Earth had eyes looking out for him
everywhere, reporting back when something was seen or
discovered that was worth telling him. Most of these eyes that
helped him were hidden among the rocks, crags, tree stumps, and
bleached skeletons of long dead creatures. The spying eyes,
more often than not, belonged to a growing pestilence that
plagued Dark Earth, as far as Nefari was concerned. This
infestation was a group of small creatures called Gimblets, which

had been keeping tabs on him and the Usher ever since their journey began.

Often, Nefari had seen these informers watching him, not quite in plain view, but hardly bothering to conceal themselves entirely, either. The Gimblets, with their pea-sized brains, didn't realize that Nefari, although having no eyes on his face when in his humanoid form, could experience all the senses through the pores of his skin. And in his other forms, even when he traveled as a swarm, he also had these same pores that allowed for sensations. His sight, which was a sophisticated form of heat sensory, came to him through thermoreceptors in his body, which acted as infrared devices. But his brand of sight didn't just allow him to see a generic image in various shades of red energy; it gave him vision that was as refined as a hawk's. No detail was hidden from him.

Even if the Gimblet was hiding behind a rock, out of sight, he could still sense its presence from the heat-energy it radiated.

Gimblets were furiously fast creatures; their little legs were capable of taking them to speeds of up to forty miles per hour. They had a complex tunnel system beneath the ground, which allowed them to travel in straight lines, rather than having to go around physical land barriers. After the headless Usher had taken his farewell plummet down into the depths of Dark Earth, Nefari had noticed, behind a mound of dirt, a Gimblet that was in surveillance of him.

About the size of a rabbit, a Gimblet's body was usually covered in black fur, often with white stripes running vertically down its back so that it resembled a pint-sized zebra. When sitting still, the creature's long black tail would curl up around its feet, and its large front paws, which acted as plows to furrow the tunnels, would rest in a relaxed, cross-footed position.

This is how the Gimblet sat, motionless, behind the hill of dirt as Nefari studied it with ominous intentions. Then, mind made up, he maneuvered himself, still manifested as a horde of flying insects, up into the air, and over the small Gimblet, without drawing suspicion. Guiding the swarm, he carefully wafted up behind it, transformed back into his humanoid figure, raised his foot above it, and just as the tiny head of the Gimblet turned to see its impending fate, Nefari stomped down hard on it with his black boot. This is how he found out the Gimblet's insides were yellow.

He detested these spies of Bramfasa. One less of them on Dark Earth was a good thing. As he wiped off his boot in the rough prairie grass, he counted at least ten more Gimblets scurrying down into their tunnels, on the way to report the dismal news to their lord.

Nefari understood that he would soon have to explain to the Dark Lord why he had made a meal of the ZiShan's head. But, wanting some fun before the tense encounter with Bramfasa, he decided to call on another manifestation of himself. To do this, he opened his mouth as wide as he could, bared his sharp teeth while wrenching his neck sideways, and bit into his upper left arm, towards his shoulder. With his sharpened eye teeth, he ripped at his own rubbery flesh, shredding it, and eventually he wrenched his whole arm loose at the shoulder.

Blood did not stain the earth; he had none in his body. He set the arm on the ground and watched as it softened back into the shapeless dark sludge. Then, up from this black mass arose one of his drooling, sadistic wolves. Nefari then proceeded to grab his left leg with his only remaining hand, wrapped his fingers around his ankle, and twisted, while also tugging forcefully. Giving little resistance, his lower leg became separated from his upper leg at the knee. Again, he set it on the ground and watched it melt into a puddle of black ooze; then, from the inky blackness emerged the other bloodthirsty wolf. Nefari sat there on the dirt for a minute, not in pain, nor pondering anything, but just waiting. Soon, both his limbs, arm and lower leg, had fully regenerated, and he stood up as if nothing had happened at all.

Then, looking at his two massive counterparts, he yelled, "Come Radulf, Bardulf." For those were the names of the two jet-black Dire Wolves. These immense Dire Wolves, extinct now on Mortal Earth, were forever linked to Nefari's dark soul. He had captured them on a mission to Mortal Earth, before their breed had died off during the Age of Ice, and had acquired their essence. He had blended with them. This merging ritual of the StyJeen, called the Rite of Assimilation, enabled his vile strain of species to become one in body and spirit with any other creature, or two of that creature in this case, through a process called "focused digestion" of the victim. A StyJeen can then call on the manifestation of this beast whenever they desire.

These Dire Wolves were no ordinary wolves. They were one hundred and fifty-pound killing behemoths.

"I would like you to find and exssssssterminate any Gimbletsss that you can, right now!" Nefari ordered them.

The Dire Wolves looked at him with submissive eyes and then gleefully started their search for the small animals, which they knew would make a wonderful mid-day meal. Depending on how many they could track down.

Nefari watched as they hunted, located, and consumed twenty-two of the minuscule creatures.

Oh, how he despised those little snitches!

CHAPTER TWENTY
A STOLEN JAR & A STRAY HAND

Rufus looked at the jar in his hands as if he had pulled off the crime of the century. What a bunch of losers those four were. He had been listening to them, perched on the other side of the basement door, the whole time they were discussing this slime. Bent down, ear to the floor, he had heard everything through the inch wide space beneath the door. Whatever this junk was that they were talking about, he had decided that he wanted it. It sounded like awesome, black silly putty or something. Like really cool slime. Kids at school made slime at home in their kitchens; they would go crazy for this stuff!

He unscrewed the lid, took it off, and looked in, keeping his distance from it for now.

Hobbs had said something about this stuff being a human hand before? Was he crazy? Frankie was really full of it.

Rufus had never understood why all of the other kids around the orphanage seemed to like him so much.

He put his hand gingerly to his face and felt the lump forming under his eye. Down in the basement, Franklin's flailing fist had made solid contact with his cheek. Yeah, Hobbs had gotten a lucky, blind punch in on him.

What a liar. Being chased by this stuff after it came down from a tree? Having flies coming from it and wrapping around his leg? He sure has played those three for a bunch of fools. They believe every bit of crap that he's feeding them, too. Well, anyway, he'd actually heard the others say they saw it moving by itself, so he had thought it was worth stealing. He laughed, thinking about how he had made them panic in the dark when he flipped off the switch, and then when they heard him coming down the steps, how they had run and hidden. Bunch of sissies.

In order to see what this stuff really was, Rufus had locked himself in the bathroom on the second level, the blinds were shut and only a single light bulb lit the room from the high ceiling. The lid was on the floor next to his foot and the open jar sat only inches in front of him. He decided that he just had to do it, get it over with. What was he scared of? He put his face down to the circular opening so that his eye was practically touching the glass and examined the contents closely. It wasn't really like silly putty, as he had thought, more like a liquid that could pretend to be a solid too. A liquid-solid globule? His Life Science teacher had called them 'colloids' or something.

As he stared even more intently at it, he saw a quality in it that he had missed at first. One that he could not quite put his finger on. It reminded him of the dark, like the same dark that still brought terror to him at the thought of peeking under his bed at night, or leaving his hand hanging down past his mattress as he fell asleep, for fear that something might grab it.

Except this was only a small piece of the dark. Come to think of it, he *had* heard Franklin call it 'The Darkness' a few times.

Shuddering now, Rufus thought he knew what Franklin had meant.

He reached up and flipped a switch off, causing the lone light bulb above him to go dark. He had remembered Hobby saying that this junk didn't like the light.

Rufus scoffed. It wasn't like it was alive or anything.

"Okay, let's see what this stuff feels like," he said out loud, although he wasn't sure why. People always talked out loud to themselves in the movies. But this wasn't the movies.

Franklin, Sami, Shad, and Parker practically flew up the wooden steps, hurled open the door, and rushed out into the hall.

"I think we need to split up," Franklin said, winded from the sprint. "Sami and Parker, you look everywhere on the main floor here. Shad and I will go upstairs and look around. I have a bad feeling about this. We need to stop him before he lets it out of the jar."

The boys took off for the stairs, while Sami and Parker started in the kitchen and began searching for Rufus.

Rufus turned the jar over and dumped the dark goop on the floor of the bathroom. He heard a solid 'thwump' as it hit the tile in one clump. With the sliver of light coming from under the door, Rufus was able to see its dark form shake like pudding. After a few seconds, the trembling stopped and it remained still. Then, almost as if it realized it was now shrouded in darkness, the slime slowly began dilating, stretching itself into a large circular shape the size of a pie pan.

Under his breath, Rufus murmured, "What the…?"

Continuing in its surprising display, the circular mass crumbled apart into hundreds of pieces, each taking the form of a black, winged insect.

"Mosquitoes?" Rufus asked, surprised at this new, but intriguing development. Maybe Franklin wasn't such a liar after all.

But he had to plug his ears when the noise of their wings whipping against the air created a buzz; one that was likely to drive a person insane if forced to listen to it for long. The legion of bugs left the tile floor, hovering upwards, but leveling out when they reached the height of Rufus's face. Quite abruptly the horde of *very* large mosquitoes (flies actually, he realized) began to pulsate up and down as one, softly at first, then more violently. Watching in disgust, Rufus saw five black spindles stretching out from the center of the swarm, four forming into fingers and a larger one into a thumb.

"Whoa!" Rufus exclaimed. "What the crapola?"

The black hue of the swarm faded and became lighter in color, and a moment later a detached human hand levitated in front of him, gently moving up and down in the air, as if on some unseen current. It began to move forward, slowly, then paused, possibly considering its options.

Startled, Rufus backed away, scooting over the tile floor until he reached the corner where the bathtub met the wall, and was prevented from going any further. In front of him, he could see the hovering hand, silhouetted against the muted backlight. He dared to momentarily take his eyes off of it to glance at the tub, trying to find something to defend himself with. Nothing, unless he scrubbed it to death with a bar of soap.

When he looked back, the silhouetted hand was no longer there. He noticed movement further away and saw it scurrying on the floor, over to the door. But the hand, coming into contact with the rays of light from the hallway seeping from under the door, quickly turned back toward him. Rufus lost sight of it after its dark form scuttled under the sink, which remained in shadows. He grabbed a washcloth hanging on the towel rack nearby, then, twisting into a kneeling position, he made his way, shuffling over to the sink. The washcloth he held spread open and was prepared to use it in net-like fashion to capture the runaway hand, if given the chance.

Then, from down the hall, he heard heavy footsteps ascending the stairs. The hand must have sensed the vibrations as well and been spooked, for it shot out from under the sink, stopped, and levitated a foot in front of Rufus's horrified face. Now, the grisly hand, having made up its mind on what to do, flew like it was shot out of a cannon right towards him.

Rufus screamed. It was a blood-curdling howl.

Reaching the top of the stairs, Franklin and Shad both jumped back when they heard shrieking coming from down the hall, no doubt someone in terror.

"That's Rufus," Shad said, fairly calmly, "it sounds like he may have already started playing with his new toy."

The hand grabbed Rufus's throat, and he used his own ten fingers to try to wrench it off. He found that it had a surprisingly firm grip, especially considering there was no arm to provide any muscle. Rufus's fingernails scratched helplessly at the strong hand, and he tried to scream again, but air no longer could pass through his throat; his face began to turn an awful shade of blue.

The bathroom door was hammered open, the lock not holding, and its hinges not even given the time to let out their eternal creaking. Franklin and Shad darted in; Franklin flipped the light switch on, while Shad ran to the blinds and threw them wide open. Light streamed into the small room and the hand released its grip on Rufus's windpipe. Franklin reached down and made a swipe for the fingers, but was unable to get a hold of any of the slippery digits. The hand, somehow knowing it must make its exit before the light drained it of all its strength, dissipated back into the cloudy swarm of loathsome flies. The mob of beating wings glided smoothly as one over to the bathtub and dove straight toward the drain. Shad and Franklin watched as the last bit of Darkness, the final insect, escaped down into the plumbing of the old house.

CHAPTER TWENTY–ONE
A WITCH & A SWITCH

Marigold woke up from a heavy sleep, very late at night, and some hours after the delivery. It had been a difficult childbirth, but it was over now. The baby had been born, and she was relieved. Getting back to Chicago could not happen soon enough. She needed to have some more of those red pills again; Bram, her creepy ex-boyfriend, had left a large supply of them for her on the counter when he left. They would help her forget all of this. True, her parents were only an hour drive from here, but she didn't see the point in a reunion right now.

She had come back to this small Minnesota town to deliver her baby because the couple that was going to adopt it and pay for all the medical care lived close to here. They had been the highest online bidders for the baby after she had advertised it on an illicit website, one which Bram had told her about before taking off. Selling your baby wasn't completely legal, so Marigold had been telling everyone that she was giving it up for adoption.

Originally, when she had agreed to come back to Minnesota to have the baby, Marigold had thought it might be a permanent move. Maybe she would stay, live near her parents, and try out a normal life. But three days away from the life she loved in the Windy City was too much, and Marigold realized she could never stay here.

A nurse, whose nametag read, 'Francine', walked into the room and asked, "Would you like me to get your baby out of the nursery for you, Ms. Tanner? You should spend some time bonding with him. Oh, and I think he's hungry too."

Marigold shook her head, "No, I don't think so. Can you just feed it some formula or something? I am not planning on keeping this baby and I don't really want to see it."

"See *him*," the nurse corrected her.

"Oh, a boy?" Marigold knew the couple buying it was hoping for a girl. She had never had her doctor tell her what gender it was, on purpose, because she thought the buyers might try to back out if they heard it was a boy.

They're out of luck now anyway, Marigold thought to herself, *they already gave me a nice down payment on the baby.*

Marigold wasn't actually sure, but she had suspicions that this couple was somehow involved in a black market for babies, trading and selling them for profit. The whole thing had felt more like a business transaction since they first contacted her. The man had even slipped one time and said something about 'whoever ends up with the baby'. He tried to cover up by saying that he meant whoever ends up being the baby's 'Godparents,' but Marigold knew better. They would sell her baby to the highest bidder, as she had done, and make a lot more money than they had paid her. Girls must go for more money, she guessed.

Anyway, she figured that whoever ended up with her baby would most likely take decent care of it. After all, it was an expensive investment.

Nurse Francine brought Marigold's thoughts back to the present, "Ma'am, have you given him a name yet? We're not sure what to write on his identification tag. Or his birth certificate for that matter."

"Um, just call him Baby Tanner. They want to name it themselves," she replied.

Nurse Francine was visibly disturbed. She looked at Marigold with grave concern and said, "Ms. Tanner, your baby needs to be held."

Marigold shrugged, "Will you and some of the other nurses hold him? I have to go back to sleep for a while." With that she rolled over, turning her back to Francine.

Recently, St. Marcus Community Hospital had started a program where they recruited senior citizen volunteers to come in and help hold the infants so that tired moms and dads could rest; with permission from the parents, of course.

On this wintery spring day of March 19th, the only elderly couple that had shown up to help with the babies, most likely because of the untimely snowfall, was Mr. and Mrs. Lighten, a heart-warming couple in their eighties. They had already passed a background check earlier that week and were excited about helping out with the overflow of newborns.

The nurses were delighted to have them there to help, considering how busy all of them had been. The man and wife, by any standard, were an adorable older couple. He wore tan slacks, pulled up too far, with a plaid, blue and red cardigan that could have easily won first place in an ugly sweater competition. His silver hair had receded far enough up his forehead to allow his bald scalp to reflect the fluorescent light above, and the aged glasses he wore barely clung to the end of his nose. It was his eyes that made him stand out to the hospital staff; they had a depth of sparkle in them that was rare.

His wife also wore a similar sweater, but with patterns of brightly colored flowers. Her smile gave warmth to anyone who passed her by, as she sat holding an infant alongside her husband. Both of them had a slight stoop to their posture, but other than that they appeared to be in good health for their age.

The two were not big talkers, but their quiet charisma and charm were undeniable. Although they were here for the first time, the nurses could tell that this husband and wife duo would give much-needed love and care to the little ones.

Charles Lighten was holding a tiny newborn girl, her perfect little fingers wrapped tightly around his thumb. As Charles put his hand on her forehead and spoke quiet words, she met his gaze with her bright hazel eyes. Ten minutes ago, the nurse on duty, Francine, couldn't get the baby girl to stop crying, but when she had handed her over to Charles, an immediate serenity came over the little one. And now the infant couldn't take her eyes off of him.

Mary Lighten sat next to him holding a baby boy. She had a bottle and was trying to get the restless newborn to drink from it. She looked at her husband and said sadly, "This poor little guy's mother doesn't want to feed him or even hold him."

Suddenly, a soothing, delicate hum came from her lips, the tune was like nothing the nursing staff had heard before; it had a magical, lulling quality to it, and any of them who stood and listened to it wished that they, too, could curl up and take a nap on the couch.

Finishing her humming, Mary said gently to the baby, "Please little one, you need to eat."

The baby squirmed in her arms for another second, then was still. He looked up at her, studied her wrinkled face, then put his mouth on the bottle and began consuming the contents of it.

She smiled down at him as he drank hungrily.

In a darkened hallway that led out of the maternity ward, Mary sensed something menacing standing and watching her. As she turned her head, the figure turned too, and Mary caught only a fleeting glance. Long dark hair; a woman. Baggy clothing. Mary was not able to detect a face before the woman disappeared down the dark hall.

She turned back to her husband and in a slightly trembling voice said, "We don't have a lot of time left Charles. We need to do this soon."

Charles spoke calmly, "I saw her too. You're right. We must be quick; they have already sent one here to watch over him. She won't come into the light, though. She can't."

Charles and Mary stood up carefully, both with precious bundles in their arms, and Charles signaled to Nurse Francine that they were ready to bring the two infants back to the nursery.

Francine was a short, stout woman in her mid-fifties. She had a face that you might see in a commercial for insurance or coffee; one you could trust. Her straight, dyed black hair was kept short, and she had silver earrings that dangled just a little too far down. As she walked over to them, she looked down at the two babies they held; the girl in Charles' arms, sleeping soundly, and the little boy in Mary's arms, looking extremely content after drinking his fill of formula.

Francine spoke kindly to them, "You two sure do have an outstanding way with babies." A second later, she asked them, "Are you going to stay for a little while longer?" The hope was evident in her voice.

Charles replied carefully, making sure he was speaking the truth to Francine, "We are. We just want to go look at the little ones in the nursery and see if there are any that could really use some love right now."

From where they stood, they could see at least ten bundled babies, most of them sound asleep, through the ceiling-high glass window that looked into the nursery. Nurse Francine walked them over to the door leading inside, reached into her skirt pocket and pulled out a key. She opened it and stepped inside. The aroma of baby powder and soiled diapers blasted their faces as they followed her into the room.

Charles and Mary searched until they found the bassinet that had the name 'Dorothy Lee Fong' written on the nametag, which hung from its handle. The bassinets were made from heavy grade steel, with wheels that allowed them to easily be pushed from the birthing room to the nursery. Dangling from the handgrips of each bassinet was a nametag that was protected by a clear plastic sleeve.

Charles laid Dorothy Fong down gently into the bed without disturbing her deep sleep. He bent down and gave her a kiss on the cheek.

Francine smiled at Charles and Mary and said, "I'll leave you two in here. I need to go check on a patient, but I'll be back shortly." Almost to the door, she paused and turned around. "Thank you so much for helping these little ones out. It means the world. I'm sure they would thank you, too, if they were able."

"They do more for us than we could ever do for them," Mary said, still looking at the baby in her arms. "We'll put this little one back and then see how the others are doing."

Francine gave them another earnest smile and walked out into the lobby, closing the door behind her.

Charles began checking the bassinets again, walking from baby to baby and reading the hanging tags, until he came upon one that said, 'Franklin Samuel Hobbs'.

"Mary, here he is," Charles said quietly.

His wife came over to the crib and peered down at the sleeping newborn in it. Below his name on the tag, it said, 'March 19, 4:35 p.m.' Mary, still holding the sleeping infant she had fed earlier, handed the baby to her husband who took and cradled him carefully in his arms. She reached in the bassinet and picked up Franklin, holding him close and snuggling his face with hers. Franklin woke up, looked at Mary, reached out and grabbed her nose.

She started sobbing… heaving, and when Charles saw her crying, he did too. After a minute, she gained control of herself and whispered to the boy, "Franklin, I am here to tell you that you are going home tonight. You are such a sick little boy. Your body can't live in this world, and The Suveran is waiting for you on Third Earth. There are so many others who will love you there too, and you will never be in pain again."

Franklin's hand touched her mouth. Mary kissed it. She held him next to her and hugged him tightly. Using her free hand, she worked with the infant's identification bracelet on his small wrist until she had unsnapped it. From a pocket on the side of her sweater, she produced another miniature bracelet that she had taken from the baby whom she had held only moments ago, who Charles now cradled. This bracelet, she then secured onto Franklin's wrist.

Tears rolled off her chin and onto Franklin's tender cheek. Charles leaned over and whispered into his little ear, "We will come to visit you soon, Franklin Hobbs. I promise."

Mary hummed softly and bounced Franklin gently in her arms; he stared at her, captivated, as the sound flowed from her lips. Soon she saw his eyes close, and she watched him as he drifted off to sleep. She carried Franklin over to an empty bassinet and laid him down onto the soft bedding. The tag attached to it read, 'Baby Tanner, March 19th, 5:28 p.m.' Mary snuggled the blanket around him, trying to provide the infant with some security his last night on Earth. She stretched out the blue beanie cap that had been lying on his sheets and fitted it around his head to keep him warm. Her tears were still falling as she took one last look at the child, now in a heavy sleep, and then walked away.

They went back to Franklin's empty bassinet. Charles leaned over and put Baby Tanner, whom he still held, carefully down into it, snuggled him in the blanket, and put Franklin's beanie on him. The baby didn't fuss. He only watched Charles keenly with his deep blue eyes. Mary bent down to put the bracelet, still in her hand, onto Baby Tanner's wrist. She stood up as the door behind them opened and Nurse Francine walked in.

"How's it going in here? I see you found Franklin Hobbs. Isn't he darling? His mom is just exhausted. I'd like to bring him to her, but she's still so out of it."

"Is she okay?" Mary asked.

"Oh, she will be. It was a long and hard delivery. She really only spent a few minutes with him this afternoon before we took him to run some tests," Francine answered. She looked at her watch, "It's 7:30 now. She's been sleeping so soundly ever since. Almost three hours. We've been bottle feeding him out here until she's up to the task herself."

Charles asked, "Would it be okay if we stepped into Angel's room and gave her some words of encouragement if she is awake? I understand her husband died only a few months ago and she is having to go through this alone."

"How did you know that her husband…?" Francine stopped in mid-sentence, "you're right. She could use some moral support, and I think you two are pretty special people. Go ahead. Her door is open."

It was dark in the room when Charles and Mary entered. Mary looked around cautiously, testing the shadows to see if anything might be lurking there.

"Should I turn on the lights?" she asked Charles.

Charles spoke softly, "They have no reason to harm her or her baby yet. It will be a long time before they figure anything out. You can leave the lights off."

The elderly couple could see that Angel was still sleeping. Mary pulled over two chairs from the wall so that they were in the middle of the narrow room, facing the bed. They sat down and waited.

When Angel woke up a bit later, frenzied and confused, Mary and Charles were there to comfort her.

CHAPTER TWENTY—TWO
A PANIC & A PLAN

Rufus sat on the floor, huddled in a ball and softly crying into his sleeve.

"Hey Rufus, I'm sorry you had to experience that. That thing must have scared you to death," Franklin said, trying not to reveal the simultaneous pleasure he felt at how justice had been served to the little thief.

"Wha... what was that?" Rufus asked, lifting his head from where it rested on his arms and looking up at the two boys standing above him. Franklin saw the large bruise under Rufus's eye where he had belted him just ten minutes ago.

Impressive contact, he thought.

Shad, suppressing the strong urge to sneeze, replied quickly and without much empathy, "That was a severed hand. What did you think it was?"

"That's what I thought it was! But how did it… I saw it come from that black junk I took from you. How did it do that?" Rufus asked, looking about as pathetic as could be.

"Rufus, it's not something I can really explain easily," Franklin said. "I'm guessing you heard me talking about it in the basement... you were eavesdropping on us, weren't you?"

"Yeah, I wanted to get you guys back. You were big jerks to me down there earlier," he shot back.

"We're not here to argue anymore about that," Shad responded, coughing up something. "What you did to us in the basement was a dirty trick. It was downright cruel! You scared us to death, and you took something that wasn't yours."

A sharp knock on the door jolted all three of them, already on edge anyway. Franklin opened it, and standing at the entrance to the bathroom was Jessy, a seven-year-old boy.

He hollered, "I really gotta go guys, please?"

"Yeah, of course, Jessy," Franklin said. "C'mon guys."

Shad leaned over and whispered, so only Franklin could hear him, "Are you sure it's safe in here for Jessy, Franklin?"

"No, actually, I'm not sure at all," Franklin whispered back, then said out loud, "Jessy, just be quick, okay?"

This got Rufus going again, "That thing... that thing might come back. It might come after us again!" he whimpered, tears still dribbling down his cheeks.

"Thing? What thing? What are you guys talking about? Why are you crying, Rufus?" Jessy said, beginning to teeter on the verge of tears himself.

"Nothing, Jessy, nothing. Right, Rufus? Nothing." Franklin shot Rufus a semi-dirty look.

Rufus seemed to catch on. He wiped his tears on his sleeve again, "Oh, yeah. Nothing, little dude. There's no floating hand or anything like that scampering behind sinks. I mean, I was just kidding around, Jessy."

"Smooth, Rufus, real smooth," Shad said. "Okay, let's go downstairs and find the girls. Let them know we found him."

He grabbed some toilet paper and blew his nose forcefully into it, before jabbing it into his pocket.

Shad left the bathroom and Franklin followed him.

"Where do you two think you're going? You're not leaving me here by myself!" Rufus got up and sprinted toward them. "That thing could be anywhere!"

"What thing? I thought you said you were kidding! Guys?" Jessy yelled, the tears exploding out from him with the force of a fire hydrant.

Franklin knew he couldn't just leave the poor little kid terrified up here like this, but he really didn't think the fugitive hand was after anyone but him... okay, and maybe Rufus.

The more he considered it, though, and remembered how his mom had been abducted, the more he started worrying about *all* the other children in the home. He looked back at Jessy and said, "Hey, Jess. Listen. You're right. There is something going on. If you hurry up and finish your business in here, you can follow us downstairs."

A few minutes later, they met Sami and Parker at the bottom of the stairs. Rufus trailed behind the other boys, a sheepish look on his face. His eyes were red and swollen, and it was obvious he'd been crying.

"Hi, Sami!" Jessy shouted, running up to her. Sami picked him up and gave him a big hug. "Hey there, Jess! These guys picking on you?"

Jessy looked up at her, a very solemn look crossing his face. "No, not at all. They are protecting me from the thing that came after Rufus."

"What do you mean?" Sami said.

"Rufus, I'm going to stuff you into the…" Parker started, but was cut short when she saw the dejection on his face. "Hey, big guy, what happened to you?"

Rufus aimed his gaze at the floor.

Franklin said, "All right. Everyone in the backyard. Let's go. We need to talk privately, and I think we all could use some fresh air anyway."

He motioned for them to follow him. They walked out onto the front porch where they found Gloria sitting and rocking one of the toddlers to sleep.

Sami spoke quietly to her, "Hi Nonna Glo. How is Greta feeling?" she asked, gesturing to the four-year-old girl in Gloria's lap.

"Oh, the poor baby's fever has come back now. I am so worried about her," Gloria replied, a canopy of anxiety hiding her normally jovial face. "The doctor has no idea what's been causing this. It's been off and on now for two months."

She put her hand gently on the girl's head. "I'm going to drive her into town to see a specialist early tomorrow morning before breakfast. They're going to run a few more tests on her. Jerod is staying here overnight, so he can be here to help you in the morning."

Jerod was the daytime attendant at the orphanage. He helped watch the children, run errands, and would also make meals now and then, although the kids were not too fond of his cooking. He was a twenty-year-old, fun-loving, yet responsible young man who loved the kids. And they all thought of him as a big brother.

Parker put her hand on Greta's hair and brushed some of it out of her face. "She's such a sweet kid. I just hope she'll be all right."

They saw Gloria looking suspiciously at the bruise under Rufus's eye, which was starting to turn a funny shade of yellow, but she didn't comment about it. Glancing at her watch, she said, "Oh, one more thing, kids. Jerod will also be in charge tonight, starting in a few minutes here. I'm going to put Greta to bed and then I have to leave to go get some groceries. I count on you older ones, you know, to help with the younger ones, like this little guy," she winked at Jessy. Her voice became sullen, "Especially now that Hank is gone."

"Of course, we will," Sami said.

They all nodded in agreement. Gloria continued, "Franklin, I think you told me you would like to cook something for everyone before Spring Break is over. Only two nights left after today. Are you still up for it? "

"Always!" he said, excited for the chance to show off his cooking skills. "Make sure you get some fettuccine noodles and Romano and Parmesan cheese. I make a pretty mean Fettuccine Alfredo."

"Okay, honey, I will. We can eat that tomorrow night. Do you know what you want to eat on Sunday night though? It's your birthday, so you decide."

He thought for a second, "Pizza is always a safe choice, Nonna Glo. You know that," Franklin answered. "You pick the kind."

"Pizza it is. I'll pick some up at the store tonight, too. Now you all be careful. Don't do anything crazy while I'm gone," she shot a look at Rufus. "You hear me now, Rufus?"

"Yeah, no problem, Nonna Glo. I uhh…" Rufus paused and looked around at the others. For a second Franklin thought he might say something about their recent adventure in the bathroom. "I'll be good. I promise," he said and managed a halfway convincing smile.

Gloria gave the little girl in her lap a kiss on the head as she waved goodbye to the children; they descended the porch steps and headed to the backyard. It was going on 7:00 p.m., but it was still light outside. After a long, dark, Minnesota winter, spring was a favorite time of year at the orphanage. The kids could run around outside until almost 8:30 at night, at which time they usually had to go in for Papa Hank's story reading. Tonight, they wouldn't have to do that.

The six children sat down in the grass, except for Rufus, who sprawled out on his stomach, still pale and looking like he had seen a ghost.

"Okay, this is what's up everyone. Rufus opened the jar," Franklin began, "he let out the Darkness that was inside it, and it turned back into its original form."

"Original form?" Sami asked.

"You know, a hand," he replied, "and it's crawling around somewhere in the plumbing of the house; it could come out anywhere at any time, as long as there's no light in the room."

Nobody said anything at first. Everyone sat staring at Franklin, wondering if he was about to suggest a solution to this very strange dilemma.

Finally, Parker spoke up, "Well, at least you're not telling us there's a runaway, murderous hand on the loose that could sneak into our rooms while we're sleeping tonight and either choke or tickle us to death!"

Rufus chuckled, and they all looked at him. "Hey, that was funny. I can laugh, can't I?" he said.

Sami responded, "Of course you can laugh, Rufus. We need to laugh a little about this or we would all go insane."

"This is a practical joke, isn't it guys?" Jessy asked, smiling nervously. "You all are punking me or something, right? I watched a show once where this guy always went around playing jokes on famous people. Please tell me that's what you're doing."

"Jess, we won't let anything happen to you, okay? You'll be with Parker and me tonight," Sami wrapped her arms around him and pulled him over to her. "You'll be fine, kiddo."

Jessy easily allowed himself to be bear-hugged by Sami. Although only a child of seven, he knew a beautiful girl when he saw one.

Parker added, "You probably want to stay close to me though, Jessy, because if that hand tries anything on you, I'm gonna break its fingers one by one."

Jessy laughed.

Parker looked over at Shad, who'd been quiet for some time now. "Hey, what's wrong with you? Are you meditating or something?"

Shad seemed completely lost in thought. He had his elbows resting on his knees and both hands on his chin, holding up his head. His eyes were closed and he seemed to be murmuring something to himself.

"There's got to be….If we could just lure it…What if…?" He opened his eyes wide, and suddenly, very animated, said, "I got it! I think I know how to deal with this thing! I'd say that by the end of the night we'll have that hand safely back in the jar! Franklin, can you get that old video camera in your room?"

Franklin thought about the relic that had sat on his desk since he moved to the orphanage. He and his mom had gotten it at a rummage sale for a few dollars and it had actually worked for a week. "Yeah, sure, but it doesn't record anymore. I just use it now for playback of movies of my mom and me."

He had been able to make some use of it for the week before it stopped recording and had taken all sorts of videos of his mom telling stories about her life before she had him.

"Oh, that's fine. We only need you to be able to look through it, not actually record anything," Shad clarified.

For the next few minutes and with a great deal of enthusiasm, he explained his idea to the others. When he was finished, Franklin remarked, "I like the way you think, Shad. I'm glad you're on our team."

"Hey," it was now Rufus who spoke up. "I was just thinking. I could help you out with this. I mean, it was my fault that thing is loose. I know I've been a jerk…a big jerk to all of you. But I'd like to…"

Franklin interrupted him, "Rufus, you're part of this whether you want to be or not, anyway. We aren't going to tell anyone else here about this. It's not worth scaring them, so we are going to need your help."

"Okay, cool. Yeah. Whatever you need me to do." Rufus reached up and ran his fingers along the area of his throat where he had been assaulted by the hand earlier. The others could still see the red finger marks that had been tattooed onto him.

He looked determined as he said, "That five-fingered freak isn't getting away with this without some payback."

CHAPTER TWENTY-THREE
A MOTHER & A MERCHANT

Angel had been sleeping for several hours when a nurse brought Franklin into her room. She awoke the second she heard his cry.

Opening her eyes, she saw an unfamiliar woman standing in front of her, a bundle in her arms wrapped tightly in a blue fleece blanket and topped with a cap of the same color.

"He wanted his mommy," the young woman said cheerfully.

Beaming at her little boy that the woman bounced in her arms, a yawn escaped Angel as she asked, "What time is it?"

The nurse answered, "It's late, almost eleven at night. You were really knocked out all day."

This she believed. She felt like she had been sleeping for days; the deepest, most tranquil sleep she could ever remember having. Confusing memories, which might have been very vivid dreams, swarmed around in her head. Didn't she have visitors at some point while she slept? Or was that a dream? Something about...ummm…, she couldn't really recall.

Funny though, she noticed that two chairs had been scooted into the middle of the room, facing her bed, and she specifically remembered them pushed up against the wall before going to sleep.

"Here you go, Mrs. Hobbs, here's your beautiful little boy," the nurse said, handing the infant to her. She helped unwrap him so that Angel could see her little one better.

Angel looked down at her sweet Franklin. His legs were kicking a mile and minute and his eyes were looking at the bright lights on the ceiling. Everything was so new to him. He had been in the dark for so many months, and now whatever his eyes took in was a wonder.

She reached down and touched his hands, rubbed the bottoms of his feet, caressed his face. Franklin tried to focus his eyes on her, but he struggled; things were still blurry.

"Hi, my little baby, you sweet little boy," Angel whispered, holding him close. She kissed his pink cheek, "I'm your mommy, Franklin, and you are my precious little one. I love you so much already!"

The young nurse stood by, watching Angel and her infant. Angel glanced up at her, "What's your name?" she asked.

The nurse was very pretty; she had a dark complexion, high cheekbones, and gentle, brown eyes. A light blue hijab covered her head and hung past her shoulders, and her black hair was tucked tightly underneath it. Her smile was kind, and she seemed to genuinely delight in witnessing a mother's love for her newborn.

"Sahra," the nurse replied. "Francine left an hour ago. She asked me to say 'goodbye' to you and tell you how happy she is for you and Franklin."

"That's very sweet of her. She was such a comfort to me during the birth," Angel said, then turned her gaze back to Franklin. It was difficult to take her eyes off of her new baby for long; he was so perfect in every way. How could he really be hers? Was she really responsible for this little human's life now? Was it really up to her to guard his health and his heart and to instruct him how to be a good person? It was a little frightening, but exhilarating at the same time.

She cuddled him close to her chest. Taking the blue cap off of him, she gently kissed the top of his head. "Oh, look!" Angel said, with some surprise. "I don't remember his hair being blonde…"

Sahra laughed softly, "They probably put a hat on him right away."

"Oh, I think we took it off for a picture," Angel recalled, "but I was so overwhelmed by the moment and everything happening…"

"He is such a little miracle," Sahra agreed.

As she studied the features of her newborn, Angel's attention was drawn to something else she hadn't seen before on Franklin. "Sahra, do you see this little birthmark on his right thigh, above his knee?" she asked.

Sahra leaned down. "Sure, I see it."

"I don't remember it being there when Francine gave him his first bath or when I held him for the first time after he was born," Angel said, disconcerted by what this discovery could mean.

The nurse grabbed a clipboard from the table. "Let me check his charts here." She flipped through a few of the pages, pausing every once in a while to read something. "Okay, no, it doesn't say anything about a birthmark. Francine must have missed it, too. That does happen sometimes."

"How could she miss it though?" Angel asked, baffled at the oversight. Especially when Nurse Francine had seemed to be such a detail-oriented person.

But Franklin was her son, and she, if no one else, should have noticed it. "How could *I* miss it?" she mumbled to herself, although Sahra heard her clearly.

Sahra replied, "You had what, three hours of intense labor before Franklin was born? You must have been completely exhausted. The records say you only saw him for…hmmm, a half-hour before you felt lightheaded and had to hand him to the nurse on duty. I'm not surprised you didn't notice a little birthmark."

Angel smiled warily. "You're right," she agreed. She had been outright drained of all energy and had barely been able to keep her eyes open.

Just then, her attention was drawn to the hallway outside, where waves of intense shouting cut through the silence of the maternity ward. It came from the room across the hall; even through a closed door, the words of a hysterical woman were audible, "What are you telling me? My baby is dead? How can this be? He was perfectly healthy the last time I saw him! What did you do to him?"

Angel could hear the nurse's voice reply something, but couldn't make out her response to this substantial accusation. She felt a deep sorrow come over her, almost as if she had just found out it was her baby that died. The heartache Angel felt at that moment was so extreme that she started to weep.

"Angel, are you okay? Do you need me to take Franklin?" Sahra asked, bending down to take the baby from her.

Angel unconsciously moved Franklin away from Sahra's reach; she didn't want anyone to take her baby from her. Ever. Even the thought of leaving Franklin in the nursery again caused her to shudder. It was her job to protect him. Swabbing her eyes with the hospital's stiff bed sheet, Angel managed to gain control of her emotions. She said, "No, that's okay. I'm okay. Just so sad for that mom and her baby."

"Angel, I'll be right back," said Sahra, heading towards the door. "I need to go get the rolling tray table to put your little guy on. I think we need to take a few more of his measurements."

"Oh, sure," Angel said. "Sahra?"

The door closed, but Sahra opened it and poked her head back through. "Can I get you something, Angel?" she asked.

"Earlier today, after Franklin was born, someone came in to take pictures with my camera," Angel began. "Do you think you could ask around and see if anyone else is available to do that right now? I would love to have some of him lying there while you measure him, with me in the picture just watching. I think it will be pretty special for him to see that someday."

Sahra nodded, "I'll ask around, I'm sure we can get someone in here for a few minutes."

Across the hall Marigold was furious; in her arms, bundled up in another blue fleece blanket, she held a baby. The nurse had just finished explaining to her that Baby Tanner had died sometime in the last hour while she had been sleeping.

The door opened and a doctor walked in the room, a grave expression on her face. She said, "Ms. Tanner. I am so sorry for your loss."

"Sure you are," Marigold said, dismissing her.

The doctor, an older woman with grey, cropped hair, kept her composure. "Your son died of congestive heart failure. I'm afraid his heart was too weak. It was not able to pump enough blood to the rest of his body."

"You did tests!" Marigold screamed. "Why didn't you find it right away? I swear, I'll sue you for malpractice!"

The doctor still remained calm. "Ms. Tanner, the tests don't always show a weak heart. A baby's heart is fragile to begin with, and a difference in the palpitations between a healthy heart and an unhealthy heart is usually not detectable."

Marigold looked down at the baby in her arms. Nine months of her life, wasted. For what? She handed the lifeless bundle to the nurse and said, "Here. I don't really know what I'm supposed to do with him."

"Would you like us to call the morgue, or do you want to spend more time with him?" The doctor was asking this question as a courtesy to Marigold but was already fairly certain of what her response would be.

"More time?" Marigold asked, exasperated. "Why? He's dead. Why would I need more time with him? Go ahead and call the mortuary. This isn't over, though. I'm pressing charges and filing a lawsuit for negligence as soon as I get out of here!"

The intensity and volume of her voice had lessened, but the venom in her tone still struck its mark. The doctor and nurse both forced a weak smile, walked out of the room with the baby, and left her alone. In their haste, they left the door to Marigold's room open.

A lawsuit might be the only way to get any money for all of the trouble she went through to have this baby. Actually, come to think of it, she might be able to win a decision in court that would make her rich, even more than if he lived and she had sold him.

Marigold was proud of herself for looking at this situation as the glass being half full, not half empty.

She thought about the couple that was supposed to buy the baby from her, how they would probably arrive soon for their purchase.

They were in for a big disappointment.

Marigold wondered if she would have to pay them back the five thousand that they had already given her as a down payment.

****

Mr. and Mrs. Lighten sat in the main reception area of the hospital where all the new patients were first admitted. They had been there all night, ever since leaving Angel's room. Positioning themselves close to the entryway, they waited in silence for the man that had purchased Marigold's baby.

It wasn't a couple as Marigold had thought, though. Charles and Mary had done their research. It was only one man, Damion Dirkman, who had been attempting to buy Marigold's baby, and he worked for the most prodigious, illegal trafficking organization of infants and children in the country.

Around eight in the morning, a man walked in pushing an empty stroller. He had a balding head with a red bandana tied around it, a long face, with an average build, and was sporting a pair of jeans and a brown leather jacket. The man found the elevator, entered it, and was just about to disappear behind its closing doors when a strong hand pushed it back open. Charles entered the cramped elevator, with Mary right behind him.

The doors closed. Charles stared at the man.

"What do you want?" the bald man snarled at him.

"I think the better question, Mr. Dirkman, is, what do *you* want with that baby upstairs?" Charles offered back.

"I don't know how you know my name or what you're talking about, old man, but I suggest you shut up!" Damion barked, lifting up his shirt a few inches, revealing a handgun jammed into his belt.

Mary chimed in now, "You know, Mr. Dirkman, it is a disgraceful thing that you do, buying and selling the most innocent of all lives. Selling them to people who may have inhumane, evil intentions for the baby. Whoever it is, and for whatever reason they want a baby, you don't care. You give it to the one who writes the biggest check."

Damion Dirkman looked at the Lightens like he wanted to strangle them. He growled, "You two working for the police or something? You have nothing on me, anyway. I'm just going up to help a friend with her baby. That's all."

"No, we aren't working for the police," Charles answered. "The police aren't allowed to make people like you just disappear as we tend to do in these circumstances."

Damion reached for his gun. He didn't have enough time though. In the next instant, Charles' aged but agile hand came down on his shoulder. Damion tried to push the old man away, struggled to free himself, but was unable to do either before his mind faded to black, like the rest of his soul.

When the elevator stopped on the third floor and the doors slid open, the Lightens, just a sweet elderly couple, pushed a baby stroller over the threshold. It was an expensive designer stroller, brand new. Still standing in front of the open elevator, Charles motioned to the nurse closest to him. She crossed the hall and approached the couple.

He looked at her nametag, "Excuse me, Sahra?" he asked.

She smiled and replied, "Yes sir, how may I help you?"

"My wife and I wanted to give this stroller to a woman here that just had a baby. Her name is Angel."

"Oh, yes, of course! She's awake right now with Franklin. Would you like to give it to her yourself?" Sahra asked.

Mary answered this time, "No, we don't want to disrupt the bonding time between them. We know how important that is. Just tell her it's from some friends that are looking out for her and her little one."

Mary reached out and gave Sahra's hand a tight squeeze. "Thank you, dear," she said.

Sahra grinned again and said, "Angel just told me she was going to need a stroller before she could leave the hospital with Franklin today. She'll be so happy!"

Charles just nodded his head, and Mary, using only her eyes, smiled back at Sahra before turning around and following her husband back into an almost-empty elevator. Only a sweaty, red bandana, still tied in a circle, lay by one wall. They waved to the nurse as the sliding door, which Charles' foot had been holding open for them, slowly closed.

CHAPTER TWENTY-FOUR
A TEAM OF TWO & A TRAP

Shad looked around the kitchen. "Okay, this is where it's going to happen. We have the best view of all the possible spots where the hand could come from, if we can lure it here. It's most likely coming from the plumbing, or possibly it's found its way into the ventilation system; another dark place for it to hide. Over there is the sink," he paused and pointed, then pointed again, "and over there are the air vents; one on the ceiling, one on the floor."

Shad gestured towards the girls' bathroom. "Then there's the bathroom sink, toilet, and bathtub in there," he said.

The downstairs bathroom, which the girls primarily used, was located adjacent to the kitchen. Anything coming or going from it could easily be seen if you stood in the center of the room.

Everyone had laughed when Shad first came down the stairs. He had been up in his room for almost an hour working on a pair of night-vision glasses for his plan, and when he was finally finished, he looked like a big goofball.

On his head was an old Minnesota Vikings hat. Hanging down from a side of the hat were three wires; one black, one green, and one yellow. Over his real glasses, he had on a cheap pair of cardboard spectacles that he had won at an arcade two weeks ago. The lenses of these glasses were thin colored plastic sheets of red and blue. Behind the two lenses were four circular red lights, taken from an old toy robot that Shad had found sitting unused in the playroom.

The red lights, two for each lens, were connected to the three wires running up to a switch, which he had duct-taped to the underside bill of his Viking's cap.

All of it was powered by a nine-volt battery tucked up above Shad's ear.

He looked like a mad scientist with a ridiculously low budget.

"Are you sure your plan isn't to get that hand to take one look at you and laugh so hard that it won't see me sneaking up on it?" Franklin joked.

Shad looked a bit confused. "Franklin, it's a hand. It can't laugh. In order to laugh, technically it would need a—"

"I was kidding, Shadrack," Franklin cut in.

"Oh, yeah, funny. You guys know what this hat and these glasses are for. I told you outside that I was going to be making a pair of night-vision goggles. I saw a video online about how to do it a few months ago. This is the perfect opportunity to use them. Pretty cool, huh?" Shad asked proudly.

Sami replied, "You're amazing, Shad! Do you think they'll really work?"

"I already tried them out in the bedroom upstairs. You'd be surprised at how well you can see in the dark with these."

Jessy looked wide-eyed at Shad and said, "How does that weird thing help you see in the dark, Shad? Aren't those glasses from a gumball machine or something?"

"No, Jessy. Actually, they're from Chucky Cheese. I acquired them with the thirty-two tickets I won playing the water gun target game. And the science behind these is fairly basic. Even in the dark, there are minuscule particles of light present that our eyes cannot detect, most of it being infrared. These glasses help me to collect all the light, even infrared light, which is bouncing around in the dark, and then use it to help me see!"

Shad took a deep breath and asked, "Does that make sense, Jess?"

"Not really, but that's okay," Jessy said honestly. "You're really smart, Shad."

"Okay, Shad," Franklin said, wanting to get back to business, "I have the camera here that you asked me about. You said something about using it in the dark?"

"Uh, yes. I inspected that camera a few weeks back when it was on your desk, and I noticed it also has infrared technology, a little more advanced than my hat, for taking videos in dark lighting. You can use it for night vision," Shad explained.

"Okay, so you and I are going to be watching for that thing. It could come in the form of a hand, black slime, or a swarm of flies. My guess is flies, since it would be able to move more freely through the air," Franklin said.

Rufus interjected, "Yeah, well the hand can move pretty freely when it's a hand too, let me tell you. And it can levitate itself, don't forget."

Franklin considered this for a second. "I did see Nefari glide smoothly up that hill with his wolves. If he can levitate, it makes sense that his hand could, too," he said.

"Uhhh, excuse me, but none of this junk really makes sense, let's not kid ourselves!" Parker interrupted.

Franklin flashed her a quick grin, "True, yet here we are."

"Well, you little…" Parker sneered at Franklin and pretended to punch him in the stomach before flaunting her own winning grin back at him.

"Anyway…" he continued, "so we don't know how it'll show itself, and remember, it may not come from the sink or the ventilation at all. It could come from another room. We need all of you to have your eyes open, scanning for any movement out there in the light. Shad and I will be here in the dark, with our night-vision, and we'll see if it'll come to us."

The first part of Shad's plan was to get the whole house lit up like the Fourth of July. Every room, every nook, and every cranny. They had even found five floodlights in the garage, ones that Hank had used for yard lights at one point and which Parker and Rufus now plugged in at various spots around the house, lighting up places where the normal lights couldn't reach. The kitchen, along with the girls' bathroom next to it, were separated from the rest of the house by a large swinging door, so it was possible to have these two rooms dark and every other room in the house shining brightly.

Franklin looked at Rufus. "Do you think you can keep the other kids playing outside for a little while? Can you get a game of kickball going with them or something like that?"

Rufus nodded his head and said, "Yeah, I can entertain them, don't worry. I know it is hard to believe, but I actually like little kids."

"Rufus with a soft side?" Sami asked. "I love it!"

Franklin looked at the orange-colored shine coming from Rufus; there was no doubt it had grown brighter in the last few hours.

"Parker, I think Jerod is in Greta's room with her right now. Do you know if she's sleeping?" Franklin asked.

"I'm not sure," replied Parker. "I'll check."

"Wait a sec. Can you somehow get Jerod outside for a while and take Greta with him? We don't want her in the house when that thing makes its appearance," Franklin said.

"Yeah, no problem. I've been known to be a persuasive person before, so this shouldn't be difficult," said Parker.

"Okay, great, you do have a way with words," Franklin told her. "Go ahead and take care of that now if you could, before we get started."

Parker nodded and left the room, heading towards the girls' living area.

Sami chimed in, "What if Nonna Glo comes back from the store while you're in here, Franklin? She'll take one look at Shad and know that we're up to something; she'll make us turn on the kitchen lights and the plan will be ruined."

"She'll be gone for another half hour," Franklin replied. "I'm almost positive. But we have to get this started now. Is everyone ready?"

They all nodded. Franklin continued, "Okay, Sami, you'll have Jessy. Keep him by you while you're turning every light on in the house. Jessy, listen. Stay as close to Sami as you can, at least in her line of sight. But I need you to flush every toilet, turn on every faucet so that water is rushing down the drain, full force, and every bathtub and sink, except for the ones here in the kitchen and bathroom. We want this place to look like a safe haven for that creep to show itself."

"Cold or hot water in the sinks?" asked Jessy, who was taking his assignment very seriously.

"Good question, buddy!" Franklin said, and patted him on the shoulder. "You choose, okay?" Then, remembering his experience in the school's basement and the extra chill which Nefari had brought with him, he added, "Maybe hot would be best."

Jessy nodded excitedly.

"Sami, you're closing all the vents around the house too, right?" Shad asked. "Oh, and blast the heat at eighty-five degrees, with the blower on."

"Already done," Sami answered.

If the hand was still somewhere in the plumbing, Shad's plan was to have the water flush it out, either away from the house, like down into the sewer, or cause it to seek refuge somewhere else in the house. Hopefully, this would be in the dark kitchen or bathroom, the only place where the water was *not* running.

His plan also included a provisional measure in case the hand had gotten into the air ducts. If this had happened, Shad thought that the hot air blowing through the ventilation system would chase it out. And the only open vents in the house for its escape would also be in the kitchen.

Where they would be waiting for it.

Franklin looked at Rufus. "Hey Rufus, it's time. Go round up the kids, take them outside. Sami, go ahead and get every light on in the house. Jessy, the water, kiddo."

Rufus left the kitchen through the swinging door, with Jessy and Sami following behind him. As she was walking out the door, Franklin gently grabbed her arm. "Sami, promise to be careful."

She met his eyes, her glow as vibrant as ever. "You know I'll take good care of Jessy."

"Of course, I mean Jessy too, but I really was thinking about you. Keep yourself safe. Please?"

"I will," Sami said warmly. "You promise me too, Franklin Hobbs."

"I promise."

She left the kitchen.

Shad had a feeling of growing uncertainty welling up inside him. "Franklin, what happens if it comes at us before we can do anything? What if it comes from above and we never even see it until it's too late?"

"Shad, I got you covered. You got me covered, right? I'll come running if I hear you yell, and you better do the same for me," he said. He laughed, trying to hide his own anxiety. "We got to trust each other now."

His roommate nodded in agreement. "Yeah, we got each other's backs."

Just then, they heard commotion in the main room. Franklin opened the door to see Parker walking by. Close behind her was Jerod with Greta in his arms. Shad ducked out of sight, it would be too hard to explain his headgear to Jerod right now. Parker looked over at them with a little smirk on her face, and she gave Franklin a nod as she left the house. Not too far behind them came Rufus, with seven or eight kids following him.

"This is all of them, the rest must be outside already," he said, giving Franklin the thumbs up before he walked out the front door, too.

Never dreamed Rufus would remind me of the Pied Piper, Franklin thought to himself, but suppressed a smile.

Sami and Jessy came down the stairs, hand in hand. "Basement?" Franklin asked.

"Done! Every light and faucet in the house that can be turned on *is* on," she said.

"And every toilet flushed!" Jessy added, mimicking Sami's tone.

Then, with some reluctance, Sami said, "Time to turn your lights out in there now, I guess,"

"All right, here we go then. Lights!" Franklin yelled to Shad, and he let the heavy door swing closed.

Shad flipped the kitchen lights out while Franklin walked to the bathroom to switch the light off in there.

Darkness fell on them, as thick as gravy.

CHAPTER TWENTY-FIVE
A SNEEZE & A SCIENCE PROJECT

Shad reached up to the bill of his cap and switched on the homemade night vision goggles. Franklin turned on his video camera. Looking at the screen on the camera, he could see shapes around him in a green tint but struggled to make out what they were. He wondered how he would ever see something as small as a hand, or worse yet, black slime.

He could see the kitchen cabinets, refrigerator, walls, stovetop, and sink; the big things were visible, although not quite clear. Being in a pitch-black room did not make him nervous, but the thought of Nefari's runaway appendage hurting one of his friends terrified him. He let the camera focus on the sink for a second, then panned over to where he thought the air vent on the ground would be. Fuzzy looking. Back to the sink. Over to the air vent on the ceiling this time. Again, fuzzy.

"Hey, how are you doing over there, Shad?" Franklin whispered into the dark. He heard the words leave his mouth, but in this blackness, it almost felt like someone else was speaking them.

"Just looking around," Shad answered. "Nothing yet, though. I can see everything really well. How about you?"

"Not so much," Franklin replied with some dismay. But then said, "Hopefully, the hand has little bells on each finger, so I can hear it coming."

"I highly doubt that would happen," Shad countered, scanning the walls, the floors, and the ceiling around the bathroom. He walked over to the kitchen area and surveyed the cupboards, countertops, and floors.

"I don't see anything, Franklin," he said, discouraged. "Maybe this wasn't such a great plan after all. I mean, that thing could just stay hidden behind the walls. It doesn't need to come out into the open."

"You forget, its whole purpose is to hurt me, or someone, so I think it'll be here," Franklin reassured him. "Just be patient."

Then his eyes began to tickle. He looked away from his video camera, rubbed them, and sat down on a kitchen chair. From behind his eyeballs, and from within the craters that held them, a strange sensation started to well up. Franklin wasn't sure how he was able to pinpoint the location of the odd tingling with such exactness, but he knew this was where it came from.

The only thing he could compare it to was the time he was being assaulted by Nefari. He had felt the same itch, almost a tickle, before the light had come; then it had beamed from his eyes, his whole face. That moment was a bit like a dream, but he could still remember it.

The sensation he felt now was very similar, and he knew something was happening to him.

He heard Shad say, "Hey Franklin, are you all right?"

"I think so," Franklin replied, not understanding just how Shad could tell something was wrong in the dark like this. "Why?"

"Well, it's kind of wild…your eyes, they're shining purple, glowing in the dark," Shad said.

Then the sensation stopped. The tingling was gone, and his eyes went back to normal. Franklin, relieved, said, "I'm fine. That was crazy, though. Something was happening to my eyes. I could feel it."

For some reason, everything was bright. Why had Shad turned the lights on in the kitchen?

"Hey, you better turn the lights off," he said seriously. "We have to keep going with your plan. It needs to be dark in here."

Behind his night vision goggles, Shad squinted, trying to figure out what Franklin could mean. It was still pitch black in the room.

He replied, "The lights are off, Franklin. What are you talking about?"

"Your hat must have fallen over your eyes, Shad, because it's as bright as the inside of a tanning bed in here!" declared Franklin.

"Look for yourself," Shad answered.

Franklin walked over to the switch on the wall that operated the kitchen lights. Off. He walked to the bathroom and looked at the switch inside the door. Off. He closed his eyes tight and squeezed them shut for five seconds, then opened them. Bright as the morning sun.

In a completely dark kitchen, Franklin could see everything like it was on a stage with a spotlight beamed at it. It occurred to him that this had to be another ability he had acquired on that miraculous night. These strange violet-tinted eyes of his were at it again.

But there was really no time to think about it.

"Behind you, Shad, turn around!" he cried, still trying to mute his voice, but leaving in the note of urgency.

Shad did a one-eighty on his feet, cocked his head to look from the ceiling, down to the ground, then over to the sink. He said, "I don't see anything. Where?"

"The air vent," Franklin said. "In the ceiling. Stay still."

He could see his old nemesis soundlessly oozing out of the vent and attaching itself to the ceiling. It reminded Franklin of a ball of tar.

When its entire form had finished seeping out onto the textured surface, it almost looked like it could be a water stain that had been created by a leaky pipe in the ceiling.

Remembering that although everything appeared bright, it was actually dark in the room, Franklin felt fairly certain the tarball did not know he had spotted it yet. Or if it even knew that he and Shad were there.

He whispered in Shad's ear, "Act like you don't see it."

"That's easy," Shad said quietly back, "because I don't."

Franklin said, "Walk around like you're still looking. Follow my lead."

"Got it," Shad said. He started walking slowly towards the bathroom, then pretended to poke his head around inside it.

Although the creature it had come from was highly intelligent, Franklin wasn't quite sure if the tarball clinging to the ceiling could detect sound or movement. He still decided to keep track of it using only his peripheral vision. This way he wouldn't give himself away by looking right at it, only from indirect angles. At the same time, however, he didn't want to turn his back on this malevolent form so that it could pounce on him when he was unaware.

"Oh no!" his roommate's distressed voice blurted out from inside the bathroom.

Dread filled Franklin. "What's wrong?" he asked, his voice only a bit quieter than Shad's had been.

"I have to… to… ahhhhh…ahhhhh…" but Shad stopped himself, momentarily.

"No, you can't!" Franklin called back.

"Ahhhhhh… chooooooooooo!"

Shad's sneeze was as loud as a shotgun and echoed through the walls of the kitchen. He shuffled out from the bathroom, stopped, and stood directly beneath the spying tarball.

"Sorry!" he whispered to Franklin.

Franklin turned quickly to the ceiling and spotted the black mass. As of yet, it had not made a move. Perhaps it didn't feel threatened because it was still under the impression that the two boys in the room had no idea it was up there. Trying to look away from it casually, Franklin hoped his sudden motions had gone unnoticed.

He also hoped Shad was not a Two-Timing-Sneezer.

No luck with that.

"Ahhhhhhhhhhhchoooooooo!"

Again!

This time Franklin observed the tarball shoot toward the vent, hide half of its mass inside it, then stop.

He cupped his hands around his mouth and whisper-shouted to Shad, "It's thinking about leaving! Walk away from it, Shad!"

Shad began to saunter around again, aiming his gaze here and there, and Franklin went over to the sink and pretended to be studying the drain. From the corner of his eyes, he peeked at the ceiling and saw that the shapeless fiend had positioned itself away from the vent once again.

"I think we're good," he said, speaking somewhat cautiously.

Backing away from the ceiling vent, Franklin slowly reached one hand behind his back towards an object on the counter, all the while trying to hide his intentions from the ever-lurking tarball. His hand grasped the coiled end of a hose attachment that led down to a powerful shop vacuum on the floor.

He easily found the metal flip switch on the vacuum, but didn't turn it on yet.

He was ready.

Then headlights swam across the walls of the kitchen.

"She's back!" Shad almost choked trying to get the words out.

Franklin took a quick look out the window. Nonna Glo was home much earlier than he had anticipated. This mission had to be finished in the next three minutes or they would lose the chance to recapture the hand until tomorrow. Franklin walked over to where Shad was still pretending to patrol.

"Shad, get the gun."

Shad reached into his pocket.

"Slowly," Franklin whispered. "Okay, do you see the vent on the ceiling?"

His friend started to look up.

Franklin stopped him, "Don't look at it! I mean, you know where it is, right? You're able to see it with your glasses?"

"Yeah, I know where it is. Is the hand by it?" Shad asked.

"Yup, but it's not the hand. It's in its slime ball form, trying to be stealthy, I guess. If you can't see it up there, aim a bit to the left of the vent. Shoot it as many times as you can."

Shad held the air pistol close to his side.

Franklin retreated, taking his position. Shad aimed the gun towards the vent, a little to the left, and fired off three consecutive pellets. Perfect shots! The idea was that that pellets were supposed to make the tarball come down from the ceiling, perhaps chase them, so that they could recapture it, but Franklin watched as the black slime absorbed each yellow, round pellet as it struck, swallowing them inside its mass. It remained motionless.

He looked out the window. Nonna Glo had opened her trunk and was reaching in to get something. Bags of groceries, of course.

"About two minutes until our scheme is up. Change of plans. The pellets aren't bothering it at all. Here, take this." Handing Shad the vacuum hose, he said, "I'm going up there."

In one smooth motion, Franklin grabbed a chair and slid it directly under the vent on the ceiling, then reached over to take a broom leaning against the wall. As he stepped onto the chair, the broom was already extended towards the ceiling. The tarball, at this point having noticed Franklin was up to something, began moving toward the vent.

After almost toppling off the chair in his rush and then finding his balance, he jabbed at the fleeing ball of tar with the handle end of the broom. It stopped moving. The end of the broom had mashed into the slime, then through it, pinning it to the ceiling. Franklin pulled back the broom handle and this time slid it underneath the ooze, using it like a pry bar, and wrenched it from the ceiling. The tarball peeled off like a sticker, clung on with one last strand of slime, then fell straight down.

Since Franklin was not in its direct path, it plummeted right past him, and as it fell, the boys saw the goo transform itself back into the hand, stop in mid-air, and hover two feet off the ground. The hand glided over to the chair on which Franklin stood, and wrapping its spindly, pale fingers around one of the wooden legs, it yanked on it. The chair tipped, and now it was Franklin's turn to plunge to the ground. He landed on his back next to the toppled chair.

"Franklin!" Shad yelled, not concerned anymore with staying quiet, "Are you okay?"

Focusing his attention on the hand, Franklin did not answer. The room was still encased in darkness, but he clearly saw the hand descend to the floor, where it lay flat for a moment. Then, stretching its fingers out, one by one in succession, it grabbed the linoleum in front of it and began pulling itself forward. He found himself a bit mesmerized by the inchworm-like motion of the gaunt fingers as they stretched, then pulled, stretched, then pulled itself over to where he lay. When it began moving up the side of his chest, the dull nails of the hand somehow penetrated the thin cotton t-shirt he wore, at the same time digging into his skin.

He hollered, "Shad, the vacuum, now! Turn it on now!"

Watching in horror, Shad frantically slid his fingers up and down around the outside of the cylinder-shaped vacuum. "I can't turn it on! Where's the switch?" he shouted desperately.

Franklin stood up, but the hand was stronger than he expected, and it clung to his chest. He ripped at it and was able to catch it off guard and throw it from him; the cold skin of the hand sending chills through him when he touched it.

Instead of falling to the floor, it caught itself in midair and floated up to his face, where it proceeded to dig four fingers into his soft cheeks. The thumb grasped underneath his chin, pushing up hard into his jaw, while its palm pressed against his mouth. Franklin tried yelling again, but only muffled cries came from beneath the suffocating palm. He clutched at it with both of his own hands and tried pulling it off, but the murderous hand had an otherworldly and powerful grip that was not about to let go. A single finger reached upwards towards his right eye, another towards his left.

In all of his twelve years, the most wondrous sound Franklin had ever heard in his life, up to that point, was the sound of his Mom's loving and nurturing voice. In a close second place, came the sound of his best friend Sami's voice, but not far behind, in third place, was the sound of that Craftsman vacuum cleaner coming to life.

"I got it, Franklin. I found the switch!" he heard Shad exclaim. Through the web of fingers plastered around his face, Franklin was just able to see the hose end of the vacuum coming down towards his head. He heard a loud slurping as the suction of the hose caught the back of the hand.

Undaunted, the hand continued to assault him.

He realized the suction was not strong enough to actually pull it from his face.

This was not in the plan, Franklin thought, and at that moment, an icy finger made contact with one of his lower eyelids. This only caused him to pry even more furiously at his assailant, but, alas, his two hands were no match for this one hand.

"The vacuum's not strong enough! What should I do?" Shad's despairing voice cried out.

Franklin wanted to yell at him to turn the lights on, but the palm of the ghastly appendage still deadened his voice.

Suddenly, he heard the swinging door slam open and lights flooded the room. The hand, instantly sensing the glare of white light on its sensitive skin, released Franklin's face, pushed off with its bony fingers and tried to scamper away. The vacuum, however, still suctioned it tightly, and instead of escaping, the appendage found itself adhered to the end of the hose. With nothing to grasp onto for leverage, it could not escape. Its fingers flailed wildly, giving it the appearance of a spider stuck on its backside. Then, in a last ditch effort, the hand changed its form back into the mob of insects and again tried fleeing the scene, its hundreds of tiny wings flapping furiously. But instead of breaking free, it was instantly sucked up into the bowels of the vacuum.

Franklin grabbed the hose and twisted it in on itself, blocking the only exit for the devilish creature.

Sami gave Franklin a nervous look. "Are you all right? I heard the vacuum going. I had to check —"

Shad, breathing even heavier than Franklin, and with a rapid heart rate to match, tore off his cardboard glasses and hat and said, "Thank goodness you did! That thing had his face. It was going for his eyes. I would have grabbed it but I …"

Heavy footsteps fell on the hard floor behind them; Nonna Glo had entered through the open door without them being aware.

"Hello, children! Would you mind helping me with the groceries? There are six or seven more bags out there in the car."

She looked at the shop vacuum and smiled. "Oh my! That is so sweet of you to do the vacuuming when it's not even your turn on the schedule. But we only use that shop vacuum in the garage. Hank uses it for his greasy messes out there. In here you need to use the upright vacuum. Here, I'll get it for you if you really have your heart set on vacuuming."

Nonna Glo started for the closet, but Franklin stepped towards her, holding out his hand and said, "Wait, Nonna Glo. We actually were using this vacuum here to help with a science project for school due on Monday. Right, Shad?"

Shad caught on to Franklin's little white lie. "Yeah, we were, uhhhh, we were seeing what size and weight of objects the vacuum cleaner could lift with its suction. The items have to be flat, of course, so that a seal can be formed. Did you know that a vacuum cleaner doesn't actually suck?" He was getting into it now. "There's really no suction force at all. The objects are not actually pulled, or sucked, into the vacuum like most people think. Instead, the pressure on the outside of the hose is greater than inside this canister here, so things are literally forced, or pushed into the vacuum from the outside." He took a deep breath, readjusted the glasses on his nose, and smiled at Gloria.

Franklin and Sami were not surprised that Shad was able to come up with this impressive soliloquy on the spot. He was great when it came to scientific improvisational talk.

Gloria looked at him with adoration and said, "That is unbelievable Shadrack, darling!" She rubbed his messy hair. "I swear you are going to discover a cure for cancer someday with that amazing brain of yours!"

Pausing, her tone changed as she asked, "Oh dear, what is that strange contraption in your hand? Are those *wires* connected to the hat?"

Shad looked down at his hand, he had apparently forgotten that he was still holding his homemade night vision glasses. "Oh, these? These are just part of the project..." He took it with both hands and fitted it back onto his head.

"Okay, maybe you should finish tomorrow, though. It's getting mighty late, kiddos."

She grabbed the handle on the top of the vacuum and said, "Here, let me empty that out. I know how Hank likes to keep it clean after he uses it."

Unhooking both side latches, Nonna Glo began to lift the round lid. Before she could, though, Sami sat down on it, slamming it back against the top of the metal canister.

She said matter-of-factly, "Oh, Nonna Glo. We can take care of all that. We'll make sure it's clean for Papa Hank. He's not coming back for a few days though, right?"

Sami's question was intended to change the subject of the shop vacuum to *anything* else, but it also happened to be a question she really wanted to know the answer to.

Gloria gave Sami a perplexed look and said, "Goodness child! You almost took my fingers off with the top of that vacuum!" But then her face relaxed and she contemplated her next words carefully. "Children, I know Hank has been acting very abnormally, but he just called and assured me that after talking with his mom, he's figured out what's going on with him. He realized he has pent up aggression towards you, Franklin, because you remind him of his older brother."

"Okay," Franklin said, thinking that this was a ridiculous excuse, "but why does that make him so angry with me?"

"Well, you see," Nonna Glo explained, "his older brother tormented him as a lad. He had a rough childhood on that farm, and Jake, his brother, made his life miserable, the poor darling. I guess you look just like Jake when he was eleven or twelve, and you carry yourself like him, too. He finally couldn't hold it in anymore and his aggression for his brother was taken out on you, Franklin." Gloria didn't even try to hide the relief in her voice as she spoke to the children.

"Poor Hank, having to hold all that hurt in for so long," she finished, wiping a single tear from one eye with her sleeve.

Franklin was stupefied that she would fall for this obvious lie from Hank, and he blurted out, "Nonna Glo, you're not serious, are you? He has never shown any aggression to me before last night. Hank has never been anything but kind to me, and now suddenly he wants to hurt me? It doesn't make sense!"

His concern about what was trapped in the shop vacuum had almost completely left his mind; Hank's return to the orphanage was, in all likelihood, a more dangerous, immediate threat to him.

"Hank had a psychotic look on his face, Nonna Glo. Something was really off about him," added Sami. "It couldn't have just been memories of his brother causing that."

Shad cut in, "No disrespect, Nonna Glo, but I think you are in bad judgment on this one. Maybe you should ask Hank to show you a picture of his brother when he was younger for some proof."

Gloria started to get a bit defensive. "Children, it sounds like you are trying to tell me that some malevolent force is at work here. That something has taken over control of Hank, and he is now a puppet forced to do its evil work on this Earth!" She looked exasperated. "You know that sounds ridiculous, right? I know you're concerned, but I have already asked Jerod to keep an eye on Hank when he gets back. Please trust me on this. If it helps you feel better at all, I also talked to his mother, and she promised me he was feeling much less agitated."

It didn't help them feel better.

Nonna Glo wasn't finished, "His mom also said he was able to burn off some steam and go deer hunting with a friend.

They got themselves a huge buck, I guess! I know he loves using that crossbow he's always telling me about."

Gloria saw the children's dejected looks and so she held out her arms wide and said, "Group hug, my little ones?" The three children stepped toward her and fell into her arms. She might have bad judgment this time, but they knew she still had a huge heart.

Jessy, who had been waiting at the door, unsure if he should join in the discussion and still a little fearful the hand might make a great escape from the vacuum, finally walked over and stood next to them. Sami saw him and pulled him under Gloria's large arm, into the embrace.

The big woman gave one final squeeze, then released them. "That's better," she said and began furiously fanning her face with her hand. "My goodness! It's hot in here! It must be at least *eighty* degrees! Did someone turn up the heat?"

No one said a word; each child merely gave Gloria their best look of confusion.

"Anyway…go ahead and get those groceries for me and then put this vacuum away." Gloria studied Franklin with something like bewilderment, "Franklin, honey, your eyes are so bright right now! A stronger shade of violet than I've ever seen them before. They're absolutely stunning!"

Then a big grin stretched across her face. "Shadrack, that hat you have on looks ridiculous, sweetie. Where did you get those wires? Did you take apart Scotty's robot? He is going to be spittin' mad at you!"

CHAPTER TWENTY-SIX
A VAPOR & A VISION

The sun had gone down in the time Franklin and Shad had spent in the kitchen. Rufus and Parker had come inside, along with the rest of the orphanage residents, and the pair was waiting at the kitchen table, anxious to see what had happened. Carrying the vacuum very carefully, Franklin motioned for everyone to follow him back out the front door, into the yard, and finally, to the old garage.

Hank's garage was next to the main house, separated only by a crumbling walkway that led to the side entrance of the orphanage. The outside of the garage had not had the updated remodeling as the old farmhouse had fifteen years ago, so it was in poor condition, with peeling green paint and deteriorating shingles clinging to the roof.

The inside of the garage was a different story. Hank had made it his own, giving it fresh drywall over the old wood siding and an oil-proof coating on the floor, which glistened as if it were wet at all times. He had built a large workbench all along the back wall where there sat many projects he was in the middle of working on; a lamp that needed new wiring, a window in need of new glass, a lengthy four-person bench he was constructing for the front porch.

One-half of the garage was being occupied by various machines. In the corner sat a John Deere riding lawn mower, and next to that was a large snow blower, critical to anyone living in Minnesota. Over further was an extensive plow attachment for the front of his pickup, and finally, a four-wheeler ATV and a snowmobile sat next to each other in the far corner. Hank would often take one or two of the children with him on these recreational vehicles for a thrilling ride in the fields, one that they would never forget.

The other half of the garage was empty, normally occupied by Hank's Ford pickup. Franklin sat in this unused space and carefully unlatched the lid from the vacuum's metal cylinder body. Above him stood Parker, Shad, and Rufus, each armed with one of the heavy-duty floodlights they had used in the house earlier. Sami sat on the opposite side of the vacuum from Franklin, ready with a jar, an even larger version of the previous one, which she had found in the basement.

Jessy had been left back in the house for his own safety.

Franklin, sweat visible on his forehead, counted out loud, "One... two... three... Go!"

He lifted the cover. The bright floodlights showered down upon them, blinding him and Sami momentarily. When they finally were able to regain their vision and see down to the bottom of the canister, there were no flies to be seen, but they immediately spotted the mass of black slime moving against the silver interior of the vacuum. It was convulsing, vibrating, and it moved quicker than they had seen it before; it seemed to be panicking as it sought shelter from the powerful rays of light battering down upon it. But there was no shelter for it, except a few stray dust bunnies that had inadvertently been 'pushed' into the vacuum's hose along with it. Needless to say, these did not provide much cover for it.

As the five of them watched, smoke, or possibly vapor, started coursing up out of the shapeless ooze. The stench that came with it was like nothing any of them had ever smelled. A stink that was not meant for human noses. Every one of them automatically pinched their nostrils together between thumb and forefinger.

"Should I put the jar on top of it?' Sami asked Franklin, still holding her nose.

"Hold on, let's watch for a minute. I don't think it's going anywhere," he replied.

The shapeless mass, still reeling from the intense white rays of the floodlights, was now letting off a high-pitched hiss. Just like the powerful stench was hurting their noses, the frequency of this noise was also painful for the children to listen to. With one hand already occupied plugging their nose, they were not able to cover both ears as well, so they had to endure the discomfort for the time being.

As vapor continued to pour out from the tarball, which was still trembling from the apparent torment it was experiencing, it altered back into the form of a hand, then, after realizing the pain was still as severe, the hand melted away and became the swarm of flies. The insects only fell to the bottom of the container, unable to fly in the intense light, and morphed back into the sludge once again. This pattern of shifting forms continued again and again, as did the horrible smell and the ear-piercing shriek it was emitting.

Throughout all of this, the kids noticed that the amount of dark matter was decreasing with every transformation, each passing second, and that only portions of the hand would manifest the next time. The hand without a thumb, then missing two fingers, eventually there was only the smooth, creaseless palm by itself, then the next time only half of it. Smaller and smaller. The flies also dwindled in number until there was only a handful left. After a while, there was nothing in the container except the pungent odor, which also hung in the air all around them, as well as the echo of its shrill, death-scream in each of their ears.

Rufus released his thumb and index finger from his nose and spoke first, "Guys, that was by far the sickest thing I have ever witnessed. Thanks for letting me help you."

"Yeah, it was nasty! Especially the smell!" Sami agreed, her voice nasally, as she had not removed her hand from her nose yet.

"No, sickest, as in *most awesome*!" Rufus explained, "I loved seeing that creepy thing fry!"

"Technically," Shad spoke, "technically, I believe the proper term to use here is 'evaporate'. It didn't fry. Or burn at all. It turned into a gas. That was why it let off such an awful smell."

"All right, well, then I loved seeing that thing evaporate. I guess I just enjoyed seeing it die in any way at all, after what it did to both me and Frankie here," said Rufus.

Franklin nodded in agreement and said, "But let's hope it's dead and not just in some other form that can regenerate itself again."

"I think the atomic particles that make it up have been too far scattered for it to become incarnate again, at this point," Shad said. "Let's assume it's dead."

"Sounds good to me," Parker declared.

Franklin lifted up the vacuum cleaner, wrapped the cord around it neatly, and put it back on the shelf where he had found it. This is how Papa Hank had always kept the shop vacuum and everything else in his garage, clean and orderly. The others followed him out into the brisk night, where the smell of rain was in the air, and thunder rumbled somewhere in the distance.

They had a while before the storm would arrive, so they decided to stay outside.

The moon was almost a full glowing circle in the sky, but it was low yet and so offered minimal light. In this setting, the darkness was extremely pleasant to the children, and Franklin wished darkness could always be this comforting to him. Above them, the stars could be seen clearly, and Shad began pointing out several constellations to the group. Leo the Lion, Ursa Major the Great Bull, Canis Major the Great Dog.

This last constellation, The Great Dog, brought back unwanted memories to Franklin of dark places where not great dogs, but immense wolves, pursued him.

Rufus was fascinated, as he had never before in his life been shown constellations in anything but schoolbooks.

"You're a smart kid, Shad. I'm sorry I used to call you a 'runny-nosed nerd' all the time," Rufus said.

Shad looked over to where Rufus stood, his silhouette visible against the porch lights. "You called me that?" he asked, not trying to hide his hurt.

Rufus tried back-pedaling. "Ummm, only once or twice, I think," he said.

Shad said, "I've been taking this allergy medicine that Nonna Glo gave me last night. She saw what I had done to my shirtsleeves from wiping my nose on them all day and felt like I should probably take something. My nose isn't quite so runny now, but I'm afraid I can't do anything about the 'nerd' part. That's just who I am."

Rufus shrugged. "Yeah, no big deal."

"I wish that allergy medicine had kept you from sneezing in the kitchen earlier," Franklin said, jokingly. "Twice."

"Oh, yeah. Sorry about that," Shad apologized. "The wires on the hat I made were hanging down and tickling my nose, and well, I sneezed. It had nothing to do with my allergies, actually," he explained.

Parker laughed at Shad. "You know, you're a funny guy Shadrack. You're not a nerd at all. You're an intelligent, unique individual who happens to be fascinated by anything with the words *Star Wars* or *Dr. Who* on it."

"You told her about that, Franklin?" asked Shad.

"Sorry, I didn't think it was a bad thing. Hey, I like watching reruns of *Little House on the Prairie* episodes. They're such a big, happy family. I'm not embarrassed," Franklin chuckled, "but I won't divulge any more of your deep, dark secrets, all right?"

Shad didn't respond, but instead asked him, "What about you, Franklin? I might have sneezed, but your eyes did something…something very strange in there tonight. They glowed bright violet, and then you thought that I had turned the lights on! What happened?"

Franklin explained about the sensation in his eyes and how the dark room looked like it was lit up. "I think it's another crazy ability that my eyes have. You know, like the other things I told you about."

"Does it still seem like it's light out here to you now?" Sami asked as she looked around the dark yard.

"No. From what I can tell, the ability only comes when I need it and leaves when I don't anymore. I can't really control it," Franklin clarified.

"That's intense, Frankie," Rufus remarked. "What other abilities are you talking about, though?"

"Rufus, for some reason I think I can trust you now, so I'm going to tell you a quick story that you have to promise never to tell a soul."

"I swear on my momma's grave, Franklin!" he replied.

For the next few minutes, Franklin filled Rufus in on what had been happening in his life.

When he was done, Rufus responded by saying, "Man, your life has sucked even worse than mine; that's the craziest junk I ever heard! But… I believe every word you're telling me after what I just saw in there tonight. Thanks for trusting me, Hobby."

Parker asked, "You guys want to chill out on the grass and look at the stars for a few minutes until lights out?" She sat down even as she asked the question.

Shad plopped down on the grass beside her before anyone else could say no. The rest of them did the same, and they all stretched out on their backs and stared up at the stars.

Sami, always the voice of wisdom, said, "Hey guys, true, this is really awesome out here, but has anyone else considered that it might not be a good idea for Franklin to be in the dark like this for so long? Shall we go inside soon?"

Franklin replied, "Thanks for thinking of me Sami, but I have you guys here. I don't want to be afraid of the dark my whole life, especially outside on a beautiful night like this. I think it's okay to stay here for a little while."

"Did you guys see that shooting star?" Parker asked. "It was right there." She pointed to a spot in the sky over a group of trees.

Shad corrected her, "That's an airplane. Look, you can see the red light blinking on its tail."

Parker looked over and stuck her tongue out at him, but nobody noticed.

"It's just a little scary knowing that the owner of that hand is out there somewhere, waiting to catch you off guard," Sami said, responding to Franklin's earlier reply.

"Yeah, I agree," Rufus said. "After that ghost that I saw last month in the woods, I get a little nervous in the dark now, too."

All the other children, almost in unison, spun their heads towards Rufus, who could sense their stares, although he couldn't see them clearly. "Uh, didn't I tell you guys about that?"

"We haven't had a lot of time to talk to you, Rufus. You know, since you became part of our group here," Sami answered.

"What ghost, Rufus? What are you talking about?" Franklin pressed him.

Rufus hesitated at first, then decided there was no reason not to tell them. "Well," he started, "I snuck outside about four weeks ago, after lights out. I had to get out of this place and just do some thinking. About life. You know? It's so quiet and peaceful out there, especially at around midnight."

Parker didn't want to let him off that easy, so she said, "Why don't you ever talk to someone here about life? Why have you always been so rude to everyone? It seems like you constantly push people away from you, even when they're trying to be your friend."

"I didn't want friends. I didn't want people to like me. I've been alone my whole life, and I'm used to being alone, now. I do better alone," Rufus said.

"Nobody does better alone," said Franklin, who lay next to Rufus. "We all need people in our lives who care about us."

"And you're stuck with us now!" Sami added.

"I have to admit, I wish I hadn't waited so long to try this 'being nice and having friends' thing out," Rufus remarked.

Franklin asked, "What sorts of things do you need to think about out there alone in the woods?" He hoped he had not crossed a line with this question, because he could see tears on his new friend's face.

"Well, when I was three months, old my mom decided she didn't want me anymore. Instead of giving me to someone so that I would be safe, she left me in a dumpster in an alleyway, somewhere in downtown Minneapolis. I guess I was there overnight until the garbage truck came in the morning. That's when the driver heard me crying. I was close to being crushed and buried in a landfill." He paused, "I have a lot to think about. Mostly, why I was left in that dumpster, and why my mom didn't care if I died."

"You know, Rufus," said Sami, "you were rescued by that man for a reason. You are important."

Rufus kept going, "I always thought it was just easier not having friends. Easier than telling people the story I just told you. Easier than being dumped again when they decided they didn't actually like me." Rufus wiped his eyes, "But I was wrong. You guys are the real deal, and I'm glad this happened. It sounds strange to say that I'm glad I was almost strangled to death by a severed hand, but if it hadn't happened, I might have never known how awesome you guys really are."

A few of them laughed quietly. "Strange how things work in this world, isn't it?" Franklin said, thinking about his own life; the ache of losing his mom still fresh in his heart. "Rufus, can you tell me about this ghost you think you saw?"

"I *know* I saw," Rufus clarified. "I was sitting on 'The Thinking Stump', as I call it... down by Lake Birdsong. You know, the lake that's sorta out in the field about a mile down the road there?" He pointed towards the street that ran by the orphanage and deep into Minnesota farmland.

"You walked all the way out there in the middle of the night? Impressive," Sami replied.

"Yeah, I was sitting there on 'The Thinking Stump', looking in the sky, sorta trying to find the man in the moon. It was a huge, full moon that night. That's when I saw someone walk out from behind a tree a few feet in front of me. At first, I thought it was Hank or Gloria that had somehow followed me, but then I saw that the person was in like a greenish light. It wasn't solid, either. More like a, what do you call it, those 3-D projections?"

"A hologram," Shad said, helping him.

"Yeah, a hologram. Walking around. Green. Then she looked at me."

"She?" Franklin asked.

"That's when I could see it was a female ghost. Young, maybe in her thirties. She looked at me and asked me something, in a garbled voice, like through a long tube or something, but I could still make out what she said…"

"What? What did she say?" Franklin asked. He sat up now, studying Rufus intently.

Rufus continued, "She said 'Have you seen…"

Franklin prodded, "Seen what?"

"That was it. She never got to say," explained Rufus, "All of a sudden, it was like she was scared and had this look on her face of panic or something. I was thinking to myself, *hey, I should be the one who's terrified right now,* but something really frightened her. She turned her head and looked behind her, said something like, 'he's back' and took off running further into the woods, then just faded away, like the hologram projector had been turned off."

Franklin, in quiet thought, lay back down on the cold grass for a minute and considered all that Rufus had just told them. He was trying to decide if he believed any of it, until the thought occurred to him that his friends had just believed every ludicrous thing he told them.

"That's a really chilling story, Rufus," it was Parker, "you need to tell that around a campfire some night."

"I guess I didn't think of it like that, though," replied Rufus. "The strange thing was, I wasn't even scared. She wasn't going to hurt me. Just needed help."

Just then a thought entered Franklin's head. An exciting, terrifying thought.

"I have an idea who you might have seen," he said.

"What? Who Hobby?" Rufus asked.

Franklin was quiet for a moment; he looked down at the grass, trying to contemplate if his hunch could possibly be true. When he raised his head, the moon, which was scaling its way up the sky, gave enough ambient light to help him recognize the looks on his friends' faces. He had piqued their curiosity and they were expecting him to satisfy it.

"C'mon, don't hold us in suspense, Franklin!" Sami pried. She reached over and lightly pushed his elbow inward on the arm that held his weight.

"Hey!" he yelled in jest, collapsing into the grass. Amid the laughter coming from his friends, he sat up and brushed off his shirt; his face grew serious. "All right," he finally offered. "What if Rufus somehow saw my mom?"

CHAPTER TWENTY-SEVEN
A SUSPICION & A SLICE OF SWISS

Later that night, Shad and Franklin lay in their beds, the events of the day playing in their minds like a movie. Their room, only large enough for two twin beds, a single desk, a dresser, and very little moving-around space, was currently lit by three small night-lights, which Franklin had brought with him from his old room back at his house.

The storm had missed them, passing to the north of Abundant Lakes. Outside, Franklin could see the night sky, stars still brilliant. He thought of the story that Rufus had told him only an hour ago, about the vision of the woman in the woods. She was searching for something. Her son, perhaps? Was she looking for him? Franklin had a strong feeling this might be the case. He had no idea how it could possibly be, though.

Shad interrupted the quiet. "You're thinking about your mom, aren't you?"

"How did you know?" Franklin answered, surprised once again at Shad's perception.

"Because that's what I'd be thinking about if I were you." He paused, "You don't think she's actually a ghost, do you?"

Franklin pondered the question, then said, "I don't think ghosts exist like we think they do. I believe in spiritual beings, but not ones that come back to haunt their old home, or school, or wherever, you know?"

"Yep," Shad agreed, "or a random forest in the middle of nowhere, like where Rufus said he saw this lady?"

"Yeah, like that. Except that the forest happens to only be a few miles from where my mom was taken," Franklin said.

His roommate got quiet for a minute. Franklin knew he was thinking about something important. Whenever Shad stopped talking in the middle of a conversation like this in the past, he had consistently come up with a profound thought.

His next question proved Franklin to be right. "Do you think she might have been taken to another whole world, as in a different realm?"

Shad was amazing, Franklin thought. He had never mentioned his suspicions to any of his friends about where his mom was, but here Shad had the same idea as he did.

"That's exactly what I think! My mom is being held somewhere in that nightmarish world where I was brought when I used my future-sight," Franklin explained.

Once again, Shad was quiet, then, "You said everything in Nefari's world was the same as the scenery around Cast Maker Canyon here in our world, right? Like the hill you were on, the fields, and the forest, although you said the trees were dead. But basically, the physical landscape of the area was the same?"

"Yeah, it was. Even the same big rocks jutting out where my bike hit. But it was different, like you said. Dying or dead. Different sunlight, different sky."

Franklin cringed at the memory of that awful place and the thought that his mom might actually be there right now.

"I've been reading some pretty amazing science fiction books that involve quantum mechanics. Do you remember the one I mentioned to you a few days ago?" Shad asked.

"Yeah, I remember. You said a bunch of scientific jargon that made no sense to me," Franklin said, laughing.

Shad nodded. "Well, part of quantum mechanics deals with the hypothesis that there is one or more parallel universes existing on the same plane as ours. Many believe there is a 4th dimension, which is what allows for these parallel worlds."

"Shad, this stuff is way above my head. Simple terms please," Franklin said.

His roommate thought about it, "Okay, some people think of the different planes, or parallels, as sheets of paper stacked upon each other. You could have an indefinite number of them. Each one is similar to our version of Earth but may have differences that we can't understand. There could also be other forms of life on those realms, walking around, living their lives right in front of us, only we can't detect them."

"Can they see us?" Franklin asked.

"Who knows? We don't know what kind of beings might live there. They could be humans, like us. In that case, they probably have the same capabilities as us, meaning they can only see what's on their own plane."

Franklin added, "But if there are different types of beings, or creatures, like Nefari, they may have the ability to step into different planes."

Shad finished his thought. "And take others back with them to their own parallel plane. Their own 'sheet of paper'."

"Like my mom..." Franklin said quietly.

Franklin Hobbs and the Quagmire of Darkness

****

Shad couldn't sleep that night. Something was bugging him and he needed to find out if his hunch was right. Franklin had already fallen asleep and was snoring softly in his bed. Shad pulled his covers off and sat up. His red flannel pajamas, which were hand-me-downs from an older, bigger boy, hung loosely on him. He walked soft-footed to the desk that he shared with Franklin, but was really only used by him, due to the fact that Franklin liked to do his work downstairs with Sami.

He opened the bottom drawer and pulled out his tablet, last year's birthday present from Nonna Glo. Only 36% power showed when he flipped it on. That would be enough though, he thought. He went online to his favorite search engine and typed in 'Full Moon' and 'Spirits', then looked through the results of the search, finding nothing that really interested him. He tried another approach; he typed 'paranormal activity on nights with full moon'.

Several of the hits that came up this time caught his attention. Browsing through them, he came upon something that he had been looking for.

After reading through the article, Shad yelled out, "I knew it!" before remembering that it was way past lights-out and others were sleeping, like his roommate for instance, who now stirred awake in the bed next to him.

"What? What are you doing?" Franklin asked, rubbing the sleep out of his eyes. "Why aren't you sleeping, Shad?"

"I couldn't. I had to check something out online. After our talk about the different planes of Earth and how we think your mom was taken to one of Earth's parallel planes, where Nefari lives, I started thinking about how Rufus had seen that spirit on a night with a full moon."

"Okay, I'm listening," Franklin said through a yawn.

"Well," Shad continued, "I did a research report on the cycles of the moon once and remembered reading all these different beliefs people have about the powers of a full moon. So I checked it out. One of the articles I just found online gave data about how, on nights with a full moon, the number of paranormal sightings went up. In other words, more people report seeing ghosts or spirits when there's a full moon in the sky! Even old Native American transcripts and other records of civilizations like the Aztecs, Romans, and Egyptians; all of them, in some printed history, have somehow expressed the significance of a full moon and how it brings out more spirits."

"How does this help us?" Franklin asked, not yet quite able to put the same pieces together that Shad had.

"So check this out. A lot of scientists who support the Parallel Earths hypothesis also believe that when there's a full moon, it somehow acts as a catalyst, or determinant, could be either, creating standing openings between realms."

"Huh?" Franklin muttered.

Ignoring the question, Shad continued, "This is thought to possibly allow the passage of light and sound waves from one plane to another in these certain 'hot spots'."

"What do you mean 'hot spots?" Franklin inquired, getting frustrated that he couldn't follow Shad's logic.

Shad answered, "There are specific spots where light and sound waves can find big enough gaps in the atmosphere of the aligned planes to transmit through…"

Franklin blurted excitedly, "And the woods where Rufus had gone to might be one of them?"

"That's right!" Shad exclaimed, then said, "I've heard one scientist use a metaphor that I really like; picture two slices of Swiss cheese, the kind with random holes in them. Each slice of cheese is one plane of Earth. If these two slices are put on top of one another, there will be places where the holes in the cheese line up, so that part of the hole, or window, may go all the way through. These are like the hot spots on Earth where openings exist for sound and light waves to travel from one plane to the other. Maybe Rufus's forest is one of these spots."

"Yeah," Franklin said, beginning to understand the science behind what Shad was explaining. "So, on nights where there's a full moon, conditions become just right for images and voices to travel through the planes of Earth. Why a full moon?"

"Well," Shad started, "I guess no one knows for sure. Possibly something to do with the gravitational pull it has, like the way it affects the oceans' tides."

"So, let me get this right," Franklin conjectured, "if Rufus saw my mom, she *was* actually there, only on a different piece of Swiss cheese!"

"Right, and your mom was able to see him as well, from the piece of Swiss cheese she was standing on." Shad's own voice had grown in enthusiasm, glad his friend was starting to make sense of it.

Franklin asked, "So, people who think they see ghosts and spirits may only be seeing other people that exist on a parallel Earth? People or things who are actually standing right in the same space as they are, but not able to be detected under normal circumstances?"

"If it's a full moon, I think that's accurate. I can't speak for other times 'ghosts' are seen. That may go beyond science."

Franklin seemed bothered, "Shad, isn't there a full moon tonight? Right now? I thought I saw one when we were star gazing earlier."

Shad grabbed his tablet and typed something in. A second later he said, "Ummm, according to AccuMoon.com, tonight was not quite a full moon. We got pretty lucky because tomorrow night the moon will be in all of its glory!"

Franklin grinned at his friend, the mad scientist, and said, "Well, then…I guess we know what we're doing tomorrow night!"

CHAPTER TWENTY-EIGHT
A LIAR & A LITTLE GIRL

There was a knock on the bedroom door. From under his sheets, Franklin peeked out at the clock on the desk; 8:13 in the morning. He looked at Shad's bed. It was unmade and empty.

"Who is it?" he called.

On the other side of the door, Franklin heard a gravelly voice. "It's me, Papa Hank. Can we talk, Franklin?"

Franklin was dumbfounded. Did this man think he could just come into his room now? Just the two of them? Alone?

"I'd rather wait, Hank," Franklin answered. He purposely left out the title of 'Papa' from his name. "I'll get dressed, and I'll come downstairs in a minute."

The deep voice came off with a gentle tone. "No problem. Whatever you're comfortable with, son. I'll be waiting for you at the breakfast table. I owe you an apology."

Franklin heard Hank's heavy footsteps walk away, down the hall, then fade altogether as he descended the steps.

Breathing a sigh of relief, Franklin slowly rolled out of bed. *This would be interesting*, he thought. Hank seemed to be trying a different technique. Playing the sorrowful victim. It had obviously worked with Nonna Glo, but Franklin knew better.

Nonna Glo had a distinct *disadvantage* when it came to believing Hank's lies. She would believe any excuse he gave her for his delinquent behavior if it meant not having to face the cold facts that something was wrong with him. Something was dangerously off.

He thought of the warning his mom had given him in her letter: *There are people in your life who are not what they seem.* How right she had been!

Of course, Franklin suspected foul play. He guessed that Nefari had somehow twisted Hank's mind. Hank might be an innocent victim in all of this. Like Nonna Glo had said only the day before, he was a 'puppet' for evil. Gloria had meant it to be satirically humorous, but she was probably right on the nose. Whatever the cause, Franklin knew he had to be extremely careful around this demented man.

After brushing his teeth and throwing some clothes on, he went downstairs, reluctantly, to the dining room. Crossing the main room, he could see Shad, Rufus, and Sami sitting very quietly at the end of the table eating their breakfast of eggs and bacon. Others were scattered around the rest of the table, eating as well. It was a large table and could seat up to sixteen people or more if they squeezed in tight. The sound of forks and knives clanking against plates was the only sound in the room.

Hank sat in the middle of them, focusing on his cup of coffee, ignoring the children around him. His facial expression was nondescript, emotions ripped from him like a pitted prune, and his curly mustache sagged down into his "I Heart Hunting" coffee mug as he pressed it to his lips.

He looked up at Franklin and suddenly came to life, "Hey, buddy! So good of you to join us."

His voice quality actually came off as pretty sincere, Franklin thought. *He would have made a decent actor in another life.*

Without rolling his eyes, Franklin gave Hank a look that meant pretty much the same thing as if he had.

"Well, I'm hungry, and this is breakfast, so I thought it would be a match made in heaven," he responded, not even trying to hide the sarcasm.

The man grinned at him. "Okay, I deserve a little heat from you. I get it. I was a jerk, and I'm sorry. I just snapped. Nonna Glo explained to you about my brother that you resemble. Heck, you are the spittin' image of him. He made my childhood a living hell, and I've never gotten past it. He's dead now, so I can't have any closure with him, and this anger is finally coming to the surface. I'm better, though. My mom helped me. She talked me through it, and I promise it won't happen again."

Franklin studied the black shine that surrounded Hank. The dark color had almost completely taken over his old glow of greenish-blue. Hank was not only being controlled by something else, but he had turned into something else. This wasn't Hank anymore.

Franklin struggled to say anything back to him. Finally, he came up with, "That makes sense, Hank. Thanks for explaining that to me. I can see why you acted like that towards me, then." He hoped this didn't sound as forced as it felt.

The others at the table looked on in silence. Franklin glanced at Sami. She looked concerned, and Rufus just looked confused.

"Okay, then. Are we good?" Hank smiled. Somehow, the tips of his mustache tickled his eyelids again.

"Yep. We're good, Hank."

"All right, but please call me 'Papa Hank', Frankie. Like you always have. I'm the same guy. Here, come give me a hug."

Hank stood up and walked around the table and reached out with his skinny arms. Franklin had no choice but to embrace him back. Hank squeezed Franklin, extra hard it seemed, but finally let go. He slapped him on the back, and his eyes twitched inadvertently as he said, "That's my kiddo. I love you, Frankie Boy."

I love you.

Those were three words that Hank had never said to him before, or any of the orphans that Franklin knew of, for that matter.

"Okay, thanks Hank," Franklin murmured.

"Well, how about you?" Hank asked. Unfortunately, he was not yet done with this sickening charade.

An awkward silence filled the dining room. Just then Nonna Glo walked in. She stood at the threshold to the kitchen, holding the swinging door open with her hip. Franklin guessed that she had been listening and now wanted to make sure it ended on a positive note. She said, "Oh, Franklin loves you too, Papa Hank. Don't you Franklin?"

Franklin looked at the ground. His words were strained as he lied. "Of course, I do. You are like a father to me, Papa Hank."

He wanted this to end. Whatever was happening here was very disconcerting, and the negative energy coming from Hank was no less than sinister.

Hank walked away to another room, seeming content that he had earned some trust back and that his recent cover-up about his brother had been convincing. Gloria went back into the kitchen, satisfied as well.

Franklin sat down next to Rufus and reached to the middle of the table where the steaming hot food sat. As he spooned some eggs and bacon onto his plate, Rufus leaned over and whispered to him, "You aren't buying all that crap from him, are you?"

Franklin laughed. "Not a chance. But it's safer for now if he thinks I am," he whispered back.

Sami studied Franklin for a second, then said firmly but quietly, so only her friends could hear her, "You cannot be alone with that man under any circumstance. You know that, right?"

"I know, Sami. Thanks," he replied back, just as quietly. "Hank's under the influence of something pretty wicked. His shine has almost completely turned now."

The children finished their breakfast and cleared the table. They brought everything into the kitchen and helped Gloria rinse the dishes and put them in the washer. Gloria, although happy that things between Hank and Franklin were better, had a look of heavy burden on her face. Her eyes had dark circles underneath them, and five or six wrinkles ran horizontally across her forehead, not normally present when she wasn't under stress.

Franklin tugged on her sleeve. "Hey, Nonna Glo. Is everything okay?" he asked her.

Nonna Glo sighed and then replied, "No, not at all. The doctor called about Greta. I took her in early this morning for some blood tests and a CT scan, and some of the results came back already. She is a very sick little girl."

Tears flowed down from Gloria's eyes, and she soaked them up with her apron. "The doctor says the scan showed a small tumor on one of her tonsils. Blood tests show it's non-Hodgkin's lymphoma. She has cancer." Gloria was no longer able to hold back heavy sobs and had to stop talking for the time being. The others came over and joined Franklin, standing next to her.

Sami started crying, too. Rufus, not wanting to show his emotions, was looking off to the side, wiping his dampening eyes. Franklin only stared ahead at Nonna Glo's bright yellow apron. On it was a calico cat wearing a chef's hat; the feline was smirking back at him. He was at a loss for words.

Shad asked her, "What sort of chances did the doctor give her?"

Gloria took a minute to regain her composure, ran her fingers through Sami's hair, who was leaning on her stout arm for support and said, "Doctor Foster gives her a 50% chance of living until she's five. She recommends starting treatment next week. The chemo is going to be a horrific experience for that sweet child. She'll lose all her hair, a lot of weight, and feel nauseous for the next 2 months."

Throughout the conversation, Gloria had either been wringing her hands together or fidgeting with her apron. Now her large arms stretched out toward the children. She moved her fingers back and forth to motion them to come to her, and when they did, she gathered them in for a hug. For only a second, Rufus grew stiff, resisting Gloria's affection, then allowed himself to fall into her arms. She hugged them all tight, droplets of tears wetting their hair. The children disappeared into her generous frame and became lost in the smell of fried eggs and bacon.

Through tear-filled eyes, Sami managed to look up at Gloria and ask, "Can we see her, Nonna? Is she in her room?"

Gloria relaxed her hold on the kids, and they withdrew a step. She replied, "Jerod is with her. She's resting. Go ahead. It would make her happy to see you. She doesn't know about the test results. I'm not ready to tell her yet."

The children nodded to imply their understanding and walked toward Greta's room.

On the way across the main floor to where the girl's bedrooms were, Rufus finally spoke. "All I can think about is Greta running around in that Supergirl costume she always has on. She wanted me to play with her a few weeks ago, to be the bad guy, and I told her no. I wanted to, but I told her no, anyway."

"She asked me, too, but I was in the middle of my book, I told her maybe later, but never did," Shad confessed. "I wish I had."

"Hey guys, we all have things we would do differently. Don't beat yourselves up over it," Sami told them. Shad shook his head in modest agreement. Rufus, on the other hand, looked down at the floor. His guilt wasn't going away so easily.

They arrived at Greta's room, two doors down from Sami and Parker's. After knocking and hearing Jerod's tired voice telling them to come in, Franklin turned the knob and the four of them entered the room. Greta lay in her bed. The children could see her little body trembling under the covers. Golden hair lay sprawled in all directions on her pillow, normally held tight in pigtails. Her back was to them, so they were not able to see the delicate features on her face. Franklin eyed the washcloth that lay stretched over her forehead.

Jerod said, "She has a 103-degree fever right now. Gloria told me to use this cold cloth to try to bring it down."

He sat on a small stool next to the bed. The kids could tell he had been there for quite some time by the three empty cans of Mountain Dew on the floor. His handsome face was unshaven, and he looked like he could benefit greatly from a hot shower. His black hair, normally parted across his forehead, hung down over his eyes in oily strands. Flipping his head occasionally in attempt to remove the hair from his face was not working, so he peered out at the children from windows of greasy hair.

He was not a tall man, just over five and a half feet in height, but he was muscular in build and more athletic than most. Currently, he wore a blue sweatshirt that boasted "Abundant Lakes Football; State AA Champions" along with a pair of blue jeans with holes worn in the knees. Although he had been a star running back on his high school team, he had always remained humble and preferred to keep a low profile. This modest demeanor of his only gave girls around the small town even more reason to compete for his attention.

Sami turned from Greta to look at Jerod, concern in her eyes as usual, and asked him, "Just how long have you been here with her, Jerod?"

Jerod kept his gaze on Greta and said, "I was with her all night. Gloria asked me if I could stay so that she could get some sleep, and then she'll take over for me this morning. She should be in here to take my spot in a few minutes. I don't mind at all. I just want her to get better." He turned his head towards them. "Are you kids here to cheer her up?"

Shad and Rufus stood awkwardly near the door, neither one of them quite sure what to do in a situation this serious. Franklin stepped forward and said, "Jerod, do you mind if I try talking with her?"

"Of course not. I'm not sure if she's sleeping or not. She's been so restless. A fever this high can give you awful dreams," Jerod told them.

Franklin kneeled down next to the bed and put his hand on the back of Greta's head. He said, "Hey there, Supergirl. I hear you've had to take a break from fighting all of those bad guys out there. We need your crime-fighting skills, so you need to get better soon."

Greta's head slowly turned, her body shifting position underneath the covers to face him. Her face was red with fever, her lips dry and cracked. She spoke softly, taking great effort even for this task. "Hi, Franklin. Hi, guys. I feel really, really sick." She paused; suddenly a distressed look crossed her face. "Franklin?" she asked.

"Yes, Greta?"

"Will you be able to fight the bad guys and monsters without me for a while? Your friends can help you, right Sami?"

Sami was holding back tears. "We're helping him while you get better. You just make sure that you *do* get better."

"Do you think I'm going to die? It feels like it to me." Greta's voice trembled with each word. She looked into Franklin's eyes. Her own blue eyes were faded and lacked the sparkle he was used to.

"No way. You're going to be fine," he answered confidently, putting the back of his hand on her forehead as his mom had always done to him when he was sick. She was burning up. He moved the cold cloth, which had slipped down to the pillow, back onto her forehead. Mustering enough strength, Greta weakly reached up and over until she touched his face. "Your eyes are so bright, Franklin. They're so pretty. Look, Sami, they look like two, bright, shining, purple stars."

Sami walked around so that she could see Franklin's face. Greta was right. His eyes were sparkling again, a beautiful shade of violet. She said, "I see what you mean, Greta. He doesn't look at many people that way. Only the really special ones. Right, Franklin?"

Behind his eyes, Franklin could feel the familiar tingling that he had experienced each time something remarkable was about to happen. He had no idea, however, what it could possibly mean this time. Clasping one of Greta's hands tightly with both of his own, Franklin said, "You *are* a very special girl, Greta. I have no doubt that you'll feel better soon. We need our Supergirl back."

As he spoke to her, he felt a surge of warmth travel slowly down both of his arms, into his hands, and then depart out the tips of his fingers. At that very moment, Greta, still holding his hands, felt a funny tremble throughout her entire body; she smiled weakly at him and said, "I am so, so tired. Can you guys come by later, though?"

"Of course, we will," he whispered to her.

Franklin laid her hand down gently on the bed and stood up. It didn't take but a moment before the serene sound of snoring rose from the bed below him. Greta lay still, already fast asleep. Her face, flush before with fever, had now paled considerably in a matter of only minutes.

Rufus stood and waited by the door as the other three exited the room. After they had left, he walked back to the bed and knelt down beside it, in the same fashion Franklin had done. In a hushed voice, he said to the sleeping toddler, "I promise I'll play with you, Greta. As soon as you get better, I'll play with you all day. I'll be the best bad guy you ever saw."

He stood up, dried his eyes with his t-shirt, and then joined his new friends out in the hall.

CHAPTER TWENTY–NINE
A PROJECTION & A PRISONER

"I never tasted Italian food that good, Franklin. Not that I've had much Italian food before, other than pizza and Spaghetti-O's. Where'd you learn to cook like that?" Rufus asked, watching Franklin closely.

"My mom and I used to try out lots of different kinds of foods. Mom would bring home expired stuff for free from the store where she worked, and we would experiment with different recipes."

Franklin thought back to how perfect his life had seemed with his mom, even though he was in a wheelchair, and even though they barely had anything. He missed it, and he missed his mom tremendously. "I got pretty good at it, I guess," he said.

"What was that stuff called you made tonight?" Shad asked.

"Fettuccine Alfredo," Franklin answered.

Parker looked ill. "Well, I think I ate one too many platefuls of whatever you just said because I don't feel so good." She was holding her stomach with one hand and putting her other hand over her mouth like she was going to be sick.

The kids had decided after supper that they would bike the mile down the road to the woods by Lake Birdsong, where Rufus had said he saw the ghost. They had told Jerod they were going on a bike ride but did not say where to. It had taken them twenty minutes to reach the lake, and the sun was on the verge of going beneath the horizon, creating a beautiful orange and pink cotton candy sunset across the water. Dusk was setting in, but the moon was a large, full plate in the sky, and it was already beginning to provide light in the absence of the sun.

The lake was out in the country, even further than Open Arms Orphanage was, and surrounded by fields, so people rarely traveled there to go swimming. Besides, the fields and forest around it were privately owned. The patch of woods where Rufus brought them was adjacent to Lake Birdsong on one side, and on the other side, it butted up to the cornfield. It was rich with different generations of trees; massive oaks and maples that had been there for over a century, mixed with balsam, spruce, and pine that had only stood there a few decades. The forest had a sleepy feeling, and they all felt it right away. It was peaceful.

The woods, and Lake Birdsong next to it, seemed to them like an oasis in the middle of a desert, only the desert, in this case, was a cornfield. The farmers who once cultivated the land had spared this patch of woods while cutting everything else down around it to use for planting crops. The lake, conveniently, had provided them with a water source for their corn and wheat.

The children left their bikes on the outskirts of the tree line and made their way through the thick foliage. As they reached the heart of the forest, visibility to either the field or lake became impossible. The great number of trees packed into this small square-mile of land made it so dense that Franklin felt like he might be a hundred miles away from any civilization.

"I see what you mean about this place, Rufus," Sami said. Evidently, she had been thinking the same thing as Franklin. "I could sleep out here every night. It's so secluded and, well, undisturbed by anything that could contaminate it."

"Like humans, you mean?" asked Parker.

Sami answered, "Yeah, humans have a way of ruining places like this."

"You guys think this is peaceful now, you should come here at midnight. Not a sound anywhere. Not even birds, squirrels…nothing. Sometimes you can hear the wind through the leaves or a big turtle plop into the lake, but that's about it," Rufus said. "Oh, and over there is The Thinking Stump."

He was pointing to where once a medium-sized oak tree had stood, but now only a two-foot stump remained. Some logs in the later stages of rot were lying next to it. One of them was a perfect home to a nest of tiny red spiders and a colony of roly-poly bugs, the other was hollowed out and looked to be a possible shelter for a raccoon or squirrel. The stump itself was not an ideal stool. Shards of wood stuck up in several places where the tree had splintered and fallen, probably blown down in a storm years ago. Sitting down on its sharp points would be painful, Franklin was sure.

As if Rufus could read his thoughts, he said, "I can only sit right at the very edge of it, otherwise I walk home with a limp." He laughed, then sat on the stump and began to look around at the trees, trying to recall his memories.

Finally, he said, "Right over there, that's the tree I saw the ghost by."

He pointed to a tall maple tree that grew a short distance away from all the other trees. Because of its mass, the tree had blocked all light from ever reaching beneath it, which prevented any plants from growing, except for a type of short grass and a velvety soft moss. These two types of flora circled the immense tree like a blanket and made it look too irresistibly perfect to Franklin. He walked over to the tree, sat down on the soft grass, and stretched out.

"Now this is where I would come to sit and think," Franklin said to everyone. Then, leaning his head against the tree, he finished his thought. "If I didn't fall asleep first."

The sun was below the horizon and darkness had slowly descended on them, as had the bugs. Large Minnesota mosquitoes were dive-bombing the children from every angle.

"These things are the size of bumblebees!" Parker yelled, swatting at one that had landed on her neck, then immediately smashing another on her leg. "I think they're trying to tell me that it's time to leave. I can't stand these flying vampires."

"*Flying* vampires?" Rufus scoffed. "That's a bit repetitive. Don't all vampires fly? I mean, that's a given, isn't it?"

Sami stepped in between Parker and Rufus, sensing her roommate's looming frustration. "Parker, you did grow up in Minnesota, right?" she asked. "You do know that the mosquito is the official state bird here?"

Franklin and Rufus were on the verge of bursting out into hysterics, but Parker didn't seem to think it was all that funny. She just continued smacking one mosquito after another, like she was choreographing a new dance.

Not known for catching onto humor or sarcasm right away, Shad replied, "Sami, that can't really be true since the mosquito is from the biological class *Insecta*, and a state bird needs to be an actual bird. You know, with feathers and a beak? In fact, the state bird of Minnesota is the loon. They're lake birds that—"

"Please stop, Shad!" Parker yelled. She evidently had lost her patience.

The others were cracking up at this point. Shad, having no idea that he was the cause of their laughter, asked, "What's so funny? What did I miss, here?"

Parker, the only one not in stitches, said, "It was a joke, Shad. Sami was telling a joke. You know, because the mosquitoes are so big that they're almost the size of birds? Get it?"

Shad looked a bit flustered at first, then a smile spread across his face. "Oh, okay, I get it. Sorry. I'm so literal sometimes that jokes like that go right over my head."

Then he added, "I do have some bug spray here in my backpack if anybody wants some."

He took off his camouflage backpack, unzipped it and reached down inside. His hand came back out holding an orange can of Deep Forest Bug Spray. Without hesitation, Parker grabbed the can from him, said, "Thanks, Shad," and begin dousing herself in it. When she finished, the others took their turns spraying it all over themselves.

Finally, with most of the mosquitoes being held off by the spray, Parker breathed a big sigh of relief and gave Shad a half-smile. "I'm sorry I'm being such a jerk, Shad… and all of you. My stomach really hurts, and I haven't been getting much sleep, either. It's making me cranky. All this stuff, between the hand and then Hank, it's unreal. It's crazy! I think I need to head back home and rest."

Franklin had already made up his mind that he was staying. He had come biking out here to this patch of forest for one reason; he wanted to witness for himself what Rufus had seen. If that 'spirit', or whatever it was that Rufus described, came back tonight with the full moon, he needed to be here. The best way to do that would be to get comfortable, sit tight, and wait. He knew he had to find out if there was any chance that his hunch was right, it might be the only way to find his mom, if she was still alive.

Thinking about it now, it sounded insane that his mom could really be trying to contact him from a parallel 'plane' of Earth. But then again, how many things have happened since his tenth birthday that could fall under the category of 'insane'?

He looked up from where he sat beneath the tree. It was dark enough now that it was difficult to even make out his friends' faces. "Hey guys, if you want to go back with Parker, you should head out with her now. I'm going to stay here for a while. I need one of you to cover for me back at the house and tell Nonna Glo that I'll be back in a bit. Tell her that I just went on a hike or something."

Parker raised her hand to volunteer. "I can tell her, but will you be back by lights out?"

"No, probably not," Franklin admitted, "but I'll have to deal with the consequences later."

"I'm staying with you, Franklin. I want to see if she shows up tonight," Shad said and sat down under the tree by his roommate. He set his backpack down next to him.

"I'm going to stay here, too," Sami announced. "You can tell Nonna Glo I'm with him. Also, we can't forget that Hank is back there now, and he's still dangerous. Parker, if you feel up to it, could you keep a close watch on him, make sure he stays around the house? If he leaves, he's probably looking for Franklin."

"Yeah, why not?" Parker replied drowsily, still feeling a great need for both sleep and a bottle of antacid.

Franklin didn't want Rufus to feel left out of their plans, but he also knew Parker shouldn't go alone.

"Rufus, I'd love to have you stay here with us, but it would be great if Parker had someone to bike back with and to help her in case Hank decides to try something," he said.

"I'll help her," Rufus responded. "Whatever you need me for, Hobby. If we see Hank acting suspicious and he leaves the house, I'm jumping on my bike and getting out here to warn you."

In the dark, Franklin smiled. He said, "Thanks, Rufus."

He stood and reached out his hand to help Shad up, who had been sitting next to him by the tree. The two of them, along with Sami, walked Rufus and Parker to the edge of the forest. The full moon helped provide some light, but it was still hard to see the condition of the terrain they were walking on. Knowing this could be a problem when riding their bikes back, Rufus pulled a small flashlight out from his back pocket.

"Thank goodness you brought one of those, Rufus! I don't want to eat any pavement on the way home. You're going to have to ride ahead of me," Parker said.

The massive, dark shadows cast by the moonlight falling upon the trees made Franklin nervous. He knew it was the perfect opportunity for Nefari to find him and carry through with the threats he had made. But unless Nefari was somehow regularly monitoring him, he might not know he's out here. Besides, he was doing this for his mom.

Shad patted Franklin on the back and declared to the whole group, "Hey, I think we almost forgot in all the excitement, it's Franklin's 12th birthday tomorrow! We really need to have a party for you!"

Franklin replied, "I don't think Hank is really gung-ho about having a party for me," he laughed. "I'd really rather not make a big deal out of it, anyway."

"We'll see about that," said Sami.

They said goodbye to Rufus and Parker, who rode away on their bikes, Rufus leading, riding one-handed, using the other to shine his flashlight on the ground in front of them. As they walked back through the woods to the large maple tree, Sami pulled out a flashlight from her jacket pocket. "Brightest one I could find, just in case your faceless friend decides to show up," she said.

"I got one, too. A hundred thousand candlepower Mega Light I borrowed from Hank's garage. It's in my backpack," Shad announced. Then, after a pause, asked, "Hey Franklin, do you think you'll be able to see in the dark tonight, like you did in the kitchen, if you really need to?"

Franklin looked thoughtful. "I hope so, but it's almost like something else, besides me, gets to decide when the right time is to use the powers."

"Eventually, maybe you can control them yourself when you get a little more experience using them," Sami added.

Stepping over a root, he replied, "That's what I'm hoping, too."

When they arrived back at the tree, Franklin shrugged. "Now I guess we just wait."

He settled back down onto the soft moss under the tree. It was much darker here, where the moonlight had difficulty breaking through the foliage and reaching the forest floor.

"Actually," Shad, said, "I brought a deck of cards. You guys know how to play Texas Hold'em? We can at least have a little fun while we wait."

"Sounds like a good plan," Franklin said. "Deal them out."

For the next hour or so, the three of them took turns playing the dealer. Shad dug some water bottles out of his backpack and Sami found some half melted chocolate granola bars in another one of her pockets. So they ate, drank, laughed, and played cards. The two flashlights they had were passed back and forth so they could see the cards in their hands. After thirty-three hands of poker, Shad had won sixteen times, ten of which he had been the dealer.

Sami pretended to be upset. "Shad, next time we play, we're using my deck of cards," she said, trying to turn her smile into an angry frown.

"I don't cheat, you guys. I play the odds and I know the percentages. If using math is cheating, I guess I'm guilty," Shad said defensively. "If anything, Franklin probably used his new 'powers' to see through our cards or read our minds!"

"Yeah, that's why I won two games," Franklin said, a droll grin on his face.

From somewhere behind the tree where they sat, dead leaves rustled on the ground.

Franklin held up his hand, signaling the other two to be quiet. He whispered to them, "Get your flashlights. Don't turn them on, but get them ready."

Something came out of the woods, something small, and scampered between the circle the three of them sat in, then ran out the other side.

"Flashlight!" Franklin yelled. Both Sami and Shad flipped their lights on and aimed the beams into the woods, towards the direction the unknown creature had run. Nothing at first, then on a second sweep of the area, Shad's beam reflected off a set of eyes watching them from four branches up the next tree over. Closer inspection showed them that the eyes belonged to a grey squirrel, which turned tail and scurried up to some higher branches.

"Okay, that was just a bit terrifying," Shad said. "I think my heart almost stopped when that thing's tail tickled my leg."

Shad and Sami turned off their light. The darkness seemed even blacker than a few minutes ago. Franklin pushed a button on his watch that lit up the digital screen. "Eleven-thirty," he announced. "We've been here over two hours now."

He let exhale an audible sigh and then lay back onto the cushiony undergrowth of the tree. Staring up at the leafy branches, listening to the calming melody they made as they gently rustled each other, he was eventually lulled to sleep. Sami crawled over and joined him, lying down on her back as well. Not wanting to be left out, Shad crawled on all fours over to the other side of his friend and leaned back against the tree.

All three of them fell silent, and it didn't take long for Franklin to give in to his exhaustion and drift off to sleep. Soon his heavy breathing and occasional snores added to the tranquility of the hushed woods.

"We can wake him if something shows up. I'm starting to think that Rufus might have been imagining everything he saw, or maybe he fell asleep out here, like Franklin, and just dreamt everything," Sami said.

As if to prove her wrong, next to the tree that the squirrel had just used for its escape, Sami and Shad watched in wonder as a green light blazed brightly for just a second, then went out. A moment later it was back and this time appeared brighter.

Shad reached down and shook Franklin. "Wake up, Franklin," he said softly, not wanting to scare away the source of the light. Sami, sitting up now, helped Shad by grabbing Franklin's arm and pulling him up towards her.

"Wake up!" she hollered.

"Is she here? What's going on?" Franklin mumbled, jolted from his sleep.

But he didn't need to ask. The green light was ten feet in front of them and approaching slowly. He watched anxiously as the glow took the form of a woman, just as Rufus had said. She was not solid in appearance but looked more like a projection from a movie camera. Not on a flat screen, either. She was three-dimensional; also like Rufus had described.

Shad was dumbstruck. The whole thing reminded him of the hologram scenes in different science fiction movies he had watched. Most notably, in his mind, was the scene where Princess Leia, in *Star Wars* was being projected out from the little droid, R2-D2.

Franklin stood up and walked closer to her. The projection of the woman seemed to move nearer to him at the same time. The children could see the woman searching, scanning the woods for something. Suddenly, she froze and stared in their direction, as if she had finally noticed the trio in front of her. A voice came out from the light. "Have you seen my son?" Pause, then, "Have you seen Franklin?" Her tone was soft and distant; it crackled as if it were on a radio station that couldn't quite come into tune.

"Mom?" Franklin asked, wonder in his voice.

No immediate reply came from the lady in the limelight. Then Franklin said louder, "Mom? Is that you?" He went closer to the woman and held out his hands, palms facing her. He brought them within inches of the green projection. The woman responded now. She held out her hands as well, palms first, and reached forward, light moving with her fingers, and she mirrored Franklin's palms, inches away.

A muted voice eked out from her. "Franklin, that's you, isn't it?" Angel reached one of her hands out even further, took a step toward Franklin, and touched her son's face. Franklin could not feel her fingers, but instead, a static-electrical sensation passed over him where her hands made contact with his skin. It wasn't painful, almost like he was being tickled with a series of static shocks.

"Mom!" He went towards Angel and tried to embrace her, but his arms passed completely through the green light. He stumbled forward but caught himself.

"Franklin, she's just an energy field, not solid matter," Shad called to him.

"Oh, yeah, that makes sense." He backed up again; he wasn't able to wrap his arms around her, but at least she was here. All the times he wondered if he would ever see her again, and now here she was, standing right in front of him.

Kind of.

For the first time in almost a year, he started to cry, really *cry*, and couldn't stop himself. Angel said to him, "Franklin, I'm alive. I'm here, sweetheart." She paused, and the children could tell she was wiping away tears of her own.

Franklin used the back of his hand to swab his face. Through his tears, he managed to ask, "How can I get to you?"

"Franklin," she said, "I have very little time... it comes back… the fields." Her sentences were broken; the words not coming in as clear anymore.

Shad walked over and stood by Sami, who had already joined Franklin's side, and said, "Light waves have a shorter wavelength and more energy than sound waves. They transmit easier through Earth's different planes. That's why her image is so much clearer than her voice. We might lose sound altogether."

No. Too soon, Franklin thought. He needed some answers before he lost her again. Desperation in his voice, he asked, "Mom, where do they have you?"

"Not sure, exactly. They took me from our home…to a place… Earth, but... different than…horrible creatures...so hot..."

"Franklin," Shad yelled excitedly, "that's probably the same awful place where you were after you crashed your bike and almost got eaten by —"

Franklin held his finger to Shad's lips and whispered, "Shhhhhh. I don't need to worry her. She's got enough to think about."

"Oh, sorry," he whispered back.

Shad spoke again, but this time he had a question for Angel, "Umm, Ms. Hobbs? Are you standing in a forest that's close to a lake right now?"

"I can see… it used to… forest... there is… stumps and…. rotting...." Angel said, her voice still breaking up, "It is…. dry here... trees... dead… close to a lake bed... no water …"

A loud clamor came to them now from somewhere behind Angel; a harsh, piercing cry. The children watched as Angel turned her head quickly to look, and when she spun back around it was clear by her face that something terrifying was close.

"The Chenoo, it found me… coming now! Franklin, listen....find me…if you don't… kill me. Please….save me…"

Angel's voice trailed off and they watched through the otherworldly projection as an enormous hand with tree branch fingers wrapped around her face. They heard her scream as she was pulled out of sight. A second later something else came into view where Angel had been standing. Another projection, only this one was at least a foot-and-a-half taller than Angel. The projected creature, which Angel had called a Chenoo, made three steps closer to them, allowing them to make out some of its chilling details in a strangely crisp picture that came from the green glow.

The most noticeable feature about the Chenoo was the set of six-pointed antlers sitting high on top of its head. The head of the creature looked to be that of an overgrown elk or maybe an antelope, except one that had been dead for several weeks. Below its antlers, the Chenoo's mangy fur and skin looked like it had been peeled off its face in large patches, some left hanging freely. On the left side of its face, where skin had torn away, its jaw, along with muscles and tendons, were visible. It pulled its lips back into a snarl, allowing them to see both lower and upper sets of glistening white points.

A skinny, gaunt neck somehow supported the Chenoo's large head, thrusting it out at a ninety-degree angle from his shoulders. Its boney arms hung down far enough to drag on the forest floor and at the end of each wrist were three long, crooked fingers, each with its own dagger sharp nail. Its legs, which it stood upright on, looked similar to the arms, but not as long and were hoofed. Matted fur covered the beast's skeletal body, but like the face, it was peeling off in some areas. The most obvious of these places was the Chenoo's chest, where strips of skin had fallen off, revealing at least half of the ribs in its chest.

Its beady black eyes smoldered from deep in its sockets as it stared out at the children. Further behind it, they could hear sobbing coming from Angel and then her mournful cry calling to her son. This time, they were able to discern her words clearly. "Franklin, help me! It's going to kill me if you don't—"

Her voice was drowned out by the sudden clamor coming from the monster in front of them. The creature opened its jaws, and out of it came not a voice, but a series of shrieks and screeches that somehow blended into one another before emerging as singular words, "She——Will——Be——Punished."

The beast turned his head away momentarily, probably to check on its prisoner, before glaring back at the children. Again, its muzzle opened up wide enough so that both sets of lengthy incisors jutted straight out from its head, and it emitted another deafening wail with enough intensity to cause lines of static to run through the image of itself being broadcast to the children.

Mucus stretched from the top of its mouth to the bottom as it spewed forth another grouping of words, "Come——Find——Me——"

From its own realm, it sneered hatefully at them for a moment before it said, "I——Eat——You——Both."

With that, the image of the Chenoo turned and lumbered back toward where Angel's cries, now weaker and less frequent, still arose. The beast then vanished from sight altogether and the greenish glow that had contained its image remained for only a few seconds longer before it faded away as well.

The children didn't move from where they stood for quite some time; they were at a complete loss for words. Dumbfounded. But even more, they were *horrified* at what they had just seen.

Finally, Sami broke the silence, "I'm sorry, Franklin. I'm so sorry you had to see that." She hugged him tight and whispered into his ear, "We're going to get her back."

Franklin was shaken. There were no tears falling, but Sami and Shad had never before seen the look etched on Franklin's face. His jaw was set tight, and his eyes... his eyes were deep purple, almost black, enraged and vengeful. He spoke low, but with intensity. "No, it's a good thing I saw that. Now I know my mom is still alive, and I know where she is. She's right here, right in this forest. If she is going to stay alive I have to help her. And I'm going to have to kill that thing we just saw."

"We want to help you, Franklin," Shad said.

"I appreciate that you guys…I don't know, though," Franklin answered. "Let me think about it."

"Any idea what a Chenoo is?" Sami asked, directing her question towards Shad.

"I never in all my life imagined they were real," a bewildered Shad answered.

Being a lover of all things science fiction, like Shad was, also meant being knowledgeable about fabled creatures, like the one they had just seen.

"I think I remember reading that the Chenoo is part of Native American folklore. I've seen drawings of these things, and none of them are as horrid as the real thing we just witnessed. I know the Algonquin tribe have folklore telling of Chenoos roaming the forests in search of human flesh."

"Thanks, Shad, that's so comforting," Franklin responded glumly.

"Do you think they can cross over to our Earth?" Sami asked.

"I'm guessing that the Algonquin tribe actually had encounters with them," Shad replied. "That means that they must be able to cross into other planes of Earth, just like Nefari is able to."

Sami thought about that. "Imagine all the monsters that we hear about in folklore, the ones that we've always been told were just made up to scare people. What if those horrifying creatures actually exist somewhere else and only make appearances here every once in a while?"

"Even Nefari, the way you described him, Franklin…" Shad began but stopped short of finishing his thought.

"What?" insisted Franklin. "Don't leave me hanging."

"…there are other stories out there on some of the online discussion boards," continued Shad, "where people recount experiences with human-like creatures without faces. Some of them even claim to be stalked by one, like you."

"Then there must be ways these things can actually get here, to our plane of Earth. To this realm. Not just as green transmitted images, but actually physically coming through something to get here," said Franklin.

"I think we should stop talking about this stuff," Sami said, becoming more and more unnerved by what she was hearing.

The forest no longer felt safe as it had when they first arrived. Before, it was peaceful. Now, it was just eerily silent. Any moonlight that was able to reach all the way to the forest floor brought no comfort to the children. The light only created spooky perceptions all around. Shadows of branches swaying in the breeze were arms that seemed to be reaching for them, and the dark patterns of rustling leaves were demons ready to pounce.

Franklin sat back down and leaned against the maple tree, which was the only part of the forest that didn't seem threatening to him. Still forlorn, he admitted, "I just can't stop thinking about what that creature is doing with my mom. I mean, do you think it's torturing her?"

"I don't know, Franklin, but I'm pretty sure it wouldn't kill her after it kept her alive this long," Sami replied. "I think it's using her as bait. That monster probably even allowed her to appear tonight, hoping you would find out and come for her."

"Yeah, maybe. I'm going to find her, too. I just don't know how to get to where she is."

"What about using your future-sight?" asked Shad. "That's what brought you to the other Earth before."

"I thought about that. But Nefari knew exactly where I was when I did that. He was waiting for me as if I had announced my entrance to his world. I need to find a way to get there without letting him, or anything else, know I'm coming."

"You need to find a wormhole," Shad said.

"Gateway, wormhole, portal…whatever you want to call it," Franklin told him.

Trying to lighten the mood, Sami giggled and spouted, "If Parker was here, she'd probably say a wormhole wouldn't be big enough for a person to squeeze through."

This succeeded in getting Franklin to laugh, but Shad only looked perplexed. "No, no, a wormhole is what they call a doorway—"

But the science fiction guru had no time to finish his definition of a wormhole before the sound of snapping twigs and crunching leaves caused all three of them to stop and hold their breath; something was crashing through the woods, coming towards them. As the unknown entity came near, its foot caught a root and sent it flying face-first, sliding to a stop in front of them. Shad's flashlight revealed Rufus lying in the dirt. At once, Franklin came to his aid and helped him up, brushing him off.

In the intense rays of Shad's Mega Light, the sweat covering Rufus's face glistened like vegetable oil. His legs wobbled this way and that, and he was desperately out of breath, but between exhales, he was able to push out two words, "He's... coming!"

"Who's coming?" Franklin asked.

Rufus finally caught his breath so that he was able to speak again. He was wide-eyed and altogether terrified as he said, "Hank's coming!"

A second later, he collapsed back onto the ground.

CHAPTER THIRTY
A TIMELY TALENT & A GRISLY GOODBYE

"Rufus, are you all right?" Sami asked him. She knelt down and helped him to a sitting position.

"Just a little dizzy…" he said, "and exhausted."

Shad had a half-full water bottle that he handed to Rufus, who gulped most of it down. "I'm feeling better now. Thanks, Sami. Thanks, guys. I just rode my bike here so darn fast. I had to tell you that you have to get out of here, *now*!"

Franklin sat down by Rufus. "Okay, we will, but hold on a second. I just need to know what you know. Why do you think Hank is coming here?" he asked.

Rufus took a deep breath. "Well, I didn't go to bed tonight because I wanted to see if he was up to anything. I figured he'd wait to do whatever he was going to do until after everyone went to bed."

With Franklin, Shad, and Sami hunched around Rufus like they were, he appeared to be under an official interrogation, especially the way Shad had the Mega Light shining down on him.

He wiped the sweat away from his forehead and continued, "A little after eleven, I could hear voices or something downstairs, so I snuck down into the living room and hid behind the couch. That's when Hank and Parker walked out of the kitchen together. He told her 'thanks' and went outside. She could have told him everything guys. I hate to say it, but there's a good chance she's a traitor." He took another gulp and drained the water bottle.

"I saw the lights on his truck going down the driveway, so I jumped on my bike and rode here as fast as I could," Rufus finished and looked up at them, shielding his eyes from the light.

"Oh, sorry," Shad apologized, as he moved the light away from his face.

"What about Parker?" Sami wanted to know.

"She went into her room. I don't know if she saw me leave or not," Rufus said.

"Don't you think Hank would've gotten here by now? If he was driving?" Franklin asked everyone.

Shad whispered to them, "Maybe Parker didn't tell him where we were, just that we were out somewhere. Or….my other thought is, how do we know that he isn't already here?"

"That's true. He could have parked out of sight and is just waiting for us, right now," Franklin whispered back. "C'mon, let's get back to the house."

The group started walking, stepping lightly and quickly, taking the same route they had used earlier that night. A few minutes later, they arrived at the edge of the forest to where the field opened up. In the light of the full moon, they could see across the expanse of the field to where the main road passed by.

Nothing yet. They found their bikes, hopped on, and started riding at a fast pace through the tall grass, anxious to leave this foreboding wood behind.

As they had nearly made it halfway across the pasture, a pair of yellow beams slashed through the darkness, aimed straight at them from the other side of the open field.

Headlights.

They heard the sound of an engine roar to life, and within moments, the lights grew brighter as the vehicle began moving towards them. The intensity of the rays blinded the children, and like a deer before it becomes roadkill, they froze momentarily, exposed out in the open. Then Franklin turned his bike around and hollered, "Ride your bike back to the woods. Go!"

The other three frantically turned their bikes and pedaled back to the edge of the forest, where they got off and let their bikes fall to the ground. Before the bikes even hit the dirt the three were already running for the thick growth of trees. Franklin followed behind them, but stopped at the tree line, turned around, and watched the truck approach him. He expected Hank to slow down and come to a stop in front of him. He expected he would have to confront Hank face to face, but the closer Hank's truck came, the more he realized the orphanage caretaker had another idea. He wasn't slowing down; in fact, he seemed to be accelerating. *Time for Plan B*, Franklin thought, although he never really had a Plan A, anyway.

Hank's truck had passed the halfway point of the field, and Franklin was directly in its path. This madman was going to try to run him over! Sure, all he had to do to escape was run into the forest, but that was only putting off the inevitable; he would have to face Hank eventually.

He remembered his curious ability to produce that magnificent light which had saved him from Nefari in the basement storeroom. That could come in handy right now. But how did he do it? What triggered it?

Franklin tried to imagine the most brilliant starlight his mind could fathom and he focused this thought to the points directly behind each eye. A ball of flaming hydrogen gas burst into his mind's eye; he pictured the sun and the immeasurably brilliant light it produced. All of this flashed through his head in a fraction of a second.

The truck was closing in on him.

The tingling came back.

And with it came the most ferocious storm of energy inside of him that he had felt yet. The next instant, his body was ablaze in a sphere of such powerful radiant light, that he lit up the entire night sky above the cornfield. Although he appeared to be on fire, Franklin felt no burn or sting. What he could feel was his energy drain from him, almost comparable to a marathon runner when they hit the "wall" and feel like they can't go any further. Five seconds of this explosive light took everything he had, after which he felt the strange power diminish and then weaken to only a glow, before everything was dark once again. Dark, except for the headlights of the oncoming truck, which seemed like only pinpricks of light in comparison.

But the damage was done. The lunatic driver had been blinded, and as he covered his eyes, he had taken his hands off the steering wheel. The truck had swerved immediately, and careened away from the course it had been on towards Franklin. Its new course was taking it directly into a large oak that stood at the edge of the woods.

The impact was loud and sent vibrations clattering through the chilly night air. The front of the pickup folded in as it plowed deeper into the tree, and Franklin could see white smoke billowing from underneath its destroyed hood. In the silence that followed, as he walked toward the truck, he thought he heard the driver whispering to him, but became aware that it was the hissing of the pressure hoses and fluid lines, which were spewing their toxic, flammable contents everywhere. The passenger door creaked halfway open, and he could see Hank in the yellow glow of the dashboard lights. Blood ran from his hair, down his face, and covered the front of his shirt. He reached out with a filthy arm and grabbed the frame of the door, then painstakingly pulled himself out of the car. His limp body dropped the ten inches to the grass below.

The smell of gasoline was strong, and Franklin knew the damaged vehicle was a ticking time bomb. Without stopping to give it thought, he ran over to Hank, grabbed both of his arms, and pulled him away from the truck. Hank offered no resistance, as his body lay motionless. When they were a safe distance away, he knelt down by Hank and put two fingers on his neck, finding the carotid artery. There was a steady pulse.

He shouted towards the forest, "Hank's unconscious!"

When he turned back, he glanced down in time to see Hank's closed eyes suddenly open wide. Like a rock from a slingshot, the man's hand launched upwards towards Franklin's neck, and Franklin felt his bony fingers grab him around the throat and squeeze it like he was juicing an orange. His oxygen supply was cut off and he couldn't take a breath. Hank used the grip he had on his neck to pull Franklin towards him, within inches from his face, his stale, hot breath causing him to gag. The hateful grin on the man's lips turned to a frown. "You little brat," he hissed. "You think just because you dragged me over here, I wouldn't kill you?"

Then, from behind them, a thunderous blast sent the stillness of the night fleeing. Hank looked over to see his truck in flames, and Franklin used the opportunity to wrench himself free from the chokehold.

Not looking back, he ran toward the forest from where his friends had just emerged. He motioned them to follow him, and he made his way through the trail which they had trampled over at least three times now, leading back to the large maple tree.

"Franklin, I thought you said he was unconscious. What's going on?" Sami yelled from behind him.

Franklin stopped running. The others slowed down and gathered around him. He said to all of them, "Listen, you guys. He tried to kill me. I thought he was out of commission after crashing his car, but I was wrong. I want you all to run to the other side of the forest, to the lake, and hide behind the cattails along the shore. Stay out of sight, no matter what happens. Don't come out in the open until I come get you, or you know that he has left. I don't think he knows you're even here, so you should be okay."

"Don't be ridiculous. He knows who we are; he probably saw our bikes. And anyway, who else is going to be here with you beside us, your best friends? It doesn't matter, there's no way I'm leaving you, Franklin," Sami proclaimed. "He'll kill you."

"We're not abandoning you, Frankie. Sorry," Shad said, a defiant look crossing his face.

Rufus, seeing that it was his turn, said, "Heck, if it wasn't for Franklin here, I'd still be feeling sorry for myself and making everybody's life miserable. I'm not leaving him to deal with that psychopath alone."

Franklin shook his head. "Sometimes I wish you guys weren't so darn stubborn, but thanks. Let's go. I'll hide with you, then."

He took off running towards the lake, ducking between trees, jumping over stumps, and skirting around bushes that lay in his path. The others did their best to keep up with him, and finally they came to a clearing where a stretch of shorter prairie grass signaled that the marshy banks and cattails of Lake Birdsong were only several feet away. They hurried over to the tall plants, whose silhouettes set them apart against the backdrop of the shimmering lake. The cattails were bent over slightly, submissive to the breeze coming in from the water. As the four children approached the soggy bank, the deep mud bordering the lake immediately surrounded their shoes, and they sunk down. Each of them took a moment to make sure their footwear was not left behind in the marsh when they lifted their feet to take the next step. After a minute, though, all of them had found a place to hide among the towering greenery.

Franklin was hopeful that Hank hadn't been able to get back up and pursue him after he had escaped. Maybe he had several broken bones that were keeping him immobile. This optimism soon proved to be only wishful thinking as the children heard Hank's deep voice bellow out from somewhere in the forest, "Hey, Frankie. Come on out, would ya? I just wanted to talk to you. Sorry about choking you back there. I was a little delirious, you know? That sure was one amazing light show you put on. Can you teach me how to do that?"

Silence trailed his question, and in an attempt to break the awkward stillness, the wind picked up and rattled the cattails together. Franklin wondered if this man was demented enough to think that he would really just pop out of hiding and declare, 'Here I am!'

From where Franklin hid, he could see his other three friends scattered, hiding no more than a few feet from him in any direction. He could see that Rufus and Shad were watching him, waiting to follow his cue. Franklin just put his finger to his lips.

The crazed voice sounded again. "Come out, come out, wherever you are, Franklin. I'm not going to be as nice if you make this difficult for me!"

If Hank got too close to where they were hiding, Franklin planned to make a dash for it, so that he could lead the maniac away from his friends. If he let Hank hurt just one of them, he would never forgive himself.

With the moon providing enough light, he was able to see Hank's tall, angular figure emerge from the forest into the clearing, twenty feet further down from where they had come out. Franklin watched him pause and look around, considering his next move. He was carrying something in one of his hands. Too hard to see what it was, though. Probably a weapon. Had he been able to retrieve it from his trunk, even after the explosion?

Then a hand wrapped around his wrist; it was Sami. She squeezed it tight and Franklin tried to smile, tried to look confident, to help alleviate her fear.

Hank's voice called out again, this time dressed in a tone of sarcasm. "Okay, if you're hiding in that swampy crap over there by the lake, I am disappointed, Frankie. First of all, I don't want to get my favorite boots muddy. Second of all, it's way too obvious. I mean, you, Sami, Shad, and whoever else is with you there, could have circled back around and found your bikes. Much better idea."

This last statement hit Franklin hard, as the maniac had intended it to. Sami was right; Hank knew who was with him.

Close by came the sound of the lake weeds being shaken again, but this time there was no breeze to bring them to life. Shad rose up on his feet, still crouched, to look over the tops of the cattails. He came back down and nervously reported, "He's got a stick or something, moving the cattails around, coming this way."

"Frank-lin? Here, Frank, Frank, Frankie! Come here, boy! Where are you?" Hank's voice had gone from sounding demented to just plain psychotic now; if there was a difference. And he was within ten feet from Sami, the closest of the four to him.

In a frenzied, but quiet voice, Franklin explained to his friends, "I have a plan, but I need you to trust me. Don't follow me when I run out. Wait until Hank notices me and comes after me, then go the other way. Get away, don't go back for your bikes, run home and call the police. Please, Sami? Please, listen to me." He squeezed her hand tightly before releasing it, trying to emphasize the importance of his request.

Before any of them had an opportunity to respond, Franklin had darted out of the weeds, jumped over the mud, and sprinted past Hank. He stayed out of the woods, right along the tree line; he wanted to be seen. It took a few seconds before Hank was able to pick up the sound of Franklin's feet sweep-swishing through the grass. When he did, he immediately turned and began pursuing him.

"There's my good boy. In this moonlight, I can almost see you as clear as day!" screamed Hank.

Franklin was running as fast as he had ever run; then, above his head, he heard the hum of a projectile whisking through the air.

Thwack!

An arrow dug itself deep into a tree as he ran past it. Head-level too. Hank was going for the kill shot. What he had seen in Hank's hand earlier must have been a bow, Franklin realized. With the amount of force that arrow had, it was probably his crossbow that Gloria had mentioned.

'Fwak'

Another arrow whizzed past him, this time within a paper's thickness of his head; he could feel his hair flutter as it jetted by and landed somewhere ahead of him.

The next thing he knew, he was flying through the air himself. He had stepped into a gopher or snake hole, and now he tumbled towards the ground headfirst. As he landed, he did his best to roll over onto his shoulder to distribute the force of the blow. His bare arms and legs took the brunt of the fall, in the way of scrapes, but he avoided any significant injuries.

Almost without missing a stride, Franklin immediately started his motion to get back up on his feet and continue running, but it was not to be, for he lost his footing again. This time he slipped on a wet, muddy patch of grass; an area of forest runoff where water collected after a hard rain. He went to the ground a second time and lay face down, sprawled out in the mud, and before he could even get to his knees, he was forced back down into the slop by a scarred cowboy boot. Hank had finally caught up with him, stepped on his back, and was holding him down in the soggy grass.

"Let me up, Hank," Franklin said coolly.

He felt the boot lift off of him, but a moment later it came back down, this time on his head, pushing his face into the mud. He tried breathing, but both his mouth and nose were submerged in two inches of dirty water. Franklin started thrashing his arms and legs, doing his best to squirm away from the firm hold Hank had on him. This only irritated the maniac, who pressed down with more force onto his head, causing him to take in a mouthful of mud. Franklin could feel the fight leaving his body; he grew weaker by the second and needed air desperately. But he knew that Hank didn't intend to let him have any.

Above him he could hear the voice of the unhinged man, as if in an awful dream, say, "This is really an undignified way to die, eating mud with your final breath. How embarrassing for you, Frankie."

Franklin's thoughts went to his mother. What would happen to her? Who would help her, now that he couldn't?

Again Hank spoke, this time from a million miles away, "I'm going to have to find your friends after I'm done with you. You shouldn't have dragged them into this. It's your fault they have to die, you know. I just can't let them tell anybody about my little episode here."

Harsh laughter was the last sound Franklin heard as he blacked out.

"Over your dead body!" shouted Rufus, appearing from the woods and charging straight at Hank, with Shad and Sami right behind him. Rufus threw his whole chunky body into Hank, who stumbled and lost his foothold on Franklin's head. Sami moved rapidly and turned Franklin over so that he was facing to the side. She opened his mouth and swept away anything that might be blocking his airway. Sludge drooled from his lips and he coughed three or four times, forcing out the rest of the mud. He turned over, face up now, and his eyes finally opened to see a very relieved Sami looking down at him.

Behind her, Hank screamed, "You little turds! Now you're all dead."

Both Shad and Rufus had begun battering Hank with sticks, until Rufus broke his branch on the deranged man's head, while Shad snapped his in two on Hank's back. They scampered towards the woods, looking for a new club to continue their beat down.

Franklin, still too weak to do anything, but now aware of what was happening, watched as Hank loaded an arrow into a hunting-style crossbow. He took careful aim at Rufus, who was still diligently searching for a weapon, and pulled the release trigger. Rufus went down instantly. The arrow struck him on his lower leg, tearing through his sports sock, and piercing his fleshy calf.

Hank did a celebratory dance as if he had just thrown a game-winning touchdown pass, then loaded another arrow into the crossbow. He lowered his aim to his next target, Shad, who had run over to where Rufus had fallen and knelt down beside him. Hank's finger was itching to let the arrow fly as he focused his mark right at Shad's chest.

Fortunately, Hank had not cared to pay attention to what Sami was up to and had no clue that she had sloshed her way over to him, on her hands and knees, through the mud. Earlier, Hank had rolled up his pant legs to keep his overalls from getting muddy. Now, like a rabid dog, Sami opened her mouth wide and chomped down into his bare leg, right in the calf muscle, gouging the same fleshy area where he had just shot Rufus.

In surprise or in agony, or maybe both, the man shrieked like a sick hyena and jerked his leg away from her, at the same time throwing his crossbow so that he could use both hands to tend to his mangled leg. The crossbow sailed several feet in the air, twirling and tottering, and landed in the cattails next to the lake. Sami still lay in the mud, spitting out pieces of skin, when Hank reached down and grabbed her arm, yanking her up to meet him at face level.

"That was a bad idea," he snarled, still holding his leg where she had opened it up with her teeth.

"Put her down you pile of dog crap!" Franklin shouted. He had regained enough strength to get to his feet and was standing several feet from Hank and Sami now. The entire front of his body, including his face, was caked in dark mud. In the moonlight, he had the look of a swamp monster that had just crawled out of the lake.

Hank looked at him and began to howl in laughter. He said, "And what are you going to do about it? Spit mud at me?"

He flung Sami down into the grass and limped towards the weeds to where his weapon had landed. Searching for only a brief second, he reached down between the cattails and retrieved his crossbow. Franklin used those few seconds to go check on Sami and help her to her feet. Further over in the grass, Shad was still hunched over Rufus, using his hand to apply pressure above the wound where the arrow was still lodged, as his injured friend moaned softly, swaying back and forth.

Franklin turned to Sami. "Can you please go back by Shad and Rufus?"

Not usually one to be ordered to do anything, she hesitated for only the briefest instant before scampering over to the other two.

Hank, still twelve feet away, down in the weeds, had engaged his crossbow and was pointing it at Franklin's head. "Franklin, I swear you have nine lives kid, but you just used your last one," he muttered, hocking up a wad of spit and launching it into the lake.

Attempting to buy a little time, Franklin asked him, "Hank, who's making you do this?"

"No one makes Hank Fulsten do anything! Seems a few days ago, I realized how much I hated your guts. Funny thing is, I don't even know what it is I hate about you. I just have this itch that I have to scratch, you know? And killing you is the only way I can figure out how to do that."

"So, the thing about me reminding you of your brother was made up?" Franklin already knew the answer to this question.

"I only got a sister, and you don't look much like her." He spit again, this time towards Franklin.

"Listen Hank, your brain is being messed with by something really evil. I can help you if you just put that crossbow down and stop trying to hurt us. We have to get Rufus to a hospital. Please, just put it down." Franklin was openly pleading to Hank at this point.

There was no attempt at humor or a sadistic quip from Hank this time; he only shook his head slowly and gave a tired grunt. But he kept his arrow pointed at Franklin's head.

It was probably a good time, Franklin had decided, to see if he had any other new powers that could help him out of this mess. He tried focusing his eyes straight ahead, staring only at the bow in Hank's hand. Specifically, his focal point was the arrow, which had been loaded into the crossbow and was aimed right at him. On that arrow, Franklin concentrated all his energy, all of his intensity, and finally all of his animosity towards this evil that was trying to ruin him.

Hank pulled the trigger.

In the split second that Hank's finger hit the release, Franklin's eyes were able to track the arrow as it came screaming silently towards him at three hundred feet per second.

The tingle behind his eyes was already there. All of his attention was fixated on the arrow, which was en route to his forehead. He concentrated his stare on it. There it was. He saw it.

Glistening carbonate point. Black shaft. Three rows of feathers at the end. Two red, one green.

Slow. Down. The. Arrow.

To Franklin, it looked like he was watching a video of an arrow shot straight at the lens of a camera, but at 1/100 of the original speed. In other words, he saw it, or rather, it came at him, in slow motion. Then, with his steadfast gaze fixed on the projectile, its speed decreased to the point where it actually stopped in midair; the carbon tip just barely touching his skin an inch beneath his hairline. With only a quick upward flick of his head, the arrow was sent hurtling into the sky, instantly resuming its original speed. Launched into the night.

Not quite understanding what had just taken place, Hank stood watching, waiting for Franklin to fall dead. He knew the shot was accurate to the millimeter; he had practiced too many times to miss one this close. That had been one of his last two arrows, so he had taken a headshot to make sure one would be enough to finish the job. So, when Franklin came running full speed at him, hurtling the top of his head into Hank's stomach, it caught him off guard. Both of them went airborne, sailing past the weeds and into the shallows of the lake.

Franklin got up right away and jumped onto Hank's chest, trying to keep him pinned on his back. The bigger man was too much for him, though. He flipped Franklin off of him and reversed the situation, sitting instead on top of Franklin, who strained his neck trying to keep his head out of the water.

His mouth began filling with water, but he was able to spit it back out as he struggled to say, "Hank…Hank." He forced out more water, then, "Whatever you do…do not look up."

Hank laughed, then mumbled, "Sure, kid."

The arrow, still being manipulated by Franklin, had been in the sky now for over half a minute. It was on the final leg of its journey back to the earth and had picked up significant speed on the way down.

Hank looked up.

The last thing he noticed before the tip of the arrow pierced his skull and came to rest in his brain was how beautiful the full moon looked that evening, suspended in the sky.

CHAPTER THIRTY—ONE
A SUPERIOR & A SCOLDING

Nefari and his two Dire Wolves, Radulf and Bardulf, stood in front of Quietus Tumulus. Around them, the surface of the planet was beginning to darken, and the intense heat was letting up. Creatures of the night were making their way above ground. Nefari sometimes considered himself to be a creature of the night, although being in the daylight on Dark Earth was not harmful to him. Some weaker creatures, however, could not even stand to be in the sunlight of their own planet.

Near his feet groveled several Creepers, slithering this way and that on their hands and knees. Once trolls who walked upright on two feet hand could exist in daylight, their whole clan had now been reduced to these pathetic nightcrawlers by one of the dark gods they had offended. The Creepers long, emaciated bodies were far out of proportion to their oversized head, which they struggled to hold up as they crawled aimlessly in search of something to feed on. Perhaps they would get lucky and come across the carcass of something that had died that day or possibly stumble onto a Monget Worm, their favorite living morsel. The wolves sniffed at them to see if they had any parts themselves that were worth eating.

The name Quietus Tumulus meant 'Death Mound' and described the tomb that Nefari presently stood in front of quite well. The mound itself was almost entirely white. It was formed from the dried, bleached bones of all the beings that had found their end here. The Lord of Dark Earth, Bramfasa, who had reigned on the Obsidian Throne for almost twelve hundred years, was a cruel god, and he found great pleasure causing torment through the torture of his denizens.

Nefari glanced up at the great skeletal walls of the mound; most of the millions of skeletons represented here were those of trolls, goblins, and ZhiShans, among others inhabitants of Dark Earth. The majority had fossilized over the thousands of years which the mound had existed.

Nefari grinned. There were no StyJeen bones to be found.

"Bonesss are for primitive, weaker, life formssss, don't you agree, Radulf? Bardulf? We are a much more sssophisssticated being than thossse that need a sssskeleton to hold them together." He spoke arrogantly, looking down at his two immense wolves that were black as the moonless night.

Both canines looked up at the mention of their names and stared at Nefari with unfeeling black eyes. In them was no sense of respect, awe, or indebtedness. They were not capable of these feelings, nor could they love, admire, or even feel friendship towards Nefari. The Dire wolves were, in truth, a part of Nefari, and those particularly useless emotions had never existed in him. Like Nefari, the wolves were only able to show emotion, such as joy or delight, if it came about at the suffering of something else, such as the Gimblets they had so eagerly and excitedly feasted on earlier. They did not fear or honor Nefari, in so much as something can fear or honor itself, for they were Nefari, and Nefari was the Dire Wolves.

The imposing dune of Quietus Tumulus was often mistaken for being the home of Bramfasa, but this solid mound was forged by bones all the way through and could not serve as a living quarters for anything. It was merely a dumping ground for the bodies of creatures which had somehow offended Bramfasa. Offending, in this case, might simply mean that they had been in the wrong place at the wrong time, perhaps minding their own business (any hapless creature, as long as it could feel pain, would serve his purpose).

The dwelling of Bramfasa was not inside the mound of Quietus Tumulus itself, but underneath it, where his bedrooms, dining rooms, dungeons, torture chambers, and banquet halls stretched for miles in every direction. So the palace had taken the name of the landmark above it, Quietus Tumulus, which rose up as a monument of death and destruction from the plains of Dark Earth.

Nefari now stood above the underground palace, looking down at the massive iron door in the flat of the earth. It resembled a manhole cover but was over ten times the size. In it was a large viewing window, where someone peering down through it would just barely be able to see the foyer to the throne room at the bottom of a long winding staircase.

Across the diameter of the circular iron door, in large letters, were engraved the words 'May King Adramel Reign Forever'.

Beneath that was a more recent engraving, its etchings containing far less muck and moss inside them than the first. It read, 'Lord Bramfasa, Dark Lord For Eternity'.

Adramel and Bramfasa were the only two kings to ever rule Dark Earth; one cast out and the other presently on the throne.

Bramfasa knew Nefari was up here waiting for him. How long he would be forced to wait was anyone's guess. The Lord of Darkness did things on his own time.

Nefari had no concern that Bramfasa would use him as one of his playthings to torment, for he played a critical role in the kingdom. Nefari was one of only several hundred StyJeen that understood and had mastered the art of gathering the souls of important beings, many times humans.

Humans such as Franklin Hobbs.

He was more skilled than most StyJeen, therefore Bramfasa had given him the Hobbs assignment; an assignment which was personal to the Lord of Dark Earth.

Personal, because it was Bramfasa's own son whose mortal soul he was taking back.

From behind him, Nefari heard a ghastly scream, a sound that touched him deeply. The melodious and agreeable harmony this shriek contained was artistic in its very nature. He knew that even he could not manage a sound this bloodcurdling, so his response to the creature able to create a noise, such as this, was as close to respect as he was capable.

He knew it to be the scream of a Drekavac, a smaller creature that resembled a deformed chimpanzee, with the powerful hind legs of a kangaroo. These legs allowed it to cover up to ten feet in a single jump and made it difficult for anything unfortunate enough to come across one to escape it.

The mouth of a Drekavac was the most noticeable feature on its heinous face. Its fangs reached five inches from both its upper and lower set of teeth, and a bite from it would quickly paralyze its victim's muscles so that it could not so much as move its eyes. This made it easy for the Drekavac to then devour them.

At times, these ghouls would find a Gateway and sneak into Mortal Earth after sundown. They were able to disguise themselves as a lost child, screaming and crying for help.

Compassionate adults, who came to the aid of the upset "child", would then become an easy meal for the monster.

At present, one of these things had mistaken Nefari and his wolves for something that was edible and had shrieked its death cry directly behind them. Nefari, although he appreciated the ferocity of this Drekavac, was annoyed and insulted at how close it had dared to come to him. Then, when it decided to leap upon Radulf and sink its needle-pointed teeth into his neck and wrap its claws around the front of his head, Nefari took it personally. Radulf's body contained no blood, and therefore he could not bleed, nor could he feel pain; he was Nefari. But he could get irritated, and so he shook vigorously, trying to throw the bothersome beast off of him.

"Bardulf, go assisssst your brother," Nefari said calmly.

Bardulf lumbered casually around to the other side of Nefari and, seeing the Drekavac clinging to Radulf's neck, made a quick open-mouthed stab at its dangling feet. Instead of tasting the blood and meat of the creature, he was kicked rather hard in the face by its muscular legs. Like Nefari, the wolves were not held together by a skeleton, and they were not able to absorb a kick with that amount of force, and so the head of the wolf broke off from its thick neck and fell to the ground.

The Drekavac released its hold on Radulf's neck. It realized too late that this animal was not going to be affected by its poisonous bite. The wolf was not made from flesh but from Darkness itself. In the next instant, Nefari's long arm reached down and took hold of the surprised creature, holding it by the scruff of its neck in front of his face. Forcing it to look at him, Nefari flashed the Drekavac a wicked grin, and although his own teeth were not as long as this creature's, they looked more formidable at the moment. His mouth expanded to its full width so that the Drekavac could see clearly down his throat into his black stomach. Without warning, a great black serpent slithered out of the cavernous mouth and wrapped itself around the startled creature's body. The snake, having been born from

Nefari's tongue, was snapped back into his mouth with the dazed monster still in its constricting embrace. Nefari's mouth closed shut.

He walked over to the decapitated head of the wolf, which had come upon a small incline, and thus, rolled down several feet. He picked it up and held it near the vacant end of Bardulf's neck. Both neck and head bubbled and festered at the wounded surface and then were drawn to each other, like opposite poles of a magnet. Back in one piece, Bardulf took his position again next to Nefari.

After hours of waiting next to the grounded iron door, at last Nefari heard a loud metallic clanking that sounded like the moving of gears, and then the great hatchway started to slide open. The expansive spiral staircase, which led to the innards of Bramfasa's lair, lay before him and his wolves. Disgusted with how long he was made to wait, he decided to take a quicker approach down. He looked at both wolves and silently nodded. No sooner had he done this than the three of them began to crumple in on themselves, their heads becoming distorted and flat and collapsing into their torsos. Torsos then melting down into black slop, and finally legs, arms, and tails disappearing into one dark puddle, which burbled and fizzed on the surface of Dark Earth.

Finally, each small air bubble from this quagmire of slime became an individual black fly, and within seconds, a monstrous cloud of them took flight, flocking together as one and diving through the open door, descending down into the dark foyer of Bramfasa's underground lair. Once in the foyer, it was not far to the Room of the Obsidian Throne, so Nefari continued his flight of the thousands, which concluded when the swarm scooted underneath the great golden doors leading to the throne room.

In the confines of the throne room, smaller masses of flies began to dislodge from the central mob, forming the budding appendages which became the head, arms, and legs of the faceless man, who no longer donned his black hoodie, but came dressed for the occasion with a jet-black suit and tie. Bramfasa, the Lord of Dark Earth, sat at the opposite end of an extensive room on the Obsidian Throne. The wolves, Nefari decided, could stay hidden within him for now. The room was dark, smelling of rot and filth, and was certainly not where anyone would expect a god or a king to have his throne.

Bramfasa loved gold, silver, and other sparkling jewels, there was no doubt about it, but he also adored death and all the delightful little ways he could surround himself with its company. He loved the specter of death, draping the walls of his throne room with it, his hallways, and especially his dungeons, where his prisoners could get a vision of what was to come.

Considering this, his throne room was still festooned with gold, silver, and diamonds in various patterns of display. All of these minerals were valuable on Dark Earth as they were on Mortal Earth because of their scarcity in both realms. But the room also had skeletal remains of all sorts of creatures. Adorning the walls of the room were the skeletons of many of Dark Earth's indigenous beings, like the rock and cave goblins, black gnomes, both large and small trolls, different species of sirens, dragons, white golems, ZiShans, and Chenoos; but also on the walls were multitudes of skeletons from the human race as well, each displayed in a different position. One was lying down, another running, some sitting; one had its leg bones swapped with its arm bones so that it stood at attention on its arms and had a leg in a permanent salute to Bramfasa. Two of the human skeletons seemed to be kicking at something unseen, in the heat of competition. Bramfasa, it seemed, was fascinated by the human form.

The floors of the throne room were covered in gold, but enmeshed throughout the gold were human bones and teeth, some forming patterns of ancient symbols, and around the border of the room the bone fragments spelled out Latin words, chants, and invocations raising worship to Bramfasa. The many decorative ceiling chandeliers, which hung in a row down the center of the room, were each made of six skulls, a burning wick extending from a hole in the top of every cranium. This helped provide some light, even if dim, in the throne room.

Being underground, the room was windowless, but in the far front corner, off to the side of the Obsidian Throne, was a gaping black hole in the floor with only a short stone wall surrounding it. From the pit came a strange glowing fire-light, which cast outlandish dancing shadows on the ceiling above it. Nefari knew this to be called the 'Fiery Void', where Bramfasa, in the rare case he was not in the mood to torment his victims, would instead plunge them down into it, thus dispelling of them.

Lined up against one wall were six StyJeen and six Groken, spaced out at even intervals. The Groken were enormous seven foot tall, four hundred pound, club-wielding trolls, with small ugly heads and very little for brains. These Groken had been trained well enough so that they could stand here for eight to ten hours at a time without belching, passing gas, or needing to eat.

The six StyJeen, which stood in formation against the wall, were costumed in their faceless, humanoid forms (it was just easier to stand upright that way, and Bramfasa didn't really want flies or greasy sludge in his throne room). One of them was Askew, the worthless StyJeen that never finished off Franklin Hobbs, like she was supposed to. Nefari couldn't believe that Bramfasa still let her live, much less serve in his court. He had known all six of these StyJeen for thousands of years and had never cared for them. He was their superior, higher in rank, so as he walked by, his head did not so much as turn one degree toward them.

On the opposite side of the room, also in an orderly line, were twelve, near-perfect specimens of Cave Goblins. This breed of goblin was over twice as tall as the treacherous little Rock Goblins that he and the Usher had encountered in the lakebed earlier. Each Cave Goblin held a large ax in their hand, the blade of which rested on the floor. A pair of tusks grew down from their upper jaw and curled back towards their faces, similar to a walrus but with greater coil. Thick whiskers grew in clumps from their pointed chins, and their green faces were heavily scarred with wounds taken in combat. The goblins were dressed in golden armor, ready to do battle for Bramfasa, although their purpose in the throne room was to look fearsome and intimidating, more than to actually serve as his protection. He had an army of hundreds of these brutes living near the Mound, ready at his command if needed.

From the other side of the lengthy room came a booming voice, "Nefari, so good of you to come." It was Bramfasa.

The king sat on his tremendous black throne, the Obsidian Throne, which had once been chiseled from a single, massive, obsidian boulder. The first God and King of Dark Earth, Adramel, had commissioned the Fire Imps, who were the master sculptors of the land, to find a stone of great size and then fashion a dark, but majestic throne from it.

Adramel had later been defeated in an epic battle with The Suveran, reigning God of Third Earth. This great war took place over two thousand Earth-years ago, and when it ended, the ancient king had been humiliated and then thrown into the Fiery Void, right in the midst of his own throne room. He still lingers in the Underneath and In-between, unable to return to the surface unless released by The Suveran himself.

Upon Adramel's demise, many imprisoned human souls were rescued from the Void, as well as the slave fields, and The Suveran claimed control over the three realms.

At least temporarily.

Bramfasa, great-grandson of Adramel, had stormed the unguarded halls of Quietus Tumulus hundreds of years later, taken back the Obsidian Throne, and assumed the position of King over Dark Earth *and* Mortal Earth. The Suveran did nothing to stop him then, and even now, after a thousand more years, he has still not disputed Bramfasa's claim over two of the three planes of Earth.

As Nefari approached the Obsidian Throne, he bowed low and said, "Your Majesssty, I had a few missshaps on the way here, and I am sssorry to ssssay that the Usher you ssssent for me did not ssssurvive the journey back."

Bramfasa was a god that could show himself in many different faces and forms. His preferred countenance looked similar to a human male and this was the one he presently appeared in. As a man, he was extremely handsome by all human standards. He believed fancy clothing was not necessary to demonstrate his greatness, and for this reason, he wore no shirt, but instead showed off his muscular and athletic physique openly.

Adornments of small bones and teeth hung from his neck and circumscribed his upper arms. His pants were black and he wore no footwear, taking pride in his lengthy toenails. Long blonde hair, braided into one rope, hung from the back of his head and draped over his shoulders, then down his chest like a serpent. His eyes were blue, his skin flush, and he had all the looks of the leading man in a movie, the ruggedly attractive hero. All the looks, that is, except for the two large protruding horns that jutted out above his ears on each side of his head. The horns were a foot in length and looked like they belonged on a mountain goat.

On either side of Bramfasa, sitting in a smaller version of the Obsidian Throne, were two Crow Wraiths staring suspiciously at Nefari. The size of humans, these advisors to Bramfasa sat arrogantly here every day, looking out over the court. Nefari disliked these two creatures tremendously. For some reason, the God of the land allowed these ravens to help him make decisions that affected all of Dark Earth. They were the ones who had first whispered the suggestion to Bramfasa that he should have a son born of a human mother.

Look how that turned out.

The folded wings of the birds hid their bodies, so that it looked like a dark cloak had been draped over them. Each had a smoldering black, curved beak, which was in slight contrast to the rest of the pitch-black feathers covering them, and their eyes were like fire as they reflected the candlelight from the chandeliers.

The Crow Wraiths, as if sharing one brain, rose from their chairs simultaneously. Their legs, which up until now, had been hidden under heavy wings, were not the spindly legs of a raven, but muscular like a human's. As they walked, their massive wings angled at a great enough distance away from their bodies to reveal two human-like arms, as well, which were separate and free moving from the wings. Instead of feet and hands, however, four sharp claws jutted from the end of the appendages.

They approached Bramfasa from each side, bending low to avoid the large horns extending straight out of his head, and each leaned its beaks into one of his ears. Nefari could see slight movements of their beaks as they whispered something to him, but he could hear nothing of what either said. Both offered their silent advice and then ended their lecture at the exact moment as the other, before leaning back and fixing their eyes on Nefari.

Bramfasa smirked. "My Crows inform me that they have heard of the Usher's demise from the many eyes we have watching for us. They also tell me about your intentional destruction of some of my other beasts, the dear little Gimblets. Explain yourself, Nefari." His smirk was gone, replaced by a wicked frown.

Nefari had known this question was inevitable, and he knew the best approach, in this case, was to tell the truth and apologize, even though this went against all of his morals.

"Your Greatnesssss, my wolvessss and I wanted to eat, and the Usher was disssressspecting *me*, Nefari of the SssstyJeen," he paused to point at himself with one elongated finger, "who hasss been your faithful sssservant for sssso many years. I do ssssincerely apologizzzze, however, for my vile actionsss." A strong tone of false sincerity was thick in Nefari's words.

Bramfasa's eyes narrowed, "You ate the head of my ZhiShan servant and then pushed his body into a chasm. Your Dire Wolves devoured over twenty of my Gimblet spies. Do you not know that everything on Dark Earth, all of its creatures and spirits, are part of me and I am part of them? Without reason or cause, I am the only one who can extinguish their lives, either by giving orders or by my own hand. If you defile them, you have defiled me." He spoke with no hostility, but on the contrary, stone-cold placidness.

"My Lord, I am ssssorry," Nefari cowered lower now, unsure when this chastisement would end.

"The life you took of the Drekavac was in defense of yourself, as was the life of that repugnant Rock Goblin whom my Usher killed. These are forgivable, but you must pay with a life for the lives of the others." Bramfasa looked at one of his Crow Wraiths. It leaned in, and again, with its beak in his ear, whispered something. He nodded.

"Where are your wolves? Let me see them!" Bramfasa demanded.

"Majessssty, they are within me now, resssting…"

Bramfasa shouted, "Now, fool! You need to show me only one."

Without further excuses, Nefari stretched his neck over to his shoulder and begin to gnaw at his arm. His jagged teeth did not take long to complete the task and his arm fell to the ground. Almost instantly, it softened and stewed back into its shapeless black form. This ooze began to bubble, then shake, and the body of the Dire Wolf named Bardulf slowly took shape in front of the group of onlookers. Nefari stood still, waiting for a new arm to regenerate. In the meantime, the shame he felt as his fellow StyJeen stood by and watched, holding in their laughter at his temporary deformity, was considerable. Askew was especially having trouble trying to keep a toothy grin off her face. He hated her.

"Ah, that is a fine looking animal," Bramfasa commented, looking the wolf up and down. "It was wise of you to merge and perform the Rite of Assimilation with two such tremendous beasts."

"Yessss, they have sssserved me well," Nefari said, wary of what was going to happen. His arm had come back in now, but the humiliation was still fresh.

Bramfasa stood up and walked down the two stairs of his throne's platform to the main floor. Close behind him trailed the Crow Wraiths. He approached the wolf. "What is this one's name?" he asked.

"Bardulf, Sire."

Bramfasa looked at one of his goblins. "Belkree," he called, "bring me a death urn, now!"

The Cave Goblin who was in formation closest to the front of the room marched to an area that had been hidden in the shadows beyond the throne. He reached out for something unseen and then walked back towards them with a dull, black vase in one hand. The 'urn', as Bramfasa called it, was somewhat pear-shaped; it was elliptical and bulging at the bottom, gradually becoming skinnier towards the top, where it crooked out again to make a wide mouth. The goblin held it out for his master to take.

"Faster, next time, Belkree!" Bramfasa said, snatching the urn from him.

He turned back toward the Dire Wolf. "Nefari, as this wolf is a part of you, I will take it, as you have taken from me." He reached out to Bardulf and wrapped his hand around one of his thick legs, yanked hard, and snapped it off. The wolf made no sound, but only looked at Nefari with question, and then, losing his balance, fell to the ground. Bramfasa held up the leg and stuffed it into the wide hole of the urn. The wolf's paw was too large to pass through, and Bramfasa and Nefari watched as it melted into a flowing mass that seeped easily down into the jar.

"Now, I could either do that piece by piece to the wolf, or you can command it to enter the urn on its own," Bramfasa said, slyly.

Nefari, wanting to move past this awful shaming, yelled out, "Bardulf, dissssband!"

Obediently, the fallen wolf began to convulse, contort, and then melt back into blackness, flowing over the ground. It bubbled, then gave birth to flies, which took to the air and dove down into the death urn. Bramfasa grabbed the lid from Belkree, put it on the urn, and handed it back to the goblin.

"Place this back on the shelf, Belkree," he ordered, though casually.

Bramfasa then leaned in next to where Nefari's face should have been. His breath was hot and sulfurous. "Do not trifle with me, Nefari," he sneered quietly, his lips quivering. "Do not think for a second that you can get away with anything in either this realm or Mortal Earth. I am God of both, and you are merely my servant. Next time you will be cast deep into the Fiery Void. You will forever join the restless soul of Adramel and the others whose misery cannot be measured."

Bramfasa turned and walked back up to his throne where he sat down again. When he aimed his gaze back at Nefari, a satisfied, smug look covered his face. The Crows followed behind at a distance and sat in their places.

Bramfasa's voice burst forth again with a snarl, "Now, how is it that you have failed to gather the eyes of Franklin Hobbs, the gifts he received from the Luminos? Are you not supposed to be my best Gatherer? Perhaps I should get one of these other six StyJeen to take your place. Maybe Askew would perform better for me." He knew the rivalry between the two StyJeen and that this suggestion would cut deeply into Nefari's ego.

Still a bit stunned at the disrespect being shown to him by Bramfasa, Nefari confessed, "My Lord, I don't know how he hasss esssscaped me both timesss. I thought he wassss weak, but he isss ssstronger and ssssmarter than I knew."

"Of course he is stronger and smarter than you thought, you twit! He is my spawn! My son! He was supposed to help me rule Dark Earth if he hadn't been ruined by that woman! His mind warped with her kindness."

Spittle flew from Bramfasa's mouth as he bellowed, and he slammed his fists down in outrage on the arms of his throne. "Now, after she, the one named Angel, has served her purpose, she will suffer as well in the fields for what she has done!"

Nefari's mouth opened to only a slight crevice, but words still made their way out, "My King, why not jusssst torture and kill her like you are apt to do? Would not her ssssoul remain here forever, then?" he asked.

Bramfasa's face twisted into an awful disfigurement, and the features of a frightful reptilian beast were revealed momentarily before contracting back to its normal visage.

He gnashed his teeth. "If I kill her, her soul cannot remain here, you fool! Have you forgotten that when The Suveran threw Adremal into the Fiery Void he took claim on souls such as hers? Her soul would go to Third Earth with him. No, but I have her under heavy guard. If you fail to kill the boy, then I will still have her. He will come for her."

Bramfasa shook his head in frustration before he continued. "The woman named Marigold, she was his real mother. The Crows had picked a perfectly despicable mother for him, one who would despise him enough to sell him for profit. I had arranged for a group of human traffickers to purchase him. My boy would have been brought up as a child slave, and the evil in him would have been allowed to thrive and fester until reaching its potential!"

Bramfasa raised his arms over his head and looked up. "Then I could have taken him back, showed him who he really was, and we could have ruled over Dark Earth together!"

He threw his arms down in disgust. "And Mortal Earth…Mortal Earth would have accepted my son as one of their own, and with his powers, they would have worshipped him!" His voice trailed off, the taste of disappointment causing him to drown in his words. "Most humans already worship me, whether they know it or not…but with him we would have owned the rest of those vermin. They would have readily made him their king."

Nefari thought for a moment. In the past, he had used a tactic with Bramfasa where he would ask him a question, even if he already knew the answer to it so that he might get back in the good graces of this smug king. It was a way of buttering him up, playing his ego against him. He tried this now, "I undersssstood that the boy'sss powerssss come from the Luminosss' gift to him. Thosssse amethysssst eyessss, which they gave him on hisssss tenth birthday? But he is ssso ssstrong, thissss sstrength mussst alsso be coming from the power he inherited from you, my Lord, doessss it not?"

The Crow Wraith on his right made a move towards Bramfasa, who immediately turned towards it. "Speak!" he ordered, his blue eyes starting to darken. "There is no need to whisper through me now."

From the Crow Wraith's curled beak arose a crafty, sinuous voice. "Yes, the abilities he has received from the Luminos are becoming stronger now, because without knowing it, he has been using them alongside his powers from Lord Bramfasa as well. On the hill where he was injured, he had unknowingly used some of his dark talents allowing him to see the future, these were powers passed down to him from his father, and so it brought him to his rightful home, here in this realm." The black bird nodded its head to signal it was done speaking.

The Crow Wraith on the left of Bramfasa picked up where the other had left off. "You need to kill him before he is able to realize the full potential of his budding power —"

Then the first Wraith spoke again, finishing the sentence, "Or The Suveran will try to use the boy *against* our Lord Bramfasa..."

The feathery devil glanced at his master, trying to decide if he should finish the sentence.

He did.

"And he *will* be a worthy adversary."

Both crows nodded their heads up and down once in unison.

Bramfasa's eyes went black as a dung beetle. The former blue islands adrift in a deep white ocean were nowhere to be found. "Kill him now, or I will slaughter you later! And by *my* name…"

He thrust out his finger and pointed to the location of the urn in which Bardulf had been cast. "I will have that wolf of yours help me murder you!"

At this point, Bramfasa's rage was transferring into visible energy. All the court could see the charged waves of fury traveling through him, seeking freedom and finally finding it, exiting through his finger at the moment he lunged his hand forward.

By the wall, a short cry of intense pain sounded, along with a loud rumble. Nefari looked over to see a gaping, green hole in the chest of one of the Groken. The troll had been trying to stand very still, holding in a belch, when the blast of violent power from the hand of Bramfasa, unintentionally as it was, struck it in the chest and left nothing in its path. The wall behind the Groken had been hit, as well. The room now had a sizable window, although it only allowed a view of the next chamber. The ruptured troll tottered, then fell backward through the newly made casement and into the pile of rubble.

Bramfasa laughed cruelly. "That brute had gotten on my nerves, anyway."

"Your Majesssssty, I will kill your boy. I promisssse you," Nefari said, holding his head high, trying to display confidence.

What Nefari knew, and he was certain Bramfasa did not, (or it would have been a topic of conversation by now) was that back on Mortal Earth there was a man named Hank who was set on murdering Franklin. This human had instructions to kill Franklin and then save his eyes in a jar for Nefari. All of this had been implanted in Hank's consciousness through a wonderfully talented little critter called a Homingryll. The Homingryll, a Dark Earth pixie with many skills, had just one that Nefari was interested in. This was its unique ability to bore itself deep into the brain of another creature by entering through the nose or mouth, whereupon, it would link together its stream of consciousness with the host's own. This allowed the Homingryll to easily plant ideas into its victim's head, which would be accepted by the victim as being its own thoughts. Nefari had plucked the winged creature from its home in one of the remaining sprite groves on Dark Earth. The chance to ruin the life of one human and be responsible for the murder of another, was all Nefari had to offer the pixie for it to agree to help.

Franklin should be dead shortly, Nefari thought, *or may already be dead, at the hands of the skinny man named Hank*.

Unfortunately, Nefari's pleasant daydream was cut short by the thunderous voice of Bramfasa, who had stood and taken several threatening steps towards him. "I will allow you one more opportunity, then I will have to deal with the boy myself. Now leave my sight."

The Lord of Dark Earth turned on his heels and went back to his throne. The StyJeen bowed in phony reverence and then began his alteration back into the Darkness from which he was made.

This prompted an urgent response from the Crow Wraiths, who immediately came to Bramfasa's side, both putting their beaks near his ear. The god listened intently before elbowing them away from him.

His lips curled back into a smirk. "Oh, one more thing," he said, the loathsome look on his face almost twisting it beyond recognition.

Nefari, who had already sunken his limbs and head down into his torso, reversed back into his previous form. When his head finally appeared back on his neck a second later, Bramfasa continued. "We know about your attempts to have the human do your job for you. The old man from the orphanage. Once again you have shown me how little I can trust you! Don't you know, imbecile, that a mere human cannot hurt that boy anymore? His powers from me combined with those of the Luminos were enough to stop you twice already! What chance do you think a human will have?"

Nefari had somehow been caught by these two sniveling crows. He just didn't know how. Never should he have underestimated how closely Bramfasa monitored activities in the overlapping planes of both Dark Earth and Mortal Earth, especially when it was something of this importance.

"Bramfassssa, I…"

He realized this new mistake before the words had left his paper-thin lips.

"Did you... just address me… by my name?" Anger and disbelief burned in each syllable of Bramfasa's words. He stood up and began walking back towards the cowering Nefari. Across his face, once again, flashed the reptilian specter that seemed to be hiding beneath the surface. Along with it, this time, the whole of his body momentarily lost its human appearance, and the scaly, rough skin of a lizard wrapped him from head to toe. A thick green tail hung from his lower back and swung to the floor. His lengthy blonde hair and great curled horns disappeared altogether and instead left an oblong shaped head and snout of a larger-than-normal Komodo Dragon. This countenance, again, only lasted briefly, and his figure flickered back to its original appearance.

"Referring to me by my name? For an offense less than that, I have peeled the skin from creatures as they begged for their lives! You disrespectful and blasphemous animal!"

Although more than six feet away, the force of his scream still managed to ruffle the greasy hair plastered on Nefari's head, blasting one or two of the black strands from its normal placement.

On his knees, Nefari bowed low to the ground, his head touching the floor. "Your Gracccce, I apologizzzze sssinccccerely. I meant no disssressssspect, I only —"

Bramfasa screamed, "Shut up, dim-witted fool! The human which you thought might be able to help you is dead. My son has figured out that his own mind's eye is very versatile in its powers, and he is getting stronger with each minute you wait. Now go and do the job. By yourself. Do not bring any more humans into it." Bramfasa pointed to the door on the other end of the room. "Get out!"

Nefari didn't even bother to morph into the swarm of Darkness. He ran out the door and didn't stop until he had climbed up all the winding stairs and exited out of the large hole above him into the warm night air.

CHAPTER THIRTY-TWO
A CORPSE & A CRICKET

Sami rolled the limp body of Hank off of Franklin and then helped her friend to his feet and out of the lake. They both sloshed up to the woods where they found Rufus propped up against a tree with Shad's flannel shirt wrapped tightly around his leg, but the arrow still protruding from it.

Shad was in a blood-spotted, white t-shirt, and he knelt by Rufus. "If I pull the arrow out of his leg, it will bleed much worse. We can let the doctors do that. But, I needed to stop the bleeding for now with pressure from a tourniquet," he explained.

Franklin walked over, shoes waterlogged and slogging through the grass, and he sat down on the other side of his injured comrade. "How are you doing, pal?" he asked. The guilt he felt was heavy on his shoulders; he knew he was responsible for the injury that his new, but faithful, friend had sustained.

As they had all begun to learn, when Rufus wasn't calling people names he was usually pretty funny, and even here he managed to make Franklin smile by replying, "Only hurts when my heart beats, Hobby." A playful grin swept across his face.

Franklin patted Rufus's shoulder. "You're a true friend, Rufus," he said. "Thanks for risking your life for me. That goes for all of you guys… Sami and Shad. You shouldn't have come back, but you did, and that's the only reason I'm alive."

No one said anything, but all shared a moment of silent understanding of the compact of their friendship. Of course, they were not going to just let one of their friends get killed.

The night had turned quiet again; faint stars dotted the sky, bowing to the moon, which gave the four friends just enough light to see each other's faces.

Sami asked the question they were all wondering. "What's the plan, guys?" They all knew that Rufus had to get medical attention, and they were not going to be able to help him all the way home in his current condition.

"I could ride my bike back and wake up Gloria. We could call the police from there," Shad offered.

"Wait," Sami said. She got up and started towards the lake, stepping carefully around the mud. As she kept her eyes on the ground in front of her, she asked, "Franklin, can you come help me with Hank? I need to get him on dry land."

Rufus saw the opportunity, however inappropriate it was, to crack another joke. "I guess he really is just a lot of dead weight at the moment, isn't he?"

Franklin looked back at him. "Very funny, Rufus."

"Someone's gotta lighten the mood here," he replied.

Franklin followed Sami as she waded into the lake where the majority of Hank's corpse had disappeared under the black water. Besides the shaft and feathers of the arrow, only the end of his nose, the tips of his elbows, and several fingers were visible above the surface of the lake. Hank's arms were sprawled out over his head, as if in the act of surrender.

"Can you help me get him out of here?" Sami asked Franklin.

Franklin followed her lead and they both reached down into the murky water searching for a hand. After they had each located one and grabbed it, they began slowly turning the direction of Hank's body, which put up little resistance. When they lifted him up and started trudging towards shore, each pulling on one arm, the dead man's face came to the surface. Franklin tried not to look, but it was impossible. Projecting up from the top of Hank's forehead was the arrow, and with its red and green feathers at the end of it, Franklin had the unsettling thought that he was dragging a demented Christmas unicorn through the lake.

The moonlight cast a haunting glow onto the lifeless man's features. His eyes remained open, as they had the instant before the arrow's death strike. The once-proud mustache, which was usually one of the most animated things on his face, drooped into its own wet frown. His mouth, too, was agape, giving him the appearance of a man who was forever in awe of something unseen.

With some effort, they were able to drag his body up into the grass. He wasn't a large man, so moving him had not been overly strenuous. Sami kneeled and started patting his shirt pockets. When she found nothing, she began searching the pockets in his jeans.

After only several seconds, she announced, "Got it!" and held up a dripping cell phone.

Drying it off on her shirt, she brought it back up to where Shad and Rufus were sitting by the tree.

"Good idea," Shad said. "Do you think it still works?"

"Let's try it out," she responded. "Some of them are waterproof these days."

Franklin came beside her as she held in the power button on the side of the phone. The keypad lit up, and after a few seconds it gave its short musical chime, signaling that it had powered on. Sami dialed 911 and when an operator answered, she gave the thumbs up sign to the others. After explaining where they were, what had happened to them, Hank's unfortunate demise, and the condition of Rufus (making sure to leave out the part about Franklin's newfound talent), the operator told her to stay right where they were and that police officers, along with medics, would be there shortly.

She pressed the 'End Call' button and then, like she had done this a million times before, said, "Okay guys, we have to get our stories to match up before we talk to the police."

For several minutes they discussed how they would explain to the police what had happened; how Hank had come after them and almost killed Franklin, and then how Franklin had finally ended up with the crossbow and shot Hank in self-defense.

"I hate lying," Sami said, "but we can't tell the police about what you did with that arrow, right Franklin? They wouldn't even believe it anyway."

"I agree," Franklin said. "Let's keep that part to ourselves."

Shad shook his head. "The angle of the arrow into the skull might be cause for questions. It's going to be difficult to explain," he said.

Franklin thought for a moment before he replied, "What if I told the police that Hank was bending down to hurt Sami when I shot him, so the arrow went in more towards the top of his head?"

Having had a few minutes to think about the events of the night, Sami finally let the horror of everything sink in. She was crouching down next to Shad, hugging her knees as she swayed her body like the pendulum on a grandfather clock. In a voice more fragile than they had ever heard before from her, she muttered, "Did this really happen? Did Hank really try killing us? He would have done anything to save us a few days ago. And now…" She pointed to his body. "Look! He's dead! He's lying dead over there on the ground!"

"I know, Sami. It's horrific, morbid, and so surreal," Shad answered calmly, digging at the ground with a twig, "almost like having a nightmare, waking up in a cold sweat and realizing it was just a really bad dream. Only this isn't a dream, but I'm pretty sure it will always be a nightmare…"

Franklin also felt the painful emotional pangs of what had just happened. But they were mixed with other feelings… something that resembled satisfaction, delight almost.

He closed his eyes tight and tried to chase these awful emotions away. Then, shaking his head, he said, "I can't believe I killed him. I can't believe it. He wasn't a bad man, something had taken control of him."

"We just can't think that way Franklin," Sami said, wiping stray tears from her cheeks. "He used to be a good man, but in the condition he was in, he would have killed all of us. Besides, if you want someone to blame, blame the freak that made him go crazy, that Nefari thing you told us about. Don't blame yourself."

Rufus, who had been quietly taking everything in, finally spoke up, "Franklin, how did you do that? How did you make that arrow stop in the air, go up, and then come back down right at Hank?"

Shad stopped his purposeless digging, flicked the twig away, and focused his attention on Franklin.

"I…I guess…" Franklin began, "I guess these different abilities I have keep coming from nowhere and surprising me. I never actually know when something is going to happen, and for the most part, I can't control when it does. Like seeing perfectly in the dark or being able to live out future events and then going back to the present. I figured I would see if there was still a trick I didn't know about and maybe try to make something happen."

"You have telekinesis," Shad said, somewhat matter-of-factly, "the power to move things with your mind."

"Is that what it's called?" Franklin asked.

Dropping his serious persona and letting his growing excitement show now, Shad exclaimed, "Yes Franklin! It's like every science fiction nerd's dream to have a friend like you!"

Franklin just shrugged, "I don't know," he said. "It has its benefits, but overall it's created a lot more problems than it's solved so far."

But even as he said this, a strange, discomforting sense of pride welled up inside Franklin's chest, and he felt like shouting to everyone, 'That's what the old geezer gets for messing with me!' He knew this reaction was not only out of his normal character but wrong on many levels. What was going on with him? It almost seemed like *his* personality was changing now.

Shad stood up and walked over to look at the arrow in Hank's head. He mumbled, talking to just himself, "I need to make sure the angle of penetration into his skull could really be created from Hank bending over. The story has to be believable."

He knelt down to study Hank's head, which lay face up, staring blindly into the night. The arrow was jutting out from just above his forehead, and blood, which had poured from the wound since his body had been taken from the water, had turned much of his hair into a sticky, red mess. Without touching anything, Shad inspected the fissure in his head at the point of entry, closely looking at the angle with which the arrow had entered the skull.

Finally, he said, "Okay," and then clearly this time, "I think that your story will work, Franklin."

Shad started to stand up when something caught his eye, "Hey guys, come take a look at this. Quick!"

Franklin and Sami hustled over and joined him. He pointed at Hank's drooping mouth. "Something moved in there. I saw it. It looked like a large insect or something."

"Well, he was in the water for a while. Maybe something crawled in," said Sami.

They all stared down at Hank like they were watching a horror movie, but without popcorn. Franklin dared to stoop his head lower, his eyes only inches from the set of pale, blue lips as he peered down into Hank's mouth.

"There! I think I saw it," he shouted, moving his head out of the way so that they could see, too.

Before their eyes, the dead man's lips began to tremble, and the children half expected a spectral voice to rise up into the chilly air. But moments later, six insectile legs, black in color, emerged from the dark spaces of Hank's mouth. Three came to rest on his upper lip, three on his lower lip. With both sets of legs now in position, whatever deviant creature this was, proceeded to use Hank's cracked lips for leverage as it lifted the rest of its body onto his face. But what came from the depths of Hank's mouth was as bizarre to the children as anything could have possibly been. A tiny creature, only an inch and a half tall, with the upper body of a man, but the lower half of a common house cricket, sat atop of Hank's mouth. Although its species name was unknown to Franklin and his friends, this was the Homingryll (Latin for man-cricket) that Nefari had chosen to do his vile work.

The part of the Homingryll that resembled a man was black, like the rest of it, and began halfway up the cricket's thorax, allowing for a pair of human arms to fit neatly before its neck began. Atop its hairless head, two small, straight horns poked through its skin, each in alignment with an eye. The upper physique of the Homingryll was quite muscular for such a small specimen, and it reminded Franklin of the creatures he had read about from ancient Greek mythology called centaurs. Centaurs were similar, except much larger and with the lower body of a horse. Regarding this creature's miniscule size, Franklin figured it was small enough to find its way into a human's brain if given the opportunity. From there, who knows? Maybe it could somehow turn a normal, kind man into a blood-loving murderer.

The hard exoskeleton, along with the segmented legs on the insect-half of the Homingryll, twitched as it anticipated its next move. Along with looking like a cricket it may have also been part lightning bug or perhaps glowworm, for it seemed to contain its own internal lantern that caused it to radiate a small amount of light. The creature must have suddenly become aware it was being studied, for a pair of translucent wings, which up to this point, had been concealed in pouches on its back, sprouted in both directions, spanning about four inches in length. Before jumping from Hank's mouth and taking flight, it turned its head and glanced up at them, allowing the children to see a malicious smile form on its miniature face.

Wasting no time, Franklin hopped to his feet and started running after the tiny creature, trying to track its faint glow before it disappeared into the night.

He called back to Sami and Shad, "I'm going to follow it. You guys stay here with Rufus and wait for the police."

"Hold on," Sami took her flashlight from her pocket and threw it to him. "You might need this to help keep an eye on it."

"Thanks," Franklin yelled back, without taking his eyes off the Homingryll.

Still kneeling in the grass, Sami took two steps backward and said, "What do you think that thing was doing in his mouth?"

Shad raised an eyebrow and replied, "Oh, I'm guessing that odd little cricket-creature was the cause of Hank's crazy behavior. Somehow it was able to reroute his neural patterns and create a new arrangement of circuitry that brought on an extreme hatred for Franklin, along with profoundly violent tendencies."

Rufus, quiet through all of the recent excitement, perked up. "You think that thing was sent by whatever is after Franklin?"

"Franklin seems to think so. That's why he wanted to follow it, I'm guessing," Shad answered.

Sami shook her head in disgust and asked, "How could it have gotten to his brain by going through his mouth? There's no passageway, is there?"

"Actually, there is a part of the skull near the sinus cavity that is very thin and it could be punctured rather easily. It might have worked its way through there, somehow. That's why you should never jam anything up your nose, you might make it to your brain."

Sami stifled her gag reflex and groaned, "Thanks for the advice."

The cry of the police and ambulance sirens off in the distance brought the biology lesson from Shad to an end. They hurried over to Rufus's side, Shad directing his powerful light at their injured friend. Sami was the first to notice that Rufus had his finger jammed way up one of his nostrils.

"What in the world are you doing?" she asked him, jolted by the gross behavior.

Rufus attempted to sound embarrassed, "Ummm... I was just seeing if Shad was right about being able to touch my brain. It actually tickles."

Shad was about to say something when Rufus slapped the ground and broke into strained laughter. "It was a joke, guys! Look, my knuckle's bent, it only looks like my finger's stuck up my nose!"

Sami and Rufus didn't respond.

"C'mon, cut me some slack," Rufus pleaded. "I'm in some severe pain here. You can at least laugh at my stupid jokes."

Perhaps earlier in the night, before anyone had died, Sami would have found this funny, but now she only ignored his vulgar joke, sat down by him, and said, "They're almost here Rufus. Hold on, we'll get you to a hospital soon."

Franklin was running as fast as he could to keep up with the Homingryll. Fortunately, it flew close to the ground, making it easier for him to keep track of its illuminated body. At one point, during the pixie's flight through the forest, Franklin lost all sight of it when its glowing abdomen went dark right in the thickest growth. Not wanting to use the flashlight and give himself away, he dared to go a full fifteen seconds without seeing it, before he was finally able to catch sight of it a few feet ahead. What he actually caught sight of was a very large, rather disturbing shadow of the Homingryll; one that had been cast on the forest floor as it flew through a rare spot of bright moonlight. Thankfully, its glow came back soon after that, and he was once again able to follow it easily.

It did not seem to be flying haphazardly, as if it was lost, but on the contrary, seemed to have a destination in mind and knew the shortest route there. Franklin tried to stay far enough behind the Homingryll so that it didn't notice him; he had no idea how keen its sense of hearing or sight was, but did not want to take any chance of being discovered. If his hunch was correct, this little brain-burrower could end up being a big help to him.

It continued through the woods and eventually came out on the far side of the trees, close to where the children had earlier ditched their bikes. Without delay, Franklin found his own bike and hopped on, so that the peculiar critter would be a bit easier to tail.

Across the field, the Homingryll flew; it seemed like it may never reach its destination and Franklin began to wonder if his theory had been wrong. Then, up ahead, the silhouette of a wide, rectangular building came into view.

Not quite sure where he was, Franklin took his eyes off his quarry for a split second to get his bearings. He realized he had come upon a farm, and in front of him was one of several barns; others stood on either side of him. Farther ahead to his left, he could see the outline of the farmhouse.

As the pixie continued to travel past the large barn, Franklin noticed a new, very high structure looming in front of him. His eyes scanned to its peak, at least fifty feet up, where he was able to make out the rotating sails of a windmill. His eyes adjusted to the new angle of light, allowing him to follow the shapes as they spun relentlessly around and around. It was an old-fashioned windmill, one that you might see on the horizon of a Dutch countryside. Its blades, fairly long, came dipping close to the ground as they spun. Probably within ten feet, he guessed.

He watched the tiny bloom of light began to ascend as the Homingryll flew upwards towards the center of the windmill. It appeared to be traveling directly for the wooden blades, which would no doubt kill it even with an indirect, glancing blow. Franklin hoped he hadn't come all this way just to watch this odd creature get crushed. Not that it didn't deserve it; it was an evil life form, no doubt, but he really hoped his hunch was correct. Troubled, he watched as it entered the blades. Its light once again went out and it disappeared into a blanket of darkness.

Wasting no time he switched on Sami's flashlight and angled the beam upwards along the path the Homingryll had taken.

There it was. The suicidal creature was flying head-on into the heart of the windmill's four massive rotating blades. Franklin could only watch helplessly as its body went right smack-dab into one of them. Upon impact though, to his shock, instead of the sound of tiny bones being crunched, he saw a quick flash of light, followed by three longer flashes, then, except for the glare coming from his own flashlight, darkness settled once again on the windmill. He immediately aimed the light at the ground, far beneath the spinning blades, and searched everywhere for the creature's tiny body, but was not able to find it.

Franklin turned his bike around, trembling with excitement, and began pedaling as fast as he could back to his friends. This was fantastic news! He had found a doorway or a wormhole or whatever it was called, most likely to Nefari's realm and to where his mom was being held captive!

CHAPTER THIRTY-THREE
A BLUNDER & A WONDER

Needless to say, the following day Gloria had put Franklin's birthday party on hold after she found out the tragic news. Hank's body had been recovered by police in the very early morning hours. Rufus had been rushed to the hospital by a screaming ambulance, and the other children were brought back in a police car to Open Arms Orphanage, where a sleeping Gloria was awakened by one of the female officers and told the whole appalling tale. The police seemed to buy the story about Franklin picking up the bow and shooting Hank as he was trying to grab Sami. No one even questioned if Franklin had ever shot a crossbow before, or how he knew how to use, much less, aim one.

Fortunately, Franklin had made it back to his friends before the police and medics actually found their location by the lake. Something had occurred to him on this short bike ride back, and when he arrived at the murder scene again, he made sure to get his fingerprints all over the handle of the bow. Just in case forensics decided to run any tests.

Rufus was back early that morning, hopping around on crutches; he had been given fifteen stitches for the deep gouge in his leg, and a large white bandage covered his wound. The arrow had somehow miraculously missed his muscles and tendons and pierced only the fatty tissue, which inspired Rufus to admit, "Oh, there's a lot of fatty tissue to hit, trust me."

Hank Fulsten's attempt at murder, which led to his own death, was all over the news; local, state, and national. He was portrayed as a man who had reached his boiling point, had flipped and gone on a psychotic rampage. Franklin and the other kids knew better, but they also knew the real story would sound insane to anyone else.

The children's names were left out of the news, as was the name of the orphanage, to protect those involved, although most locals knew who Hank was and where he worked, anyway. Police detectives spent most of the morning questioning the four kids.

Asking questions like:

"Why were you out there to begin with last night?"

"What were you doing in the woods before he came?"

"How did he know where you were?"

"Why did Hank want to kill Franklin?"

The four of them answered as best they could, trying to tell the truth, without giving too much information. They explained that they were there because they had heard the woods was haunted and wanted to see for themselves, but did not know how Hank knew where they had gone. Yes, Hank had been acting strangely toward Franklin lately, and they were not exactly sure why. Maybe something to do with Franklin reminding him of a brother he hated.

Eventually, Gloria was able to politely sweep the police out the door, knowing she needed to protect the children from having to keep reliving the traumatic events of last night over. Besides, with almost no sleep, they kept dozing off while answering the officers' questions.

Gloria herself was utterly heartsick. She thought she had known her long-time friend so well and couldn't understand how he had hidden this terrible, dark secret from her. Franklin wanted so badly to tell her the truth; that Hank was a good man, as she believed he had been. He knew, though, that the time to reveal that much information was not now.

Completely exhausted, the four of them sat on the couch in the living room, the same couch where Franklin had sat for Hank's book reading only three nights ago. *So much has happened since then,* he thought to himself.

"Oh, children," Nonna Glo walked over to where they sat, still in her blue robe, eyes puffy from crying. "Children, I am so sorry that I did not listen to you about Hank. I can't believe I was that ignorant. You knew all along something was wrong, and I just kept wanting to believe the best about him." She came and maneuvered her large body into the middle of them on the couch. Sami rested her head on Gloria's spacious arm, while her other arm served as a teddy bear for Shad as he wrapped his hands around it and held tight.

"Rufus, how is your leg, honey?" she reached over across Shad and grabbed Rufus's hand.

"Let's just say that being a chubby kid has its advantages, like when someone shoots you with a crossbow," he said, squeezing the fat on his lower leg.

Gloria laughed. "Like I always say, having a little extra weight on your body will usually help you more than it hurts you. You keep that wound clean. I'll help you change the bandage later."

She looked over at Franklin who sat next to Sami. "Franklin, can you forgive me for not believing you?"

Franklin stood up and walked to her. He leaned down and gave her a tight hug around her neck. "There is nothing to forgive, Nonna Glo. You trusted your friend. You look for the good in people and overlook the other stuff. You had no way of knowing he would do anything like that."

Gloria laughed. "What would I do without you kids? I am so thankful you're okay." She started to get up, but then stopped and sat back down again. "Hold on, pumpkin! You're twelve today! I swear to you that we'll have a party and cake when you get home from school tomorrow. We'll have pizza tonight. I already got that. Okay?"

"Don't worry about it, Nonna Glo. I really don't need anything," Franklin said sincerely.

"Hey Gloria, can you come here?" It was Jerod. "You have to see this."

He was motioning to her, waving his hands excitedly.

She patted Sami's head, which was still resting on her arm, and squeezed Shad's hand one more time, then stood up and sighed. "It sounds like good news. I could use some of that right now," she said, taking off in the direction of Greta's room.

The whole orphanage had been woken when the police pounded on the door in the middle of the night, and every one of the children had stayed up to see what was happening. Because of this, most of them were still sleeping late into Sunday morning. Up until now, this had included Parker, who presently emerged from her bedroom, stretched, rubbed her eyes, and walked towards where her friends sat in the living room.

When the four children had arrived back last night, Parker had hugged each one of them, and her concern for them seemed genuine. She had cried when they told her about what they had gone through after she left them in the woods. "I am so sorry that I didn't stay to help you guys!" she had proclaimed over and over to them.

Now Parker plopped down on the shag carpet in front of the couch, facing them, knees bent upwards and held in place by her lanky arms, which wrapped around them. Her black hair, usually down to her shoulders, had hurriedly been rolled into a bun on the top of her head. Her eyes were lacking their familiar twinkle, and she looked as tired as the four of them felt.

In her sleepy condition, it took her more than a few seconds to realize that Rufus had returned and was there with them. When she finally did notice that he was sitting in front of her, she was a bit befuddled. "Rufus!" she exclaimed. "When did you get back from the hospital? Are you all right?"

"Not very long ago and not a big deal, you know?" He answered, puffing out his chest and using a tough voice. "Just a mere flesh wound, nothing too bad." He laughed loudly; a tired, almost crazy kind of laugh. The others only managed a smile.

But Rufus wasn't quite finished. "I guess I won't be blazing fast when I run anymore. I mean, like I usually am; at least for a while until my leg heals."

Parker sat unmoving, staring at Rufus blankly as if he was a complete fool, until she finally lost it, started cracking up, and fell backward on the shag rug, still laughing.

Franklin decided it was a good time to fish for a little information from Parker, so he asked her, "Hey Parker, what happened last night when you got back here?"

Just as Gloria had trusted Hank, Franklin also believed in Parker. He hoped it wasn't true that she could have somehow helped Hank find them last night.

"Well," Parker said, looking at the ceiling, focusing on nothing in particular, "I made sure Hank was here, in the house. After he did his rounds upstairs in the boys' rooms he was working on the sink in the kitchen, so I went in and talked to him. I wanted to get a feel for things, you know, see if he was still acting strange."

Sami chimed in, "What did you talk to him about?"

Parker's eyes settled on Sami's concerned face, she replied, "At first I just asked what was wrong with the sink, and he seemed to act pretty normal."

She looked at Franklin now. "Then he asked where you were, Franklin. He wanted me to tell him where you and Shad had gone, cause you weren't in your bedroom," Parker said.

"What did you tell him?" Shad asked. He leaned in a little closer to Parker, in anticipation of what she would say. She turned her gaze to the long strands of shag on the carpet, where her pointer finger had several of them wrapped around it.

After thinking for a moment, she finally said, "I... I told him you went on a bike ride. He pressured me to tell him where you went, and I said you went to Cast Maker Canyon. I thought he would never find you. You were over a mile away in the other direction from there, so I went to bed because I still felt sick. I had no idea there was anything to even warn you about. I promise you guys."

She finally lifted her head and faced all of them, her eyes were deep puddles as they went from Sami, to Shad, to Rufus, and stopped on Franklin. "I would never have told him where you were, Franklin. That would be like trying to kill you myself! You don't think I would do that, do you?"

If she was lying, she was really convincing, Franklin thought.

"No, Parker," Franklin looked at Rufus. "No, of course we know we can trust you. It's just so strange how Hank found us."

Shad was the one looking at the ground now. He wiped both his palms across his face and kept them there, covering up his eyes.

Parker scooted closer to the couch, so that she was looking directly up at him from the floor. "Hey, what's wrong Shad?"

In a muffled voice, he softly declared, "I am the biggest idiot in the world, that's all. I think I figured out how Hank found us." He took his hands away from his face. "Franklin, you can punch me right in the nose if you want. I deserve it."

"Whatever, Shad. C'mon, what happened?" Franklin pressed him.

With a 'here goes nothing' kind of sigh, Shad lifted his head and confessed. "When we were heading down the stairs last night, Jessy came out of his room crying, he said he had a nightmare. I walked him to his room and tucked him back in. He asked me where I was going with a backpack. I wasn't even thinking. I told him that I was going biking to Lake Birdsong. It seemed so innocent at the time. I never even thought about it again, until now."

Rufus slapped Shad's knee. "Man, that's something I would have done. Really stupid, Shad! No offense or anything."

Shad shook his head. "You're right, Rufus! So dumb of me! Hank must have talked to Jessy on his rounds, and Jessy told him about us. Parker, he was probably just asking you where we were to see what you would say, to see if you were suspicious of him at all, or if you would actually tell him the truth. I'm guessing he wanted to know if he needed to get rid of you later, too, after he dealt with the rest of us."

Shad's head went back down and his hands came up to support it again, this time going to his forehead, where he pulled at his bangs. "I am so sorry, Franklin. I really put us in danger with my stupidity."

Franklin reached over to pat his friend on the back. "It's not like you were trying to hurt us, Shad. You were just trying to comfort Jessy, and you slipped up. Anyone could do it."

Rufus reached out and punched Shad on the shoulder, a bit too hard. "You big butt head!" Shad turned to him in surprise but saw that Rufus had a toothy grin across his face.

"Ouch! That really hurt Rufus," Shad mumbled, rubbing his shoulder.

Franklin had not yet had time to tell about his experience following the Homingryll or the discovery of a possible door to the other Earth. He thought now might be a good time. "Hey guys," he said, interrupting Shad right before he punched Rufus back, "I found something I need to tell you about. I followed that little creature that came out of Hank's mouth. It flew all the way to a farm—"

"Little creature? What all did I miss?" Parker asked, interrupting him.

But at that moment they all turned as Greta's tiny, but lively voice, came from across the room. She was running towards them with her Supergirl cape waving behind her. "I'm looking for bad guys," she yelled. "Any of you seen a bad guy?"

Before they knew it, she had jumped onto the couch with them. Rolling over the first three of them, she stopped when she got to Franklin and sat up in his lap.

Her face was rosy, not feverish rosy, but healthy looking, and she said with delight, "Thank you, Franklin!" and then grabbed the back of his head, pulled it down to her, and kissed his cheek.

"Wow," said Franklin. "What are you thanking me for?"

"For making me better!" she answered, as if he should have known this fact.

"Greta, I didn't do anything, but I am happy you're feeling so much better!" he said, hugging her, wondering what could have caused this drastic change in her condition.

"Yes you did, silly," she smiled at him. "You grabbed my hand before I went back to sleep. I felt something tingle, like you had one of those practical joke, shocky-thingies in your hand, but it didn't hurt me. Then I woke up and I was better! My fever is gone now, and I can run around!"

Gloria came running into the room. "Greta, you need to stay in bed. We want you to keep resting now." She came over and picked Greta up and held her close. "I am so happy you're feeling well, sweetheart."

Gloria looked down at Franklin. "She swears it was you, Franklin. You made her better."

Franklin just smiled. He remembered now; the sensation that had passed through his hands into Greta's. Could it really be possible that he might have the ability to do something as remarkable as healing this girl? He thought about how he had been healed himself, two years ago from today. Whatever had healed his legs, whatever power of Light that had performed that wondrous miracle, may have gifted him with the same ability.

"Greta, go on back to your room now. Okay, sweetie? Hop in bed," Gloria instructed.

"Okay, Nonna Glo. Bye Franklin, Sami, Parker, Shad. Bye Rufus!" She ran halfway across the shag rug, then stopped and turned back. "Oh yeah, Rufus, I heard you tell me that you would play with me when I got better. You remember? When you thought I was sleeping?"

Rufus appeared confused at first, but then made a bad-guy face and held his hands up like monster claws before he broke into a goofy smile. Greta waved at them one last time, then flashed her own mischievous smile as she ran back towards her room.

Gloria stayed facing them. "The doctor is coming today to take some more tests," she said quietly to them. "But Jerod and I really think something incredible happened to her last night. I can't explain it, but she's just as spirited and energetic as she has ever been!"

Franklin looked over at Sami, who was already there to meet his gaze. Something had happened. Franklin was sure now, too.

He would bet his life that her cancer was gone.

CHAPTER THIRTY-FOUR
A SPITBALL & A SWIRLY

It was a marvelous, March morning. The air was crisp, but not cold, the birds had started their morning choruses, and for most kids, it was a time of year that meant three months of freedom was only a sprint-to-the-finish-line away. This fact, however, was nowhere near where Franklin's thoughts were as he got ready for school that morning. His mind was in one place, and that was the windmill. He wanted to get back to it as soon as he could.

Thinking about that cadaverous-like beast putting its skeletal hands on his sweet, loving mom made his blood boil, which, he noticed, caused a bit of a tingle behind his eyes. But he had to have some sort of a plan. He couldn't just be led right into a trap, either.

Telling his friends about how he had followed the mini, mind-controlling minion to the windmill and how it had flown right into the spinning blades and disappeared, had sparked their enthusiasm, as well as curiosity. They had all pledged to go with him to save his mom, but he knew that bringing them would be a mistake. It would make it too difficult to rely on any sort of cloak-and-dagger approach, and he was certain that stealth would be absolutely necessary to survive and succeed in that place.

On the bus that morning, kids were all doing their share of complaining. Spring Break had been good to them, and it was hard, for all but Shad, to return to early mornings and responsibilities again. Shad was very thankful to get back to the routine that school brought, along with the extensive school library that held all of those science-fiction books that needed reading.

Franklin sat next to Shad and Rufus, and Parker and Sami sat in the seat across the aisle from them. The bus driver had grunted hello to them as they stepped on the bus, but it was obvious that he was also disappointed to be back. Conversation was minimal on the ride there, as none of them wanted to discuss their thoughts on a crowded bus, and small talk just seemed out of the question.

For other kids, though, talking was all they could do. Franklin and his friends could hear the whispered questions and conjectures of others around them, children not from the orphanage, trying to figure out which orphans the psychotic man had tried to murder. No doubt, by the end of the day, everyone in the whole school would know it was them.

When they stepped off the bus, Franklin saw someone that made him cringe. It was Brad, the bully, with his buddies gathered around him. They were at the top of the stairs, right outside the school's glass entrance doors. Many other students were standing around, too, trying to get a look at some yellow sheets of paper posted on the exterior brick wall. Franklin remembered the principal announcing that the updated list of honor roll students would be posted when school started up again. Kids were pushing and shoving trying to get in close enough to read the small type, even kids like Brad, who Franklin knew had no chance of making the list. It was in this crowd, a few minutes later, that Franklin accidentally stepped on the bully's foot.

Brad was big, even for a seventh grader; taller than anyone else in the grade. He already had a voice that was five decibels below all the other twelve and thirteen-year-old boys and had noticeable red chin hairs that were growing in number every day. The bright, red and curly hair on his head assisted in making his eyes appear to be a demonic shade of orange, although they were actually light green.

On past occasions, Franklin had seen Brad flirt with Sami, and he knew the bully hated the fact that Sami paid no attention to any boy *but* Franklin. Having his foot stepped on didn't hurt Brad, but constantly being shown up by the blond-headed freak did. For this reason, he decided to shove Franklin as hard as he could down the concrete steps.

Franklin was completely caught off-guard and flew through the air down the three steps to the sidewalk below; the breath was knocked out of his lungs upon impact. Instead of getting up right away, he closed his eyes and lay back down. His body ached and it was easier to stay put for the moment. But, to his further dismay, a few seconds later, he felt a cold shadow fall upon him, and he opened his eyes to see Brad standing there, blocking the sun. As he looked straight up at the bully who had the blue sky behind him, Franklin was able to get a clear view of Brad's shine radiating out from him. It was a dark green glow, which he interpreted as the bully's strong insecurity in himself. Franklin knew that this insecurity, or self-doubt, had created a boy who sought to make those he was jealous of feel equally as bad about themselves as he did.

Brad knelt down, climbed onto Franklin, and pinned his arms to the ground with his knees, then sat on his chest. Franklin knew that struggling would be pretty futile, seeing that Brad weighed at least twenty pounds more than him.

"What are you doing, Brad?" he asked, not afraid to look right into Brad's shifty eyes.

"I'm doing to you what I've dreamed about doing since the year started; something that I should've done a while ago to put you in your place!" Brad sneered.

"You've been dreaming about doing this? C'mon, Brad. You gotta get a little bit more of a life if this is your big achievement for the year," Franklin quipped. He knew that Brad had a short tolerance for insults, but he really didn't care at the moment.

Franklin knew that right now would be a really bad time to use any of his powers. It probably wouldn't go over very well with others, and by now, a crowd had gathered around the two boys. Franklin saw that his friends were at the forefront of the congregation.

"No, freak, I've dreamed about doing this," Brad positioned his face right above Franklin's face and snorted up a big ball of phlegm. He started to let it leave his mouth and fall towards Franklin's face, then, as it was about to break free, he sucked it back up.

Shad and Parker made a move toward Brad, but two of Brad's over-sized buddies stepped in front of them. Rufus, still fairly immobile on his crutches, looked on helplessly.

"Get off of him, you creep!" Sami cried, as she squirmed her way through Brad's bodyguards and grabbed him by the arm. This only further provoked the bully, and he let the wad of saliva drip even lower this time before inhaling it back into his mouth.

Brad's face was red when he turned to Sami and snarled, "What do you see in this guy, Sami? He's a purple-eyed freak!" He yanked his arm from her and let the phlegm ball plunge down once again, but this time it went too far for him to be able to reverse its course. It landed splat on Franklin's nose and then dribbled down both sides of his face.

"Oops," Brad said mockingly, putting his hand up over his open mouth in jest. "Did I just do that? I guess I let it slip."

He stood up but continued to loom over Franklin as he spoke. "That's what I dreamed of doing, freak!"

Franklin was still pretty sore from his fall down the stairs, but it was nothing compared to the humiliation he felt at that moment. Sami knelt next to him and grabbed a tissue from her pocket. She gave it to Franklin and he wiped his face off, then she helped him stand up.

"You are an absolute jerk, Brad!" Sami yelled at him as he walked back up the stairs and through the front doors, his buddies still giving him high fives.

Brad looked over his shoulder. "Your loss, babe," then disappeared through the door.

The anger that burned inside of Franklin was not obvious to his friends, and he wanted to keep it that way. When the bell rang, although still filled with rage towards Brad, he was able to casually remark, "We better get to class. Thanks for helping me out, Sami, and the rest of you guys for trying."

"You need to teach that guy a lesson!" Parker said, making a fist and slamming it into her other hand's open palm.

Rufus added, "Yeah, I'd love to see him eat some of his own—"

"Rufus," Sami said, cutting him off, "that's disgusting!"

"What?" Rufus asked. "I was going to say 'words', eat some of his own words." He laughed. Franklin nodded in agreement but didn't say anything.

"Why didn't you just try out those new talents you have again? The telekinesis that you used on Hank? You could have easily gotten Brad off of you," Shad pointed out.

"Too many people watching," Franklin answered, "and I'm not even sure I could do it again, you know what I mean? Like I did with Hank's arrow."

Unfortunately, that was the truth. In the last twenty-four hours, ever since it had happened, Franklin had tried to remember everything he could about those few seconds, trying to pinpoint precisely how he had stopped that arrow in mid-air and made it shoot straight up into the sky. He could not, however, recall what he had done in the heat of that intense moment. Everything was a bit of a blur. And then controlling the arrow's path in the air once he had stopped it? Having it come back down precisely onto Hank's head? He had no clue how he had managed that, but he had an inkling that it was all through his subconscious thoughts. Meaning, he was controlling it without actually knowing he was controlling it.

Heck, he wasn't even sure how to activate the night vision that had allowed him to see in the dark kitchen two nights ago.

Abundant Lakes Middle School was for kids in grades five through nine, and it had around three hundred total students. Sami and Franklin were in the same homeroom class with Mrs. Dwight. She had a combined group of fifth and sixth graders, something the school was trying out. Rufus was further down the hall in Mr. Darby's class of only sixth graders, while Parker and Shad, both in fifth grade, were on the middle school's second level.

This was Franklin's second year in a row with Mrs. Dwight, and he still looked forward every morning to homeroom time with her. She always made her classroom a safe and equal environment for all students, no matter their social-status in the school. She was by far Franklin's favorite teacher, and he could tell that Mrs. Dwight had considerable regard for him as well. He suspected she had requested that he be in her class again, because in most cases, students were more than likely to be assigned a different homeroom teacher each year.

After his mom had disappeared in September of his fifth-grade year, Mrs. Dwight had expressed to him many times the sorrow she felt for him. At the same time, though, she encouraged him not to give up, that he still had a whole life in front of him, and only he had the ability to do something valuable with it. She had also assured him, in the past, that if he ever needed anything, she was there for him. Franklin knew she probably treated all of her students as kindly as she treated him; the best teachers have a way of making every student feel like their favorite.

"Good Morning, Franklin and Sami! Did you two have a fun Spring Break?" Mrs. Dwight asked, greeting them at the classroom door. Her pink shine, which radiated from her, was as bright as ever, Franklin noticed.

"It was very eventful, I guess you could say," Sami replied.

Franklin assumed that she had not heard about the events that had taken place yesterday. That was okay with him.

He added, "I learned a lot about myself, too, so that's a good thing."

This, he thought, *was certainly true. He had learned plenty about himself.*

"Oh, fantastic. It is so good to see you both again," Mrs. Dwight said, hugging each of them as they walked past her.

Franklin hugged her tightly back and then walked to his assigned desk. Sami's desk was on the opposite side of the room, and right as the last bell rang, they both took a seat. At the front of the classroom hung a smart board, a massive computer screen that most teachers at their school used now instead of whiteboards. Mrs. Dwight had always put a quote across it in the morning to help encourage her students throughout the day. But this one made Franklin drop the pencil he had just taken from his backpack.

It said: *Darkness cannot drive out darkness; only light can do that. Hate cannot drive out hate; only love can do that.* - M.L. King Jr.

He looked over at Sami across the room and pointed at the screen. She nodded her head; she had seen it, too. It was strange how perfectly it applied to Franklin's current situation, and he committed the great Reverend's wise words to memory.

"Okay, students, good morning and welcome back from Spring Break," Mrs. Dwight said. "It is so good to see all of your smiling faces again. Now, can anyone tell me what they think the quote on the board means?"

A fifth-grade girl name Brandy raised her hand in the corner. Mrs. Dwight pointed to her. "Yes, Brandy? What do you think it means?"

"I think it means the only way to treat people who try to hurt you is to be nice back to them," she answered.

Franklin put his hand in the air. "Yes, Franklin?" Mrs. Dwight said. "Do you have something to add?"

"Well, If someone has a dark nature, like born from Darkness, then treating them with more Darkness is only going to make them worse," Franklin paused. "You have to shine Light on them or show them kindness and love. That is the only way to deal with hate."

"Well done, Franklin. You too, Brandy. Martin Luther King Jr. knew that African Americans would never get what they wanted by being hateful and using violence against the ones that hated them. So, he led nonviolent marches and demonstrations to show that his people were serious about getting equal rights, but were not willing to hurt anyone. The white people who hated the African Americans were brought into the light and made known to the rest of the nation, as were the violent acts that they had committed. This was the start of the Civil Rights Movement and one of the early steps in helping Blacks receive equal treatment," Mrs. Dwight finished.

The phone on her desk rang. She picked it up and after a moment said, "Yes, I'll send him right there." She put the receiver back. "Franklin, dear, you are needed in the office," she announced.

Oh no! He thought. But asked, "Did they say why?"

He looked over at Sami who looked nervously back at him.

"No, I'm sorry. I have no idea why," Mrs. Dwight told him. Then she asked, "You're not in trouble are you?"

"I don't know…" Franklin looked bewildered. *Was it something to do with the Brad incident?* He wasn't sure.

Mrs. Dwight chuckled. "I'm kidding, Franklin dear! I can't imagine you doing anything to get yourself in trouble."

As Franklin ambled toward the door, he gave her a meager smile. "Yeah, well, sometimes I'm not so sure, Mrs. Dwight."

The office was back in the direction of the school's entrance. On the way, Franklin remembered that he hadn't taken the time to scrub his face off with actual soap since Brad had contaminated him with saliva, so he took a quick detour into the boy's room. After washing at the sink, he took a second to study himself in the mirror. His blonde hair was mussed up from the earlier encounter on the sidewalk. Besides his hair, scratches were also plentiful on his face from where hanging branches had caught him as he ran for his life from Hank. It also seemed that the freckles on his face had multiplied since he was in the sun every day last week.

Even so, he thought that wearing his nicest plaid, button-up shirt and clean jeans made him look like a normal boy, not an orphan. He quickly rebuked himself for thinking that way; of course orphans were normal! They just weren't always as well taken care of. In his case, though, he was very well cared for and loved. Gloria and his friends had made his life feel rich, but not quite complete. Not without his mom.

He moved his face closer to the mirror. His eyes, although only light purple in this dark and dingy bathroom, were definitely purple.

The toilet in the stall next to the sink flushed.

Maybe Brad and the others who had pointed this out were right; maybe he really was a freak. Who else had purple eyes? No one, that's who.

In the mirror's reflection, walking into view behind him, came Brad. He had a smirk on his face, and Franklin knew that something offensive was about to come out of his mouth.

"Hey, Freaklin. You ready to make another one of my dreams come true?" he asked, taunting Franklin. "Have you ever wondered what it would be like to have your head in the toilet as it was being flushed? Just like—?"

"Not really," Franklin interrupted him, "but I was wondering what sort of animal could have died in here to make a smell that awful, but when I saw you, everything made sense."

Behind him, Brad's face turned redder than his hair. He made both hands into fists and held them up for Franklin to see. "I should knock you out, you mutant," he said, "but there is a strict no violence rule at this school, so instead I'm going to give you a swirly…put your head in the toilet. Maybe it'll turn your eyes brown."

Brad sauntered up to Franklin, who had not yet made any move to escape. He grabbed Franklin's arms and held them behind his back, then started forcing him to walk over to the stall he had just left.

Voice impassive, Franklin announced, "Brad, I'm only going to tell you this once. Let me go, or you're going to be sorry."

A cackle erupted from Brad. "Sure, I will, Freaklin." He forced Franklin into the stall and leaned him down toward the open toilet. With one of his hands, he began to push the back of Franklin's head closer, while the other hand continued to restrain his arms.

Meanwhile, Franklin was concentrating intently, trying to recall how to summon his power of telekinesis.

With his head being forced towards the toilet, everything in his field of vision was upside down and on the floor…like

Brad's feet. He focused on those two abnormally long feet with every bit of mind-power he could muster together.

Dirty laces. Scraped leather. Focus! Fading Nike emblem. Threads hanging.

He felt a tickle start behind his eyes.

The cesspool of water was only inches away from the top of Franklin's head, and Brad let go of him with one hand momentarily while he reached for the lever to flush the toilet.

Finally, Franklin knew his eyes were about to do something. The bully's obnoxious laughing had been constant but stopped suddenly as his feet slipped backward, and he lost his grip on Franklin's arms. He continued skating backward, until all at once both his feet left the ground and lifted towards the ceiling, flipping Brad upside down as they went.

"What the heck is happening?" A panicked look came across Brad's face, and his eyes went wide. "What's going on? Franklin, help me!" he shouted.

In only a few seconds, Franklin had Brad turned entirely upside down, suspended in front of him. They were face to face, as they had been earlier on the sidewalk, only now Franklin had the advantage.

"Are you doing this to me? How are you doing it? Please stop, Franklin! What are you doing?" Brad blubbered, on the verge of tears.

Franklin looked at Brad, then looked at the toilet, and slowly his captive began to float over to the ceramic bowl. Then, he stopped him so that he hovered directly above the rusty toilet water.

"Hey Brad, I gave you fair warning. I told you that you'd be sorry. Now when we are done here, I expect that you will leave me alone and never bother me or even speak to me again. Do you understand?"

Brad's face was starting to turn as purple as Franklin's eyes, much of his body's blood had found its way down to his head, and blacking out seemed to be inevitable if he was not put back on his feet soon. "Let me down, Franklin. I won't bother you anymore!" he cried out.

"Okay, whatever you want," Franklin replied, not hiding his broad smile.

Slowly, he let Brad down. Straight down, head first into the murky water of the toilet. Brad's pathetic pleas only added to Franklin's delight. When all of his hair was immersed and the waterline came to his eyebrows, Franklin reached out and flushed the toilet. The water swirled around and around, and Brad's hair swirled with it, twisting his red strands of hair into an upside-down, self-serve ice cream cone.

"Oops! Did I do that? I guess I let it slip!" Franklin said, intentionally mocking Brad.

In between pitiful sobs, Brad managed to squeak out some desperate questions. "What are you? How are you doing this?"

Franklin slowly brought Brad up out of the water, then turned him upright, while still in the air, and finally lowered him to the ground. Water dripped from his coiled and swiveled hair, soaking his clothes and the floor around him.

Franklin let more than a little laugh escape. "Look at your hair! I guess I know now why they call it a swirly," he said.

The bully, mouth agape in fear, still managed to look perplexed as he pushed his way past Franklin, out of the stall, then sprinted past the sink and kicked open the door. Without once looking back, he took off down the hallway to his homeroom class, running his fingers through the squirrel nest on top of his head as he went.

Franklin heard the hollow wooden door smash into the wall outside, then a few moments later, close gently with only a click, as it was caught by its spring hinges.

He couldn't help but laugh out loud.

CHAPTER THIRTY-FIVE
(UN)FAMILIAR FACES &
(UN)PLEASANT FACTS

The rest of the way to the office, Franklin had one overpowering thought. And that was how good it had felt to do that to Brad. In fact, not good, it was actually a fantastic feeling seeing Brad get what was coming to him. The look on his face, while he was hanging upside down, had been priceless. Franklin thought that if he had a camera handy and could have taken a picture, he would have hung it in his locker to cheer him up on a rainy day. He still had a broad grin on his face when he stepped through the office doors.

The administrative assistant, Ms. Dewey, sat in a desk facing him as he walked in. "I'm glad you have found something so funny this early in the morning. I try not to laugh before noon, myself," she said dully, without changing the frown on her face.

Trying to be friendly, Franklin faked a chuckle and said, "Hi, Ms. Dewey. How's it going today?"

He had always imagined Ms. Dewey to be better suited as a grumpy librarian, not someone who was supposed to be the face of the school, for anyone coming to visit. With her glasses, short curly gray hair, permanent grimace, and most importantly, her very low tolerance for almost everything, she would do much better giving people threatening looks so that they returned their library books on time. Some might say she was cantankerous.

"Hello, Franklin. I'm doing no better than I usually am on any working Monday. Mondays are awful. You have some visitors. In the waiting area."

"Visitors?" He was relieved, thankful that it wasn't anything about his scuffle with Brad before school. He didn't need to bring that episode back into the light *or* the one he just had in the bathroom. "Do you know who it is?" he asked.

"No, Franklin. I don't make it my business to try to remember all of your acquaintances. And please, tell them that from now on the best time to visit you is during lunch hour, not right when the day is getting underway," she said crossly.

"Okay, I will. Thanks, Ms. Dewey," Franklin replied. This had actually been one of his more pleasant conversations with her.

"Down that way," she mumbled, pointing to the adjoining hall inside the office.

He walked slowly towards the end of the room, which turned a corner and eventually opened up into the waiting area. Trying to think of who could possibly be here to see him was giving him a headache; he had absolutely no idea. Unless it was Gloria. Or could it be the police? Asking him more questions? He hoped not.

Turning the corner, he could see the rows of chairs ahead where visitors were asked to wait. The only people sitting down there currently was an older couple. Probably someone's grandparents, Franklin guessed. He was about to turn back and go ask Ms. Dewey if whoever was looking for him might have left, when he heard his name being called. "Franklin, right here. It's us that came to see you."

It was a soft, female voice. The elderly lady was looking at him, her face bright. "My name is Mary Lighten, and this is my husband, Charles. It is so nice to finally see you again."

Charles, he thought. *Charles?* Why was that name familiar to him? His brain decided not to respond to this question just yet.

Although it was spring, they both wore colorful green and red sweaters that might have been bought in the early 1990s. The old man stood up and wiggled his glasses closer to his eyes. He wore checkered green pants that were pulled up way too far, and Franklin could see most of his blue and red socks beneath them. Leather sandals finished his outfit. The elderly lady also got up and took a step towards Franklin. He noticed that her green skirt looked like it was handspun from wool and might have come straight from a colonial museum. She also wore glasses, and short silver curls covered her head. The old man's head was partially covered by grey hair, but only on the sides and the back. Both of their skin had the typical creases and crinkles of someone their age.

But even from ten feet away, he could see that they had eyes that were both penetrating and gentle at the same time, and somehow they were familiar to him. He also had a peculiar feeling that they knew all about him as well. Heck, somehow they already knew his name. And the shine emanating out from each was glorious. Both had beautiful colors of yellow, blue, orange, and outlining the glow was a brilliant purple.

"Hi. Ummmm, I don't think we've ever met, actually," Franklin said, racking his brain to try to remember when he might have come across this pair before. Could they be his long-lost grandparents that lived in Europe somewhere? He doubted it. They had no reason to come see him; at least they never had before.

"Oh, yes Franklin, we met you on the day you were born, twelve years ago." Mary's kind smile, as she spoke, set Franklin at ease. "Of course you wouldn't remember, but we both held and cuddled you."

"Really?" Franklin asked, becoming energized. "Then you must have met my mom?"

Speaking with people who knew his mom was rare, and it was always special to hear any stories that others had about her. His own memories of her had been strong but were starting to fade, and this upset him.

He needed to find her soon.

"We did," Charles finally spoke. "We talked with Angel. She is an incredible, loving woman and mother, and we know how much you miss her."

Franklin just about dropped to the floor. "Miss her? How did you... Do you know where my mom is? If you do, you need to tell me!" he demanded.

"Franklin, we have an idea, like you do, where she is," Charles replied. Then he paused to think, considering where to take the conversation from here.

After a while, he continued. "We know about you. We know about your life. We know about the poverty you and Angel lived in for years. We know about the car accident, the years of being a paraplegic and having to use a wheelchair, and the miracle that took place two years ago."

Franklin was unsure how to respond, but before he could, around the corner came Ms. Dewey, looking like someone had just returned a book that was a month overdue. She spoke sternly, "Franklin, your grandparents, or whoever you two are, need to finish up with your get-together here. You need to get back to class, and they need to leave and find another time to talk to you."

When she finished chastising them, an awkward silence fell over the room. Franklin was unsure if he should say something or not...but then a faint melody started to dance around them, waltzing through the air, an enchanting lullaby. The humming triggered a hazy memory somewhere in his subconscious. Why was this tune familiar to him?

After suspiciously eyeing all of them, Ms. Dewey discovered that the sound was coming from the motionless mouth of Mary, who stared off into the distance.

Then, with her face wrinkled and her eyebrows raised in disapproval, Ms. Dewey informed Mary, "Humming is not allowed in the —" but she stopped short.

Something resembling a smile took form on her face. Because of the lack of using this expression in the past, her cheeks had not been adequately stretched out, so the grin was not allowed to wander too far in either direction.

She pointed to a door near them, still 'smiling', and said cordially, "If you need more privacy, you three are welcome to go outside and take a walk around Sunfish Lake, behind the school." Her voice was sweeter than syrup. "Franklin, just try to be back before next rotation, in about 45 minutes." She turned and retreated towards her desk. Franklin, Charles, and Mary could hear her mumbling to herself as she walked. "... Lovely tune... such a beautiful song."

Charles turned on his tiptoes and declared, "It's certainly a majestic day!" He headed towards the door and asked, "Shall we go for a walk?"

Franklin and Mary followed him.

Sunfish Lake was only a stone's throw from school, or maybe a few throws, depending on how strong your arm was. They walked through the lawn of the schoolyard, then into the longer weeds of the neighboring field. From there, Franklin led them to the worn pathway of trampled grass that kids used as a shortcut to access the lake.

Charles waited until they had been outside for only half a minute before he said, "Franklin, we know about what happened with Hank, and we're very concerned for your state of mind."

Franklin's first instinct was to ask how they could possibly know all of that, but he had learned in the five minutes since meeting them that the Lightens weren't normal people. So, instead, he just replied, "Yeah, it's been hard for me to stop thinking about what happened, but I'm all right."

"Are you?" Charles put his hand on Franklin's shoulder. "You killed an innocent man."

At this remark, Franklin could feel the blood rush to his face. The tone in his voice was one of frustration more than anger, as he said, "How can you say that? He was going to kill all of us!"

But Franklin knew Charles was right. Hank *had* been innocent.

Charles continued, "You should not have deliberately taken Hank's life. His mind may have been hijacked, but inside he loved you and was desperately trying to stop himself…but the creature that controlled him had too tight of a grasp on his brain's frontal lobe, where emotions and most thoughts are managed."

"What could I have done though? He was going to kill me. He had already shot Rufus!" Franklin argued, recalling Hank's demented laugh and murderous eyes. Not to mention that steel-toe boot, which had held his face down in the mud until he had passed out.

This time Mary answered him, "Yes, that is true. Had you not stopped Hank, the most likely outcome was that you and all of your friends would be dead, as would Gloria and a handful of other kids at your orphanage."

Still unwilling to admit his fault, Franklin demanded, "Then what could I —" Mary, however, was not done.

"You had to stop him. Yes, Franklin, no doubt," she was stern now, but with a tender tone, "but you could have figured out a way to do it without killing him."

"But that creature inside him—" Franklin protested.

"Would have eventually given up and left him alone," Mary said, finishing his sentence.

Franklin's thoughts again drifted back to two nights ago. He remembered the anger he felt when he took control of the arrow and sent it plummeting down into Hank's head. True, he didn't know how he had been controlling it, but in his subconscious, the fury he felt must have taken over. He also remembered the feelings he had afterward, the feeling of pride for what he had done and the strange sense of uninvited jubilation which came surging through him like a river gone wild; jubilation over killing Hank. He hadn't understood why he had those emotions; Hank had been his friend.

Thinking out loud, he finally asked, "What in the *HECK* is wrong with me, then?"

Charles rubbed his chin, scratching at beard stubble that wasn't really there, and said, "We're here to help you sort that out, Franklin. You're an incredibly special boy, but you need to be careful to keep those gifts, which make you so special, from turning you into something else. Something you don't want to become. As you have found out, you also need to be very careful of the male StyJeen that calls himself Nefari. He will not stop pursuing you until he has what he needs."

"My eyes, you mean?" Franklin asked.

"Yes, your eyes, the source of your strength," Mary replied.

The path through the grass brought them to a small wooded area and then came to an abrupt dead end at the shore of Sunfish Lake. Here, the path turned into rocks and dirt and branched off in either direction around the small lake; Franklin gestured for them to take the trail to the right.

With enough room on the path for the three of them to walk side-by-side, Franklin took his place in the middle. He had so many questions for them! He started by asking, "How did you know all those things about me? About my mom?"

He looked from one to the other, and when they didn't respond right away, he asked, "What were you doing at the hospital when I was born?"

Charles looked mindfully at Franklin for a few seconds, then turned his eyes back to the bumpy trail ahead of them and spoke. "Let me answer that by telling you something else first, Franklin."

Mary looked across at Charles and nodded her head in approval. He continued, "Mary and I are not humans," he said with some pause. "We only appear to be human. The Suveran has given us the ability to take several different forms; this is our preferred form to take, and the one we most often appear in."

Franklin stopped in the middle of the path, and his companions walked only a few more feet before stopping, too. This revelation should have surprised Franklin more than it did, but he knew of another creature that could also take on human form. Nefari, however, without a face, wasn't nearly as convincing as these two.

"Okay, I can believe that," he said, "but *what* are you then? If you aren't human, I mean."

"We are the Luminos, the Beings of Light," Charles answered.

The sun shone brightly on most of the lake and brought a fine shimmer to its rippled surface. But where the trio was walking beneath the canopy of trees, it was shady, and the wind gave Franklin goosebumps. High above them, branches of maple and oak trees were being entertained by the breeze, sounding their playful rustle to any creature close enough to hear. Mary glanced up, but it was with concern, not wonder, that she did so.

Charles touched her shoulder. "It's okay, Mary. It's only the wind."

She smiled at him. "Oh, you're probably right…only the wind."

He turned back to Franklin, who also had his head cocked upwards to peer at the noisy trees. The old man thought carefully about his next words. "Franklin, it was me who visited you on your tenth birthday while you were asleep. I healed your legs and gave you many of the gifts which you have been using. These are gifts from The Suveran, God of Third Earth."

This got Franklin's full attention. Stunned, he asked, "And are you the one who unlatched my car seat and opened the door so that I could fall out?" He looked both of them in the eyes, one at a time, trying to gather information from those oceans of knowledge that stared back at him.

Not waiting for an answer he already knew, he asked the next one. "Did you do it because you thought the tree branch would have killed me?"

Several feet from shore, a fish jumped, sucking in a mayfly that was skimming just above the water's surface. Again, Mary was startled by this simple sound from nature, and Franklin wondered what it was that caused her to be on edge like this.

Her kind voice answered his last question, "Yes, Franklin, I was the one who helped you that day." Her hands reached out and grabbed both of his, and the warmth that came from her touch helped to settle his racing thoughts.

"My mom never mentioned seeing you, though," he replied.

"No, she wouldn't have been able to see me, sweetheart."

"Oh," was all he said, figuring now wasn't the right time to try to understand this particular mystery.

Mary continued, "The Suveran gave us the assignment of protecting you, and so that's what I did. We can't see the future, The Suveran does not allow it, but we are able to see the most likely outcomes in a situation, and I just knew that branch was probably going to end up right where your tiny body sat."

Holding back tears, she said, "I'm so sorry for what happened… for crippling you. You were such an innocent boy."

Franklin leaned towards Mary and pulled her in with a tight hug, and she gladly returned the embrace. When he finally let her go, he said, "Mary, thank you for saving my life that day. Being in a wheelchair for eight years wasn't fun, and sometimes it was downright awful, but it made me who I am. It made me strong."

He turned to Charles and hugged him just as hard, then said, "And thank you, Charles, for healing me that night, for letting me walk again."

The affection they showed towards him right at that moment, the expression on their faces, was what Franklin had always imagined loving grandparents would be like. It was a good feeling.

He started down the trail again, and Mary and Charles walked with him. As Mary ambled along next to him, Franklin watched out of the corner of his eye as his new friend, in the guise of an elderly woman, searched the shadows in the forest. Was she worried about Nefari coming after them?

The path on this side of the lake was muddy. Having been hidden from the sun's rays, it had not yet had the chance to dry out from the early morning rainfall. To avoid the soggy spots, they had to detour through the taller grass beside the path. Franklin kept quiet for a minute, processing his thoughts. He watched the motion of his feet as he walked and absent-mindedly kicked at a stick, only to find out the hard way that it wasn't a stick, but a solid root that almost broke his toe.

Grabbing his foot in pain and hopping on one leg, he asked, "Why me? What's so special about me that you went to all that trouble to see me on the day I was born? Why was that faceless woman trying to get to me when I was two years old? Why is this nut Nefari trying to kill me now? Why did you heal my legs and give me these eyes with such extraordinary powers?" He took a breath, thought about asking something else, then decided to hear the answers to these vital questions first.

For the next fifteen steps they took down the lakeshore path, no one said a word. Then Mary spoke, slowly, so that the delicate information she was conveying to him would have time to sink in. "Franklin, you are not like other people, either."

"Am I like you? A Luminos?" he asked, somewhat hopefully.

"No, Franklin. Part of you is human, from your mother, but part of you is like your father…" Mary paused, "like your father who is from a place called Dark Earth."

"Dark Earth?!" cried out Franklin. He had spoken louder than he intended to. A bit quieter this time, he asked, "You mean that horrible place I went on my bike, where everything was dead? Isn't that where Nefari lives?"

He stopped again, this time walking over to the shore, stomping directly through the mud without any attempt to step around it. This was not the answer he was looking for, and it was too far beyond belief for him to accept.

Sunfish Lake had only one small beach with actual sand, and that was on the opposite shore from where the three currently stood. The rest of the lakefront did not boast sandy beaches, but instead, the shoreline was made up of millions of small pebbles and some larger stones. Franklin scanned the stretch in front of him, where water gently lapped up to the land, and seeing what he wanted, reached down and picked up a few of the flatter rocks. Looking back at his grey-haired friends, he again noticed Mary acting strange, this time watching the surface of the water out in front of where he stood. But when she noticed his stare, her eyes softened, and her face lost its nervous edge.

Franklin said, "My father died a few months before I was born. My mom wasn't lying to me. She wouldn't." He pitched the stone, side-armed, and it sailed into the lake. They all watched as it skipped once, then dove down into the water. "So what do you mean my father is from Dark Earth?"

He skipped the second stone; this one took three jumps off the surface before it nosedived down.

"I know this is difficult to hear, Franklin, but your father was not human," Mary explained. "He was, and still is, a being from Dark Earth. The inhabitants there consider him their god. His name is Bramfasa."

Franklin looked wide-eyed at both of them for a brief moment, his blonde hair blowing back across his face, then he started laughing, chuckling, snorting, chortling; trying to keep himself under control at first, but then, after a few seconds, he no longer held back, his laughter became loud and obnoxious. Charles and Mary waited patiently for him to finish his outburst. He finally stopped to say, "You expect me to believe that? That's the craziest thing I've ever heard in my life!"

"What we're telling you sounds absurd," Charles acknowledged. "I get it, but think of all the absurd, unbelievable things that have happened to you in the last two years! You have been pursued by a man without a face. To anyone else, that would sound ridiculous. We just told you that the two of us weren't human, and that didn't even make you flinch."

Charles came over to the shore and put his arm around Franklin's shoulders. "Listen, Franklin. You're not like your father. You were supposed to be, but you're not. And we want to keep it that way."

He realized his new friend was right about the preposterous, outlandish events that had happened to him in the last two years. He had no reason not to trust what these two were telling him. But the son of a Dark Earth god? It couldn't get much worse than that. Could it?

"Franklin." Mary approached him from the other side, she grabbed his hand and held it in her small, wrinkled fingers and said, "There is one other thing we need to tell you."

Seeing the confusion and pain already in Franklin's face caused Mary to struggle with her words," A woman… a woman…her name was Marigold. She was at the hospital the same night as your mother, to have her baby, too. She… Marigold had been seeing a man, dating him, named 'Bram', that's what he called himself, what he told people his name was…but it was short for Bramfasa. He had disguised himself as a human. She became pregnant and eventually ended up giving birth to a boy that night at the hospital."

Franklin's brain started swimming circles in his skull. The pieces of the puzzle were starting to fit together, and he didn't like the picture they were forming at all. He thought about the photograph of the baby his mom held, how there was no birthmark, and then the photo that suddenly showed up of a woman holding an infant *with* a birthmark. Deep down, he had already known…those pictures could only mean one thing.

Then he recalled who's name was on the photograph. How had he had forgotten?

"It was you!" he exclaimed, looking at the old man. "You sent the picture of her, didn't you? I remember now, it said 'From Charles, To Angel'. It was a picture of this Marigold woman you're talking about, right? She was holding *me,* wasn't she?"

"It was time your mother figured out the truth as well," he said. "That's why I sent it."

How could it be true that Angel was not his real mother? Tears welled in Franklin's eyes, overflowed, and streamed down his face. Mary dug into her handbag and pulled out a handkerchief, which she used to wipe his wet cheeks.

Taking the cloth from her, he dabbed the corner of his eyes, and with a voice filled with ever-increasing desperation, he asked, "Why? Why did my mom take me from that other woman? Why would she take me if I wasn't hers?"

In the precise, yet comforting voice, that Franklin had already grown to appreciate, Charles replied to him, "Marigold was going to illegally adopt you to a group of very corrupt people. These people would have then resold you to the highest bidder. Franklin, you could have ended up a slave or worse. Marigold, when she was younger, had once been a good person, but she let Darkness take over her life. Bramfasa made sure of that."

Mary reached her other arm around Franklin and hugged him, pulling him close to her. Franklin put his head on her shoulder, sobbing quietly. As the colorful, wool sweater soaked up his salty tears, he thought about how strange it was; he had just met this remarkable couple only thirty minutes ago, but he felt like he had always known them.

Franklin lifted his head and said, "I don't understand, Mary. How did I end up with Angel, then? How did I go home with her? What happened to the baby that I saw her holding in the picture? Her real son?"

The real Franklin Hobbs, he thought.

Closing his eyes, Franklin tried to picture his mom, her beautiful, reassuring smile... she was, and would always be, his mom.

Then another obvious truth struck him. "Is that why you two were there in the hospital?" He looked at Charles, then Mary. "Did you switch me with the other baby?"

Charles looked down. If there was a way he could have spared Franklin from this pain, he would have happily tried, but the boy had to know what really happened. He answered, "Angel's baby had a chronic heart problem, Franklin. The Suveran had told us the baby was born sick, so we knew, even before the doctors did. When we had the two babies alone in the hospital nursery, we switched you with him. We gave Angel to you, and we kept you from a life of misery and a future in Dark Earth."

He looked up, directly into Franklin's eyes. "We gave you to Angel and kept her from the pain of having to deal with her own beloved baby's death." Charles stopped talking. He waited to see Franklin's reaction, hoping with all of his heart that the boy understood.

For more than a minute there was silence, silence that carried no awkwardness along with it. Franklin again used the handkerchief to wipe away the remaining streaks of tears on his face, and when he finally spoke, he said with conviction, "This doesn't change anything. Angel is my real mom, as far as I will ever be concerned. Thank you, Charles… Mary. Thank you both so much for what you did. When you gave me to Angel, you saved my life."

Above, a gull cried out to its comrades, relaying whatever messages scavengers of the sky need to communicate with one another. The sharp, sudden squawking caused Mary to jump ever so slightly. But Franklin noticed it. She was still agitated about something.

"We were only following The Suveran's plan for you," she said, but her eyes told Franklin how much she truly cared for him. "He saw a great amount of potential in what you could become."

He scrunched his face into a puzzled grimace. "Really? Even with my father being who he is?"

"Your father chose to be the evil that he is, Franklin. He chose a long, long time ago. We all have a choice. You had a choice, too, and Angel helped you choose what's right by loving you and showing you the power of kindness," Charles explained.

Kindness. Franklin felt a pang of guilt sweep through his conscience just then, thinking of what he had done, not only to Hank, but to Brad as well. A lump of remorse built up in his throat. How absolutely *unkind* he had been to the bully! Right after he had explained to his whole class what he thought Martin Luther King Jr. meant when he said that Darkness cannot drive out Darkness, he had gone and taken revenge on Brad.

Then he thought about Hank again. Dead. His lifeless stare peering into Franklin's soul. And somehow, in some way, he had enjoyed it. He did not want to become like Bramfasa, but he knew there was a part of him that could easily be persuaded into continuing to take this budding anger of his out on others.

Again, he looked at Mary; she was really starting to make him nervous the way her eyes kept scanning the area.

Finally, deciding that he had to know what all this trepidation was about, he asked, "Hey guys, is there something that you're worried about right now? You know that Nefari can't come into the light. And it is pretty sunny out today."

Charles shook his head. "You're a perceptive lad, aren't you? No, Nefari is only one breed of the dangerous inhabitants from Dark Earth," he said, "of which there are many. There is one particular group of creatures that Bramfasa has assigned to find Mary and me, to either gather or kill us if they can. This breed is not affected by light, like the StyJeen that has been hunting you. We have found, though, that these creatures, which pursue us, only reveal themselves where they will not be seen by humans. So never in public spaces. But, when we go off on our own, like we are now, it is important that we are ever-watchful. Always vigilant."

"Is that what you keep looking for, Mary?" Franklin turned to her and asked.

"Franklin," Mary said, "they always seek us... once we were taken as prisoners to Dark Earth. We were tortured in extreme ways by Bramfasa. It happened hundreds of human years ago. We managed to escape...."

Her voice trailed off. The memories were visibly disturbing to her. She recovered quickly. "That said, we have been out here in the seclusion of the woods far too long. Bramfasa has undoubtedly tracked us by now... and not just us. You, too."

"Don't you have the ability to stop this thing that pursues you? Don't you have powers, like the ones you gave me? Powers that they should be afraid of, too?" Franklin asked.

Mary sighed. "Yes, but we are never guaranteed to win any of these battles here on Mortal Earth, nor are they. And these creatures are big, if there's more than one, they are very difficult to fend off."

"Could they kill you?"

Mary's gaze met the sullen eyes of Charles, and her own expression became melancholy as well, expressing the sorrow it would cause either of them to lose the other. She said, "They could, Franklin. Being immortal, as we are, only means we won't die naturally of age or disease, but we can still feel pain, and our present lives can be ended by the same things that could kill any human."

"Why doesn't The Suveran intervene and help you out?" Franklin asked, wondering what the fearless leader of Third Earth does while his Luminos are out here being stalked and tortured.

Charles thought for a moment. "Franklin, if every time one of us, a human or a Luminos, was in trouble and The Suveran stepped in to save us and win our battle for us, we wouldn't really be living; there would be nothing on the line, nothing to risk. Accomplishments and rewards would be meaningless. Bravery and valor would cease to exist. Anyone could do anything they wanted, without cause to worry."

He paused to study Franklin, and when he was satisfied that the boy was listening, he finished, "No one would need to make a tough decision to do the right thing, the good thing, because there would never be any prospect of danger, anything to fear. Does that make sense?"

"I guess," Franklin replied, shrugging. *But not really*, he thought.

Not too far off shore, about six feet above the water, a group of brown and white seagulls had begun flocking together. They had answered the earlier cry of their lone friend, and now at least thirty birds hovered above a small area of the lake, which appeared darker than the surrounding water. The seagulls took turns swooping down, letting their yellow feet graze the water, before they fluttered, like a kite given more string, back to the flock. In their tiny birdbrains, the darkness in the water somehow meant food.

Franklin figured it was probably a sizable school of fish that the gulls were following. In the past, he had seen dark spots in the water which turned out to be a thousand or more minnows swimming within flipper distance of each other. But those schools of fish he had seen were never the size of the shadowy murkiness that the gulls were currently fascinated by.

"Strange," Franklin uttered under his breath.

Charles stared earnestly at Franklin, who again felt no awkwardness, but as if he had known this kindhearted man forever. He said, "Franklin, we are aware of your intentions to attempt a rescue mission, and we want to help you get your mom back, but…we can't go with you." He shook his head. "We are not able to enter Dark Earth ourselves, not again. But we won't leave you unprotected. We are going to send you help, a different type of Luminos that will travel with you, if you let her. She will be an extension of your eyes and ears, helping you however she can. Her name is Nellie, and she will remain your protector until you no longer need her."

Protector? Franklin liked the idea.

He replied, "Okay, but how will I know who she is?"

His question went unanswered; a splash came from the lake that gave him the impression something like a meteorite had just crashed into the water. Franklin turned to look. Not something going into the lake, but something coming *out* from the lake. From the darkened water, which the gulls had found so curious, emerged an immense arm, coated with dull, metal armor. Lake weeds were knotted and tangled around it, hanging from it, and it reminded Franklin of the swamp monster that had once terrified him in a *Scooby Doo* episode. The hysterical cries of terror, which came from the birds, echoed out from the lake and must have sounded like the screams of humans to any ear within hearing distance.

Quick as any frog's tongue snatching a fly, the alloy-clad arm burst upwards into the midst of the gulls, grasped three or four birds in its large fist, and pulled them back down into the murky depths. Thousands of bristling bubbles, left in its wake, blanketed the water's surface. In the next moment, the bird-eating beast surfaced closer to shore and stood to its full, colossal height.

It stared hatefully at its audience on land.

CHAPTER THIRTY-SIX
A CLASH & A CALAMITY

"What is that thing?" Franklin asked, turning frantically towards Charles and Mary.

"That's a Groken. A troll from Dark Earth; the beast we were telling you about," Charles said, with only a bit more urgency than his voice usually contained. Then he added, "There must be a Gateway at the bottom of the lake that it came through."

He grabbed Mary's hand. "We need to leave, now." His tone now held the dire quality that was to be expected.

But Franklin, before being whisked away by Mary, who in turn had grabbed his hand, was able to take in a glimpse of the horror this creature cast. As the Groken stood in the lake shallows, only its lower legs and feet remained hidden by the water. Guessing at the depth of the lake where it stood, Franklin figured that the monster was over seven feet in height, its shoulders were broad and upper legs swelling with muscle. Its torso, along with both arms, were covered in an armor of simple fashion, but which looked to be a very durable metal. Dents and stains marked the chest plate where the Groken had taken blows from opponents in the past.

No armored helmet concealed it above the shoulders, and he could see that its head, a grotesque display, was too small for its hefty body.

Whatever brain could fit into that tiny head, Franklin thought, *probably doesn't provide him with many keen insights.*

Vile little eyes looked out between bushy eyebrows and wrinkles of ancient skin. Its lips, which curved into a frown, still had feathers clinging to them from its recent snack. The largest feature on its face was a long, sagging nose that drooped almost as far down as its top lip, which stuck up to meet it. In one of its hands was a sword, possibly iron, that it dragged behind it, slicing through the panicked water.

Waves were sent cascading in all directions as the Groken began its clumsy trudge to shore. It lifted its sword high and swung it in circles, cutting the air and shouting in a dull-witted voice, "Luminos! We found you!" It smashed the sword down into the water.

One seagull, lacking almost as much intelligence as the approaching troll, had remained close by, still hoping for a free meal. Instead, however, it was hacked into two congruent pieces as it hovered in mid-air.

Finally, breaking the stupor that had descended on him, Franklin heard Mary's voice yell out, "C'mon, let's go!" as she pulled him toward the forest. The scampering trio plowed through young trees and low bushes, running as fast as they could.

"What did he mean *we* found you?" Franklin hollered so that Mary could hear him over the loud fracas they were creating. He received no answer, as she was focused on mimicking the quick movements of Charles, who dodged and danced around nearly impassable obstacles in their path.

A tall oak tree came crashing down next to them, the topmost part of its trunk landing only feet away and creating a mess of branches and leaves on the forest floor. Emerging through the web of green foliage created by two adjacent oaks, appeared a second Groken. This one, rather than carrying a sword, swung an iron-spiked ball around the circumference of its head. In Franklin's vivid, but odd imagination, he was struck with the impression of one small planet orbiting an even smaller planet.

He had seen these types of weapons in movies about the Middle Ages before and recognized it as a type of mace. The metallic sphere was as large as an average basketball, and it was attached with a crudely made chain to a white, angular handle that the beast clasped. The handle itself looked like it might be the leg bone of some unfortunate creature. Kudos to this ugly thug for finding a creative and practical way to use the remains of a meal.

The troll swung his mace and it exploded into a large maple tree, causing it to come crashing down mere feet behind Franklin. Up ahead, where the forest ended and the grassy expanse of the schoolyard began, Charles was frantically motioning them to hurry.

The mace-wielding Groken showed surprising speed as it pursued them, and his bird-eating partner was not far behind. When Mary and Franklin caught up to Charles, he reached out and put his hands on Mary's arms, held them there firmly, and calmly said, "Go, Mary. Protect Franklin. Take him back to the school."

Franklin was not able to show the same steadfast composure as Charles when he shrieked, "No way! I want to help you fight!"

Mary took both his hands and tried to coax him to come with her, but he would not budge. The first Groken appeared around the bend, coming fast. Because the iron ball was kept in constant circular motion as he advanced, several more trees came smashing down, falling towards them and sending fragments of tree limbs hurling at them. Before Franklin knew what was happening, he had been lifted into the air and was moving towards the direction of the school. Mary was five steps ahead of him and running. Both her and Charles, like Franklin, possessed telekinetic abilities, and he was discovering now what it was like to be on the 'receiving' end of this unique talent.

He looked like a stage mime pretending to be confined in an invisible box as his arms and legs flailed in the air, without any effect. He cried out, imploring his captor, "Mary, please let me down! I can help Charles! Please, you have to let me help him!"

Looking back towards the forest, he saw one of the Groken advance upon Charles, who stood still, waiting. Then, in front of the old man, a fallen tree danced to life and he propelled it through the air, sending it crashing down onto the monster's back, momentarily knocking it off its feet. The other Groken came storming down the wooded path, approached Charles and swung his sword wildly at him. The old man was able to skirt gingerly out of the way.

When they had traveled far enough so that they reached the back of the school, where thankfully there were no windows for students to look out and witness what was taking place, Mary finally stopped running, and Franklin, too, stopped in the air behind her.

"Stay here, Franklin!" she said, using a commanding tone that Franklin had not yet heard from her. He was left suspended above the ground as she turned back toward the melee and surveyed the battle scene.

Not wasting any more time, she charged back to help Charles, who had just lifted up one Groken with only a flip of his head and thrown it into the other, causing both to go tumbling backward.

Franklin desperately wanted to go help his friends, and he decided to try a different escape tactic.

Fight fire with fire, he thought.

He focused on the ground beneath him, fixated on it, concentrating in the same manner he had stared at Hank's arrow, and then today, at Brad's shoes. It seemed that giving something his complete attention with both his mind and eyes was what created the telekinetic link between the object and his thoughts.

The grass.

Skinny green blades. Trampled on and bent. Bumblebee bullying a clover. Emerald points bending.

He felt the familiar tingle pulsing through his eyes, which had begun to take on a violet glow. Then, as metal shavings are drawn towards a magnet, he began pulling himself towards the ground. It was working! With this approach, inch-by-inch, he was able to overcome the force Mary had used to hold him up, and slowly he brought himself down to the grass. He guessed, that had Mary remained with him, he would not have been able to do this, but when she left, the force holding him up had diminished.

When at last he alighted on the ground, he still half-expected to be held in the place where he stood. But with a foothold for his feet to push off of, which he did not have while suspended in the air, he was able to move freely forward. He ran with all the strength he had. In front of him, he could see Mary ducking under the mace that buzzed past her head. These two senior citizens looked to be in their eighties, however, they moved with the agility of skilled athletes. The humor of what he was witnessing didn't escape him but laughing now was out of the question.

Franklin understood that they were, in fact, ageless, and this human form was only a disguise. Even so, the two brutish trolls were slowly overpowering them. He could tell Charles was growing tired; his ability to move things telekinetically was waning. Finally gaining the outer perimeter of the battleground, Franklin watched as the old man, again with a twitch, sent a partially buried boulder flying into the chest of the Groken who carried the sword. But because Charles was not at full strength, the massive rock had only a fraction of the velocity on it and barely affected the beast at all.

As Franklin charged in, he stared at the same boulder, which had seconds ago landed harmlessly at the feet of the Groken. It was as burdensome and heavy as it looked, but with fresh strength and strong concentration, he lifted the boulder straight up into the air. Surging upwards, the rock did not hit the Groken directly, but skimmed past it, slamming into its chin and then snagging the bottom of its drooping nose, shaving half of it off its face. This sent the beast sprawling to the ground in pain.

As the boulder reached the apex of its flight and began its descent, the half-ton rock became too much for Franklin to handle any longer. It came careening back towards earth, exploding down onto the legs of the same Groken that had just taken it in the face.

Bones crunched.

His screams of agony were resounding, and Franklin worried about teachers and students possibly hearing the beast. But there was no time for a thought like this, for no sooner had he disabled this Groken, than the other one, seeing what happened, came charging towards him in revenge-filled hysteria; snorting, spitting phlegm, and swinging his mace high above him.

The spiked ball smashed down into the ground next to Franklin, launching a gust of dirty air into his face as it passed him. In his rage, the Groken had thrust the mace downward with such force that it sunk completely into the dirt, which had been softened by the early morning rain. Try as he might, the beast could not recover the mace; it was held steadfast by the covetous earth, suctioned down by the mud.

The other beast, the one with the crushed legs, still lay in the grass, groaning in pain with the boulder planted soundly on him. His green blood had spilled onto the ground all around where he lay. He had attempted several times to move the rock and prop himself up, but as of yet, he had not succeeded.

The Groken who could not retrieve his mace, instead bent down and grabbed the sword of his downed comrade, lifted it up, and with the speed of a helicopter blade, slashed it horizontally through the air, in the direction where Charles stood. Although exhausted, Charles managed to jump backward, out of the blade's path, but not before he had been nicked in the shoulder.

The old man grabbed his shoulder in pain, and without taking his eyes off the beast, he yelled, "Franklin, you have to leave! We haven't come this far just to have you killed by one of these Dark Earth savages!"

But when there was no response, he turned to look where Franklin had been standing, at the spot where the spiked ball was still lodged in the ground, but the boy was gone.

The Groken made another slash towards Charles, this time reaching him before he was able to dodge the blow, and gouged him across the chest, ripping through his sweater and deep into his flesh. He was sent sprawling to the ground, and his glasses flew from his face. There was blood where the sword had carved him, but more noticeable than the flow of red was an intense white sliver of light that came blazing through the gash, up from inside his chest.

The old man looked up at the Groken, who had traipsed over to where he had fallen. The grisly creature had positioned the sword so that it was raised up high, with both hands grasping it, his pronged elbows pointed out to either side, and the glistening steel tip aimed straight down, ready to be driven through Charles.

But then Charles heard Mary scream to the Groken, "Hey, over here you thug! Come over here and fight me!" Unlike

Charles, Mary still had strength left in her because she had not had to fight off two Groken by herself. She held her hands straight out, palms facing outwards and open towards the beast. As the Groken began the downward thrust of the sword's point, which would pierce Charles' heart and be certain death for him, intense bursts of fiery light were thrown from Mary's palms, hitting the Groken squarely in the chest and knocking it off of its feet.

Mary was ready to give it another blast of light-energy, but before she had the chance, the all-but-forgotten troll, who had been lying on the ground and had finally managed to roll the boulder from his legs and pull himself up, reached out and knocked her backward with a such a powerful blow from his fist that she flew through the air, slamming into a tree. Her lifeless body slid down the trunk and crumpled on the forest floor.

The lame Groken began to laugh in imbecilic convulsions, exposing his rotted brown teeth to anyone who could handle looking at them. The other joined in the glee with a few lethargic guffaws of his own, then turned his attention back to Charles. Remarkably, the wounds that Charles suffered to his chest had almost completely healed. However, this healing had sapped even more of his energy. He had tried getting to his feet but stumbled again onto his back as the Groken prepared to deliver the final blow through his heart, from which there would be no healing.

Then, from somewhere above the great beast, came a loud and defiant scream. "Nooooooo!"

Hoping to gain an advantage, Franklin had climbed up to an overhanging tree branch, launched himself into the air and plummeted down onto the back of the monster. He slipped, but then regained his footing and scurried up the scuffed armor, onto the troll's broad shoulders.

Charles, still lacking strength, was nevertheless able to seize this opportunity. With haste, he crawled over to the troll and wrapped his arms tightly around both of its legs. The

Groken, being attacked on two fronts now, dropped the sword it clung to and began to thrash his arms, reaching over his back multiple times, attempting desperately to grab any part of Franklin that he could, while at the same time kicking his legs trying to fling Charles off.

Franklin had found a small seam in the troll's armor to use as footing, but his wet shoes slipped from their perch as the Groken moved about wildly. His legs went careening from the creature's back, but his hands stayed linked around its throat and he rode the Groken like an upright bull. The wild movements of the Groken's dance made Franklin's legs swing about as if he were a rag doll.

He was finally able to gather in his legs, and he placed them back in the notch on the Groken's armor that served as a footrest. With his arms still wrapped firmly around the mighty neck of the Groken, Franklin swung himself to the front of crazed beast so that he was face to face with it.

The surprised Groken brought his hands up to grab the annoying boy who clung to his neck, but before he could reach him, the oaf lost his balance. The combination of Charles desperately trying to hold the monster's legs together, along with Franklin dragging it down by its neck, gave the brute no choice but to tumble to the ground.

In the meantime, Mary had shaken off the blow dealt to her by the Groken and was on her way to help Charles and Franklin. With cat-like movements, she picked up the abandoned sword, and running part of the way and sliding feet-first the rest of the way, she positioned herself in front of the flailing troll, which at this time Franklin was still riding like a bronco. She left the sword vertical, pointing up to the heavens, while she held the hilt against the earth. When Franklin swung around to the front of the creature, and it started its downward plummet, she let go of the handle and backed away to avoid being crushed by its great armored body.

The sword, as susceptible to gravity as any solid object, was not able to balance itself in this straight-up position for long, so Mary gave it a little extra help, focusing her thoughts on it and keeping its pointed end in the direct path of the falling beast.

Franklin used his feet to push off the troll's shoulders, and in doing so was able to thrust himself away before it crash-landed on top of him. The Groken fell fast and hard, and it was skewered by the sword, right through its chest, before it slid all the way down the edges of the blade to the hilt resting on the grass. Mary's placement of the sword had found the troll's heart, and it was dead on impact. The sword still stood, point up, covered in the green goo of its victim.

Both Mary and Franklin, after breathing a sigh of relief, rushed over to Charles, who lay on the ground, exhausted. Franklin asked, "Charles, are you okay?"

Charles wiped some perspiration from his forehead using the heel of his hand and answered, "I'm okay, Franklin. Thanks to you and my old friend here." He turned to look at Mary.

She nodded back at him, her eyes twinkling. Franklin sensed an unspoken language between the two.

"It got you with the blade, didn't it?" Franklin asked. "But I don't see any wounds on you."

"We have the ability to heal many types of wounds and diseases, but it takes much of our strength. That is why Charles has grown so tired now," Mary explained. "I don't even know how he managed to wrestle with the legs of the Groken like that."

The mood among the three was upbeat. Even Charles managed to make himself laugh. "That overgrown Proboscis-nosed Monkey never had a chance. He was eating out of the palm of my hand!" he joked weakly.

"Proboscis-nosed Monkey?" Franklin asked.

"Google it," Charles answered. "You'll see the resemblance."

Franklin felt an air of contentedness settle over him. For the first time since his mom had disappeared, he felt like he truly was with family. Sami was his best friend, no doubt, but these two felt like home. Mary was like his grandma *and* a kick-butt superhero at the same time.

'Super Granny'. Or maybe, 'Grandma Wonder'. He'd have to think about it.

Franklin looked at Charles. He wasn't such a slouch himself, he thought, grateful the old man was not really any worse for the wear. He heard Mary say, "We'll take care of the mess here, but you need to get you back to class, Franklin. I don't want you getting into trouble."

He turned to Mary just in time to witness a peculiar thing... something red fell onto her, just below her shoulder, adding to the color of her already vibrant sweater. His mind gurgled and fogged over, and he had the distinct feeling that everything was moving in slow motion, including his thoughts. He looked closer and saw that nothing had actually landed on Mary, but something had, in fact, penetrated her from her backside and gone all the way through her, bringing bright red blood with it.

It was the Groken's sword, and from behind her the crippled monster had been crouching to stay out of view, but now raised his head into Franklin's line of sight. It said in its simple, sluggish voice, "You got one. Now I got one."

While the three had been resting and laughing, they were unaware that behind them the other Groken, the one whose legs had earlier been smashed by the boulder, had slowly been advancing towards them, pulling itself through the grass with its legs dragging uselessly behind it. It had gotten up onto what was left of a knee, and in one of his hands was the sword that it had retrieved from the chest of its dead partner. Then, from behind Mary, he had run the blade through her back.

In horror, Charles screamed, "Mary, no!" and he moved close to her side, taking her in his arms. Franklin shook away his muddled thoughts and sprinted several feet away to the spot where the mace still lay embedded into the mud. He grabbed the chain and yanked as hard as he could. Nothing happened. He put the chain down and concentrated fiercely on the spiked sphere, focusing... on… one... thing.

Tingling.

The mace started trembling in the ground and then, with an audible 'Fwupppp', ripped free from the suction that held it.

Franklin picked up the handle. The ball was heavy, but still lighter than he had imagined it would be, and using all of his muscle he was able to whirl it around his head. It gained speed with only the flick of his wrist with each rotation. With his telekinesis, it would have been easier, but it felt like this needed to be a bit more personal and hands-on. He looked up. The murderous ball certainly did not have the speed it did when the burly troll had swung it, but it was traveling fast enough for his purposes.

Careful not to disturb its circular path, he trekked softly, but with determination, back to where the Groken was still squawking and snickering about what he had done to Mary. Slowly, Franklin began to change the course of the mace, so instead of swinging it around his head above him, it was now gradually going up and down, coming close to the ground in its motion. The wounded troll, finally seeing what Franklin was up to, made an attempt to move away. Too late. The mace smacked him in the thick armor covering his chest and sent him skimming along the ground until the friction of the grass brought him to a stop. Franklin, eyes radiantly purple and filled with tears, was not finished yet. He kept the mace in its circling pattern; *around, down, around, up, around, down, around, up around, down —* and then the mace abruptly stopped. The troll, groveling in the grass, had given the spiked ball reason to pause, and just like that, its head had become two sizes smaller that day.

Franklin looked down at the gory sight he had caused and felt no remorse for the death of the evil creature.

Running over to where Charles held Mary in his arms, he knelt down to be at eye level with her. Mary's face was pale. She was struggling to breathe, and her eyes were rolled back so that only the whites of them were visible, but with effort, she slowly brought them back down to focus on Franklin.

"You did good, Franklin. You did so good," she struggled to say, her mouth barely parting far enough for the words to come out.

She tried to speak again, lips pursed, and with great exertion, she was able to say, very faintly, "So strong," and then she slid her hand over to rest it on his. Franklin held it tightly. The tears flowed freely down his cheeks, softening the caked-on dirt that covered his face. Mary looked once more at Charles and somehow willed her mouth to form a smile. Charles kissed her forehead. She put her lips back together and quietly began to hum the tune that had been so familiar to Franklin earlier in the school's office. Her eyes stayed open, but only for a few moments before they glossed over, and finally, the soothing sound coming from her lips ceased.

Franklin leaned over and threw his arms around her neck; he cried to Charles, "Why couldn't she heal herself like you could?"

The old man shook his head. He, too, was crying. "It pierced her heart. The Groken knew it would be fatal."

"She's really dead? You mean you'll never see her again?" he asked, not concerned that his voice was cracking with every other word.

Instead of answering his question directly, Charles gently laid Mary on the ground so that she was facing upwards. He nodded his head toward her and said, "Watch."

It was difficult for Franklin to look at Mary like this. Lifeless. He forced himself to, however, because Charles had asked him. Nothing in particular had taken place in the seconds since she had passed, but as he kept his attention on her, his pause turned to wonder, then awe, as her whole body took on a rich shine, radiating out from inside her, and grew into a blazing, fire-like glow. Flames seemed to dance over Mary's entire body, but he did not look away, although his eyes began to ache. The light seemed to grow more blinding by the second, and just when he thought it was too much, and he would have to avert his eyes, the radiance coming from her gradually began to lessen.

And as the light finally faded enough so that Franklin could gaze at her without fear, he could see that Mary's body was no longer the same. Her skin, hair, face... all of the distinctive features about her, had been consumed by the brilliant glow, and now she was simply... well, she was *light*.

She was, after all, a 'Being of Light', he remembered.

Face and torso, arms and legs, although seemingly pure light, were still part of her form, and with the latter, she stood, facing Franklin and Charles. As an airplane can leave behind a trail of smoke in the sky, Mary's afterglow remained lingering in the air where she had been, giving away her movements. Only for a moment did it last, though, before it dissipated.

Franklin and Charles stood up, not wanting to miss this wonderment, but also out of reverence for what Mary had become. No words came from her as she held out her arms high into the sky, face upwards, her whole body ablaze with light. Her head turned one more time towards them, then, the radiant shine that gave her shape began to break up like vapor, scaling off from her and taking to the air. Franklin had the impression, although he knew it wasn't true, that she had been formed from millions of fireflies, which were now flying away into the woods, over the field, and scattering in all directions. Even on a golden day like it was, the shards of brilliant light were visible as they receded further away, until finally, Franklin could not see them anymore.

"She's not gone, Franklin," Charles said, turning his gaze away from where the last fragment of Mary's glow had been, before finally answering the question from several minutes before. "She's just not a physical being anymore."

"I thought," Franklin searched for the words, "I thought you two were already Luminos, Beings of Light? What was that, then?"

Charles nodded. "You're right, I am. It might help to think of me as existing in a pupa stage, not quite having reached my full potential or capacity, as Mary has now. She has transcended in the higher echelons of Third Earth inhabitants. She will not have the need to take on the form of other beings or creatures, like we both have been doing for thousands of years. As I am doing right now."

"Will I see her again?" Franklin asked, wishing for everything that Mary could still be with them right now. The grandmother he never had.

Charles placed his hands on each of Franklin's shoulders and looked him in the eyes. "You will. So will I. I'm sure she wants to see us, too. But listen, Franklin, I can tell you without a doubt that she would want you to leave these woods now. It isn't safe. Another one of those thugs could be on the way," he said.

Franklin gave him a tight hug, then asked, "What are you going to do with these dead trolls, here? You can't really leave them laying around."

"I have a way of making things disappear sometimes. It'll take a lot of strength and concentration to make these two just evaporate, but if I can't, well then, I guess that's what deep lakes are for," he said with a wink.

Franklin wanted to laugh, but couldn't. Instead, he asked, "When will I see you again, Charles?"

"I'm not sure, but I hope it's sooner than later."

He was silent for a moment. "Franklin, your powers are strong, like Mary said. You are becoming a force to be reckoned with. But be careful. Don't forget some of your powers were passed to you from Bramfasa. They can..." once again he chose his words carefully, "....they can affect you. They can change you, if you let them."

Franklin watched as a ladybug strolled slowly across a leaf in the dirt; he felt too ashamed to look at Charles for the moment. How could he tell his old friend that he had *already* started being affected?

He couldn't. All he said was, "I'll be careful. Bye, Charles." Turning towards his school, Franklin took off running.

Charles yelled after him, "Bye, Franklin. Remember, keep an eye out for Nellie! She'll find you!"

The old man looked over at the two dead Groken lying in the dirt. *This might take a while*, he thought.

CHAPTER THIRTY-SEVEN
A QUERY & A QUEST

Franklin made it back for the start of his third-hour class, which was Biology, where he had to dissect a crayfish. *Not really a big deal after I just smashed in the head of a troll*, he thought to himself as he cut open the smelly crustacean. At lunch period he saw Sami and only briefly relayed the events of the morning to her as they munched on the school's version of a hamburger. But he was just too exhausted to relive everything over in detail again.

She was understandably horrified at what he told her, but Franklin could also see the relief on her face that he hadn't been hurt.

He said to her, "Oh, and I learned that we were right about the clues in the baby box. There was something going on. It turns out my birth mom isn't really Angel, after all."

Sami listened as Franklin explained what had actually happened at the hospital on the day he was born, as told to him by Charles and Mary. She seemed to understand that the specifics were not important right now, so she asked no questions.

Franklin left out the part about his dad being an evil god named Bramfasa.

He also 'forgot' to tell Sami about his encounter with Brad in the boy's bathroom. He was ashamed of his actions and didn't want Sami to be ashamed of him, too.

The whole time he spoke, he was distracted by the memory of Mary, the memory of how she had disappeared into a million points of light. Beautiful. Celestial. Sad.

After school, on the bus ride back to Open Arms Orphanage, Franklin relayed to his friends the plan he had been devising.

"I'm not going in the house at all when we get home. I know that Gloria is throwing a party for me and I feel awful for leaving, but I have to get to my mom now; I might have already waited too long. I'm grabbing my bike, heading to Lake Birdsong... and then to the windmill."

Sami reached around her head and began gathering together her long black hair, and as quick as anything, had put it into a thick ponytail. She said, "I'm coming with you, Franklin Hobbs. I hope you know that." She looked at him like a mom disciplining her child.

"I am, too," Shad said. "I might be able to help somehow."

"I wanna come, too." It was Parker, leaning forward from the seat behind Franklin. "What do you think?"

Rufus knew his leg might not be up for the task, especially when it was such an important and perilous mission like this one. He sat next to Shad, not feeling left out, but not feeling particularly useful in any way.

"Okay, guys, listen," Franklin said, turning to each one of them as he spoke, "this is not like the movies where everything turns out just fine in the end. Something really bad could happen to any of you, and I don't want that. I've been thinking about this, and I think I need to do it alone."

Sami's face paled, and she turned towards the window, saying nothing. Parker nodded and replied, "Is there any way we can help, though?"

"I'm not sure. I wish I knew more."

Shad adjusted his glasses as he said, "Franklin, there is one thing that I might be able to do to help. Maybe. I've been doing a little internet research about high-powered walkie-talkies, like the ones Hank has in the garage, and how, sometimes, they pick up very strange signals."

"Like what?" Franklin asked.

"Like voices and noises that aren't necessarily from this world. It sounds ridiculous, but I've read the same things on more than one website, in discussion boards on the 'paranormal'. The sounds people hear sometimes on those things have no way to be explained, unless someone is playing the *same* joke on different people all around the world."

Shad paused, making sure Franklin was still interested, then continued, "Some of the people on the different discussion boards think that sound waves come from other versions of our Earth, like Dark Earth, and are being picked up by these high powered walkie-talkies."

"Kind of like how we saw Franklin's mom in the woods," Sami commented. "But I thought that was only possible on nights when there was a full moon?"

"Yeah, but that might be just light waves that can only come through during a full moon. Sound waves may be different. I don't know for sure," Shad said. "But we can find out. If both of us had a walkie-talkie, one here on our Earth, and one on the parallel Earth you're going to —"

"Okay," Franklin laughed as he broke in, "that would be great if you guys want to hear me scream as I get eaten by a troll, but otherwise, I'm not sure about it."

"Well, I just thought if you did need to tell us something important or needed our help, that it would be good to have. Just so we know how you're doing. But I'm not even sure if it'll work, anyway, and I guess it's just one more thing for you to carry," Shad said. Franklin could tell his friend was a little hurt at how his idea had been mocked.

"Actually, Shad," Franklin said, "I think it is worth a try. If nothing else, it would keep me from getting lonely."

Shad tried hiding a smile, but it was obvious he was pleased. "Okay, then. I'll get them ready when we get back."

"What's wrong with a cell phone?" Parker asked. "Maybe he can even text us some pictures of this place."

"Cell phones need satellites," Shad said. "In the place where Franklin is headed, I don't think satellites are very popular."

Parker gave Shad her best 'whatever' expression.

The bus pulled up to the end of the long, gravel driveway leading to their orphanage. The five friends got off the bus, along with several other younger kids who the bus had picked up at the elementary school on its route back. Franklin went straight to the garage, where his bike was parked. Sami followed closely, and as he was checking the air in his tires, she knelt down on the floor with him and put her hand on his back. He turned his head towards her.

"Franklin, please let me come with you. I want to be there to help you if you need it, if something happens to you," she said softly.

"And I don't want anything to happen to you either, Sami," he replied. Looking at her, Franklin realized he had never seen her eyes this big before, or this beautiful. He leaned in and kissed her on the cheek. "I'm not going to be gone for long," he said. "I promise I'm coming back."

He stood up, took Sami's hand in his, while at the same time using his other hand to guide the bike out the side door of the garage. There was still plenty of daylight left, but Franklin was getting anxious to start. Rufus and Parker were standing on the front porch of the house, waiting for him.

Rufus yelled, "Franklin, Shad said he would be right back. He was getting some batteries for the walkie-talkies."

Franklin put his kickstand down, letting go of Sami's hand, and walked over to them. The screen door opened and out came Jerod. Behind him, in hot pursuit, were several of the younger kids. He had been filling Hank's position for the time being as the second full-time caretaker with Gloria. Still so young, Gloria wanted to make sure it was right for Jerod, so she was calling it a 'trial'. She also called it this to lower the children's expectations, knowing how disappointed they would be if he decided that life at an orphanage, full-time, was not for him.

"Hey, guys," Jerod said, waving at them. "How are all of you holding up? You had a pretty rough experience yesterday and not a lot of time to process it before going back to school."

The children looked at each other, unsure of how to respond. "I just tried not to think about it," Sami said, honestly. The others nodded their head in agreement.

"You let me or Gloria know if you need to talk about it." Turning to Rufus, Jerod asked, "How's your leg, bud?"

Rufus replied, "Actually, I ditched the crutches for most of the day. It's not that hard to walk on. Just hurts."

Jerod smiled, nodding approvingly, "You're a tough kid, Rufus." Then, smile fading, he asked, "Franklin, what about you? You okay?"

Franklin didn't need to think about this question for long, he had been pondering it ever since his discussion with Charles and Mary. "I will be. It's a pretty hard thing to let go of. It'll take some time," he said.

"You can't feel bad Franklin, he was trying to kill you." Jerod reached out and patted Franklin's shoulder. "We all loved Hank, the *old* Hank, but whoever that was needed to be put down."

"Yeah, I guess," was all Franklin could say.

Changing the subject, Jerod asked, "Well, how was school today?" Out of the screen door ran Greta. She maneuvered her way through the other young children and jumped on Jerod's back. He bent down so she could climb up to his shoulders.

"Not bad," Rufus said, "but it sure was hard to say goodbye to my bed, and the habit I'd gotten into of taking an after-breakfast nap."

Parker blurted, "There's this guy at school named Brad. You need to go and kick the crap out of him, Jerod. He's the biggest bully."

"I wish I could help you with that," Jerod laughed, "but I'm guessing the police would want to have a talk with me afterward."

"Franklin can handle him, though," Sami said. "He just doesn't want to hurt him, right?" She glanced at Franklin.

"Umm, yeah. Actually, he and I had a talk, and I don't think he's going to bug me anymore," Franklin said as he scratched his head and looked down at the peeling paint on the wooden deck boards.

"All right, Frankie!" Rufus exclaimed. "You kicked his butt, didn't you?"

They were all looking at him, waiting for an answer. Sami nudged him with her elbow. "Did you do something to him?" she asked. Franklin stared at her now, trying to figure out what he would tell his friends, especially with Jerod right there. Luckily, Shad came out through the screen door before he could answer. It slammed shut behind him.

"Franklin," Shad said, out of breath and panting, "I looked everywhere and finally found some Double A batteries in the kitchen drawer. I tried them in the walkies, and they're fresh. Here you go." He handed Franklin one of the black walkie-talkies.

In his excitement, Shad had not noticed Jerod standing right there. But Parker, trying to cover up his blunder, joked, "Okay, Shad. What are you two going to be doing with those? Playing cops and robbers?"

"Or are you two just such good friends that you always need the other one right there, only a button-push away?" Rufus kidded, trying to help.

After Shad noticed Jerod was standing there, his face turned red. He took his glasses off sheepishly and cleaned them on his shirt.

In a curious tone, Jerod asked, "Franklin, you have your bike parked over there and now a walkie-talkie. Anything you want to tell me?"

Realizing there was no use in trying to completely hide what he was doing, Franklin conceded. "Jerod, I have something I have to do. I can't go into detail, but you have to trust me that I'm doing the right thing."

They all looked at the young caretaker, waiting to see what he would say. "Does this mean I should tell Gloria to postpone the party? She's already made the cake," he replied. "How long will you be gone?"

"I don't know. I'm going to try to move as fast as possible, though." Franklin dared to ask the next question. "Can you cover for me with Gloria, so she doesn't worry?"

Jerod looked intently at Franklin, then the rest of them. He nodded his head. "I'm gonna lose this job as soon as I start, but I was a kid once, too. I know sometimes there are just things you have to do. You've got a good head on your shoulders. I trust you. You be careful, though. Promise?"

"Promise," Franklin said, holding out his hand for a handshake to seal the deal.

Instead, Jerod grabbed him and gave him a hug. "One question, though," he said, letting go of Franklin, a sly smile on his face. "Does it have anything to do with a girl?"

Glancing away, Franklin hid his own grin. He looked at Sami, who was trying not to laugh. "Ummm, kind of, I guess," he said. "Yeah, it does."

At least he was telling the truth.

Greta, who was still propped up on Jerod's shoulders reached down and patted Franklin's head. "Hey, guy! Guess what the doctor said? I'm all better! And so I said back to her, 'I know, only thanks to Franklin'!"

"That's so cool, Greta!" Franklin said.

Sami walked over to her and tickled her under the arms. "It's cool because now I can tickle you again!" Greta shrieked in delight, jumped off Jerod's back, and ran into the house.

Once she had left, Jerod whispered, "Cancer's gone. They ran more tests and she's all clear. The doctor says it's a miracle. She double-checked the blood samples from two days ago, and there were definitely cancer cells in her blood at that point. Not anymore, though."

Not wanting to run into Gloria, Franklin asked Rufus if he could go in and grab his backpack for him. While he did, Sami and Parker went into the kitchen and found some high protein energy snacks that would last for at least two days. Shad grabbed two six-packs of water bottles, and along with Hank's powerful Mega Light flashlight, he loaded everything in the green, nylon pack.

"Oh, thanks, I almost forgot," Franklin said as Shad handed him a black knit hat, one that was meant to be pulled over the entire face, with holes for the eyes and mouth. A 'burglar' mask, Shad called it.

"For stealth, when necessary," his friend told him.

Franklin took it and stuffed it into a side pocket of his backpack.

After everything had been packed, or so he thought, Sami handed him his windbreaker jacket, which she had grabbed from inside.

"You don't know how cold it gets there at night," she said.

Doubting that the place he had seen when he encountered Nefari on Cast Maker Canyon could possibly get chilly, even at night, he took it from her anyway and jammed it down on top of the water bottles. He tried to zip up the pack. It didn't want to close but finally surrendered to his tugging. Franklin was reminded of the time that Shad had brought home so many library books that he had ripped open his entire backpack and ruined it.

Yep, almost that full. But these were essential items he had to have with him (except for the jacket). He threw the bag over his shoulders, clipped the walkie-talkie on his belt buckle, and hugged all of his friends goodbye.

Shad said, "Keep the walkie-talkie on, if it works, maybe give us some updates."

"I will. Thanks, Shad."

"Here," Parker reached out with something in her fist. He took it in his palm and saw that it was a red camping pocketknife. She said, "This thing came in handy more than once when I lived on the street. It's good for opening cans, sawing wood, unscrewing things, or slicing into someone's skin," she laughed. "At least that's what my grandma tells me, I never had to use it for that last one, thankfully."

"Thanks, Parker," Franklin winced at the thought but knew it might come down to something like that. "Hopefully, I'll only need it to whittle a stick for roasting marshmallows. If I use it for anything more violent, I promise I'll think of you," he said, stuffing it down into his front pocket.

"Ummmm, Franklin, I don't think we have any marshmall—" was all Shad could get out before Parker stopped him.

"It was another joke, Shad," she said.

"Oh, got it," he replied.

Sami stepped up to Franklin one last time as he hopped onto his bike seat. She reached out and took his hand, squeezing it tight. "You be careful, Franklin. Don't make me come rescue you!" she said, her face contorting as she tried to hold back tears.

Rufus exchanged a private look with Shad that said, *See, told you they were more than friends.*

Franklin put his fingers together so that they were straight and held his hand to his forehead. He saluted Sami. "Yes, ma'am! I will!"

Then he waved one last time to all of them as he pedaled down the driveway. When he reached the paved road, he took a right and started towards Lake Birdsong.

CHAPTER THIRTY-EIGHT
A PROTECTOR & A PORTAL

Above him, white clouds drifted lazily on their blue, pathless journey, and the sun was giving up its tug-of-war match with the western horizon, slowly being dragged into oblivion. Franklin figured he had three hours left of light, and he pedaled at a brisk pace down the lonely country road. Only a few cars whizzed by him, going both directions, and no one in the vehicles turned their heads to pay him any heed, reminding him that he really was all alone. He felt a strange kinship with all the death-row prisoners out there that might be eating their last meal.

Franklin knew that soon, if the windmill Gateway worked, he would be on another sinister Earth that didn't know what clouds were, or blue skies, either, for that matter; at least from what he had seen the last time he was there.

Thoughts of his mom pushed him along faster than anything else could. Imagining her alone and scared, having been beaten by the Chenoo regularly for the last year and a half, he pedaled harder, realizing that every second could make a difference in whether he found her alive or not.

If he and Shad were right, his mom was being held in the forest where they had seen her projected image. The windmill Gateway would most likely bring him to the corresponding point on Dark Earth, which was less than a mile from the woods. The only problem was, he had no idea what the terrain would look like on that alien Earth. The Gateway might end up taking him to the middle of a lava-filled volcano, for all he knew.

No. From what he could tell from his limited time on Dark Earth, where he had experienced the parallel version of Cast Maker Canyon, the terrain of the land was almost the same as his Earth. This included the landmarks and topography; perhaps at one point, the two parallel planets had started out being identical. He greatly doubted there would even be a hill, much less a volcano, where he exited the Gateway, if it was farmland here on this Earth.

The ditch on either side of the road had been neglected by lawnmowers for a long time and was filled with high-reaching overgrown grass and weeds. This made it nearly impossible for Franklin to tell what he was actually seeing when up ahead, one area of the thick foliage seemed to be thrashing and moving about. Whatever was creating this mayhem in the weeds piqued his curiosity. Was it a struggling animal? He couldn't stop. He was in a hurry, and his mom came first; stopping to check on anything else right now was foolish, so he sped by without so much as looking down into the ditch, for fear he would see whatever it was in the weeds and be forced to stop, out of guilt.

Pathetic whimpers came wafting up to his ears from somewhere below him, which only made him pedal faster.

A hundred feet down the road, his conscious got the better of him, and he turned his bike around. When he reached the general area where he had heard the cries, he got off his bike and slowly waded down through the waist-deep grass. He heard the pain-filled whimpers again and adjusted his direction. Suddenly, right in front of him, out of the weeds, an animal's black muzzle appeared, followed by a furry black face. Just as quickly, it sank back down into the grass. He bent down and reached his hand into the unknown, and his fingers found deep, soft fur. Franklin flattened out the greenery all around the area with his feet and arms, as best he could, until he was finally able to see the animal before him; a dog. A big, black, shaggy dog.

Through fur that partly hid its face, the dog looked at him with helpless eyes. Franklin could tell what a sad life it had lived by the way it stared at him, almost as if it seemed to be expecting the worst to happen again. He saw the duct tape that was wrapped tightly around its muzzle, which was why it could only whimper and not bark. Its two front legs had also been duct taped together.

At one point, the dog's rear legs had been taped, too, but Franklin could see the slackened loop of grey tape hanging down; the dog had at least managed to work its back legs free from their shackles. The only movement the poor creature could manage was upward thrusts, using its hind legs to push off the ground, which had first caught Franklin's attention from down the road. Someone had hogtied this beautiful dog like a calf at the rodeo and then thrown it into the ditch, leaving it to die slowly.

As he sat there, carefully unwrapping the tape from the animal's front legs, trying not to pull out its fur, Franklin realized he didn't have to travel to Dark Earth to encounter evil; there was still plenty of it in this world, too.

Amazingly, the dog was not scared of him and sat quietly while its legs were freed. When he finished, Franklin started on the tape that held its mouth closed. As soon as the last bit of bondage had been removed, the dog, realizing that this human was good, stuck out its tongue and began licking Franklin's fingers. Franklin laughed and petted the dog on the head. It had the smoothest, most beautiful fur he had seen or felt on an animal before. The dog rose from its prone position on the ground, and Franklin was surprised at how large it was. It looked to be over one hundred pounds.

As a young boy, his mom had given him a book about different breeds of dogs, and he had spent hours upon hours looking through it. Although he and his mom could never actually afford to buy or take care of a dog, he had always dreamt about owning one. He recognized the one in front of him now from that well-used picture book of his; it was a Newfoundland or Newfie. He was reminded of the extreme faithfulness of this breed, and the great measures that they had been known to take in order to protect their owner.

It was too bad that Gloria didn't allow pets at the house, especially large dogs like this.

Something else, too. Since he had gained the ability to see auras around people, he had *only* seen them around people, never animals. But now that the friendly animal stood up in front of him, he could see that it had the most beautiful blue and pink shine surrounding its entire frame. *What a very strange dog,* he thought.

The canine stared up at him, wondering what Franklin's next move would be. He didn't have time to take it anywhere. Against his liking, Franklin made the tough decision that he would have to leave it here for now and just hope he could find it on the way back, after he had rescued his mom. Then, maybe he could find a good home for it, someone who wanted a very large, but sweet-tempered dog. Who knows? Maybe his mom would even let him keep it if they found a house big enough to have a pet bear.

"I have to go, but I'll be back, buddy. I promise," Franklin said, petting it one last time on its soft head. "I know you can't understand me, but I'll find you a home if you wait for me." The dog looked at him with eager eyes and then hung its tongue out and began panting.

"Here, eat this."

Franklin unzipped his pack and took out a protein bar, unwrapped it and held it out for the dog, who eagerly chowed it down. He then opened a water bottle and held the dog's muzzle angled slightly upwards while he poured some in its mouth. Again, it swallowed the water with vigor, letting the water rush down its throat, lapping the stray splashes that landed on its fur up with its tongue. Franklin noticed that the dog's slobbery jowls grazed against the water bottle, but he still took a guzzle from it himself after the dog was done. He was never one to worry too much about germs.

He got up and turned to leave, but felt the dog right at his heels, ready to follow him. He looked back at it and was surprised to see the big dog making eye contact with him. It whined, put its paw up to Franklin's leg while wagging its tail fiercely, then barked twice in quick succession, all the while keeping his big, brown eyes on him. Franklin knew this Newfie was trying to tell him something, but he didn't have the time right now to interpret dog language.

He needed to go.

The dog turned over on its back and threw its paws up in the air, trying to get his new human friend to rub its tummy. Unable to resist its adorable insistence, Franklin succumbed and gave it a few quick strokes on its furry stomach.

"I gotta go. I'm sorry," he said. Seeming to understand him, the dog's head tilted to the side as it remained on its back.

He again stood up and walked away, hoping the Newfie would not follow him this time. It didn't. Climbing back up the ditch and hopping on his bike seat, he took one last look at the black dog, now laying on its stomach, head down on its paws, but watching Franklin's every move as diligently as ever.

Franklin started pedaling, moving away, trying to convince himself he was doing the right thing by leaving it behind.

After fifteen more minutes of biking, he saw the field next to Lake Birdsong, a large field, covering forty acres of land. Being here brought back a sudden pang of fear and guilt when he thought about what had happened only days ago, how he was responsible for ending a man's life. To his relief, he felt no sense of pride anymore over what he had done, and he had no anger left for Hank. But he did feel a sudden surge of nervous joy, knowing that this was also the forest where his mother was being held captive, although in another realm.

He swerved off the pavement and navigated his bike carefully down the steep ditch, then took off riding into the field. Instead of going to the forest, he stayed to the left, trying to remember the exact direction he had followed the strange little winged creature. When he was confident that he was heading in the right direction, he stopped his bike so that he could get a quick drink. It was a warmer-than-average spring evening, and he knew he needed to stay hydrated.

As he took off his backpack, unzipped it, and took out another one of the water bottles, in his periphery vision, not too far behind him, he noticed something racing towards him. Something black. He recognized it immediately. The dog was approaching him rapidly, and he laid his bike down to greet it. But he wasn't ready when the eager dog leaped upon him, knocking him over and licking his face like it was covered in peanut butter.

After he regained a sitting position and was able to get the dog to stop slobbering all over him, he said to it, "Hey, you followed me this whole way? How did you keep up?"

The dog only pawed at him until Franklin grabbed its leg in his own hand and held it. With his other hand, he held up his water bottle to its mouth, like before, and tipped it back. After letting the dog drain the bottle, he said, "What do you want, doggy? I can't help you right now."

It cocked its ears and turned its head to the side. It barked and jumped up on Franklin as he sat there in the grass, putting its two front paws on his shoulders. That's when Franklin noticed that it was wearing a collar, which up until now, had been hidden under its mess of thick fur. He grabbed the collar gently and twisted it around until he found a metal ring that held a red tag on it. Looking closely, he saw that it said NELLIE in capital letters, engraved across it.

A little bell rang in Franklin's head. Nellie. That was the name of the Luminos that Charles said they would send to help him. A dog? Was this really who they had sent?

Not that he minded too much. He wrapped his arms around Nellie, which only made her start to lick his face again, this time even harder.

"Okay, okay, girl. You can come with me. But you don't know what you're getting yourself into," he said.

Although she seemed content seconds ago, at these words from Franklin her demeanor somehow grew even more joyful; her tail wagged vigorously as she gave him one more lick across the face.

"C'mon then," he said.

Franklin got up and stretched out his legs again, then, straddling his bike, he sat down and took off in the direction of the farmhouse. He pedaled hard, and Nellie was able to keep up with him as he rode his bike at top speed. After ten minutes, he could see the four-bladed mill looming in the distance. Not only did Nellie keep up with him, but she was able to run ahead now, leading the way. To his right, a red sign stuck out from the ground; written in messy script was a warning that he was entering private property and needed to stay off. In smaller letters, at the bottom, it said, 'Trespasers well be delt with harshley'. Just like that, misspelled words and all. Two days ago, when he had taken a slightly different route in the dark, this homemade sign had gone unseen, and even now, he paid no attention to the warning it gave.

Up ahead the windmill looked foreboding, as it churned fast enough to make butter out of spring air. It seemed to be waiting, daring him to enter its rectangular, wooden blades. Franklin accepted the dare whole-heartedly; there was nothing he wouldn't do to get to his mom back.

Moments later, Franklin and Nellie were in the small compound of the farm, with the windmill right in front of him and other smaller buildings scattered about. He bent down to pet Nellie. "We're here, girl, but you're going to think I'm crazy when I show you what we have to do."

Just then, a shotgun blast rattled the quiet evening, echoing off the buildings, and sending chills through their bodies. Several yards away a patch of sod exploded, sending the dirt airborne around them.

"That was a warning shot!" A man's angry voice yelled out from somewhere close by. "Get off my property you loser, or the next one will take out your mutt!"

Franklin's 'fight or flight' response kicked in, and flight seemed like the best option at the moment. He hurriedly pedaled his bike to the building that lay at the base of the windmill. Looking back, he saw Nellie remaining steadfast at the spot where they had just heard the blast. Her ears were perked, and she looked attentively from one building to the next.

"C'mon, girl! Follow me!" he yelled at her.

Unable to locate the source of the gunshot, Nellie decided it was time to run. She took off, catching up to Franklin, who waited anxiously at the door. As she reached him, from somewhere behind them another deafening blast sounded. A split second later, a baseball-size hole was torn into the wood planks of the building.

Throwing his bike on the ground, Franklin turned the knob, which he fully expected to be locked, but instead found that it opened rather easily, and he was sent stumbling through the door, landing on the hard cement. Nellie followed him in and then leaned her head down, nudging his hand with her cold nose.

"I'm okay, Nellie. Don't worry," he said, trying to reassure her, while at the same time wondering to himself just *why* he was reassuring a dog.

The room they found themselves in looked like it hadn't been used in quite some time. Dead beetles and rodent droppings covered the floor where Franklin had fallen. When a mouse scampered in front of them and then into a small hole in the wall, Nellie immediately chased it and let off a chorus of semi-playful barks.

"Girl, try to be quiet," Franklin whispered. Nellie walked back to him with her tail down and gave him a look that Franklin interpreted as an apology.

Still on the ground, he used his foot to kick the outside door shut before he stood up and surveyed the room, trying to find a place where they could hide, if they had to, from this new madman in his life. The building they were in served as a foundation for the windmill, as well as housing a staircase to get up to it.

Apparently, the room was also a storage area for massive bundles of old, rotting hay. Franklin had not seen any cattle or horses around, so these bundles might have been sitting here, collecting mold and dust, for a long time. They were stacked to the ceiling on three sides of the room and as far out as the middle, leaving only narrow hallways to walk down. The fourth side of the room was left clear of hay to allow easy access to a small control board that sat on a table. Most likely controls for the windmill.

Next to the control panel was a door that said, 'STAIRCASE TO ROOF' on it, this time printed neatly and with all the words spelled correctly.

Franklin darted for this door, with Nellie close behind him. He tried turning the handle, but it was locked. Instead, he heard the sound of the entrance door opening and looked back to see a shotgun poking through the space between the wall and door.

They moved fast towards the nearest stack of bundles, and upon reaching it, Franklin pulled one of the rectangular prisms of hay out. Fortunately, none of the bales collapsed, and it created a space where he and Nellie could squeeze in and stay out of sight. He crawled into the hidey-hole with the dog following and heard the door slam shut just as he pulled her in. The space would have been tight if it was just him, but with Nellie, it was downright cramped. She backed up close to him, and he ended up with a clump of fur in his mouth.

The man's snarly voice boomed from ten feet away. "That's you, isn't it, Jack? You're back to try to rob me blind, aren't you? I'll kill you this time. Just give me a clue where you're hiding, so I can put some buckshot in your behind."

What else could go wrong? Franklin thought. *Now I'm being mistaken for some enemy of this crazy farmer named Jack!*

Definitely not an ideal way to start his mission. The man had seen him clearly enough to take a shot at him outside. Couldn't he tell he wasn't this 'Jack' guy? He might be a lunatic. Or intoxicated. Or perhaps, both.

Franklin thought about trying to reason with this man, but stepping out to show the farmer that he wasn't actually 'Jack' was a bad idea; he might get shot just because this guy has an itchy trigger finger. He decided to wait it out.

The small opening, which their hidey-hole provided, allowed Franklin to see down the tight corridor created by the haystacks. It was at the end of this corridor that the man appeared, poking his rifle into cracks and crevices as if the 'Jack' he was looking for was the size of a mouse. The farmer was large, mostly in his stomach, and wore a dirty, white tank top with tufts of chest and back hair sticking out around his neck. The stubble on his face looked to be about three days out from being shaved, and his hair may not have seen a brush in twice that amount of time.

He reached back behind the corner of the haystack and wheeled Franklin's bike into view. He must have retrieved it from outside where Franklin had left it.

"Is this your bike, Jack? A little small for a guy like you. What happened to your fancy truck? Oh, and tell me, where's the money you stole from me?" As the man spoke, his speech became more slurred and his voice grew increasingly toxic with each word.

Franklin watched him walk back around the corner and out of sight, then heard the sound of his bike clattering onto the cement floor. "You might need some new tires on this here guy, though."

Silence. Then, the blast of a shotgun cracked through the musty air. A few seconds later, another explosion sounded. "Yup, you're definitely gonna need some new tires."

The man continued in his search for Jack, his loud cowboy boots giving away his location with each step. Just when Franklin thought the farmer might give up and leave the building, his hefty frame came back into view around the corner. He began squeezing his way through the cramped hallway of hay and towards their hiding space. Franklin watched as his dull black boots shuffled past them, towards the control board, before turning around and lumbering back in their direction.

"Well, now, looks like someone pulled out a bale of hay here," the man said.

Franklin saw him kick the bale that he had left out, conspicuously, in his rush to hide.

The farmer continued, "Almost like they were trying to hide under there. Let's just have a look." The barrel of the shotgun poked into their space. Nellie looked at Franklin and cocked her head to the side, seeming to ask what his plan was. Franklin thought about using his latest talent against this man, but after what had happened to Hank, he was skeptical. He didn't want to seriously hurt this guy, and he had not completely figured out how to control his telekinesis. What if he threw him against the wall and killed him on accident? Besides, the man was holding a shotgun, Franklin didn't even know if he could do anything to stop buckshot.

It didn't matter. Nellie had decided to take control of the situation herself. Her body had grown tense and Franklin sensed that she was about to move.

He yelled, "Nellie, wait!" and held her as tight as he could.

But when the barrel of the gun disappeared from their limited view and was replaced instead by the man's sweaty face, Nellie rushed out, escaping Franklin's hold, and startled the farmer enough so that he fell onto his back. As Franklin poked his head out from under the stack of hay, a burst of gunpowder sounded, and the pellets tore into something not far behind him.

The gun had been jolted from the farmer's hand on impact with the hard floor, and Nellie bolted to him, securing her jaws around his throat. As Franklin scurried out of the hidey-hole, he saw the man sprawled on the ground, panic on his face as he gazed up at Nellie.

"Hey, call your dog off, please? Her teeth are on my throat!" he said. His voice had lost its edge, but his words still slurred into one another as he looked desperately now at Franklin.

Franklin glanced over at the door that accessed the roof of the building. The shotgun had fortuitously blasted through the lock and the door now swung open. He reached down and picked up the shotgun, then threw it behind the nearest stack of hay bales.

He approached the farmer, who was doing his best to remain perfectly still as he was held in place by Nellie's sharp cuspids.

Calmly, Franklin spoke to him. "Listen, mister. I don't know who Jack is, but I'm not him. All my dog and I need to do is get to the roof of this building, and we'll leave you alone."

Spittle flew from the man's mouth as he emphatically yelled back, "Go ahead. Just call this mutt off!"

"C'mon, Nellie. Let's go," Franklin said, already climbing the stairs. Nellie looked down at the petrified farmer between her jaws. Her look was harsh, and she allowed a low, intimidating growl to bubble from within her throat. After a few seconds of this final warning, she released his neck and ran toward the door, up the stairs, and after Franklin.

"Stupid dog. Stupid kid!" the man yelled from below them. "Where's my shotgun?"

After four flights, Nellie finally reached the top of the staircase, where she found the door open. She stepped out onto a flat roof coated with tar and small pebbles. To her left, she saw Franklin standing on the edge of the roof, at least a forty-foot drop to the ground. But what really caught her attention was that only a few feet in front of him, the four massive blades of the windmill spun at such a rapid rate that the gust of wind they created made it difficult for her to hold her ground. With some difficulty, she walked over to where he stood, and both boy and dog were cast in a strobe light effect as the sun shone through the spiraling sails.

Franklin looked down at his new friend. "Thanks for what you did back there. I think you actually made that jerk wet his pants."

Her tongue caught Franklin's hand in the air as it came down to scratch behind her ears, and she licked him with unfettered affection.

"Girl, listen. You don't have to come with me. But I'm not going to lie, it would be really good to have you along," Franklin said to her.

Nellie glanced behind them at the open door they had just come from and sounded off an urgent bark. Franklin spun around to see what she had seen, and there, stepping from the staircase onto the roof, was the robust farmer, who had by now recovered his shotgun. He quickly spotted them and began staggering in their direction. Franklin noticed that the man looked even more disheveled than he had earlier; his grungy tank top had a long rip running through it, and somehow he had lost one of his black boots. As he stumbled, an empty whiskey bottle fell from his pants pocket onto the pebbled roof, sending shards of glass flying in all directions.

He bellowed, "Where you going to go now, kid? I got you point blank. First things first, that dog is dead."

His trembling arms raised the shotgun up to his shoulder and he took aim at Nellie. A split second before the shotgun boomed, however, Franklin shouted, "Now!" and with his hand on her collar, both he and his dog leaped into the precariously revolving blades of the windmill.

Trusting what he saw two nights ago, when the bizarre, tiny half-man, half-cricket creature had flown into the sails and vanished, Franklin jumped outward towards the middle of the mill. Nellie, trusting Franklin, jumped with all her might in sync with him. Wood splintered from one of the windmill's blades as the buckshot from the shotgun burst forth, missing its intended target.

Waiting to find out he was wrong, waiting to feel the pain that came with being broken into bits by huge wooden slats, Franklin's whole body tensed up, preparing for the worst. But instead of being dealt a deathblow by the blades, he experienced a sharp jolt of electricity throughout his body, bringing him to convulse in uncontrolled spasms, and just when he thought it was too much for him, it stopped.

Then, weightlessness found him. His body was being pushed along now, as if on a current of air. Clouded light crept into the channel he traveled through, and around him in the haze he heard shrieks of seen and unseen ghouls. He had the feeling they were imprisoned, stranded in this space that he assumed was in between parallel dimensions. Some of them crawled or walked, always in awkward, jerky motions, coming close to him. He pulled away at first, but then realized they could not hurt him.

The ghouls would claw at him, but would always stop short of actually reaching him. It was as though he were traveling in a protected tube, while everything else was stuck in this intermediary zone. This all brought to mind a book he had read when he was eight, *Charlie and the Great Glass Elevator*. In the book, the boy Charlie and his family, along with a crazy man named Willy Wonka, are shot into space, where they can see all the wonders and dangers around them from the safety of the elevator they are riding in.

But this wasn't outer space, and he wasn't in an elevator. Was he? His body suddenly collided with something spongy, like foam, and although it was solid, it somehow allowed him to pass through it. A type of membrane. When he came through to the other side, he had the distinct sensation that his body was beginning to deconstruct and turn to liquid form, his molecules no longer held in one place, but moving around each other haphazardly.

That was all he remembered.

CHAPTER THIRTY-NINE
AN ENEMY & AN EAVESDROPPER

Unfortunately for Nefari, he was not privy to information he needed without actually finding it out for himself. Some creatures, like Bramfasa or Bramfasa's Crow Wraiths, just knew things. Sometimes because informants told them, but also because they possessed a greater power of knowledge than others. Creatures like Nefari had to get their information directly by discovering it for themselves, usually. He wished he could be all-knowing. It would make things easier.

In recent days, he had not been able to keep an eye on Franklin, waiting for an opportunity to collect what he needed. Bramfasa had demanded his presence at Quietus Tumulus, and that had slowed him down. He had not been able to stalk the boy in the shadows as he had in previous times, like when he found him outside his house before daylight arrived, or when he caught him alone in the school's dark basement. So now, as he waited in the space underneath Franklin's mattress for the boy to come up to his room, climb in bed, and finally go to sleep, he grew a little excited. He really needed to collect the boy's eyes.

He had no reason to think Franklin would not be coming to his bed tonight.

The door to the room opened, and underneath the bed the Darkness tremored with anticipation. The lights came on, but fortunately for Nefari, the rays of white poison could not reach into his hiding spot.

"I hope Franklin's okay," he heard a voice say.

He knew it to be the voice of the boy Shadrack Wence, roommate of Franklin. This news disappointed Nefari. It meant his little Frankie was not here tonight.

"Why don't you call him on the walkie-talkie and see if it works?" another boy asked.

This was the voice of the chubby boy Rufus, whom Nefari had seen lounging around and sulking in previous visits here before. He had spent moments in all the orphans' rooms at one time or another, under their beds or in their closets, just to pass the minutes while waiting for Franklin to return. This boy, Rufus, was usually an outcast, almost always by himself, crying in his room. It made Nefari's black heart suffer to see that he had made a friend.

The boy Shadrack spoke again, "I don't want to disturb him, though. What if he's hiding from some monster and suddenly my loud voice comes across on the walkie? I'm really curious to see if the sound waves will find their way to Dark Earth, but we need to be patient."

Dark Earth? That's where the kid had gone then. Nefari's black mass lay still now. He would wait until the room was dark again to come out from under the bed, then he would leave the house and travel through the nearest Gateway back to his Earth.

CHAPTER FORTY
A DARK EARTH & A DISAPPEARANCE

Somebody was torturing him and he couldn't wake up. His face! It felt like it was being ripped from his skull! He had to wake up, right now!

Franklin finally opened his eyes in a delirium, ready to fight for his life. He found himself lying in the middle of a field, on the soft remains of decomposing prairie grass. When he figured out what was actually happening, he laughed with overwhelming relief, then reached up and grabbed Nellie around the neck and hugged her.

"Good girl! You were just trying to wake me up, weren't you?"

Nellie had been licking his face for the last ten minutes with her warm, slobbery tongue. Now she stood by happily and wagged her tail. Her long black fur, like Franklin's hair, was tousled and tangled from the trip through the Gateway. Franklin sat up and looked around. He was in unfamiliar territory.

"Hey girl, we're definitely not in Kansas anymore!" he exclaimed.

Nellie gave him her best inquisitive look, and her tongue lolled from her mouth as she panted from the heat that they suddenly found themselves in.

"It's from a movie. The Wizard of Oz," he said, scratching his head. "Shoot, that makes you Toto, and me, well, I guess Dorothy. Never mind then."

It must have worked, he thought. *The windmill! It must have had a Gateway in it!*

He knew if it hadn't, he and Nellie would be in about two thousand different pieces right now.

A question came to him. Was the door of the Gateway that they had just exited somewhere above him in the sky, just as the Gateway in the windmill was almost fifty feet in the air? He had never before considered that possibility. If this were true, at the very least he would have sustained multiple broken bones falling from such great a height. This in itself was evidence that the Gateway must have opened on the ground, not up in the air fifty feet.

If *this* was the case, then it was also worrisome to him. Not that he wished he had fallen five stories to the ground, only that he truly had no idea where the entrance to the Gateway back to his Earth was. How would he locate it? Then again, if it were five stories in the air, how would he have been able to get back to it anyway? Build a staircase?

And, if the Gateway back to Earth was on the ground somewhere around him, Franklin was nervous that he might accidentally step through it without trying and would end up back where that crazy man waited to blow him away. Or, maybe he would just fall fifty feet to his death off of the barn roof. So many horrendous possibilities, and all of them were chances he had to take.

Getting to his feet, he surveyed the area. Brown crispy grass almost exclusively surrounded him, except for an occasional patch of dirt; nothing that looked peculiar or that would serve as an optimal spot for a portal. There was also the possibility that the Gateways only worked one direction, and maybe there wasn't a Gateway…or what did Shad call it? A *wormhole*? Maybe there wasn't a wormhole anywhere near here at all that would take his mom and him, plus Nellie, back home.

The thought of being stuck here in this place was something he couldn't wrap his mind around, so he decided to take one problem at a time for now. This little hiccup in his plans would need to be dealt with later.

The land where he stood was on higher ground. Before him was a gradual hill that sloped down to a ravine. It looked like at one point in time, the small canyon had been keeper of a river, but in the last century it had been overgrown by weeds. Franklin remembered that the crazy man's farm, where he and Nellie had almost met a ridiculous end, was also on a hill. He knew Pleasant Acres River flowed through that area of farmland back home, eventually meeting the mighty Mississippi somewhere south of the Minnesota border. This must be the bizarro version of Pleasant Acres River, so he needed to head away from this riverbed in the opposite direction. East. Towards the sun?

Franklin was reminded about something peculiar…well, something *else* peculiar about this place. He had noticed it in his brief time here before; the sun set in the east instead of the west.

He wasn't a huge science guy but felt a little like Shad when he concluded that this parallel Earth must be located in a parallel solar system as well. Could it possibly be a mirror-image solar system in this case? Exact opposites? At any rate, by the sun's position in the sky, he figured it to be about the same time here as it was back home, and that meant he had an hour or so until sundown.

Glancing at his watch, he found the digital display cracked, leaving the time impossible to decipher, but he guessed it must be about 6:30 at night. In Minnesota, it had been about sixty-five degrees outside when he left. The heat here, however, was intense, probably over a hundred degrees. He was a sweaty mess, and he'd only been here a mere three minutes, or at least *awake* three minutes. He had no idea how long he'd been out cold, with Nellie trying to slobber him awake.

As he had been on his previous visit here, he was again chilled by the sun's threatening color. There was no cheerful yellow gleam coming from it to tell the inhabitants of the planet that everything was going to be okay because the sun will rise again in the morning. On the contrary, the sun rising again in the morning meant a sky that would, like every other day, be painted with a poisonous orange hue. Not to mention an Earth that would be encased in light akin to the glow coming from the evil innards of a jack-o-lantern. Oh, and then there was the unbearable heat it would bring.

There was nothing here in this dead field; no farmhouse or barn, no windmill, no crops, no homes of any kind. It was desolate. Signs of life were non-existent, which he was grateful for. Any creatures living here must exist in the shade or hide underground during the daytime hours.

Franklin dug a bottle of water out of his backpack and held it up to show Nellie, whose tongue was finding it difficult to stay in her mouth. After they both had taken a swig, he put the remaining water back into his pack.

His mom, or the image projected of her, had told him she was being held in a dead forest, with a lakebed somewhere nearby it. So, that's what he would look for then. If this Earth did have the same layout and topography as his home, then he knew what direction to go to find the dead forest and the dried up crater of Lake Birdsong.

The use of landmarks to help him stay on the right path would be difficult; everything was so different here. Either dead, dry, or not there at all. But he could find her. He had to.

As he walked briskly towards the setting sun, due east, he became distracted by some extra weight pulling on his jeans. That's right! His walkie-talkie! He had completely forgotten it was there. He loosened the clip and took it off. After inspecting it, he was relieved to find it undamaged, at least visibly.

He pushed the side button and held it close to his mouth. "Shad, are you there?" Nothing. Only fuzzy static. He tried it again. "Shad, Sami, is anyone there?"

Again static crackled, then a voice broke through, very soft and faint, but it was Shad's voice. "Franklin, is that you? You're there?"

"I'm here. I made it. It was crazy, and you wouldn't believe how hot it is."

"Really? Good thing you brought so much water."

"Yeah, thanks for remembering that."

Shad's voice didn't hide the thrill he felt as he said, "This is an amazing scientific breakthrough, you know? You may be the first human to ever cross to a parallel Earth!"

"Besides my mom, you mean."

"Yeah," Shad said. "Sorry. Are you okay?"

"We're fine, yeah. We had a little trouble at the windmill, but it worked out. I'm on my way to Lake Birdsong right now."

Sami's voice burst through the small speaker, much louder than Shad's had been. "*We*? Who's with you?"

Franklin smiled to himself, it didn't take much to get Sami riled up. "I picked up a friend on the way to the windmill. A dog named Nellie. I know it sounds weird, but she's helping me. I'll tell you more, later."

"Okay. A bit strange, but I'm glad you're not by yourself, at least. Be careful."

"I will. Better go now. Bye, guys."

"Bye, Franklin," Sami said.

He put the walkie back on his waist. Shad had done it again. Who else would have thought that a simple device like this would work to communicate between two different dimensions? He chuckled. Nellie, walking right beside him, looked up at him and started wagging her tail, just happy to see him happy.

It was only about a mile's distance from the windmill to the forest, and he estimated that he had already walked half of it. By now he was almost completely drenched in sweat as it cascaded down his back and stomach and bulldozed into the scrapes that he had endured from his encounter with Hank. The sweat also ran into his mouth. He was too tired to prevent it from doing this, and it reminded him how much he disliked the taste of salt. This brought on his thirst again, and he thought about getting more water but decided to wait until he got to the forest. He needed to conserve it; his mom would probably need some, too. Nellie seemed content; she was panting and obviously hot, but not suffering at the moment as she ran up ahead of him.

The fields to the north of him, which was the same direction his orphanage would be, were quite extensive here, and Franklin could see how flat the land actually was in this part of Minnesota. *Well, not really Minnesota, but close enough*, he thought.

He could see for miles over the open land, so why couldn't he see the forest yet? Squinting his eyes, he thought he detected movement far out in one direction of the field. It could just be the heat playing games with him. He closed his eyes tight, then looked again. This time he saw more than just movement, he saw quite a bit of activity, and he was able to recognize the figures of humans moving to and fro.

He remembered seeing this odd sight when he lay helpless on Cast Maker Canyon! Figures that looked human, well over a thousand from what he could tell, were working in the field out there! Not all of them could be people, though.

Some of them were way too large. But what were they doing on Dark Earth? Could there be a race of humans living here, too?

Maybe he and his mom weren't the first humans on this planet after all. As before, he saw the large piles of dirt that the workers seemed to be adding to or taking from with shovels. He couldn't tell which.

They weren't more than a quarter-mile away and only a bit farther north than the direction he was traveling. He considered getting a closer look to see if his mom was in that group, but decided he would stick to his original plan; hopefully, he would come to the woods soon.

After twenty more minutes of trudging along through dirt, sand, and decay, the scenery around him finally started to change. Sticks and stumps started to appear every so often, then more frequently, until finally, not too far up ahead from him, he saw a forest of dead trees. They had blended in almost perfectly with the surrounding brown field, so Franklin had not been able to see the forest until he was almost upon it.

Although exhausted, he started running towards the graveyard of trees, Nellie close at his heels. Taking in the full sight ahead of him as he sprinted, he saw that most trees, although dead, were either still being held up by their own trunk or were leaning against another tree, while a lesser number had already decayed to the point that they had fallen to the ground. He took this to mean that some of the trees had been able to hold out without water for longer than others, their roots reaching further down. But nothing remained alive in this forest, he was certain of that. Not one bit of green dared to show itself in this oasis of rot.

Sitting off to the south of the forest was a tremendous indentation in the surface of the earth. Sections of it looked to go down twenty feet deep into the ground. The vast crater seemed to have an area that was similar in size to how Franklin remembered Lake Birdsong. This was the right place, he was sure of it.

He came to the very outskirts of the jungle of tree limbs and trunks and peered in. But seeing far into the labyrinth of trees, although there were no leaves, was almost as difficult as if it were a green forest; the tangle of lifeless wood blocked every angle of his vision.

He knew his mom was probably not going to be wandering around like she had been the night of the full moon when she appeared to him and his friends. Was she locked or chained up somewhere in this mess? If so, she must have had a way to escape, especially since Rufus had also seen her the month before. Because of these previous escapes, Franklin figured that now her captor had probably made it much more difficult for her to find a way out. On the other hand, it was also a possibility that the Chenoo didn't care if she left, because he knew there was nowhere for her to go.

His mom had said something about the Chenoo coming back from the fields. The fields? Maybe she meant the fields where he saw those humans working earlier. And the bigger creatures he had seen out there among the human workers? Was one of them possibly the Chenoo that was holding his mom prisoner? This might mean that he was not guarding her right now, but would be back eventually.

The sun was closing in on the eastern horizon and would be disappearing soon, leaving him in darkness on this strangely skewed Earth. Time was not on his side.

Franklin became aware that he had not seen Nellie in several minutes, and when he looked around, she was nowhere in the vicinity. He imagined that she might have gone into the forest ahead of him to explore the strange new smells.

He risked being heard by anything lurking nearby as he called out into the woods, "Nelllllllie!" He cupped his hands around his mouth and yelled, "Hey girl! Where are you?"

Nothing. He tried not to breathe as he listened for any sign of his lost friend.

Then the smallest of cries drifted to him, carried in the sweltering currents of heat. It did not come from the direction of the forest, but from somewhere above him. Franklin looked up, and there to his left, high up in one of the trees that still remained standing, he saw his black, furry companion dangling in the air. Something had her.

CHAPTER FORTY-ONE
A SNATCHED SIDEKICK &
A STACK OF SKELETONS

Nellie was hanging helplessly by her front legs. The creature holding her was some sort of a large bird, like an eagle, but Franklin thought it also looked furry. Too far away to tell.

"Hold on, Nellie! I'm going to help you!" he screamed.

Knowing it had been spotted must have unnerved the predator, because it deserted its perch in the tree and glided into the sky. It flew low enough for Franklin to see it more clearly, and he saw that it was an eagle, but only in part. The other half of it was something like a fox.

Of course, he had never seen or even heard of an Enfield, and he wasn't interested in what it was, anyway. The only thing he knew was that Nellie's two front legs were being held tight by the very large talons of the raptor-like animal. The powerless dog pivoted her head to look at Franklin as she flew by him; her eyes conveyed to Franklin that *she* was the one who was sorry to have let *him* down. His heart sank as he started giving chase to the creature that clenched his dog so tightly.

But then Nellie's survival instincts took over, and the Newfoundland started kicking her dangling legs furiously, while at the same time snapping her jaws at the Enfield's hind legs, which held her.

Should he try using his telekinesis to drag the fox creature down or make it release Nellie? He didn't want Nellie to fall and not be able to stop her from hitting the ground.

He had to do something, though. And fast. The flying predator was putting distance between them.

Focus on the animal. Focus. The talons. Nellie.

Franklin was trying, but there was no tingling behind his eyes. He felt nothing.

It seemed that his gifts were not effective on Dark Earth. But supposedly his father was from here! His powers had to work! Maybe the creature that had his dog was just too far from him.

The pair moved steadily away from Franklin, flying higher into the sky, back towards the direction from where he had just come. He was still running but could no longer keep up with them. After a few minutes, he stopped and hung his head in disgust. There was nothing he could do.

Nellie, not one to give up easily, was finally able to reach her head far enough up and to the side so that she could snag the leg of the creature with her teeth. Her jaws held tight, and she bit down as hard as she could. The Enfield let out a painful shriek, and although it came from its head which looked like a fox, it sounded like the cry of an eagle in distress. As it screeched, both of its talons released their grip on Nellie. The Enfield had made the quick decision that instead of ripping its prey apart back at its nest, it would have to drop the dog now and let gravity kill it.

But Nellie didn't drop. Stubborn as she was, she refused to release the Enfield's leg from the clutch of her jaws. And the big dog's weight, as she hung from only one of the Enfield's appendages, made it impossible for the creature to stay in the air, and so they both started on a quick descent to the ground.

Meanwhile, Franklin had raised his head and was looking back up into the darkening sky to where his furry friend had just been carried away. He wanted to pay Nellie the respect of at least watching her until she was out of sight. Although the ebbing light made it difficult to see clearly, what he *could* see made his heart skip.

It was Nellie, but now she was dangling by her mouth and from only one leg of the Enfield. The Enfield was whipping its broad wings up and down wildly, while Nellie's weight pulled it steadily to the earth below. Franklin started running so that he could be there to help her when the two animals reached the ground, but he wasn't fast enough.

Nellie came crashing down to the dirt with the leg of the animal still firmly in her jaws. But, with the fox creature flapping its wings the entire time, it had slowed their descent so that they did not crash-land with enough force to get hurt.

They landed fifty feet in front of Franklin, the Enfield landing on top of the Newfoundland. There was a tussle; Franklin couldn't see exactly what was happening, but Nellie had finally released its leg from her jaws and was lunging in again, mouth first, trying to get a hold of a body part more tender than a leg; like the fox's throat. This caused the Enfield to fly several feet up into the air, where it hovered above its prey, wings whipping rapidly, making quick darts in at Nellie, but now going for her eyes. It knew that blinding the dog would bring a certain end to this fight.

But it discovered that attacking Nellie from her front side was futile. The big dog was snarling, baring her teeth, and she was quick to block any attacks from the sharp talons of the Enfield with her own strong jaws.

Franklin was almost to them but saw that the Enfield had changed its tactics again and was now attacking the dog from behind. It was trying to grab Nellie with its talons, but this time by her hind legs, so it could carry her away upside-down. This would place Nellie's muzzle far enough away so it wouldn't be in danger of being bitten again. The Enfield darted in towards the hindquarters of the big canine, but Nellie kept turning swiftly to face it each time it tried.

Only a few more steps and he would be there to help her, but then he watched as Nellie stumbled just once while she was turning toward the Enfield, preventing her from being able to fully face it. This slight miscue cost her, for the eagle talons were successful in grabbing her under the rear haunches and pulling her off the ground.

As Nellie was hoisted upwards once again, Franklin went airborne, vaulting himself towards his dog, catching her around her wide front shoulders and pulling her back to the dirt. In the next instant, he jabbed his hand into his pocket and seized the camping knife that Parker had given him. With one hand holding Nellie, and the other hand holding the knife, he had to use his teeth to pry the blade out from where it was tucked next to the can opener. Franklin reached around Nellie, all the way to where the Enfield was frantically trying to untangle its talons from the dog's fur, and he plunged the knife into whatever flesh of the creature was available. The knife, which only had a short blade, dug all of its two inches into one of the tender front paws of the fox. A miserable cry arose from the Enfield as it finally freed itself from its one-time prey and flew away.

Similar in the way that a sunset back home often throws out beautiful pink and purple light, decorating the sky right before dark, the sun here no longer cast its dreadful orange color, but instead, it created a hideous spectrum of green hues that lingered on the horizon. It was into this putrid green sunset where the Enfield disappeared.

As it departed in rapid fashion, the red camping knife fell from its injured foot, landing blade down in the dirt in front of Franklin and Nellie.

Franklin threw his arms around his friend's furry neck. "Nellie, I thought I had lost you!" he exclaimed. His face went into her downy fur, and she turned her head back and slobbered on him with her tongue, but only for a moment before barking twice. Franklin realized Nellie was the one reminding him that they had to hurry now.

"You're right, we gotta go."

He picked up the knife, wiped it off on his shirt, and put it back into his pocket.

The sun almost setting meant that the sweltering heat had begun to let up, though it was still hotter than an average summer day on Earth. After finishing off one of the water bottles, they hurried back to the edge of the dead forest, which was further away than Franklin had remembered backtracking in his frantic race to save his dog.

Peering into the jungle of waste and trying his best to see through the tree limbs and trunks, he said out loud, fairly certain that Nellie could understand him, "We're going to have to just work our way into this mess. Be on the lookout for anything."

Franklin jumped up on top of the closest branch in their path and climbed over it. This is how he started to work his way into the heart of the woods. Nellie had a much easier time with the trek, she could duck under many of the branches that Franklin had to clamber to get over or circle around them quicker than he was capable of doing.

There was still just enough of the strange green sunset seeping into the woods to allow them to see where they were going, but Franklin knew he would need his flashlight soon. He assumed that his ability to see in the dark would probably not work on Dark Earth, just as he had tried without success to conjure his telekinetic powers to stop the Enfield.

Although Shad had made sure to pack spares, conserving the batteries of the Mega Light was very important for two reasons. One, he did not know how long he would be on this dangerous planet, and therefore he needed to be deliberate in its use. And two, the white light that glared from this high-powered flashlight was a possible weapon against Nefari. Franklin cringed at the thought of a surprise encounter with his frightening nemesis.

He knew that Nefari could tolerate daylight on this planet. The ghoul had done it earlier, when Franklin lay on Cast Maker with a severely broken leg. He also realized Nefari might be waiting to make his move at night, when a surprise attack would be easier.

He wondered about Nefari; he had not seen him in several days. Why not? And Bramfasa? Would he, at some point, encounter this diabolical god that supposedly fathered him? Could he ever be capable of being as corrupt as his father? Or had Angel, as Charles and Mary told him, negated that evil heritage through her intense love for him?

Some of his new abilities may have come from his father and therefore might work on Dark Earth. He could keep trying. The question was, should he use his father's powers? Might he continue on the downward slide that he had been on with his anger and pride and become like his father? He didn't want to find out.

He reminded himself about the farmer, how he could have easily killed him back there at the windmill if he had chosen to. Either with his own strange, new talents or by directing Nellie to sink her teeth down into the man's neck. But he had not even considered that dark thought. Maybe he hadn't inherited any devilish genes from Bramfasa after all.

He came back to the present and saw that in the mere minutes his mind had been meandering through these questions, the light had diminished considerably. With no moon or stars to speak of, ambient natural light was non-existent, making it impossible to see some of the smaller obstacles. He couldn't afford to sprain an ankle, so he switched on his flashlight.

Nellie had disappeared again. He had seen her venture on ahead a few minutes ago but had not seen her since. Her black fur blended in with the night so perfectly that unless he had his flashlight trained right on her, she would be no more visible than a shadow. Of course, if she barked, like she *suddenly* did at that moment, it would help drastically. It wasn't her loudest bark, but rather a hushed 'woof', like she knew that being covert was necessary. Franklin begin moving towards her muted sound and aimed the flashlight in the same direction. He thought he noticed the beam of light reflect off of her shiny coat.

Arriving at the point where he thought he'd heard Nellie, his light revealed her standing there at attention while she waited for him, her eyes already pinned on him as he emerged between two leaning trees. When he didn't immediately come over to where she was, she swiveled her big body in a circle, then pawed at the air.

"Okay girl, I'm on my way," he said as he cautiously began to approach her.

Nellie wagged her tail in response.

Right then, if Franklin's nose could have jumped off his face and fled, it would have, for the stench of death hung in the air here, thick and overpowering. Holding his nose and trying not to breathe, he scanned the forest floor with his light. The remains of logs, blackened by fire, were scattered around him in a four-foot diameter. Ashes littered the dirt as well, spanning further out than the charred wood.

"Someone or *something* has had a lot of campfires here," he said in a low voice, pointing his light at Nellie again. "But what's that awful smell?"

In response to his question, she started pawing the ground beneath her, then she looked at him imploringly, urging him on with a flurry of whimpers. He walked to her, got down on his knees, and inspected the ground where she had been pawing. Remains of a dinner; bones, small pieces of rotting flesh, and bloodstains adorned the earth. The raw, discarded meat had attracted tiny scavengers; green, spirally worms moved over the surface of the flesh and poked their heads up like gophers from within it. This was no doubt the source of the horrid smell. As he stood up and aimed the beam further out, he saw that the scattering of bones extended for several feet, coming to an abrupt end at a high pile of similarly discarded remains. Franklin stood back up and could see that the mass of bones stood taller than he did, and that some of the yellowing remains must have been as large as the bones in his own body.

"A graveyard that doubles as a kitchen *and* a dining room," he muttered quietly.

Whatever had eaten animals with bones this large must be a very formidable creature itself; like the Chenoo, for instance.

Franklin felt certain Nellie had found the location where the Chenoo came to rest at night after being in the fields all day.

A thought entered his mind that was so repulsive he had to shove it out immediately, only to have it bully its way back in.

The pile of bones. He had to see it. Stepping quickly, he covered the distance to the pile in only a few seconds. The rank odor, which engulfed it, was almost as repugnant as it had been near the decaying flesh. His fear was confirmed. Although he was no expert, some of the remains in the pile looked human.

Moving around it, disgusted as he was, Franklin carelessly stumbled over a larger bone that had come to rest on the ground. Before falling, he was able to catch himself, using several other bones jutting from the center of the pile for support. The force of his weight rattled the pile, causing a single bone to roll off the top. As it jostled its way down the hill, a unique, hollow tone reverberated from each bone it struck, resulting in a haunting tune. Finishing its disturbing trip to the ground, it rolled to Franklin's feet and came to a rest at his shoe. He aimed his flashlight down and saw a large skull at his toes. He didn't need to look too closely to see that it was a human skull. His first thought was that it probably had come from one of the human slaves he had seen far out in the field.

But his mind drifted to a more appalling possibility. Could this skull belong to his mom? Could her remains be somewhere in this collection of death that had accumulated in front of him?

His immediate attention shifted elsewhere. Next to the pile, the beam of his light caught something else, not a bone this time, but something that caused the light to reflect back into his eyes. Something very out of place. What type of shiny, glittering item could possibly be around all this death? He bent down and saw a small object of metal pressed into the dirt. After prying it out of the hard earth with his fingernail, working without the aid of the flashlight, he held it in the palm of his hand, but with a closed fist, hesitant to reveal it.

A persistent dread had been heavy on him since he entered the forest, and it had seemed to be moving him towards this moment. Shining the light now down on his hand, Franklin slowly opened his fist. In it was a small silver-plated figure of a mother kneeling down and holding her young son tight in her arms.

It had hung on his mom's neck since the day Franklin was released from the hospital after the accident. One of the nurses, who had grown attached to both Angel and Franklin over the six weeks he had spent in intensive care, had presented it as a gift to her. His mom used to tell him how she wore it every day, since then, as a reminder of how blessed she was that he had survived. Now here it was, next to the remnants of some gruesome creature's kill.

Any question he had about whether his mom was still alive or not had been answered.

CHAPTER FORTY-TWO
A RUN-FOR-HIS-LIFE &
A REUNION

He squatted there in the filth, quietly crying. But as the reality of his mom's death… no, not just death, but the savage and barbaric last few moments of her life, came to his mind, his chest began heaving, and great, loud sobs escaped him.

In the dead woods where he sat, his wails of grief only added to the morbid backdrop.

His mom had most likely spent her last minutes alive, before being torn apart, knowing she was going to be dinner for that beast; knowing she would actually provide it *nourishment* with her own flesh and eventually just become more bones to add to the growing pile. This gave Franklin both incredible sorrow and extraordinary, raging fury, at the same time. His anger caused the tears to flow even harder, and the only thing he could think to do was to pound his fists into the ground, again and again, until they both bled.

The ground beneath where he rested had become damp with his salty teardrops, and soon his fists were covered in both blood and mud. Nellie came and laid next to him, not disturbing him, but just *being* there for him. Unconsciously, one of his hands went to the fur on top of her head, and he petted her. This calmed him somewhat, and after his sobbing had subsided to a point where he thought he could talk, he took the walkie-talkie from his belt, held it to his mouth, pressed in the talk button, and said, "Anyone there?"

Crackling. Silence. More crackling, then, "Franklin, we're right here." It was Sami. "Are you all right?" she asked. "Did you find her?"

Looking at his mom's necklace in his hand again, he swallowed hard, holding back the impulse to once again burst into tears. "I found her," he answered, putting the necklace into his pocket.

The despair in his voice had already given away what he had not yet actually told them, and they understood.

"Franklin, I am so sorry." Sami's voice had the quality of someone crying softly. "You tried to help her, she knows that."

Again, tears were begging to escape the corners of Franklin's eyes, like hot magma pushing against the crust of the earth. But he knew crying wasn't going to do his mom any good now. He had made up his mind what he had to do.

"Franklin?" Sami asked with some urgency. "Franklin, come back home now, okay? Please just come back." She released the button and waited for the crackling of the walkie-talkie that always sounded before his reply. Nothing.

"Franklin, are you there? Are you all right?" She was almost pleading with him.

He was silent for another moment, then he pressed the button in again to talk, a new quality in his voice now, "No, I'm not all right. I don't think I'll ever be all right again. But I am going to avenge my mom's murder; I'm going to butcher that monster. I'm going to kill it first, then I'll come home."

Shad grabbed the walkie, against Sami's wishes, "Franklin, it's Shad. Please listen. Just come home now. We'll get a plan together and then you can punish that creature; we'll help. Don't try it now, your anger is clouding your judgment."

"Thanks for caring guys, but I have to do this. If I die trying, then at least I died trying. If you hear from me later, it went well. If you don't, well, it didn't go so well. I love guys. Over and out." He turned off the walkie completely; he didn't want to give them the chance to try to talk him out of this. His mind was set.

Franklin stood up and headed for the cover of the woods, frustrated that he didn't even have time to grieve properly for his mom right then. The Chenoo would be back soon, and he didn't want to be such an easy target. "C'mon girl, we need to hide somewhere," he said, gesturing for Nellie to follow him.

After panning the trees with his flashlight for a few seconds, he decided that the best place to stay out of sight, while also remaining at a close proximity to the Chenoo's camp, was behind the very heap of bones where he believed his mom's remains to be. The field where the humans had been working was to the north, and the bones had been discarded on the south side of the campfire. Hiding there would most likely give him the best vantage point of the Chenoo returning from the field. He would wait for it to fall asleep, for he assumed the creature slept, and then figure out the best way to kill it.

The flashlight in his hands had been on this whole time, and he realized that this might have been a mistake. It may have already given away his position to his enemy. He at once flipped it off and walked toward the back of the bone pile. He took his backpack off, threw it to the ground, then crouched down, moving to a position where he was laying on his stomach. Unzipping a side pocket, he took the black mask out that Shad had given him and stretched it down over his face, past his chin, and down to his neck. If there was ever a time to be covert, this was it.

Nellie lay beside him, resting her muzzle on his back. Her ears were perked and ready. When that thing did come back, she would hear or smell it long before Franklin would. He tried to picture the foul creature in his head; he recalled it being the vision of death, with its skin hanging down and its bones in clear view. Strangely, it had many similarities to an elk or deer, except the fangs, which Franklin was pretty sure deer didn't have. He remembered what Shad had said regarding the Native American folklore about Chenoos; how they craved human flesh.

He thought of his mom again and cried into his hands.

As Franklin lay under the canopy of the dead trees, which sat under the moonless night, his eyes began to close. He tried several times to open them and stay alert, but he could not fight the alluring beckon of sleep. His mind and body were exhausted, and he drifted into an uneasy slumber. His dreams were filled with faceless monsters, bloody fights, narrow escapes, and brutal deaths. Nevertheless, his body rested.

In the middle of one of these nightmares, he was roused awake by Nellie's wet nose nudging his arm. At once he remembered where he was and what he was waiting for. It was not clear to him how long he had been sleeping, but he guessed it had been at least several hours.

He inched his head far enough out into the open, beyond the mess of bones, so that he could see. The blackness was intense. Without the flashlight, he could see nothing in front of him. He doubted he could even make out his own hand if he held it in front of his face.

His other senses were alert, too, and his ears, even through the knit hat, picked up the sound of twigs snapping underfoot of something. Nellie was standing next to him out in plain view, but Franklin was fairly confident that she would not be visible. The crunching had stopped, and now the sharp crack of limbs being torn off of a tree came every few seconds, followed by the loud racket of what must have been an entire tree smashing to the ground.

Silence came for a short period of time but was then replaced by the distinct sound of an ax smacking wood, over and over. Then the creature, which by now Franklin concluded had to be the Chenoo, began walking again, and he could distinctly hear it dropping the cut logs into a pile. Somehow, Franklin smelled the fire before he saw the small flames on the forest floor. With the aged and dry wood being used as fuel, the flame didn't take long to become a blazing fire, which crackled and spat into the night.

In the firelight, Franklin was able to see his ghastly adversary, sitting on what was left of the fallen tree. The Chenoo looked just as Franklin had remembered it from the cryptic projection several nights ago. Large chunks of skin peeled from its obscene torso and face, exposing rib bones and laying bare one side of his jaw. Gangly arms hung to the dirt, three fingers on each, with sickeningly sharp nails. Its legs, also too long for its body, were bent at the knee as it sat so that it looked to be insect-like with its elongated appendages contorting both this way and that. On the end of a short muzzle were finely pointed incisors, the top set of white daggers extended down over the lower, occasionally opening up so that its tongue, which reminded Franklin of a white eel departing its lair, could catch the saliva that was drooling from its mouth.

The Chenoo drooled because in front of it lay a bloody, dirt-covered carcass that it had dragged behind it through the forest. Franklin could not make out exactly what it had chosen for its dinner, but it was a beast almost as large as the Chenoo was itself. He watched as the lanky arms reached in and grabbed one of the dead creature's legs; the sound of ripping flesh could barely be heard over the excited grunts which the Chenoo made.

Franklin had assumed the fire was to cook the meat, but now he saw that cooking was not a priority with this beast, and it proceeded to eat the animal raw. In less than a minute, it had consumed the entire leg, leaving the bones. It then gnawed as much of the remnants from those as possible, too, before tearing another appendage off the victim in front of it.

As the Chenoo was finishing his second helping, it paused, and its black nose starting bobbing up and down in the air. A breeze had come in from the south through the woods and brought with it a scent that must have interested the predator. Franklin grew nervous as he watched it sniffing the air; he should have considered the possibility that it had the olfactory senses of a bloodhound and then chosen a hiding place downwind of it. But there had been no breeze earlier, anyway. In fact, he had never even felt a breeze in this dimension of Earth until now. *Perfect timing*, he thought.

It was too late. The Chenoo tossed down the half-eaten leg, inhaled the strands of flesh hanging from its mouth, and in the same blood-curdling shrieks that it had used when they heard it before (but from the safety of a different dimension) it cried, "Putrid——human——stench."

Standing up, the awful creature stretched to its full height of over seven feet, raised its long arms high, while simultaneously thrusting out its skeletal chest and tilting its head towards the sky. It issued the murderous cry of a predator commencing a blood quest, then moved from the fire in the direction of the bone pile where Franklin hid.

In his mind, Franklin's plan had him with the advantage of remaining undetected, while sneaking up on the Chenoo as it slept (if it slept) and somehow killing it. But being hunted by this Dark Earth monster in the night, on its home turf, was not part of his strategy.

The grisly predator gave itself one last whiff of the air and then took off in a long-legged sprint towards Franklin's hiding spot, its spidery arms trailing behind it in on the ground.

Already on his feet, Franklin whispered to Nellie, "Let's go. Now!"

He left the backpack where it lay, but grabbed his flashlight and took off running into the woods. He kept the beam of light directed at Nellie, who had sprinted out in front of him. His face would have taken a great whipping as he ran through a barrage of twigs, but fortunately, the mask he had put over his head protected him. The dog continued looking back to make sure he was close behind her, and it seemed to Franklin like she wanted him to follow her. So that's what he did.

Running for your life in a dark forest full of stumps and fallen trees is not easy, and it only took one time for Franklin to misjudge how far he had to jump over a log to send him crashing to the forest floor. For the split second he lay there, he recalled the bloody scene of the Chenoo eating the leg of whatever it had just dragged into camp. Only his imagination changed the scene so that it was *his* leg the beast had just ripped off and was devouring like a drumstick.

Nellie immediately came back to encourage him to get up and be fast about it. She didn't have to bark twice, he was up in a flash and sprinting once again.

Franklin knew the monster was gaining ground in its pursuit of him; the sound of its big body crashing into trees was getting closer, and it would be upon him very soon. Following Nellie was like practicing a trust fall with your friend. In a trust fall, a person must have faith that their friend will catch them as they fall backward towards the ground. So as his dog, for whatever reason, began to circle back in the direction they had come, Franklin followed willingly, because he trusted that his new companion had both of their best interests in mind as she chose this route.

In the middle of her circular trek back around, Nellie suddenly veered to the right, cutting directly toward the campfire that both dog and boy could see burning ahead. Franklin flipped off his flashlight. He wondered what she could be thinking...

should he really trust a dog with his life? Again, he reminded himself that this was no ordinary dog.

Twenty feet from the fire, Nellie stopped, as did Franklin. They both looked back and saw nothing, but heard trees snapping as the Chenoo kept running straight, not knowing they had made a sharp turn back to his camp. The same breeze that had given Franklin's scent away earlier, now carried his distinctly human smell away from the Chenoo, helping to keep it off his path. For now, anyway.

Smart dog, Franklin thought. *But what was her plan now?*

As they approached the fire, Franklin made sure to sidestep the twisted, torn animal that lie in the dirt, the one that had just served as a late night snack for the Chenoo.

Nellie ran past the fire, and Franklin continued to follow her, but then he stopped when she did and watched as her ears twitched and came to life. Had she heard something? She moved a little farther away from the blaze, ears still alert, but now putting her nose to the ground as well.

"Nellie, what are you doing? We have to either run or turn and fight this thing. There's no time for sniffing!" Franklin said in a whisper, becoming exasperated by his dog's lack of worry.

Nellie paid no heed to him, but she continued to concentrate all of her attention on what her nose was telling her, and did this for the better part of ten seconds. Then her paws suddenly came to life. In the light of the fire, Franklin could see her padded feet clawing furiously at the ground. It gave him the impression that the dog's feet, like the dog itself, had minds of their own.

The 'burglar' mask covering his face had gotten somewhat twisted and was blocking part of his vision in both eyes. Probably not the best time to have poor eyesight, considering it was already hard enough to see. Not only that, but the mask was completely soaked in his sweat. After ripping the suffocating cap off of his head, he flung it into the fire. So much for stealth.

The cool breeze felt good on his unmasked face, but this relief only lasted a moment before dread replaced it once again. Best guess: they only had a few minutes, maybe less, before the Chenoo would come back to his home base.

Behind the pile of bones sat Franklin's backpack where he had left it. He retrieved it, knowing it had critical items for survival. Items he would need, assuming he wasn't another meal, served cold, for the monster pursuing him.

Returning to the fire, he found Nellie still digging frantically. He turned the Mega Light back on and pointed it down, trying his best to cloak the stray beams of light so as not to signal their position to the Chenoo. Then, getting close to the ground, he inspected the area where the dog's paws were at work. Nothing had been uncovered yet. A small pile of dirt that Nellie had excavated was all there was to show for her efforts.

A bone-chilling screech rang out from somewhere in the woods. It didn't sound very far away.

"Let's go!" he said quietly, moving past Nellie, ready to run again and this time take the lead himself. His foot kicked something hard, not a stick. Looking down, he could see an ax lying in the dirt, the one that the Chenoo had used for chopping wood and, most likely, the bodies of past victims. He decided it might come in handy, and so he stowed it away in his belt loop.

"C'mon, girl!" He was close to grabbing Nellie's collar and dragging her away when the firelight allowed him to catch a glimpse of something at the bottom of the hole where she dug. Inspecting it with his flashlight, Franklin saw a rusty iron ring, about the diameter of a pop can. The ring reminded him of the old handle used to open the cellar door in the orphanage yard.

"I see it," he told Nellie, who finally stopped digging upon hearing these words. She backed up, giving him room, and he reached down and gave it a hard tug. When the heavy ring moved ever so slightly upwards, he used both hands to begin sweeping away more dirt. Nellie joined him, and soon the two had cleared a larger area around the ringlet, allowing Franklin to discover that they were atop a series of wooden slats that had been fashioned to make a trapdoor.

A door in the ground? For what? he wondered.

But even as this question came to his mind, something else, akin to hope, sprang up in his heart.

He asked, "What did you find, girl?"

Nellie stared at him earnestly, then looked at the door in the earth, then back at Franklin again, all the time wagging her tail. He took the cue from her and stepped down into the three-foot-square clearing where they had both worked to move away the dirt.

Bending down, he got both hands around the ring and was about to pull up on it when a thought occurred to him. He realized that lifting up a door that he was standing on was probably not going to work.

Franklin glanced over at Nellie to see if his new friend was capable of laughing at his stupidity, but she only looked on patiently.

Instead of standing inside the hole which they had cleared, he hurriedly positioned himself on the outside and bent down to once again try to lift up the ring.

As he pulled on the ring, the door in the ground lifted just an inch, but it was enough to allow him to hear a weak cry coming from beneath him. Someone had been yelling down below, in the earth, the whole time, and only Nellie had heard it!

But the low throaty growl that suddenly burbled forth from his dog as she peered into the woods told Franklin that they were out of time. Fifteen feet away in the dark came the sound of branches snapping, giving way to something big; no doubt the Chenoo was returning. Franklin gave the door everything he had, pulling up hard, and to his surprise, it came up easily, tossing off the rest of the loose dirt as it did.

He held it open with one hand and flipped the flashlight on with the other, aiming it directly at what lay beneath the door. What he saw was a crude, wooden staircase descending down. Wasting no time, Franklin pushed Nellie onto the stairs, grabbed his backpack, and just as he heard heavy footsteps lumbering towards him from the darkness, he slid under the partially elevated door and let it shut gently above him.

He waited in the dark, at the top of the stairs, for a minute, making sure the Chenoo had not spotted him. When he was fairly certain it had not, he started to climb down the stairs.

His foot missed the first step, however, and he tumbled all the way down to the bottom of the pit, jarring the flashlight free from his hand and causing the light to go out. Uninjured, he sat up and looked around. Because of the darkness, he wasn't sure if his eyes were opened or closed, and he had to blink several times in order to find out.

If it's possible, he thought, *it might be even darker down here than up there!*

To his comfort, he felt Nellie's furry face brush against his own, right before her warm tongue found his cheek.

"Thanks, girl. I'm okay," he said softly. Then, pausing momentarily, he addressed the darkness, "Who's down here with us? Who's voice was that I heard?" His hand searched through the dirt around him until he found his flashlight.

All varieties of evil played out in his imagination. Fantastic fiends that might currently be sharing this hole in the ground with him danced in his mind's eye; this hole that may very well end up being his own grave.

But he also imagined the possibility that it was something else entirely, and it didn't take long for him to find out the answer.

"Franklin?" It was a voice so sweet that called out to him from the darkness, and he got up and moved swiftly to its source, without pause. Shuffling forward, he found his mom's open arms waiting to embrace him. The feeling of her holding him once again, a feeling he never thought would be possible, was even more miraculous than the night his legs were restored. He wanted to hug her forever, and it seemed that he might, but Angel finally relaxed her grasp and released him, instead taking both of his hands in hers.

Remembering to keep his voice low, Franklin exclaimed, "Mom, it's really you! You're alive!" His face was wet with tears, "I… I found the necklace the nurse gave you up by the bones and thought that you had…" His voice faded. Finishing the sentence wasn't necessary.

"The first time I escaped," Angel whispered back, struggling to speak at all through her free-flowing tears, "the Chenoo threw me on his shoulder and carried me back here. The necklace must have been ripped from my neck because I haven't had it since that night."

Her hands went to Franklin's face; this time they were real flesh and blood instead of a hologram image. She tenderly rubbed his cheek, wiping away his tears. "Franklin, can I see you?" she asked.

He fidgeted with the flashlight, which had cracked apart just a bit in his fall, until he got it to turn on and then held it out far enough to illuminate himself. The tears in her eyes twinkled as she gazed at him. She held him tightly again. "My Franklin, you came for me, sweetheart," her voice was weak. "But you shouldn't have come here," she took a deep breath, "because wherever we are now is a living hell."

"Mom, there's no lock on that door up there," Franklin said, a bit bewildered. "Why haven't you left? Just gotten out of here?"

She hesitated, thinking about her answer, "I knew when I saw the image of the boy sitting in the woods one night, that if I kept trying, I might be able to contact you, too…so I went out every night before the monster would get back from wherever he went. I kept looking for you, until you finally came two nights ago." Angel sighed and gently put her hands on his face again.

"But after the Chenoo caught me the last time, a few nights ago when I finally found you, he started piling dirt on top of the door so that I couldn't just lift it to get out anymore."

Franklin remembered having to dig down into the ground and sweep away the dirt with Nellie, in order to uncover the wooden boards of the trapdoor above them.

"But earlier," he said, still not understanding, "when you were first brought here, you could have left…"

"Where would I go?" she asked. "I knew the best chance of you ever finding me was to stay here, stay in one place."

Finally, Franklin nodded his understanding. He reached into his pack and pulled out a bottle of water, opened it, and handed it to his mom. She took it and thanked him, gulping it down in between bites of an energy bar that Franklin had also fished out of his backpack. He sat down in the dirt once again, and his mother joined him.

Franklin wanted to be able to see his mom, too. It had been so long. He pointed the light in her direction, making sure not to blind her with the intense beam. His first thought, upon seeing her, was how her beauty had not been diminished by the cruelty she had been subjected to. She was filthy; dirt streaked in all directions across her face, and her long brown hair was black with mud. Even through the grime, he could see how pale her face was. How sickly she appeared.

The clothes she had on, the same ones she must have been abducted in so long ago, were tattered rags. Her frame was so thin now that she looked emaciated to him, literally starving to death. Her arms and legs were scarred by the many beatings that she had no doubt endured, and some of them, deep lacerations, were possibly infected. Streaks of dried blood ran down her neck, starting at a large gash that was visible through her matted and thinning hair. A wound on one of her legs etched a path from her knee down to her ankle, probably slashed by one of the bladed fingernails of the Chenoo.

Something was off, a bit strange, but in the thrill of finding her, he tried not to dwell on it. He didn't know why, but his mom had no shine about her. Nothing. Nellie's pink and blue shine had been bright, even on this tainted planet. But his mom's colorful aura, which Franklin had always been able to see ever since the night he had been healed, was missing.

He asked himself what this demon Chenoo could have done to her that would make her shine disappear.

Whatever had happened, whatever horrible things it had done, his mom was still here. In front of him. He would rescue her, and nothing would stop him.

In a hushed voice, Franklin declared, "I'm going to get you out of here, Mom. We're going to wait until that thing falls asleep, and then we'll leave."

He watched as the muscles in her face struggled to create a smile.

During their reunion, Franklin's heart had skipped a beat whenever the sound of the Chenoo's bony feet scraped the wooden slats above them. He was grateful for the darkness outside and that the firelight's intensity was waning, because it hopefully would keep the predator from discovering that dirt no longer covered the top of the trapdoor. Assuming it had any brains at all, that discovery would certainly give it a clue that the door had recently been opened.

A few times they heard the beast's shrill cries, although muffled through the thick boards. Franklin knew it was probably cursing in frustration about having let him get away. But now all sounds of movement and screaming had stopped, and it was silent above them.

Before Franklin could say anything else, Angel grabbed his hand and whispered, "He's listening for us now. We need to be still and keep our voices low."

Franklin aimed the beam at the ground, just to provide some light. He wasn't ready to switch it off yet, not down here. In the corner of the underground cell, on the other side of his mom, were two bowls made from the caps of skulls, one with some small meat scraps in it and another that must have been used for water. His mom had been treated like a common animal.

They sat down and looked up into the muted darkness, waiting to hear some sign that the Chenoo had started moving again.

"I don't think it can hear us," Franklin said. "We've been quiet, and that wooden door is hard for sound to penetrate. I couldn't hear you yelling at me until I lifted it up."

"That's true, Franklin," Angel agreed.

Thinking about this now, Franklin was puzzled. How *had* his mom known that he was above her? Why had she been yelling for him? The Chenoo was a big creature, and hearing *it* walk above them was not difficult, but he and his dog hadn't been loud…except for…maybe when Nellie had been digging so stubbornly.

"You must have heard the dog scratching on the door up there," he concluded, confident this must be right.

In the murky light provided by the flashlight's beam, which was currently directed to the side of the pit, Franklin had noticed his mom's face was tense, but now, with his last words, here expression relaxed.

"Yes, the dog. I heard it scratching," she said, almost imitating the cadence of his voice.

As if on cue, Nellie came over, plopped down next to Franklin, and put her head on his lap.

Angel, noticing Nellie for the first time, scooted backward on impulse. "A dog?" she asked emphatically.

Franklin could hear the surprise in her tone, but there was also something else in the delivery of the question. Possibly an undertone of worry; he wasn't sure.

"Ummm, yeah. You just said you heard her scratching above on the door, right? Mom, you love dogs. You always told me that," he said. "You're acting a little funny. Are you all right?"

Instantly, he knew how insensitive this question sounded and he could tell that his mom wasn't sure how to answer it, either. He tried correcting his mistake, "I'm so sorry, Mom. Of course you're not okay. You've been a prisoner down here for more than…"

Angel grabbed his hand and squeezed it. "It's all right, Franklin. You don't need to apologize."

"This is Nellie; my dog and my friend. I've known her for less than a day and she's already saved my life more than once."

Nellie didn't look up. Her head remained on Franklin's lap, and she kept her eyes low.

Franklin nudged her, trying to get her to stand up and go greet Angel, but he was unsuccessful. Newfoundlands were definitely a stubborn breed.

"Just reach over and pet her, Mom," he said finally.

Angel's eyes widened with fear, although Franklin, still prodding Nellie, did not notice.

Franklin finally looked at his mom and saw that she was frozen, waffling on what to do.

"C'mon. Nellie's gonna love you once she gets to know you."

With a few more of his insistent prompts, Angel finally agreed. Slowly, she reached across Franklin to pet Nellie's head. But before her hand actually touched her, the dog gave a deep, guttural growl.

She jerked her hand back, frowned and muttered, "Dumb dog doesn't like me."

Franklin looked at his mom questioningly. This wasn't something she would have ever said before. It appeared that being a prisoner on this morbid version of Earth for so long had given her personality a sharp edge.

He turned to his dog. "Nellie, why did you growl, girl? That was bad!" Franklin said, scolding his furry friend. "This is my mom!" But then he softened, continuing to scratch her behind the ears.

Answering his own question, he said, "I think she must smell the Chenoo on you."

Angel gave Franklin a timid smile and took one of his hands, "Franklin, you need to stop talking so much. We'll have plenty of time for that after we get out of here, honey."

Above them, the silence was broken by three whacks on the wooden door. Bawomp! Bawomp! Bawomp!

The slats shook, loosening crusted dirt that snowed down upon them. Franklin jumped to his feet and extended his hand to help up his mom. Weakly, she took it and stood up.

"Does it do that very often?" Franklin whispered to his mom.

"Never," she shook her head despondently, "the most it does is open the door to come down and give me food and water once a week…sometimes hit me."

"Then it knows, Mom! It must be able to smell me or Nellie again." His voice didn't quiver from fear when he spoke, but rather had the steady quality of someone in control. "Do you know of any way to hurt this thing?" he asked.

Angel's voice, on the other hand, had the tone of defeat when she answered him, "No, I don't, or I would have tried it already." She thought for a moment. "But you can see that its body is slowly rotting away. Its skeleton is exposed throughout it, and it keeps getting worse. I don't know how, but it still has a voracious appetite, and it's very powerful, even though I don't see any muscle on it," she replied.

"It's like the dead that come back to life in that television show. It must have supernatural strength," Franklin said.

Angel begged him, "I don't want you to try to help me, just run if you can…when he opens the door."

The creaking of old hinges punctuated her sentence. Nellie had already positioned herself in the space between where

Franklin stood by his mom and the bottom of the steps, ready to protect him.

Franklin flipped his flashlight off.

Above them, the wooden door was flung wide open. The Chenoo's violent screech deafened the trio momentarily, but a second later they heard its heavy footsteps descending the stairs. Then it was there. They knew, even if they couldn't see it, that it stood directly in front of them, blocking their only exit.

Dying now was not an option; he had come this far to rescue his mom, and he wasn't going to leave her alone again. He had only one idea, his only real hope. Franklin focused his thoughts, directing his stare into the darkness towards the Chenoo.

He hoped he had been wrong earlier and that his gifts would work here on Dark Earth. At this point, even if he had to call on powers that Bramfasa had given him, he didn't care. This was a dire situation. If he couldn't pick up the monster and throw it to the ground with telekinesis, then maybe he could at least blind it, like he had Hank, so that they could escape past it, possibly even lock it down here in its own cell.

Focus. Chenoo. Focus.

The tingling began behind his eyes, and he could feel the warmth coming to him; he could see the glow of a dim light began to radiate out from him. But almost as soon as it had started, the sensation faded.

In the void directly in front of them, the Chenoo burst forth with an outcry that sounded faintly like laughter. The smell of the rot coming from the creature made Franklin gag; he imagined this must be similar to the stench of a decomposing corpse. Seeing once again that his powers were not responding to him, he instead decided to just use what he had, so he aimed the flashlight at the spot where he figured its ugly face was and flipped it on.

In front of them, they could all see the beast shade his eyes from the powerful beam. It stumbled over Nellie and came crashing down onto the ground next to her. She immediately pounced on the Chenoo and started thrashing at its exposed neck with her teeth.

Franklin used the opportunity to grab his mom's hand and usher her hastily up the stairs. He wanted to help Nellie, but first, he had to get his mom to safety.

"Mom, head over there," he pointed to the north, upwind of where they were, "and find a tree to climb." Before she could protest, he ran back towards the hole.

As he approached the dugout, he could hear Nellie's terse, threatening barks coming from below. He stopped at the top of the stairs to think. Another one of his powers would come in handy right now; he had found out from the StyJeen that this particular one *was* from Bramfasa, and so it might work here, on Dark Earth. And, it would be helpful before just rushing into the fight.

Franklin closed his eyes and meditated, for only a second, on his current situation and the different options he had right at that moment. Choosing one of them, he found himself sprinting down the stairs; he took the ax from his belt and had his flashlight readied. He was just in time to see his dog airborne, hurtling into the packed dirt wall of the underground cell. She smacked against it with an audible thud, let out a short whine, then slumped to the ground and fell silent.

Before he even had a chance to swing his ax, from behind him the Chenoo's two spidery arms emerged out of the dark and wrapped tightly around his chest. Its three angled fingers on each hand dug deep into both sides of his torso, penetrating into muscle. He screamed in pain, but this only made the Chenoo grasp him tighter. Franklin struggled to take air into his lungs, but when he did, the skeletal arms squeezed it right back out of him. To his horror, he felt a hot, needling pain in his shoulder so intense that he forgot about his lack of oxygen. The pain suddenly became more extreme, and he heard the sound of something being ripped apart next to him. When he turned his head, the hot breath of the beast was in his face. In the dark, he could hear its teeth grinding down, chewing the flesh and muscle that had been torn from his shoulder.

On the verge of losing consciousness, Franklin fought to bring his thoughts back to when he was still at ground level, at the top of the stairs, not yet having descended into this agony.

Then he was there, standing, pondering his options again. His gift of future-sight had worked, as he thought it would, and he had seen that going back down into the pit would have been a fatal mistake.

CHAPTER FORTY-THREE
A RESCUE & A RIBCAGE

Franklin stood at the top of the dugout trying to figure out what he should do now. Below him, Nellie's barking had stopped, and he heard a short-lived whimper rise from the hole beneath him. She had just been smacked into the wall as he had seen only moments ago.

Shining the flashlight in a circumference around him, desperately looking for anything that might help, he spotted a rope, about seven feet long, tied around a tree. When he picked it up, he saw that it looked to be made of braided fibers from a root or other part of a plant, but still seemed as strong as any manufactured rope he had used before. On the free end of the braided rope was a slipknot tied to create a loop; the Chenoo probably used it to fasten around the necks of his meals, keeping them fresh right here at his campsite until he was hungry.

Setting the flashlight down, but aiming its beam at the tree, he pulled the camping knife from his pocket and cut the rope loose. When gathering it up, he saw that he had misjudged the full length of it at first, and that another eight feet of slack had been lying next to the tree which he had inadvertently cut off. He picked it up and using a double fisherman's knot, secured the two lengths of rope back together, giving him about a fifteen-foot cord.

Franklin wasn't exactly sure how a long rope would help him yet, but he had nothing else at this point. He positioned himself to the side of the open doorway and waited, flashlight extinguished, for the Chenoo to emerge from the hole. He didn't need to wait long. The massive antlers came up first, followed by the rest of its sickening body.

Almost in a state of panic and without any ideas to go on, Franklin recalled how he and Charles had brought down the troll the day before by making it lose its balance.

It's something, I guess, he thought.

Although being in such close proximity to this stomach-churning behemoth went against his better judgment, he had to act quickly. The Chenoo rose up out of the hole. Franklin couldn't see it very well, but he could hear it grunt, smell its rot, and feel the cold chill that actually poured from its body. As of yet, it hadn't noticed him crouching next to the hole, and fortunately, it came up facing away from him. When both of the Chenoo's feet had stepped off the last stair and onto ground level, Franklin reached the rope out and brought it around its bony ankles, then grabbed it with his other hand so that he had its legs caught in a lasso.

He pulled it tight.

Not expecting an assault of this nature, the gangly creature took a step forward and toppled to the ground.

Franklin wasted not a second before reaching down to his belt and grabbing the Chenoo's ax, while at the same time scampering to where the beast had fallen. He raised his hand high and came down hard, hacking the blade of the hatchet into the back of the beast's head, near the center where its racks of antlers began. The ax blade easily cut through its loose skin and wedged neatly into its skull. He pulled it out, and again lifting it up, came down with as much force as he could muster, this time right below its neck, trying to reach its spinal cord. The ax went down and dug into bone once more, where it held fast and prevented Franklin from retrieving it this time.

All of this was in a matter of seconds, and as the beast realized what was happening, it was able to react much more rapidly than Franklin had thought it could. It propelled itself upwards by pushing off the ground with its outstretched arms, jumped into the air, and then turned its lanky body back over, somehow landing on both feet. Before Franklin could move to get out of the way, one of its arms shot out and three spindly fingers wrapped around his neck. It lifted him off the ground, angled its head back, and once again emitted its wicked shriek. This time, from such a close range, Franklin's eardrums were rattled.

Franklin twisted fiercely back and forth, his legs whipping freely in the air, but to no avail. The Chenoo, not wanting to kill him quite yet, did not grip his throat tightly enough to deny him oxygen. Nevertheless, being dangled helplessly in the air by the neck made it difficult to breathe.

With the other arm, the Chenoo reached around its own head and pulled the ax out from his back, then held it up for Franklin to see. The hatchet looked minuscule in his spacious palm. Franklin saw that there was no blood smeared across the blade. It was as clean as if it had pierced dry sand. The beast tossed it to the ground, then using his terrible one-word shrieks, his muzzle inches from Franklin's face, screamed, "I'm——Already——Dead."

So violent were the shrill screeches, that the brittle branches hanging nearby shook, some falling to the forest floor. The Chenoo's hot breath was forced into Franklin's face and up his nostrils. The smell of death was intense, coming from inside the creature, and Franklin had to keep himself from gagging before he struggled to reply in wry fashion, "I guess that explains... why you smell like roadkill."

His intent was not to hurt the Chenoo's feelings, although he hoped it did. He was really trying to keep the beast's attention on him so that it wouldn't notice his leg. A moment ago, the rope had somehow ended up across Franklin's feet when the Chenoo lifted him up by the neck. Now, he raised his foot up slowly, so that he could reach down and grab the end of it with his fingertips.

The monster, eager to get a taste of his coming meal, coiled out a dry, white tongue speckled with rot, from its mouth. Starting from Franklin's chin, it licked him slowly and deliberately, savoring every inch, up to his forehead, leaving behind a trail of ivory skin flecks.

The pale tongue crawled back into its mouth, and the Chenoo bared his finely edged teeth for Franklin to see.

"Okay… that's enough!" Franklin countered, straining with each word. "You went way too far…. What am I supposed to do …with that repulsive memory…now?"

Meanwhile, Franklin's fingertips had finally made contact with the coarse fibers of the rope, which he pulled up into his hand and clutched tightly.

The Chenoo only stared at him with its deep-set, barren eyes, not offering a response.

"How about I do a little…open chest surgery on you?" Pulling up the looped end of the rope that he held, Franklin thrust his arm forward, fist first into the deteriorating body of the creature. His hand, along with the rope, went right through the muscle lining, into the Chenoo's hollow chest cavity.

While the beast had been licking him moments ago, he had somehow managed to devise a plan, and this was the first part. As for the rest of it, he wasn't very confident.

Moving his hand freely now around inside its chest, brushing against shriveled lungs and a withered heart, he finally located the back of the rib cage, and he looped the rope around the thickest part of the Chenoo's ribs that his hand could find. Two ribs actually. He pulled the slipknot tight and tugged on the rope to see if it was secure. It didn't budge.

Having nerves that also must be dead, the Chenoo didn't feel pain. This gave Franklin a few seconds before the creature actually noticed that a hand was digging around inside him.

When it finally did figure this out, it threw Franklin to the ground, knocking the breath from him. But he could see he had been successful; the rope hung from the hole he had made in its chest, still attached up inside to its rib cage.

The enraged Chenoo exhaled a throaty gargle before it began thrashing its claws across Franklin's face, giving him sets of matching gashes on both sides of his cheeks. Then, with his strong hoofed feet, the monster delivered blow after blow of painful kicks to his ribs.

Franklin's eyes had been closed for the entire beating thus far, but now they opened wide. He glowered at the Chenoo with a strange, feral stare. Even in the blackness of the night, his purple irises were visible as they began to glow softly. But within seconds, the purple hue in his eyes gave way to a new color.

Orange.

Soon the orange flared from his sockets so brightly that his eyes appeared to be on fire.

At the same time, everything around him became visible, and he could see clearly even in this pitch-black night of Dark Earth.

He noticed something... or somebody... running out from behind the pile of bones towards him, and a yellow beam from a flashlight bouncing as the person ran. Not his mom. He knew that. But in the midst of the painful beating at the hands and feet of the Chenoo, he could not get a clear look at the person.

Another hard rib kick forced a grunt from him, and then he felt the skin on his chest open as the Chenoo's nails ripped through his shirt like tissue paper.

But he now saw who it was sprinting like a mad person towards the Chenoo. The shine emanating from her as she ran was unmistakable; bright pastel colors. Sami had come to help him. She must have found her way to the farmhouse, to the Gateway hidden in the spinning blades of the windmill, and then somehow to this dead forest.

For some reason, instead of being grateful to see her, he grew angry. In profound pain and bleeding from several deep incisions, Franklin still found the ability to scream, "Sami, what are you doing? I thought I told you not to come here! Can't you just listen for once?"

His voice was harsh, and he was furious that she had not stayed back at the orphanage, like he had told her to. His level of anger surprised even himself. Why was he acting this way towards his best friend, who at the moment was risking her life for him?

"You needed some help," was all she yelled back in reply, as she crossed near the fire pit, only feet away from the Chenoo now.

The beast paused in its focus on Franklin and looked at Sami. The flashlight she held, which was aimed at its head, allowed her to see its monstrous antlers turn towards her. Warning Sami to stay away, the Chenoo lifted its head in the air and screeched its deafening cry, but it didn't slow her down.

As she neared, she threw the flashlight to the ground and raised her arms above her head. Her hands had been concealed at her sides until this point, but now Franklin could see that both fists were clenched around a single bone fragment, about a foot long. It looked like the thick leg bone of an animal, one that had been snapped in a way so that sharp splinters stuck out from it on one end.

"Sami, stop. It'll kill you!" He screamed at her.

But she wasn't stopping, and he could detect no fear in her expression as she charged the beast, who was still poised over Franklin and holding him down with one hoofed foot. The Chenoo casually stretched its gangly arm out to swat her away, but instead, Sami ducked, maneuvered under it, and lodged the bone deep into the creature's flesh beneath its shoulder.

At this, the Chenoo, undaunted by the bone fragment in its side, swung its arm back the other way and cuffed Sami squarely in the back, throwing her face first into the dirt. Its three fingers groped around under its arm until it found the splintered bone and pulled it free. Then, leaving Franklin laying on the ground bleeding, it trudged towards Sami.

Sami was just turning herself over, dirt etched into the skin on her face from the head-first slide she took. She sat up and balanced herself on the skinned palms of her hands. Even in the dark, she knew…she could *smell*, that the Chenoo was perched right over her, his legs on either side.

The beast still held the sharp bone fragment in one of his hands, and as Sami tried to scoot away from underneath him, his other hand reached down and lifted her up by her ponytail, the tips of her toes still touching the earth.

She screamed brazenly at it, "Let me go, you Sasquatch!"

Like it had with Franklin, it only stared at her with its unfeeling black eyes, saliva draining from its pointed teeth. His other arm shifted and Sami felt the stinging shard of bone pressed hard against her neck.

Irritation and outrage still held Franklin in a strong, trance-like grip, but hearing Sami scream finally snapped him out of the spell that had come over him, and he sat up.

It was time for the next part of his plan.

Thinking fast, he took the other end of the rope that still lay next to him and knotted it around a nearby tree trunk, one that looked to be well rooted into the ground.

It was then that he caught sight of another beam from a flashlight, maybe two, centered on the Chenoo's head. He heard a loud *Twanggg* and the sound of something whizzing through the night air. He saw the Chenoo recoil after receiving a firm blow in the face from a small, but compact object. The creature flinched and almost dropped Sami. A second later the Chenoo backpedaled again as another projectile came hurtling towards it and tagged it on the shoulder.

Then, *Thwack*! The Chenoo's head jerked back as it was struck below its eyes, a large chunk of facial flesh falling to the ground, exposing its left cheekbone.

It released its hold on Sami, and Franklin was surprised as the beast shrank back into the woods, out of sight. The rope that he had tied around the trunk lifted off the ground and pulled tight as the injured creature must have traveled its full span and was now tugging against it.

Franklin was reminded of the time Hank had taken him and some of the other orphans fishing for Walleye. His own fishing line had gone tight, right before he hooked and then reeled in a three pounder. On the other end of his line now, though, he had caught something much more sinister than just a fish with dead eyes.

Franklin managed to stand up, although the agony in his body fought him with every muscle he had. He began hobbling slowly toward Sami when another flash of movement caught his attention. Running towards Sami, holding his glasses firmly onto his face with one hand, was Shad, and not far behind him was a limping Rufus. Franklin could see that in both their hands was a contraption that looked like a homemade slingshot attached to the top of a flashlight.

Rufus yelled, "That'll show that Cheboon, or whatever it's called, not to mess with us! Score one for the fat kid!" he paused but wasn't done. "That's me by the way, Shad. I want to make sure you don't think I'm calling you—"

"I get it!" Shad's voice yelled out from the dark.

Glancing down, Franklin saw the rope go slack again and fall to the ground.

The Chenoo was coming back.

He cried out, "Shad, Rufus! Get Sami out of there! It's coming back! It was a trick you morons, you didn't hurt it! You couldn't have, it's not even alive!"

Surprised, Shad shined his light in the direction of Franklin's voice and saw his friend staggering towards him.

"Stay there, Franklin. I got her!" he yelled.

Sami lay on the ground struggling to get her body to respond, still trying to recover from the hard blow that the Chenoo had given her on the back. Shad was almost to her, ready to help, when out of the darkness extended a long and crooked arm with a three-fingered fist on the end that smacked him across the head. His glasses were jostled from his face, and he was sent airborne into the pile of bones, which crashed and clattered down on top of him.

The Chenoo stepped out from behind a nearby cluster of dead trees that hadn't yet succumbed to their rot. It made a move towards Sami, but before it reached her, Rufus arrived on the scene. He had dropped the slingshot and retrieved a butcher knife from his back pocket that he had taken from the orphanage kitchen. He flailed it wildly at the beast, but only whiffed in the air. The Chenoo grabbed Rufus by his shirt and flung him towards the open door of the pit. He rolled over the earth twice and then disappeared down the hole. After falling five feet to the bottom and landing on his butt, he shouted at the top of his lungs, "You big, dead, dumb Chedoon!"

Franklin figured Rufus had that coming to him for getting into a fight he had no business getting into. He stopped and sat down on the ground ten feet from the creature. His eyes were no less orange than they had been during the extreme beating, which he had endured a few minutes ago. In fact, they began to glimmer even brighter now as he concentrated on the Chenoo, focusing on the creature's grotesque face, trying anything to rekindle his powers of telekinesis.

The final part of his plan.

Focus. Chenoo. See it. Hold it. Throw it.

Finally, Franklin felt the tingle behind his eyes strengthen and gain the severity he was waiting for. But it was different than before. It was painful this time; the pounding in his head was intense, and his brain felt like it was on the verge of exploding. He needed this to happen right now. It had to happen!

His orange eyes took on a haunted demeanor as they cast their stare directly at the undead creature. Franklin screamed out, "Hey you diseased moose! Are you ready to meet your maker?"

The Chenoo let out a series of grunts through its nose and turned its attention back to Franklin. Its mouth spread out into a smile of sorts, crackling what skin it still had around its muzzle like thin plastic. It took a casual step in his direction, still letting its six fingers drag behind it.

That was it.

With great thrill, Franklin felt the power burst forth from his body and watched as the surge of pent-up fury caught the Chenoo in mid-step. He savored the look of confusion on the face of the simple-minded beast as it was flung with powerful force, as if by a full-on tempest, away from where it stood by Sami.

The end of the rope, which Franklin had earlier plunged into the Chenoo's chest cavity and wrapped around part of its ribcage, was still being held firmly in place, and the other end remained attached to the very solid stump near Franklin.

Something had to give.

It only took a split second for the slack in the rope to disappear, and the monster, entirely astonished, reached the end of its leash like a whip cracking in the air. Now it was Franklin's turn to sound off a victorious howl as the Chenoo's chest burst open, its ribs and other skeletal fragments wrenched from its body.

Most of the creature continued to move away at a rapid pace, while some very important parts of it were left on the looped end of the rope.

But Franklin needed to make sure it wouldn't be bothering them anymore. Painfully, he made his way over to where the creature's feet could be seen jutting out from behind a knotted tree trunk; upon closer inspection, he discovered that the lower torso of the Chenoo was by itself, torn from the rest of the body. This didn't stop its gangly legs from thrashing this way and that, trying with all their might to bring themselves to a standing position.

A little further on, he saw the top half of the once terrifying creature. With no rib cage left to speak of, the Chenoo's upper body had ripped away easily from the rest of it, and Franklin found its antlers, head, neck, shoulders, and arms all together and unscathed, having come to rest against a fallen tree. Beneath its neck hung only tatters of loose skin; no blood or vital organs were in the vicinity. Franklin wondered if this beast even had a stomach with which to digest all the meat it consumed.

The beady black eyes glared up at him with deep hatred, and it pulled back its lips in a snarl. One of its arms lurched towards him, claws outstretched, but Franklin had made sure to stay out of its range. The half-of-a-Chenoo tried without success to flip itself over, perhaps thinking it could chase down Franklin by scratching and pulling itself forward through the dirt.

"You're pathetic," was all Franklin could think to say.

CHAPTER FORTY—FOUR
A TANTRUM & A TRICK

His plan had worked after all, he thought, although it had almost cost him his life, as the monster had thrashed him easy and often. The pain in his ribs was still sharp, but it was his head that was pounding. Absolutely pounding! The ache behind his eyes had not subsided at all, even after he let loose his fury on the Chenoo.

Franklin walked to where he had left his friends. His eyes had not yet lost their savage orange glow, and the same rage began welling up in him again when he found them.

"Hey!" he bellowed loudly as he came upon them. "What in the world were you three thinking?"

Sami had managed to crawl over next to Shad, who by now had emerged from the heap of bones that he had been buried in. She looked up at Franklin and calmly said, "Rufus is okay, in case you were wondering. We're all going to be okay, I think."

He shrugged off the comment and knelt next to them. In a gruff tone, he asked, "Why did you try messing this up? I had everything under control, and you could have ruined it…and gotten all of us killed while you were at it!"

Although Franklin knew they couldn't see him in the dark like he was able to see them, Sami still watched him. Even in the pitch-black night, it felt like she could read his thoughts, see right through him; her brown eyes were wide, searching his unseen face. Not only that, instead of relief in her expression and tone of voice, relief that the Chenoo was no longer a threat, there was sadness.

She asked, "What's wrong with you, Franklin?"

The anger in Franklin hadn't subsided. "Wrong with me?" he asked, with clear-cut sarcasm.

"Yes, you!" she said loudly. "You're acting horribly! We came because we knew you were in danger. We came here to help you!"

He tried to control his fury, but it continued to spew from him. "Trying to help *me*? I had to save *your* stupid lives!"

Sami sat all the way up, leaned in and brought her hand back, almost like she was thinking about slapping him for that last comment. Instead, she looked closely at his face and said, "Franklin, there's something really different with your eyes. They're not right. They're bright orange, not their normal violet."

By now, Rufus had found his way up the stairs and out of the pit and was stumbling his way towards them. When he finally arrived, he tripped over Shad's abandoned flashlight and fell flat on his stomach. Looking up at them from the ground, he said, "Bro, you're acting like the tail end of a donkey. It was her idea to come here and risk her life to try and help you. We couldn't have stopped her even if we tried. You'd be dead right now if she hadn't run at that Chegoon and stabbed it."

Franklin considered this. That was probably true.

He only said, "It's pronounced Chenoo."

"Okay, Chenoog, whatever. Who cares, anyway?" Rufus said.

Shad leaned over and whispered something into Sami's ear. She nodded her head and then reached over to Franklin with both arms and wrapped them around him, squeezing him tight. Shad scooted over on his knees and joined her, then Rufus, not wanting to be left out of the hug-fest, got up and tried throwing his arms around the group as far as he could reach.

This only piqued Franklin's anger, and he yelled, "Knock it off, losers! Leave me alone. I don't feel like hugging you right now!"

He thrashed his arms and legs, but to no avail, and even in the frenzied and distraught condition he was in, he still knew that using any of his powers to get them off would be overkill. There was no escaping; he couldn't budge them. After a few more tries of pushing and squirming with the same result, he gave up and just let his friends embrace him. As he did, his temper started to gradually recede. He could actually feel the rage leave him, and his head stopped hurting, too.

A flood of shame suddenly saturated Franklin down to his core. How could he have treated his friends with such hostility? The warning that Charles had spoken only yesterday came to his mind, *"Be careful to keep your gifts from turning you into something else. Something you don't want to become."*

Things had gotten a little out of control.

A moment later, he joined in the bear hug with as much vigor as his friends.

Trying to get an apology out amidst the tight embrace of three others wasn't an easy task, but Franklin managed to say, "Sorry about acting like that, guys."

His friends released their grasp and backed up to give him some space before Sami spoke for all of them, "We forgive you, Franklin." Shad and Rufus nodded in agreement.

He felt normal again. The orange gleam in his irises was gone, and after blinking his eyes open and shut several times, he discovered he was once again as blind as any of his friends were in this darkness.

Shad reached to the ground and grabbed his flashlight, then aimed it downwards. With the light it provided, Franklin could see his friends' faces. All of them were eagerly watching, seemingly waiting for an explanation to account for his aggressive behavior, but it didn't come.

Instead, Franklin exclaimed, "I can't believe you guys came for me!" He reached out and found Sami's hand, gave it a prolonged squeeze, and said, "Thanks, Sami. Thank you, guys. You did save my life. I was pinned down pretty good by that... that Chegoon." With his elbow, he nudged Rufus jokingly in the side as he said this. Then, looking from one friend to the next, he asked, "Is everyone okay?"

"I think we're all right. Bruised maybe, and some of my hair is still falling out from when I was dragged around like a cavewoman," Sami said, then looked at the deep scratches on Franklin's face. "But you... you look like you need a trip to the emergency room," she finished.

Franklin laughed, "Don't think we'll find one of those around here. I'll be all right. Just scrapes and bruises. Possibly a few cracked ribs. Hard to say."

Just then, Angel came running towards them. She yelled, "Franklin, you did it! You killed the Chenoo! Something I wish I could have done eighteen months ago. You're such a brave boy!" She grabbed him and held him tight. Shad's flashlight was still giving off enough light so that everyone could now see Angel, and she could see them.

Franklin hugged her back, but the whole time wondered if his mom had actually seen *how* he had killed the Chenoo, or at least stopped it, by using his telekinetic powers to throw it through the air. Shouldn't this make her a little curious? Down in the pit, he hadn't mentioned to her anything about his new abilities. It's possible, though, that in the dark she hadn't actually been able to see anything and had no idea what had happened.

Turning, he saw the look of utter surprise on each of his friends' faces, "Everything all right, guys?" he asked.

"I guess we all thought you were hinting on the walkie-talkie that you had discovered that your mom had... umm, had died," Shad explained. "No offense, ma'am," he said, embarrassed, making eye contact with Angel.

Franklin remembered the long-distance conversation he had earlier with them. "I'm really sorry, but I hadn't had a chance to tell all of you yet. I thought my mom was dead, until Nellie found her!"

He shuddered, suddenly remembering Nellie.

How could he just stay here and talk like everything was okay, when his dog was down in that hole in the ground, still hurt? Maybe dead.

He needed to check on her right away.

"Mom, can you explain to them how I found you? I have to go do something. Will you guys wait here for a second?" He sounded flustered.

Sami started to ask, "Do you need—"

But Franklin interrupted her, "I'll be right back, Sami. Nellie needs me."

Checking over by the door to the pit, where he had first rumbled with the Chenoo, he found his flashlight, flipped it on, and then, despite the pain in his side, flew down the steps to the floor of the underground room. His flashlight immediately showed him the black lump of fur; his Nellie was sprawled out on the ground where she had landed.

Franklin put his face down into the thick coat that covered his dog and said softly, "I'm so sorry, girl. I'm sorry I couldn't help you." Then, with both hands, and with all his might, he scooped her up and held her limp body in his arms. She was very heavy, and carrying her hundred-pound frame was more than a struggle. His ribs ached with every step, but slowly he willed himself to carry her up the stairs. Once at the top, he laid her on the earth so that he could rest and then called to Rufus to come help him. Together they carried the dog's body the rest of the way over to where his mom and friends waited.

Laying Nellie's body down next to Angel and shining the light on her black, shaggy form, he said, "Mom, this is who found you... not me. I got us here, but Nellie did the rest. She died trying to… to protect us." He did his best to keep a steady voice.

Sami ran her fingers through Nellie's fur. "This is the dog you told us about over the walkie?" she asked mournfully. "She's an incredible dog, Franklin. Where did you get her?"

"Some old friends gave her to me. They knew she could help me out."

Shad's hand went to Nellie's nose. "Franklin, her nose is still wet and cold."

"Yeah, I'm sure her whole body is probably cold by now, Shad," Franklin responded glumly.

"No, no, when a dog's nose is wet and cold, it's a good thing. And feel this," Shad held his hand in front of Nellie's open mouth. "There's warm breath coming from her."

Franklin put his hand where Shad's had been, in front of Nellie's muzzle, and sure enough, heated dog breath engulfed his fingers.

"She's alive?" Franklin asked, not quite believing it.

In response, Nellie's head lifted a few inches off the ground. Franklin sensed her movement and aimed his light toward her face; he saw her eyes reflecting the light back to him, like two pools of the purest water.

The pools blinked.

As implausible as it was, she was still alive. Nellie was gazing directly at him, and the sound of her tail thumping against the ground only added more evidence to this marvel.

Franklin bent down and hugged her. "Nellie, you're alive? You scared me! I thought that thing had killed you!"

His dog did what she did best when greeting someone, she slobbered on his hand, and then she turned and licked Sami too, who was still rubbing her back. Franklin continued patting her head and scratching behind her ears.

"Good girl! You tried protecting us!" he said. Nellie put her head on his knee, only moving her eyes to look up at him.

Then Nellie noticed Angel sitting behind Franklin. The big Newfoundland kept her head on Franklin's knee, but a deep growl, again, came from down inside her throat. Slowly, she sat up, shaking off some of the stiffness in her joints, and perched next to Franklin. Her growl grew in intensity and became more audible as she lifted up her jowls to show her teeth to Angel.

"What's wrong with that dog?" Angel asked with obvious irritation. "I think you ought to leave her here when we go. She'll fend for herself."

Franklin shot his mom a look of 'no way!' but remained quiet.

Angel moved a few feet farther away from Nellie, but the dog continued in its persistent growling, offended by Angel's very presence.

Franklin reprimanded her, "Nellie, this is my mom. She is the reason we came here! You need to stop growling at her, right now. I mean it!"

The Newfie grew silent and went back to licking Franklin's hand.

Shad, who had been sitting quietly, cross-legged in the dirt, stood up and walked over to where Franklin sat. Franklin noticed that Shad's glasses were cracked on one side, but at least he had found them and would be able to see. He bent down and whispered in Franklin's ear, "Can I talk to you privately for a second?"

They walked far enough away from the group so that they were out of earshot, and Franklin said, "Yeah, what's up, Shad?"

Shad moved next to his friend, keeping his back to everyone else. "Hey, I know you're really excited right now about finding your mom, but I need to tell you something, or I would feel remiss."

"Okay, sure. What's wrong?"

"Well, I was just thinking after you left us at the orphanage, last night," Shad said, a bit hesitantly.

"About what?"

"The night we saw your mom's vision in the woods. A few things didn't add up when I had time to think about it."

"Okay, I'm listening," Franklin said, trying not to let his growing frustration show in his voice.

Shad continued, "Well, don't you think it was a bit of a coincidence that she appeared to Rufus so close to where our home is? And that he happened to live at the same orphanage as you?"

"It worked out nicely, I agree," Franklin said.

"Yeah, it did, but there's more than that." Shad took a deep breath and sighed, then said, "How did your mom know that thing was called a Chenoo?"

"Huh?"

"Your mom, when we saw her image in the woods that night, she told you the *Chenoo* would be back for her. How did she know it was called a Chenoo?"

"It probably told her," Franklin responded.

"Maybe, but that thing didn't sound like a big conversationalist. Right? So it probably didn't tell her. Then how did she know?" Shad moved closer to Franklin so that they were face to face. He whispered, "Do you think she'd been studying American Indian monsters before she was kidnapped?"

This question came off as sounding more sarcastic than Shad had intended

Franklin was beginning to lose his patience. He wanted to be back with the rest of the group, especially his mom. "Umm, probably not, Shad. Please, get to your point."

"My point is, I'm not convinced that's your mom out there," he shook his head. "I'm sorry, Franklin. It's too convenient that we were able to see her in those woods. Too easy. I mean, how did she keep escaping so that she could appear to both Rufus and you? You think that monster would have let her escape a second time? And it was a slip up when she told you it was a Chenoo that had abducted her. How would she know the technical name of it? I had only heard of a Chenoo because I happened to be interested in ancient mythical monsters. I had actually seen some drawings of them on the internet before."

"I don't buy it, Shad!" Franklin said angrily.

"Well, what about the way your dog doesn't trust her? Why is Nellie growling only at her?" Shad reminded him.

"No, sorry, Shad. That's my mom there. I know my mom; she's beautiful, loving, and intelligent, just like the lady you met out there. My mom!" Franklin said this, trying not only to convince Shad at this point but also trying to convince himself.

But even as he did, something else that had been nagging at his thoughts finally occurred to him. Not only did Nellie have a shine, but Shad, Sami, and Rufus all had bright colors radiating from them, too. Colors that Franklin was used to seeing back on his Earth but was somewhat surprised to see here. His ability to detect the auras surrounding them was strong, even in this dark dimension of Earth.

He remembered down in the hole, when he first saw his mom, he had thought it was strange that she didn't produce a vibrant shine like she always had before, a shine that was symbolic of her kind and gracious spirit. He had dismissed it then, thinking maybe the pain she had suffered over the last months had caused her spirit, and the shine around her, to recede and ultimately disappear.

But the more he thought about it, he decided that his mom's strong character, her spirit, could never be taken from her, no matter what she had gone through. Not from his mom. So where was her shine then?

Franklin let out a heavy sigh. He didn't want Shad to be right about this.

"Okay, how can I prove that this hunch of yours is wrong? What do I need to do?" Franklin asked, finally succumbing to his friend's prodding.

Shad thought for a second. "Is there anything that just you and your mom knew about, that just you two shared? A joke? A song? An expression?"

He racked his brain trying to think of anything. With his head resting in the palm of one hand, he said, "Okay, I got something."

"All right," Shad said. "You want to fill me in on what it is?"

"You'll figure it out, just keep your ears open."

The two walked back to the rest of the group. They found Sami and Rufus sitting on either side of Nellie, pampering her with affection. Angel still sat farther away, keeping her distance from the dog. They joined them, sitting down in the semi-circle.

"Hey, I got some food in my backpack that Sami and Parker fixed me up with. Let's eat a little," Franklin suggested. "We need some energy for our hike back." He began passing out water and granola bars to everyone.

"Save some water for later, though," Angel suggested. "It gets awfully hot here when the sun starts to come up in the morning."

"Speaking of Parker," Franklin said, "she must have chosen to stay behind, huh?"

"No, she came with us," Sami explained. "At the farm, though, that man started screaming at us, and he had a gun. We were afraid he'd shoot us, so Parker volunteered to be the decoy, while we ran to the windmill. I didn't want her to do it, but she insisted. Parker wanted to help you Franklin; she took off in the opposite direction on her bike, and we watched as the farmer chased her off his property before he came back for us. We were already almost there, at the building beneath the windmill, so we had plenty of time before he made it to us."

"Wow, Parker is something else! Never knew she was so brave," Franklin exclaimed. "That guy was nuts! He would have killed Nellie if he could've aimed better. And I'm pretty sure he would've shot me next."

Angel's soft voice sounded now, "You kids are all so awesome. Doing all of this for me? How can I ever thank you?"

"Ms. Hobbs, we are so happy that you are safe and can come back with us," Sami said. "Franklin has told me so much about you, and I'm looking forward to spending more time with both of you!" Her voice gave away the thrill she felt.

Angel replied, "That's sweet of you, Sami. Franklin, you have made such fine friends since I've been gone."

"I have, you're right," he agreed. He paused for a moment before changing the subject. Then, taking a bite of his granola bar, he said, "Well, this isn't exactly a three-course meal, but it'll do until we get back home, huh Mom?"

"Of course it will, Franklin. I haven't eaten anything but leftover meat scraps for quite awhile," she laughed quietly. "So, this is an absolute treat for me."

"When we get back, Mom, let's make our favorite meal to celebrate your homecoming," Franklin suggested, a new tone in his voice.

"That sounds like a great idea, Franklin! I can hardly wait!" Angel clapped her hands together. "I'll be so happy to get out of here!"

Franklin pressed her a bit, "Mom, I can't exactly remember the ingredients that I need, you know, for our favorite dish?"

Angel sighed. "Oh, I don't know, Franklin. Let's not worry about it now. Let's just wait until we get back home."

"Oh, okay," Franklin said. But he wasn't going to let her off that easy, so he asked, "But do you remember the name of our favorite dinner and dessert? We would have it every few weeks if you were able to get the ingredients that we needed from your store. What's it called again?"

Angel's voice began to show some uneasiness and the early tones of annoyance. "Franklin, please. It has been a long time since I made anything for dinner. I'm very tired right now and I think it's time to leave this place. Nothing good can come from staying here. I've seen quite a few of the creatures that wander this planet, and we don't want to meet up with one."

While Angel was talking, Sami came over and knelt down by Franklin. She whispered into his ear, "What are you doing, Franklin? Your mom's exhausted and ill. Why don't you wait until later to ask her these questions?"

He whispered back, "I'm almost done. Just bear with me."

The black of the night was starting to fade as dawn had the inkling of an idea to arrive. No longer was every movement and expression concealed by the dark, but noticeable to the discerning eye.

Angel had seen the whispering, and she looked a bit vexed as she turned to Sami and Franklin and said, "Franklin, it's not polite to tell secrets in front of others. Is there something wrong?"

He had decided that honesty was the best policy in this case. He said, "Mom, there's just a few things that don't make sense, and I really need to know what's going on."

"All right, honey, but can't this wait until we get home?" she was almost pleading with him.

"No," he said, "it really can't wait. You need to settle something before we leave."

"What?" Angel asked indignantly, not even bothering to conceal her anger anymore.

"Like I asked before, what was our favorite meal we used to make together?" Franklin repeated.

"I don't know, Franklin! Tacos? Burritos? Who cares, anyway?" Angel yelled, surprising both Sami and Rufus. Shad and Franklin, though, by now had been half expecting this outburst.

Franklin hung his head and shook it in disgust. He said, "Mexican food, Mom? You didn't even get the right ethnicity." He looked her in the eyes, they were beautiful eyes, but he was ready to make a sudden move if he had to. "It's always Italian food. Our favorite was Chicken with Marsala Risotto made with Marsala wine, cremini mushrooms, and fresh spinach, topped with chicken breast, seasoned with rosemary, thyme, and garlic. Apple crisp for dessert. Sparkling grape juice for both of us, that is, if you were lucky enough to find some that had expired at your store!"

All five of them, plus one dog, sat unmoving on the ground as the darkness of the planet began to lift. But only Rufus and Shad were positioned at an angle that allowed them to see Angel's face as she turned away from Franklin, and they witnessed it distort into an inhuman, deviant form, for only a moment before snapping back to its original beauty. The two exchanged a frightened look.

"Franklin!" Shad yelled. "Wait—"

"Hold on, Shad, I got this," Franklin interrupted.

Rufus gasped, "But—"

"I got this, Rufus," insisted their friend.

Angel regained her composure and said, "Franklin, I knew that. Italian, of course. I only forgot. Do you know how hard it's been here for a year and a half? I don't even remember who I am some mornings. You know how badly that beast abused me over and over?" Angel put her head down into her open hands and began sobbing. She looked up with a tear-streaked face. "It was horrible, Franklin."

This was ridiculous, Franklin thought. He couldn't stand to see his mom relive those grisly experiences with her former tormenter. Of course this was his mom. He had been foolish to listen to Shad. He kneeled in front of Angel, putting his arms around her and pulling her close so that he could hold her. She rested her head on his shoulder and looked off to the side. Her eyes were closed, and her dark hair was partially draped over Franklin's back.

"I'm sorry, Mom. I'm sorry I doubted you. It's just that there were some things that didn't seem right."

Rufus couldn't stand it anymore. "Franklin, that ain't your momma, unless she gets really ugly when she's upset," he blurted out.

Franklin gave Rufus a semi-dirty look.

The sunrise was in its early stages, providing enough light now to see details. As Franklin spoke to his mom softly, continuing to embrace her, the other three children watched while, in only a few seconds, Angel's features transformed from human into something far less. The skin under the ragged clothes she wore went from smooth and pale, to scaly and grey. Underneath the scaled skin was no longer Angel's gaunt frame, but a carved and muscular one. On the hand that grasped Franklin's arm, Angel's short, dirty fingernails transformed to grisly black, then grew out until they curled in on themselves.

Her face was now covered with a black, see-through cloth, a veil, that billowed down from her hairline, but below the veil hung long strands of greasy, ashen grey hair. She still rested her head on Franklin's shoulder, and through the transparent veil the children could see her eyes were no longer shut, but open wide, staring, unblinking, into the woods. They were pure white eyes, with only the slightest black grain of a pupil. The rest of her face was grey in color and seemed to have the same scaly skin that was on her arms and legs. A set of thin and cracked lips turned down into a frown.

Shad screamed, "Franklin, it's not your mom! Get away from her!"

Franklin pushed her off his shoulder, and at the same time Rufus pounced on the veiled mutant, grabbing her scaly forearm. He tried to pull her away from Franklin, but as he did, his hands slipped right off her arm, and he went flying backward. A glutinous, gooey substance hung from her skin.

"Yuck! It's like fish slime on her," Rufus yelled.

Taking back his hand, which was still in the grasp of her scaled fingers, Franklin then reached down and seized both of her arms tightly. The woman seemed to have no objection and did not fight him.

He stood up, but remained low to the ground, making sure to hold this thing at arm's length. "What did you do with my mom?" he yelled into her shrouded face. Again, there was no protest or argument from the veiled mutant, even as Franklin shook her roughly.

Nellie got up and rushed to the scene, barking wildly at the thing that had been Angel, and was about to spring on her when Sami grabbed her collar.

Angel's sweet voice still arose from the creature like a misplaced melody. "If that dog touches me, I will kill it. Keep it away. I am doing you a kindness by giving a warning." It was a threat that all the children believed, and although Nellie tugged to be free from Sami's grasp, she held her tight.

"Sami, keep her with you," Franklin said. "Nellie, stop. Please. It's not hurting me."

The dog subsided somewhat and eventually sat down at Sami's feet. She continued to watch the creature closely, waiting for it to make a move.

But it only looked up at Franklin and said, "You asked about the human named Angel. Your father has been holding your adopted mother himself, at Quietus Tumulus, his palace. Bramfasa would never leave a prisoner as important as her in the care of a dimwitted Chenoo. Believe me, Son of the Most High."

"Son of the Most High?" he asked, surprised at the creature's unnerving title with which it had addressed him. "Is she still alive?" he screamed.

"I wouldn't know," the thing answered.

"Who… I mean, what are you then?" he demanded. "How did you make yourself look and sound exactly like her?" The anger began to rise in him again.

"Lift my veil," she said, still using Angel's voice.

Without hesitation, he reached for the veil that hung just beneath her scorched lips. Sami grabbed Franklin's arm. "Wait, Franklin. I don't think that's a smart idea. You don't know what she's capable of."

It was good to finally see Sami again without having to use a flashlight. He could see the genuine concern in her eyes that he'd grown used to from his best friend.

"I know, Sami, but I need to see her face," he said, his thoughts seeming muddled. "I can't really explain why, except I thought she was my mom."

"Hold on, Franklin," Shad demanded, "what did she mean when she called you 'Son of the Most High'? And who is this Bramfasa guy?"

Franklin felt like he had just been caught doing something wrong. "Well, I guess I should've told you guys what I found out yesterday about my father. It's a little humiliating, though."

"Humiliating?" The scaly woman asked, and even from beneath the veil they could sense the bewilderment on her face brought on by Franklin's comment. Looking up from her sitting position, she declared, "Your father is the Lord of Dark Earth! He is exalted here! You should feel unabashed pride being his son!"

"Whoa," Rufus said, "you're like a prince or something, Hobby? That's the bomb-diggity!" He laughed, "I'm guessing this father of yours is pretty evil, though, right? I mean, if he's god of this awful place."

"Yeah, he is," Franklin admitted.

Sami didn't seem to share Rufus's opinion, that this new information was the 'bomb-diggity', and she looked a bit stunned when she spoke, "I thought you told me..." she started, but stumbled over her words. "I thought you told me that your father died before you were born?"

"I swear, I had no idea, Sami," Franklin pleaded. "It doesn't mean, by definition, that I'm going to be just like him. It's up to me how I turn out, and Charles and Mary told me that my mom helped in making me into a good person."

"Wait, was your mom married to this Bramfasa?" Shad asked, unable to close the floodgate of his questions.

"That's the other thing. I already told Sami this. I found out Angel isn't my biological mom."

"Oh geez, I'm sorry about that," Rufus offered.

"Thanks, but it's okay. I'm over it," Franklin sighed. "She will always be my one and only mom."

"I don't understand, though. If he's your dad, why does he want you dead?" Shad asked.

Franklin's face scrunched up, and he answered, "I don't know. I guess my existence threatens him, somehow."

The friends had almost forgotten about the Angel-imposter sitting in front them, but they were snapped back to the present when the scaly woman repeated, "Lift my veil," showing not one sign of frustration after having been completely ignored. Her voice had now shed Angel's tone. It had become an octave lower, but not unpleasant, and with a singsong quality.

Franklin turned his attention back to the woman and reached for her veil. Very slowly, he lifted away the black, lacy fabric, each inch revealing more of her bizarre facial features. The grey-scaled flesh became more vibrant, somewhat whiter, as it was unveiled, perhaps from not being baked in the sun like the rest of her body. Her white eyes stared up at him, pupils dilated now to pebble size. On either side of her face, her stringy black hair was pulled back far enough to show two holes in the side of her head, which served as her ears. The transparent slime, which seemed to cover her whole body, and was the reason Rufus couldn't get a grip on her arm, was thick on her face, and it glistened in the rising sun. She was not hideous, nor truly frightening, but she evoked emotions of contempt in Franklin that would any creature, human or not, that had just deceived a boy into thinking his mother was with him again.

When the veil had been completely lifted over her head, showing the entirety of her face, she spoke to all of them but one word.

"Watch."

The Angel-imposter stood up and became as unmoving as a statue for a full ten seconds. She appeared to be thinking about something, making a decision. In the next moment, though, they witnessed her face, as well as her body, change back to a smiling image of Angel, whose familiar features now appeared incredibly creepy to all of them. She remained like that for only a second before she morphed into a stumpy, knotted-faced troll, at least two entire feet shorter than Angel's countenance had been.

Again, after a short period, she became a creature that was much larger than her original form; her body contorted and stretched until it was towering over them. Franklin recognized it as one of the Groken he had fought and that had killed his friend, Mary. Soon the Groken's body shrank and became a horned ghoul, looking much like the images of a demon, that all of them, at some point in their lives, had seen in a horror movie. Sami shuddered at this alarming sight and moved closer to Franklin. Thankfully, this grim figure didn't last long before it transformed into a small creature, only half the size of the children and covered in black fur. At first glance, it seemed to be something you might cuddle with, like a large stuffed animal, but when it turned and revealed its face, all of them took a hurried step back. Rufus was so shocked that he stumbled over his own feet and fell forward, almost crashing down onto the suddenly very *uncuddly* looking munchkin.

After a few more mutations, the creature finally returned to her original scaly form. She pulled the veil back over her face and sat down, motioning for the four children to do the same. They sat around her, no longer fearful of her strange appearance.

In her distant, melodic voice, she said, "Son of the Most High, I am not here to hurt you. I would not harm a hair on your divine head. I was part of their plan to entice you to come here. I am a Grey Siren. My name is Alluda, one of the ancients of Dark Earth."

This was practically right out of the books that Shad had been reading, and the look on his face was similar to that of a toddler opening a tricycle-shaped birthday gift. He asked, "So, you can make yourself look like any other creature you want? You're a real life shape-shifter?"

Alluda answered, "We call ourselves 'replicators'."

"You said you don't want to harm me," Franklin replied, "but you helped out that creature that wanted to chow down on me. I guess I don't get it."

Alluda waited before she spoke again, then said, "The Chenoo was commanded to kill you by our Lord Bramfasa. I could not interfere with that command. My instructions were to study your mom, learn her movements, voice, mannerisms, sift through important personal information in her memories, and then become her, become Angel Hobbs, in order to draw you here. If I had refused to follow the commands that he gave me, Lord Bramfasa would have made an example of me. Please forgive me, Son of my Lord."

He ignored her plea for forgiveness. "And the necklace I found?" he asked.

"Your mother's," Alluda nodded, "taken from her for the very purpose it served, making you believe I was Angel."

"Why would Bramfasa need to use you as a decoy, Alluda? Why not just use my actual mom to lure me here?"

Her mouth curled into something of a scowl as she said, "It's not that simple. Your dear mother refused to play along, even at the threat of being subjected to torture. She threatened to take her own life if Bramfasa tried using her as bait of any kind. But he still needs her alive."

Franklin's face turned red and he clenched his teeth. "Please, just tell me where my mom is being held!"

"If I knew, I would tell you, Son of the Most High. But she was taken away from Bramfasa only yesterday," Alluda replied.

"Taken? By who?" Franklin demanded.

"I repeat, if I knew, I would tell you. Something came in the night and plucked her from Bramfasa's dungeons. Something with great ability, strength, and cunning, for it was a difficult task," Alluda told him.

Franklin tried to let this sink in. What could it possibly mean?

"Another thing," she continued. "I found out only very recently, when a messenger came to me before you discovered me in the pit, that Bramfasa's orders have changed. He no longer wants you dead, but wants you taken to him alive."

"I guess he'll be relieved to know that Franklin killed his Chenoo, then," Sami interrupted. "Why didn't you say something to that nasty creature? Or try to stop it?" Her questions sounded more like a reprimand. "You could have saved a lot of trouble!"

"Talking to a Chenoo is like talking to a rock, besides, it had no idea I wasn't actually the mother of Franklin, either. Bramfasa thought it would be better that way," Alluda explained. "I tried to do what I could to help you escape it, and thankfully, with the dark powers and intelligence your Father passed on to you, his son," she nodded towards Franklin, "you were able to kill it before it partook of your flesh. But now you must be taken back to your Father. He is not a patient Lord."

Stepping forward in front of the other three, one hand solidly on her hips and the other still holding Nellie's collar, Sami asked, "And do you think *you're* going to take him?"

"Human child, it is not my job. I've been told that one of our Lord's trusted Shadow Chancellors is marching here with a battalion of warriors to do just that." She turned to Franklin. "My Grace, I would never harm a hair on your head or force you to do anything against your will. You may reign someday here on Dark Earth, and I wish to remain in your good graces."

Franklin shrugged. "Well, if that happens, I suppose you will be," he said.

But his masked sarcasm was lost on Alluda, and she bowed her head and responded, "I am forever thankful, Son of the Most High God."

"But you must tell me who you think took my mother?" Franklin adjusted his voice to sound more formidable. "Do you have any idea at all?"

Then, almost in unison, all of them, including Alluda, turned their heads towards the south end of the forest. From that direction came a steady pounding, the cadence of a distant clattering of many heavy feet, marching as one. At the same moment, they noticed that the earth beneath their own feet had begun resonating, in a time consistent with the distant rhythm.

Franklin turned to the Siren, "They're coming, and by the sound of it, your king sent his entire army. We have to leave here now! Please tell me!"

Trying to be of some assistance, Shad politely said, "Alluda, please. If you could just give us your best guess."

Alluda stared at the sky.

Rufus decided to try and help also, "Please, ma'am. Uh, I mean, fish-lady, tell him. It's his mom. I mean how would you feel if your mom was taken from you?" he asked.

Alluda only continued to look straight up at the rising sun, her thin, parched lips turned upwards into a smile. "I was required to burn my mom alive and consume her ashes when I was but three centuries old."

"Ooohhh, that's rough. I'm sorry for your loss," Rufus said sheepishly.

Alluda ignored Rufus, stood up and shuffled right past him, then, facing the sunrise, she stretched herself out, arms high into the air. The grey scales covering her body started to shimmer orange and then burst into a fierce, but concentrated fire. Through the dancing flames, her captive audience watched as her body began melting, dripping like wax, until there was no physical sign left of her.

In the corner of his eye, Shad picked up movement. When he looked over he saw a dark presence hovering above them.

"Guys, over here," he said.

They all turned to see a spirit that appeared as a thick, floating column of transparent black vapor; the orange of the sky beyond was still visible through its misty form.

The spirit began to soar around their heads, weaving in and out of them; it passed right under the legs of Nellie and came out the other side. The dog barked wildly at it, turned in circles, and snapped her teeth around the trail of dark haze that flowed behind it, but it went through the dog's mouth like smoke.

The children tried following the spirit with their eyes as it moved, but it traveled with such electric speed that it was almost impossible. As it continued to fly above and around them, they grew dizzy, but more so, they became annoyed. Alluda seemed to be acting like a bothersome child the way she carried on with this silly display.

After a few moments, the spirit slowed down and alighted inches above the ground. From its flowing black body emerged a silver head with a face, that in contrast to the rest of its ashen shape, was breathtaking. The straggly hair of the Grey Siren was gone, and only long, silver curls hung from the bewitching head of the specter. Beneath these curls was an angelic face, with the proportions and symmetry of a goddess, as if it had been sculpted by Michelangelo himself, from a block of polished silver.

Sami couldn't help herself. "You're absolutely beautiful!" she told Alluda.

The spirit opened its elegant lips and let out a laugh, and in Alluda's deep voice it said, "All Sombre Angels are beautiful if they choose to be. I am only replicating a Sombre Angel, but it's a form I covet over all others."

The children could hear that the cadence of the marching feet was closer now, louder. The army of beastly warriors had already reached the forest. Vibrations in the ground were stronger, and the added sound of crashing and crackling logs created even more of a clamor that intensified their feeling of impending doom.

Franklin looked at Alluda, wafting lightly in front of him. She was quite an amazing sight, but she had also completely frustrated him now, and so he started walking away.

"C'mon, you guys. She's playing games with us. We need to get out of here. They're only minutes away."

Nellie also felt the sense of urgency, and she tugged at Sami's pant leg with her teeth, trying to get her to follow. Sami was having difficulty taking her eyes from Alluda's magnificent appearance, but finally fell in step behind Franklin, as did Shad and Rufus.

They had only taken a few steps when they heard the Sombre Angel speak, "Wait!" she said, "Son of the Dark Lord, know that I only help you because you are heir to the throne of this world. If these other three were not your friends, I would have brought them to the work fields by now. I am still a faithful servant to my King Bramfasa and the protection and furthering of his kingdom. But... I am torn because I also have allegiance to the blood that courses through your veins, and so I can tell you just a little. "

Franklin stopped and turned back around. "Okay, go on," he said.

"Whatever took your mother from Lord Bramfasa's dungeon was not from Dark Earth, that I know," she hesitated. "It was a rescue mission. Over two hundred Cave Goblins and Groken guarding the palace were murdered, and the palace was left in shambles. Not one witness was found alive to speak of the onslaught."

The spirit whisked up into the sky head first, but not far before traveling back down towards them, gliding right at their faces. As it neared, the lovely features of the Sombre Angel's face morphed into the face of a monster, one that a child might imagine hiding under their bed or in their closet. Pointed teeth flashed white. Its black eyes looked like they would swallow their souls, and as it sped towards Shad, he tried to duck, but the nightmarish face of the poltergeist barreled right into his wide-eyed, terrified face. But to his surprise, it passed through his cranium without any blood splatter, or any sensation at all, and then out the back. It continued through the other three children, permeating their skulls or torsos as they stood in line behind Shad. Finally, Alluda appeared again behind them, and they had to quickly turn to face her.

The replicator had altered back to her former angelic countenance and was once again captivating in her form. She whispered to Franklin, but so all could hear, "Go now, or you will be caught. Your friends will be tortured and thrown into the Void, and you will be made to do Bramfasa's bidding. Travel to the slave fields, hide amongst the dead there."

"The Void?" Franklin asked.

"You have been there. The space between Earthly dimensions, where imprisoned spirits and beings exist in the state of absolute oblivion…"

Franklin remembered the bizarre feeling of being in the 'Glass Elevator' with the creatures clawing to get at him. He must have passed through the Void, which explains the lost souls trying to hitch a ride with him.

"….an eternal abyss of misery, the Underneath and In-between," as she finished, her sing-song voice trailed off into a whisper, and with that, the Sombre Angel flew back over their heads and towards the area of the forest where the approaching army marched.

Rufus shook his whole body like a dog trying to dry its fur off. "Ooooooooh, that gave me the absolute heebie-jeebies!" he said. "Why did she go through us like that?"

"Because she could," Shad countered.

Nellie chased after the Sombre Angel, deep into the woods, hurling the most ferocious barks she could manage at the apparition. When the dog finally felt that the shifty spirit had traveled far enough away from her friends, she turned back to find them, tail wagging.

CHAPTER FORTY–FIVE
A SCOUT & A SLINGSHOT

Shad had stashed away a backpack, upon first arriving with Rufus and Sami in the forest, and he now retrieved it before they left on the next leg of their journey. Thankfully, he did, because it contained five precious water bottles and more food. Having decided to take Alluda's advice of traveling to the slave fields until the coast was clear, they hurried through the forest and exited the north end. Franklin believed the scaly woman truly was trying to help him, even though she was probably just as evil as any other creature from this realm. Besides, if they tried heading west, back to the Gateway where they had all been deposited into this world, the approaching battalion of soldiers would almost certainly spot them.

Franklin led the way through the field of sparse grass and decay, with Nellie at his side, Sami and Shad close behind, then Rufus, with a noticeable limp, taking up the rear. The heat was already a factor and kept them from traveling as fast as they otherwise could have.

There was no discussion as they made their way early on; the gravity of the current predicament they found themselves in was heavy on their minds. About a quarter mile out into the field, the group stopped and looked back at the woods to see if they were being pursued yet.

Shad, who had the best eyesight of the group with his glasses on, suddenly said, "Down, everyone!"

Without questioning him, they all pressed as low as they could to the ground. Shad took a pair of binoculars from his pack, poked his head a bit higher, and peered through them. He handed them to Rufus, who squinted as he put his eyes to them, shook his head, said, "Oh boy," and passed them to Sami. She looked through the glass lenses, grimaced, and passed them directly to Franklin.

Franklin took them from her and got on one knee. He steadied his elbow on his other knee as he looked through the binoculars. Around the entire perimeter of the woods that he could see were hundreds of goblin-like creatures, each clad in golden armor. The parts of them not covered showed green skin, which could be seen on their faces, hands, and lower legs.

Franklin could also see that each had a pair of tusks, like an elephant, curling down from its mouth and then back up into a point. An ax was the weapon of choice for most, but some held spears longer than they were tall. He wondered if one of these thugs was the Shadow Chancellor that Alluda had mentioned, but he guessed that this great captain was still farther back in the woods, giving orders. Surely with a name like 'Shadow Chancellor' it would be a more dignified looking creature than the likes of these rhino men, anyway. They were a fearsome looking lot, and he guessed there were more of them patrolling inside the woods that he couldn't see. It wouldn't be long before they realized Franklin was no longer in among the sticks and stumps, and they would storm the fields, probably dispersing in all directions searching for him.

To his dismay, his prediction came true sooner than he thought. Watching through the binoculars, he saw them form into parties of ten to twelve goblins, which then began marching into, what Franklin assumed, was an assigned direction to search. Several winged creatures that had been in chains until now, and out of sight behind the group of warriors, were brought out into the open. Immediately, the creatures flew ahead of the search battalions and swooped low to the ground, scanning for signs of life.

He crawled back to Shad and handed him the field glasses. "Okay, guys," he said, "no rest for the weary. They're trying to track us and are sending some sort of flying scouts ahead of them. We need to stay low but move fast. The slave fields aren't too far away. I saw them on the way here."

For the next thirty minutes, the five of them crouched low as they walked, trying to keep themselves below any remaining foliage that might help hide them. It was exhausting, and they all discovered how walking in this position takes additional muscle strength. They stopped only to take occasional water breaks.

It was mid-morning, and the sun was not yet at its highest point. Shad's digital pocket thermometer already showed that it was a blistering ninety-five degrees out, humidity probably pushing it up to one hundred and twenty-five degrees. The heat affected Nellie more than the rest; her black fur absorbed the sun's rays and made her as miserable as she could be. Although her strength had begun to diminish and her tongue hung from her mouth, she still managed to maintain an upbeat and positive spirit, providing the rest of them with an intangible energy that even their granola bars couldn't give them.

She would occasionally run on ahead of them, every five minutes appearing again to make sure they were still coming. Rufus, Shad, and Sami had fallen in love with the Newfoundland

and found an extra spring in their step every time she came around to check on them.

It wasn't easy to talk while they were walking at this pace, but something had been weighing heavily on Sami's mind, and she sped up so that she walked at Franklin's side.

"Franklin?" she finally asked.

"Yeah, what's up, Sami?" Franklin replied.

She considered her next words carefully. "You seem like you feel better now. Do you?"

"I'm still sore from being used as a soccer ball by that brute, and I have some nice deep scratches on me that I'm hoping don't get infected, but I'll make it," he answered. Then, "How about you?"

Franklin slowed his pace and turned to look at his friend, whom he realized was as pretty as ever, even in the unflattering orange light of the sun.

He said, "I think we have a few minutes to rest. We've put some pretty good distance between us and those gremlins."

They all stopped and sat down in the knee-deep foliage. When Nellie plodded over to the middle of the group and lay on her back, Shad and Rufus peppered her with attention. Shad rubbed her tummy, while Rufus used her as a pillow.

Sami said, "To answer your question, Franklin, I'm sore, too, but that's not what I meant." She paused, "Do you remember how you were acting, right before you ripped that horrible thing in two? And the way you treated us afterward?"

Behind them, Rufus reached into Shad's backpack and took out a water bottle. He guzzled down a third of it and then held it out for Nellie.

"Well…" Franklin started, trying to recall exactly what he had said and done. He remembered the guilt he felt for the way he had acted, but nothing specific. "I must have been desperate to stop that creature from hurting you guys. It had just tossed Shad and Rufus, and it had been holding you up by your hair while putting that sharp bone to your neck. I wanted to keep it from hurting you. That's all I remember. But…I know I felt like a jerk afterward."

Shad, overhearing their conversation, said, "You mean, you don't remember how furious with us you were when you first saw us? You told us we were getting in your way!"

Sami continued Shad's thought, "And then after that, you yelled at us again. You said that you saved…and I quote, '…your stupid lives'."

"Really?" Franklin asked. "I guess that part is kind of a blur. I remember you guys hugging me…"

Rufus laughed and said, "Yeah, it was actually a form of cruel torture for you to be in the middle of that group hug. You hated it at first. I think you called us all idiots."

"Losers," Shad replied.

Rufus gave Shad a look of surprise, "C'mon Shad! Now you? Really?"

"No, Rufus. He called us *losers*, not idiots," Shad said, a bit agitated.

Sami tried to guide the discussion back to where she wanted it. "Your whole personality had changed, Franklin," she explained. "You were not the same boy we all love."

At this comment, Shad and Rufus exchanged a funny look and Rufus mouthed the word 'love?' to Shad so that nobody but him saw.

"Something happened to you. I almost…well, I felt like slapping your face, Franklin! But I would never do that…you were just so…so mean," Sami said, a somber note in her voice.

She looked right into his eyes and put her hand gently on his cheek. "And your eyes, they didn't have that incredible purple shine like normal. They were a very awful shade of orange…that sort of glowed in the dark," she said, and shivered as the memory came back to her.

"Really? Orange?" he asked. "I guess I vaguely remember you saying something…I realized that I had acted differently. I felt really guilty about it and still do. I know I've had a lot of anger recently, since the thing with Hank." Franklin was studying each of their faces as he asked, "Did I really act that awful?"

"Worse, you acted like a total blockhead!" Rufus said, half-joking.

"Blockhead?" Franklin asked, "Do I look like Charlie Brown to you or something?"

"Well…now that you mention it…yeah, kind of," Shad said, letting off a series of chuckles and chortles that made it sound like he was choking on steak.

Rufus playfully punched Franklin in the shoulder, "I guess that makes Shadrack here Charlie Brown's friend; that really smart dude who sucks his thumb and carries a baby blanket everywhere, huh?"

"You mean Linus," Shad said, no longer laughing.

Sami rolled her eyes in annoyance and, once again, redirected the conversation. "You *did* act awful, Franklin," she said, and he noticed that she still sounded hurt.

Rufus's fist hadn't hit Franklin very hard, but the truth suddenly did.

His powers…the ones from the Luminos, which Charles had given him the night before his tenth birthday, would not work here on Dark Earth. At least they hadn't yet. He had tried them several times. But because he was in Bramfasa's realm, *his father's* realm, the powers that he had inherited from him… well, *they did work.*

Thinking back to the battle with the Chenoo, he remembered that he had used his future-sight again, this time to avoid being eaten alive in the pit. The first time he had used it, when he had been on his bike, it had somehow transported him to this very realm, only over on Cast Maker Canyon, broken leg and all.

He recalled something Mary had told him, "We can't see the future, The Suveran does not allow us…"

That had to mean that future-sight was an ability that his father had bestowed on him, not the Luminos, and it probably had triggered other abilities passed down to him from Bramfasa. That might explain the extreme headache he had when using those powers on the Chenoo.

If his eyes had really taken on an orange glow, he was calling on powers that were dark and dangerous and shouldn't be called on. It's true, he used the powers to kill the Chenoo, but he allowed them to change him, to make him more like his father. Even if he was only angry and hateful for a few minutes, that was too long.

They had affected him. Had they changed him permanently, though?

Although he had the same abilities when he was back on his home Earth, like the telekinesis he had used on both the Grokens there and the Chenoo here, they were not from the same giver. He had summoned his dark powers while here.

But all that *still* didn't explain why he had felt so good after killing Hank, and then, to a lesser extent, giving Brad that awesome swirly. He had used the powers from the Luminos then. Or could it be that it was a blending of the two, a composite of the powers from both sides, and that Bramfasa's influence over him had extended past just Dark Earth?

And maybe he was more like his father than everyone, including himself, had thought.

An acute need to apologize again to his friends struck Franklin like an uppercut to his conscience. "Sami, I am so, *so* sorry for treating you that way; all of you guys," he said, turning to each friend and looking directly at them, his violet eyes showing the depth of his regret.

He didn't give them time to reply before continuing, "It was right after I used the gift of seeing into the future. After I saw myself getting killed down in the pit…that's when I started feeling different. I think—"

"Hey, bro," said Rufus, flashing his genuine, million-dollar smile that Franklin had learned by now to love, "we get it. Just do your best not to do it anymore. Try to be chill."

Franklin nodded.

Shad broke his train of thought, "Franklin, I think you need to be careful here. It makes sense, now that I know who your father really is. You were 'becoming', just barely, but becoming nevertheless."

"Becoming?" Sami asked.

"We use that term in science fiction to explain that someone is changing, becoming something different. In this case, something dangerous. Franklin was using his powers from his father, and because of that, he was *becoming* more like him," Shad explained.

"Yeah, makes sense," Franklin said. He didn't know how Shad always figured these things out so quickly, but he definitely didn't want to scare Sami anymore about him 'becoming', or whatever.

He stood up halfway, still crouching, and said, "All right, we better get moving." He took Shad's wrist and looked at his friend's watch. "It's eleven o'clock, and the hottest part of the day is still coming. I'd like to be in some shade before that happens."

"Let's find some shade, Shad!" Rufus said, with a little more than just a chuckle. "Get it? 'Shade Shad'? They're almost the same word except that shade has an 'e'?"

His laughing stopped abruptly when he realized he was the only one doing it. "It's kinda fun to say, Shade-Shad..." Rufus's voice trailed off.

All three turned back to look at him, straight-faced, too exhausted to even give a pity chuckle at his corny humor. Nellie, who was still resting on the ground but had rolled back over, had her head down on her paws. She didn't lift her head, but only shifted her eyes upwards so that she could gaze at Rufus. When

Rufus finally looked down at her, she barked twice, almost as if scolding him for his ridiculous attempt at a joke.

"What? Bad joke?" he asked shamefully.

Rufus reached down and rubbed his leg where he had been injured by Hank's arrow, wincing quietly in pain as he massaged it, trying not to be heard. Franklin saw this, though, and also noticed that the once white bandage on his wound was not only filthy, but also had a large red circle where blood had soaked through.

"Your wound has opened up again, Rufus. I don't even know how you're walking at all," he commented.

"I brought some first-aid cream and more bandages for it," Sami said. "I thought this might be a problem. Shad, I stuffed them in your backpack."

"I'm sorry, guys. I didn't want to be a burden. I just wanted to help. I'll be okay," Rufus said glumly.

"Man, you're a tough dude. I'm impressed," replied Franklin. "Let's find some shade and get you doctored up."

Not too far, fortune had it that there was a boulder, a very large boulder, jutting up from the ground, angled outwards, and high enough to cast a good sized shadow beneath it. The group trekked over to it, and Rufus was the first to roll himself down into the space under the rock, yelling, "Blessed shade!"

The area was wide enough for the rest of them to comfortably sit by him, protected from the sun's unforgiving rays.

Shad found the bandage and ointment in his backpack and handed it to Sami. She immediately began to work on Rufus's wounded leg.

"Looks infected," Sami said, unwrapping the soiled bandage. "It's a good thing we're cleaning it up now."

Rufus tried not to cry out in pain as she wiped the dry blood off his leg with the inside of the old bandage, and then applied the clear ointment onto the wound with her index finger.

"That is incredibly painful, but thank you, Sami," Rufus said, blowing air out from his mouth, then sucking it back in with short, quick spurts, trying anything to dull the pulses of agony.

When she finished putting the clean bandage on, they sat quietly for a moment and the thought of sleep entered all of their minds, but they knew it was out of the question. Staying a good distance ahead of the battalion of savages, which was probably still right on their heels, was vitally important.

"Shad," Franklin said, "can I see those binoculars?"

Shad dug into his pack, pulled them out and handed them to him. Franklin crawled out from the ditch and into the open. He put the lenses to his eyes and directed them towards the area of the field that they had just traveled. "The search party must be pretty far behind. I don't see them," he hollered back to his friends.

But almost before he had finished speaking, the binoculars came flying back into the dugout at Shad, with Franklin close behind them. "Everyone, get as close to the rock as you can and lay down!" he ordered.

He followed his own advice, his back flat against the ground beneath the rock and watched the sky. Although the boulder provided shade, it didn't hide them from sight if something or someone looked down at the right angle. Franklin lay in between Rufus and Sami. He reached his hand over to Rufus and asked quietly, but with the same intensity, "Do you still have that slingshot you blasted the Chenoo with last night?"

"Yeah," Rufus whispered, somewhat apologetically, "but I never actually hit it with my slingshot. Think I was wide left every time. I kinda celebrated and made it sound like I had done something…but that was really Shad that hit it."

"Can you get it for me?"

"Right here." Rufus reached into his back pocket and pulled out the slingshot. He put it in Franklin's hand.

"What's going on, Franklin?" Sami asked, grabbing his arm to gain his attention.

"You know the winged beasts that I saw earlier, part of the scouting party that's looking for us? One of them was about two hundred yards from here, coming this way," he answered, trying to stay as calm as he could, "and I'm pretty sure it noticed me."

Feeling around on the ground with the palms of both his hands, Franklin searched for rocks to use as projectiles. "If it did spot me, it'll be here any minute."

Shad noticed what he was doing and said, "Hey, I got some stones in my pack, Franklin. No slingshot, though. I left that back in the woods."

"I'll need the rocks," he replied. "Can't find any here."

He held the slingshot up and studied it, recognizing it as one of the two that Shad had made earlier that year out of some rubber tubing he found in the house. Using dental floss, he had attached the tubing to either side of a tree branch that was in the shape of a 'Y', and in the middle of the stretch of tubing there was a square of fabric for the pouch. Recently, he had added a flashlight, which was taped to the bottom of the slingshot. It seems that Shad had known he might be taking aim at something in the dark, as he had at the Chenoo last night.

Franklin removed the small flashlight and gave it back to Rufus. In return, Rufus passed several stones to Franklin that Shad had given him.

The four of them lay there. Waiting.

"Franklin?" It was Sami.

"Yeah?"

"What if you don't kill it?"

"Then it heads back to deliver the message that it found us. They'll send their whole platoon this direction."

They saw its large shadow before they actually saw the creature itself. It flew twenty feet above them, and they could see it was not a bird, but some sort of fur-covered critter, around five feet long. Its leathery wings curled in a delicate slope away from its body as it glided through the sky. At the moment, it was not flapping these wings but seemed to be floating on a current of air. When it glided closer to the ground, they were able to see that they were dealing with something like a large bat, but a bat that possessed an uncanny human resemblance as well.

Its legs were long and trailed behind it; large flat feet pointed down to the ground. A pair of small hands also hung beneath the wings; they were easy to spot because each hand was wrapped tightly around a tiny animal of contrasting color to the bat. One of the helpless creatures it squeezed was white, and the other, a little larger, was pink, probably furless. The children watched as one of the hands reached up to its mouth, which opened wide to welcome the smaller of the creatures. It chewed the animal for only a moment before it tilted its head back to aid in the swallowing of its meal.

Its pointed ears protruding from the top of its head moved sideways like they were on a swivel, and on its fuzzy face, two thin, yellow eyes scanned the boulder, which was now in front of it.

"I think I'm going to pass out. That's the biggest rodent I've ever seen!" Rufus exclaimed.

Shad had to correct him. "Technically, Rufus, it's not a rodent. That thing looks like a bat, and bats are in their own group called 'Chiroptera', which I believe means, "hand-wing."

"All right then," Rufus said. "It's a huge chipotle. Whatever."

Shad ignored the ridiculous mispronunciation. "If it really is a bat, it relies equally as much on its echolocation as it does on its eyesight during the daylight hours."

Franklin looked a bit confused. "I thought bats were blind," he commented.

"Nope, they can see things as well as us, but in the dark, when they can't see, their echolocation works by itself. Right now, it's using both senses, though. Listen, do you hear the loud clicks coming from it?"

They all held their breath while listening intently to the sky. Sure enough, they detected a series of sharp, fast ticks coming from the creature that glided in circles above them. The sound faded, but only for a few seconds before they heard the pattern of clicks again.

"Even if we're hidden in the shadow of the boulder right now and it can't see us with its eyes, if any of those sound waves are bounced back to it and shows movement down here, it'll sense it," Shad explained. "We need to remain perfectly still and we might be okay."

Franklin watched as the monstrosity of a bat started to flap its wings furiously, trying to slow itself down before quietly gliding low, only feet above the ground. It was on the hunt for Franklin, whom it had most likely seen out in the open earlier. The four of them became horizontal statues, except for their eyes, which followed the bat wherever it went on its rampant search. After a minute, thankfully, it seemed to be flying away from them.

A mouse-like animal scuttled from underneath the rock where they lay and ran past Shad and Rufus, then out into the open. It had been hiding with them the whole time. Franklin caught a glimpse of the furball as it scampered back to him and disappeared down a shallow tunnel.

Its movements had attracted the attention of the bat.

"We got a problem here, guys," he uttered under his breath. He put a rock in the pouch of the slingshot and took aim at the bat, which had already altered its course and was now coming toward them. He pulled back the rubber hose as far as he could, and as the bat flew near them, he let the stone fly. It rocketed towards the creature, dead center at its head. But, at the last second, the bat dipped slightly and the stone went right between its pointed ears, not even skimming it. What the narrow-miss did do, however, was alert the bat that something was not only hiding beneath the rock, but that something was also trying to kill it.

Franklin threw the slingshot down. "So much for the element of surprise. This isn't going to work."

His head came to a rest back on the ground and he stared up at the angry animal, whose intentions seemed to have shifted from a 'search and report" mission to a 'search and destroy' revenge job.

Sami knew what Franklin was doing, and she began to plead with him. "No, Franklin, don't try it here. Not again. It's not safe. Please stop!"

He paid no attention to her.

Focus. On. The. Bat.

The bat had definitely decided to ignore Bramfasa's orders, which according to Alluda, were to bring Franklin back to him alive. The creature was gaining speed as it dove straight down upon them, yellow fangs readied.

Franklin's head started to ache horribly, but he felt the familiar tingling sensation once again.

As he was close to harnessing his powers, Sami let out a horrifying scream. Something had fallen from the sky and landed on her head. His concentration was lost, and he turned to help her. Lying on her lap, after first bouncing off her head, was a smallish, pink animal, dead as a doorknob. Having been squeezed in the bat's hand, its eyes were now hanging out of its head, and a pasty tongue stuck out from its mouth, just as it had in the seconds before its death. The bat had decided that the best option was to first rid itself of its lunch before attacking, so it had dropped the pink critter, and now climbed back up into the sky, ready to proceed, once again, in its assault on the children.

The tiny animal that slumped across Sami was indeed hairless and looked like it might be in the feline family. Franklin brushed it off her and lay back down. He looked up and tried to concentrate once again.

The bat had regained its speed and trajectory and was close to being upon them once more. He was running out of time.

Sami yelled, "Stop, Franklin!"

Focus!

Only a few seconds left before —

Thwaaack!

The top of the bat's head exploded as a stone rocketed into it, hitting it right between the eyes. Its limp body came barreling to the earth, twirling around in the air like a practiced ballerina as it fell. It face-planted into the ground next to Nellie, who had stood up moments ago and readied herself for a counter-attack. They all felt the barrage of dirt that sprayed them upon its impact, and Nellie hastily shook her body, ridding herself of the sand that had bathed her.

After their initial shock, all eyes turned to Rufus, who couldn't hold back a smile; a smile which started from one ear and went to the other. He held the slingshot high in one hand in a victory pose and yelled, "See ya, sucker!" as he sat up.

No one said anything to him. They only stared.

"What?" he said. "Are you guys really that surprised I hit it?"

CHAPTER FORTY-SIX
A BLINDFOLD & A BLACKOUT

Franklin reached over and smacked him on the back, "Of course not, Rufus. That was incredible! Thanks for covering for me when I choked."

"Good job, Rufus. You really came through in the clutch there," Shad added, his pale face betraying how scared he had been.

Nellie ambled over to Rufus, jumped up on him and slobbered on his face, her way of congratulating him, too.

"Thanks, girl," Rufus said to her, not bothered by the slob. "I'm glad I could finally help."

Sami was quiet, but she went to Rufus and hugged him. Franklin had a feeling he knew what was bugging her. "Sami, I'm sorry. I just didn't want that thing to hurt any of us."

She looked at him. Tears had welled up in her eyes. "You need to promise me you'll stop! Franklin, you *have* to promise. I've had too many people in my life let me down. Not you, too!"

"Sami, I …"

"I couldn't stand to see how you changed, earlier. I'd rather that bat carried me away than have to see you like that again. Please promise me you won't try using those awful powers again while we're on this planet, or parallel Earth, or whatever it is." Her face was wet, and she was trembling.

"Okay, okay, Sami. I promise. I won't try using them here again," he said. What else could he tell her? He pulled her close to him and held her tight.

Shad was kneeling on the ground, busying himself by organizing his pack, putting the slingshot, leftover stones, and flashlight away. Rufus just stood there, feeling a bit awkward. He finally said, "Okay, time to be moving on people. There might be more of them nasty bats."

Then, looking over at the heap of fur and leathery wings that lay in a pile only a few feet from him, he said, "That thing looked freakishly human, too. It gives me the heebie-jeebies just thinking about it!"

Starting at one hand, Rufus's body began shaking and contorting. The gyrations traveled up his arm, through the center of his body, his head, down the other arm, and then ended with a final quivering in the fingers of his opposite hand.

"See?" he said. "That was the heebie-jeebies! I got them bad that time!"

Franklin tried to hold a straight face, but couldn't stop himself from cracking up, and soon Shad and Sami were joining him, laughing at Rufus, or rather, with Rufus, who was also snorting and giggling.

It was now midday, and the heat was more suffocating than anything any of the children had ever experienced before. The pile of bat, which had been dead for only minutes, was already starting to steam and smell in the sun's fury. Nellie, like a typical dog that didn't want to waste good meat, had decided to make lunch out of the pink critter that had fallen from the sky onto Sami. She had been busy with it for several minutes, but now came back to the group and nudged Franklin's leg.

Finally gaining his composure after the laughing frenzy, Franklin said, "Okay, girl, you're right. We need to get going."

He snatched up the binoculars and wandered a few feet away from the boulder's shadow. Facing north, he peered through the lenses.

"There," he said loudly. "I see the workers in the field up ahead. Not much farther, forty minutes at the most."

"What are we going to do when we get there?" Rufus asked.

"Blend in, make it difficult for whoever is looking for us, or if that doesn't work, hide. Maybe find more water and try to cut back towards the Gateway, staying off the beaten path," Franklin answered.

He remembered that he wasn't even certain if there was a Gateway to take them home.

"Wait, what about your mom?" Sami said. "What are you going to do now, Franklin?"

"I have to think of my next move. I need more information if I'm going to find her, and I have a friend back home who might know something," he answered, wondering if Charles had any knowledge of his mom's 'rescue mission', if that's what it was. If The Suveran had been planning this mission, and Charles knew about it, why hadn't Charles said something to him before he risked his life coming here?

They continued to move forward at a brisk pace, despite the scorching sun, and came upon the work camp thirty-five minutes later, without any further incident. Staying out of sight, they surveyed their surroundings. One of the first things they noticed was that, off in the distance, past the tormented slaves, was an imposing hill of rock. It was Cast Maker Canyon. Next to it, another dead forest. They had traveled far enough north to reach a region that was eerily familiar to them.

"That's our hill, guys. Cast Maker," Franklin said, "and this must be the slave camp I saw after I crashed my bike." Franklin remembered the frightening experience, seeing the spectral vision of Dark Earth for the first time, the wandering slaves in the distance…and not understanding where he was.

"We must have already passed Open Arms Orphanage, or at least where it is back on home Earth," Shad pointed out. He shook his head. "This parallel universe thing is absolutely amazing!"

"I could do without it," Sami remarked placidly.

Their attention returned to the horror show before them, the crowds of humans toiling in a small area of the field. They saw that every so often, spread around the outskirts of the camp, were fifteen to twenty-foot high piles of dirt. The humans were bringing shovelful after shovelful, never stopping, always adding to the mountain of brown and red earth. Some climbed the dirt pile to the very top, stumbling and falling on the way, to drop off the contents of their shovel. Others stopped halfway up and emptied their haul, while some simply threw it at the base of the mountain. It almost seemed like they had each been assigned a spot to drop off their load of dirt every time, in order to keep the hill in balance.

Strangely enough, there were other mountains that were being dismantled by slaves, the dirt brought back to fill in the massive craters that had been dug earlier.

It was one of these mountains, where currently no slaves climbed or deposited their shovelfuls of dirt, which the children and dog decided to hide behind as they scanned the slave camp.

Thousands, probably tens of thousands, of human workers were toiling at their senseless but eternal task of digging or filling in holes. Franklin thought that the only way the craters could have gotten as deep as they were, was if other workers, down inside the holes, were passing up dirt to the slaves at the top. And who knows? Maybe a level of workers below that, as well. Regardless, it didn't seem like they ever stopped or were allowed breaks, and there was no water visible anywhere that they could drink.

Most of the slaves, both men and women, were dressed in rags, and some of them, the men, had nothing except a cloth covering their waist. These prisoners had most likely been here for a long time, years upon years, for they looked to be completely lifeless, any sparkle of humanity gone from them. It appeared that they simply existed to toil, sweat, and barely escape death every day.

Some of the laborers had clothes that were not as ragged. Franklin guessed that these humans were probably newer recruits to the slave fields. He could tell these captives still hadn't had their spirits completely broken like the others. Every once in a while, one of them would attempt to speak to a fellow slave near them if they could do it without being caught. All of the slaves were covered in filth and either had open wounds, scars, or both, covering their exposed skin. Some were missing a hand or an entire arm, and these slaves struggled with the work in a mighty way.

Scattered throughout the mass of despondent slaves were Chenoos that looked very similar to the one which they had encountered the night before; the one that now lay in pieces back in the woods. Some were taller, shorter, or were at different stages of decay in their undead bodies. Another group of the guards were muscular creatures that looked like large trolls, and Franklin recognized at least one to be a Groken. Some of these hulking guards had the heads of bulls, even boars.

Every slave driver they saw had a cruel whip made from the tough hide of an animal, and each whip came with sharp metal fragments tied to the end of its leather strands. These were meant for taking chunks of skin off the victim when the whip was snapped back.

In the five minutes that the children stood there, watching in dismay, they saw at least three of the slaves receive a thrashing for either pausing momentarily in their labor or talking to another slave. In horror, they witnessed one of the Chenoos pull out a long dagger and use it to slice off the hand of a man who had fallen and been unable to get back up. The Chenoo then wrapped the man's stump in his own ragged shirt, hoisted him up, and handed him back his shovel.

"What's happening here?" Sami cried. "This is the most awful form of torture I've ever seen!"

No one had an answer for her. Nellie came over and sat by her, hearing the distress in her voice, and Sami ran her fingers through the dog's silky fur.

"I can't believe it," Shad responded after a minute. "How do they get away with this? Why doesn't somebody stop them?" His brows were furrowed in anger, and his face was crimson red as he spoke.

Franklin answered, "I really don't think anyone back home knows about this place. How would they?"

Rufus was crying, not outright bawling, but he was so shaken by what he saw that tears were streaming down his face. "Actually, I'm pretty sure I've heard of this place. We *have* to help them, guys! We can't leave these poor people like this."

Franklin shook his head and answered, "You're right, Rufus, I just don't know how we *can* help them right now. We would have to recruit some more people back home to come here with us." He sighed, "But, for the time being, we ought to stay right here anyway, behind this hill, out of sight. Stay here until dark, and then cut back to where the windmill Gateway is."

A man of about fifty years old, shirtless, wearing nothing but rags, came wandering close to where the children were hiding, and he began digging a new hole. He had been burned badly from the sun. Blisters covered him, some of which were open and oozing. While he worked, he stared blankly ahead; his movements robotic as he drove the shovel into the ground, pulled up dirt, walked to a newly forming pile twenty yards away, and emptied it. There was not a slave driver or other worker in the near vicinity, and before anyone could stop her, Sami ran out from behind the cover of the hill where they hid. She stepped in pace behind the man as he came back for another shovelful.

Tapping him on the shoulder, she said, "Excuse me, sir?" He didn't turn around or even stop walking. She tried again, only this time grabbing his elbow. "Mister, come with me. We'll get you out of here!" Again, no response.

Not one to give up, she reached over, took his shovel from him and tossed it on the ground, then grabbed both of his shoulders and swiveled his body so that he faced her. The man's gray hair was sweat-plastered to his forehead. Cracked and blistering, his face remained expressionless as he looked down at the ground.

"Can you hear me?" she asked, almost yelling this time.

Suddenly, his hands reached up and grabbed both of Sami's wrists, yanking them from his shoulders. The slave lifted his head up and looked her right in the eyes. What she saw made her body go limp. Earlier, she had not been able to see the man's eyes as they truly were. She had thought, or assumed, as all of the children had, that although they were glazed over, his eyes were otherwise a normal white hue, with blue, green, or possibly brown irises. She saw now that they were not white, but instead transparent, and she could see deep down into them, and what she saw inside was blackness. She saw Death.

"I can't leave," he growled loudly. "No soul can leave here, you wench! Don't you know what this place is?" Sami tried wriggling free from his leathered hands, but he held her tight.

"Please, let me go!" Sami cried as loud as she dared.

Then Franklin was there, pulling at the man's fingers, prying them off of her wrists. The man's hands were cold, stiff, but his grip was strong, and it took everything Franklin had to finally force him to release one of her arms. But as soon as that hand let go of Sami, the man grabbed Franklin's upper arm, right below his shoulder. Instinctively, Franklin swung his other fist at the slave and connected with his chin, sending him stumbling backward, and causing him to release his hold on both of them.

"C'mon, Sami!" He grabbed her hand and ran back to where the others were. Behind them sounded a high-pitched, almost inhuman cry. They looked back at the man and saw that he had regained his feet and had his hands cupped to his mouth. He was wailing at the top of his lungs, "Bahhhhhhhhhhhh!" until finally he ran out of breath and stopped.

Almost immediately, he erupted again, this time yelling, "Freeeeeeeeeeee soooooooouuuuuuullll!"

Slave masters from every corner of the work camp heard the commotion and came racing towards the hysterical slave. He screamed a third time, back to his original cry of "Bahhhhhhhhhhhhhhhh!"

Then he went quiet, and as if nothing had happened, he bent over, picked up his shovel, and began to dig his hole once again. But the damage was done; nine or ten guards were in full sprint towards the man. Surely, they would scour the area to see what had caused the outburst.

"Go, go!" Franklin yelled at his friends. Nellie had already scampered ahead of them but was looking back, urging them on. "Follow Nellie. She's trying to lead us out of here!"

Franklin watched as his friends ran after the dog, who brought them out into the open field again into a patch of higher growth. Just as the camp overseers came into view, the children and dog dove headfirst into the grass, out of sight.

All but Franklin.

He had been about to take off, following Nellie as well, when he heard another sound that caused him to pause.

"Where's Franklin?" Sami asked, panicking.

It wasn't the blaring cry of another slave or the gruntings of the guards as they came closer to investigate. It was an all too familiar sound that he had heard more than once before, but his mind was racing too fast to remember exactly where.

"I thought he was behind me!" exclaimed Rufus.

It was the most awful, deafening roar, like thousands of buzzing vermin had come together to feast on a decomposing corpse. Franklin looked down at the ground, where the noise seemed to be the strongest. It was black. He could not see his feet. Both shoes had been entirely engulfed by an immense swarm of over-sized flies.

Nefari had indeed found him.

Pivoting around on their stomachs, the three children stuck their heads up high enough to peer over the weeds. There was Franklin. He had not moved since they left, and his expression told them something was wrong, although the children could not see anything immediately threatening him. About five guards were talking with the slave who had screamed, probably questioning him. It wouldn't be long before these slave drivers went around the mountain of dirt to find Franklin.

"Man, Franklin needs to get his butt out of there, like now!" Rufus said.

"Does it look to you guys like he's struggling to move?" Shad asked.

Sami grabbed the binoculars from Shad's bag and used them to look at Franklin. Not wanting to believe what she saw, she said slowly, unsteadily, "Something is covering the bottom of his legs. Something black, like mud, or—"

Rufus finished her sentence, "Darkness. It's the Darkness he told us about."

Franklin swatted at the flies, but that chased them away only momentarily before they returned to the rest of the swarm. The wicked insects wrapped around his lower legs like shackles and wouldn't allow him to move an inch, no matter how hard he struggled. The number of flies seemed to be ever increasing, and he finally saw that they were pouring out of a small opening in the hill of loose dirt, which he stood next to.

Within a few seconds, the flies had multiplied to what must have been hundreds of thousands, and they had now buried Franklin up to his waist. They battled and bit each other, trying to squirm their way to his tender skin. Some had crawled up the cuff of his jeans and were inside his pant leg. The sensation of countless tiny wings beating against his skin felt like needles and brought him to the verge of screaming.

But he remembered his friends hiding in the field, not too far out, and he knew that any cry he uttered would put them in danger of being discovered by the overseers.

He now understood that using the abilities he had was dangerous in this realm ruled by his father. It was starting to make sense to him why. It brought father and son closer together. When he used his powers against the Chenoo in the woods, he thought he could almost feel someone other than himself with him, helping him.

Bramfasa.

Using his abilities here on Dark Earth was changing him, like Sami had said. If he continued to use them, this evil might consume the only half of him that was human. He would end up being just like his father. And he had promised her...

But there was no choice right now. Being a prisoner in his father's realm was not a better option, and that was assuming Nefari wasn't going to just murder him, anyway.

Franklin glared at the swarm of insects covering him. Concentrated. There it was, the incredible pain again, the tingling. Then a stir of energy began to pulsate from behind his eyes; his eyes which had already begun to take on their orange shine.

He found himself suddenly full of unexplained rage, hatred for all things. Disgust. But before his pent up fury could be released and directed onto the swarming pestilence of insects that was Nefari, everything went black. He couldn't see. The swarm had covered his face like a mask, and his energy focus was lost.

In the next instant, his entire body disappeared inside the massive horde of misery.

Like in a nightmare, Sami watched as her best friend was swallowed up to his chest by the swarm of flies. She had to do something! As she got up to run to Franklin's aid, Shad reached out and grabbed her arm. "Hold on, Sami. You need to stay here."

"Let me go, Shad!" she cried. "I'm going to help him!"

"You'll get yourself killed! Sami, I promised him I wouldn't let you, or any of us, make any more daring rescue attempts that would put our lives in jeopardy."

"Well, *I* didn't promise him. Let me go!" she demanded, trying to take Shad's hand off of her.

He tried reasoning with her. "Between the Chenoos and the other monsters over there, not to mention that swarm of flies, which we know is Nefari, you would never make it, Sami!"

She looked pleadingly at her other friend who was hiding with them. It was an unspoken request, and Rufus knew it was up to him to cast the tie-breaking vote.

He shook his head slowly but decisively. "I promised him too, Sami. I told him I would protect you if it came down to it."

While they argued, Nellie slipped out from the tall grass and ran towards Franklin.

Flies were forcing their vibrating bodies past Franklin's closed lips and into his mouth; he had already swallowed several, but more kept coming, finding their way to the back of his throat, cutting off his oxygen supply. Some were digging down into his closed eyelids, trying to reach the treasures that lay behind the thin, protective skin. Franklin took two blind steps and stumbled, falling into the dirt. Some of the flies were thrown off of him upon impact with the ground, but they immediately returned to the spot where they had been, as if on an invisible elastic string.

Unsure what to do now, Franklin started rolling around on the ground, like a person on fire trying to extinguish the flames. This managed to throw more of the flies off, even crushing some. Using his hands like shovels, he then scraped away great quantities of the vile pests from his eyes, allowing him to see for a moment before they regained their wings and came back.

But then, as fast as they had swarmed him, the flies were off of him, only the ones coating his eyes persisted. He remained on the ground, trying to recover his strength when he heard directly above him Nefari's serpentine voice spew forth, "Ssssso good to sssssee you, Franklin. I wassss beginning to wonder if I should ever encounter you again."

"What do you want?" Franklin asked, still trying to wipe the flies away from his eyes so that he could see his enemy.

Nefari towered above him, the humidity of the day glistening on his smooth, featureless face. "The ssssame thing I have alwayssss wanted," his nemesis retorted. "You, dead."

Franklin countered, "I guess you didn't get the news. My father wants me alive now."

"Oh really? No, I didn't get the newsssss, sssssso, I cccertainly can't be exxxpected to allow sssssuch a deplorable outcome," Nefari taunted him. "Your father will undersssstand, I'm sure. If he doessssn't, well, maybe it'ssss time to sssssee him try hisss sssstrength againssssst the mosssst powerful SsstyJeen on Dark Earth."

Nefari had been working on other techniques of summoning his Dire Wolf that did not involve ripping or biting off his own appendages; that specific method was inconvenient as well as incredibly humiliating. He opened wide the hole in his face that served as a mouth, and after gagging and retching, a steady stream of black jelly oozed forth. Part of his dark soul. This amorphous substance took shape on the ground where it was spewed, and it formed into Radulf, his lone surviving wolf.

The Dire Wolf sat on its haunches, looking up at its master and waiting for a command. Franklin cleared away the flies just long enough to see the wolf before the insects were able to block his vision again.

"Why don't you call your swarm off of my eyes and let me take a good look at you. Fight like a man…" he paused, "or a pile of black sludge, whatever you are," Franklin said, daring to taunt Nefari back.

No response came from the StyJeen, and Franklin continued, "It looks like you only have one wolf now. Did something happen to the other cuddly fellow?"

Nefari still didn't answer, then, "Yessss, your father took Bardulf from me. I *will* take my wolf back, and then I will feed Bramfassssa to both of my wolvessss."

Franklin decided to keep it going, "Sounds like there's a little feud between you and Daddy. Are you planning a revolution on Dark Earth or something?"

"Enough!" Nefari screamed. "Radulf, go tear off that boy'sss armssss!"

The wolf, only a short leap from Franklin, bent his hind legs to make the jump, but before he could take flight, he was knocked over sideways by a charging streak of black fur. Nellie had made her move, coming to Franklin's rescue, and although a large dog, she was still only a fraction of the size of Radulf.

Nevertheless, her momentum provided enough force to knock the Dire Wolf off of its feet and send it flying towards Nefari.

"What issss thissss pathetic creature?" Nefari asked, looking with utter disdain at Nellie, who was growling as savagely as she ever had. Her lips curled as she showed Nefari every tooth in her mouth.

The faceless fiend reached his hand towards Nellie, but quicker than a blink, the dog launched itself, jaws first, into the air and took a hold of his greasy palm, ripping the hand from his wrist.

"Again?" Nefari screamed.

By now, the devil wolf had shaken itself off and was up again, lunging himself at Nellie's throat. Nellie, sensing more than actually seeing the coming onslaught, met Radulf's teeth, instead, with her own open jaws and clamped down on the wolf's lower muzzle. The two tumbled to the ground, and Franklin could hear the feral snarling and gnashing of teeth as they fought.

Nefari casually picked up his hand, looked at it without interest, and mumbled, "Sssstupid animal."

In that brief window of opportunity, Franklin, who had finally managed to wipe away the insects from his eyes long enough so that he could get his bearings, rolled his whole body over twice, bowling into Nefari's legs. This caused the StyJeen to fall to the ground, and immediately, Franklin pounced on top of him and tried pinning his arms down.

But this amount of contact with the being of pure evil shot a streak of agony through both his body and spirit, and suddenly his mind's eye became a movie projector, playing out scenes from his life. The loneliest, most brutally painful events he had ever experienced surged into his consciousness as if they had just happened.

He saw his birth mom, Marigold, from the viewpoint of his own infant eyes, pick him up and glare at him, not with tenderness as a mom should, but with disgust, and then hand him back to another to hold. He felt the terror as he flew out of his mom's swerving car, still in his car seat, then felt himself bounce along the unforgiving pavement. Then again, he had to experience the utter hopelessness that he had felt after his mom had been taken from him, leaving him desolate and abandoned.

With his soul being tormented by the past, and a tsunami of pain welling up throughout his arms and chest from holding down Nefari, Franklin was unable to retain his consciousness any longer, and he collapsed to the dirt.

CHAPTER FORTY-SEVEN
A CAGE & A CADAVER

Sami, Shad, and Rufus watched from their hiding place as Nefari stood over Franklin, who was desperately trying to swipe at something covering his eyes. They saw the black Dire Wolf form upwards from the ground and make its move towards their friend, and then they gasped as Nellie sent her body hurling into the drooling mongrel, knocking him over.

"We have to go and help Franklin!" Sami screamed at her friends, and with that, she gave one final twist and pull, finally freeing her arm from Shad's hand. Before he could regain his grasp, she had jumped up and was already on her way to Franklin.

Shad and Rufus also bolted from where they hid, chasing after Sami, whom they had vowed to Franklin they would protect. He had brought this request to them privately, earlier that morning, when they had stopped to rest in the field, and Sami had been busy giving Nellie some water.

With a great bit of poor timing, the loud raucous created by the two canines had attracted the attention of a pair of nearby guards, two Cave Goblins that had hung back to torment the slave who had screamed at Sami. The agitated guards, both clad in shining armor, and one being of greater size than the other, came running to see what was creating the bedlam. As they rounded the corner of the dirt ridge, they practically ran into Sami. Dropping his whip to the ground, the smaller of the two guards grabbed her by an arm and jerked her to him.

An instant later, Rufus and Shad, trailing right behind Sami, had to slide to a stop in the dirt to keep their momentum from carrying them into the back of the guards. One of them had its lanky arms wrapped around Sami's waist as she screamed wildly. By the look of question on his face and drool coming from his mouth, it seemed that he was trying to decide whether to eat her now or share her with the others later.

The larger Cave Goblin stood in front of the one who held Sami. He carried no whip or other weapons in his hand but had a small hatchet fastened to his waist. He seemed to be a captain or chieftain over the other, and he made the quick decision for the smaller one by screaming to a different guard, one who had started running towards them.

"Rujin, bring the cage, now!" he ordered at the top of his gruff voice. He then turned back and said to the lesser goblin in front of him, "We will *all* feast on it, Jojin. Don't even think of feeding on it now unless you also want to be part of our meal."

Jojin, the goblin who held Sami, glowered resentfully back at his captain but refrained from tearing into his prisoner just yet. The two boys, still laying at the feet of the chieftain, looked up in terror as the hulking green creature bent down and grabbed both of them by their feet, snatched them up in the air, and slung each one over a shoulder.

Sami was not going to be taken easily and shouted, "Let me down you deformed oaf, you pile of rancid cow manure!" Her fingernails dug deep into the tough flesh of Jojin, who slapped her head in an effort to stop her.

A cage was brought out directly by the guard named Rujin, who was a ZiShan, a guard of lower standing because of its low intelligence. Like the Usher who had escorted Nefari earlier to Quietus Tumulus, the seven-foot tall creature looked like a cross between a saggy-faced troll and a furry gorilla. Using irregular tugs, it pulled the metal crate behind it with a rope of twisted weeds and hemp. Then, while using its thick fingers to untie the knot that held the cage, it spoke slowly, "Here Juma, here cage. You gonna share humans with me? Never saw live ones here before. My mouth water."

Juma barked back at the ZiShan, "No! Not for you, dimwit! Jojin and I are dividing the meat on these humans with some of the other guards later." He snatched the cage from Rujin, who looked dejectedly away from him.

Rujin mumbled under his breath, "You not allowed to eat them. We ordered to bring live humans to JinJin."

Juma looked at Rujin with agitated revulsion as he asked, "What did you say?"

The ZiShan turned back to Juma, an ounce of courage in him now, as he repeated, "You not allowed to kill live humans. Not for us to do. I tell JinJin."

JinJin was the supervisor of the slave camp and reported directly to Bramfasa.

Satisfied and somewhat proud of himself, Rujin began ambling back the way he had come.

The rusted ax that had dangled at Juma's belt was now in his hand, and before Rujin had taken three steps from him, Juma lifted it up high, for the ZiShan was almost a half a foot taller than he was, and brought it down on the tattletale's head, embedding it in his skull. The troll toppled to the ground.

"What Jinjin doesn't know, won't hurt him. Besides, I'm hungry," Juma said. Reaching down, he put his foot on the fallen beast's hairy face for leverage and pulled the ax from its head. Blood covered the blade, and before he put it back in his belt, he brought it to his mouth and slurped the gore from it like he was eating a slice of grapefruit.

Looking at Jojin, Juma commanded, "Throw Rujin's body in the cage with the human children. He can be part of our feast."

In the meantime, Nellie and Radulf had carried their death brawl farther out into the field. Nellie, who was physically no match for Radulf, had taken her share of deep gouges from the bites and slashes of the Dire Wolf. This was all a part of her strategy, sustaining painful injuries in exchange for leading the wolf away from its master. Her instincts told her that the Dire Wolf, which was made from the essence of the StyJeen, was not at its peak strength unless it was in close proximity to Nefari.

The cage was a small, six-foot-square enclosure with a hinged metal door. Tired of her unrelenting hollering, Jojin heaved Sami through the door of the cage like a sack of grain, wherein she tripped over the uneven floor and went sailing head first into the bars on the opposite side. Her screaming stopped suddenly, and she made no noise at all as she lay on the floor. Juma then swung both Shad and Rufus by their feet through the cage door. As they sailed into the small space, their bodies battered against the cell's ceiling, and they landed sprawled out on the floor, Rufus on top of Shad. They sat upright, just an instant before the ZiShan's dead body came flying at them through the door, knocking them both back down. The rusty door was slammed shut and locked from the outside.

The two boys tried with all of their strength to scoot the dead weight off of them, while wiggling and squirming out from under the rancid smelling body at the same time. Finally, they were able to free themselves from the corpse, and they used their feet to push it as far from them as possible. Which wasn't very far.

Clearly, this oversized gerbil cage was used regularly to hold meals for the brutish slave drivers. Inside the cage, it reeked of stale urine and fear, the fear of desperate animals that had been held captive previously inside of it. The three children could barely fit into the cage by themselves, and with the massive troll's body, it was almost impossible to move at all. Sami remained on the floor, silent and motionless, her eyes closed.

"Hey…hey, is she all right?" Rufus frantically asked Shad, who was checking Sami's neck for a pulse.

"I don't know. Her head is bleeding quite a bit, but she has a slow pulse," Shad answered quietly.

In between the rusted metal bars, the two boys, now on their knees, could see the smaller goblin named Jojin turn its attention towards Franklin, who had only just moments ago fallen from his position on top of Nefari.

"Franklin, watch out!" Rufus warned his friend.

Juma, the one in charge, came over and started to rattle the cage. "Shut up, you filthy humans!" He wrapped his burly hands around the bars and shook the cage harder, laughing wickedly as the boys lost their balance and toppled over again.

As Jojin approached Franklin, he saw that the scene had changed from what it was only seconds ago. It had gone from a wrestling match between two people, to the boy now laying on the ground, covered in a dark slime, struggling to get up. In fact, the tall man without a face had disappeared altogether.

Seeing another easy meal, Jojin stomped over to Franklin, reached down and pulled him up by the arm. The slime had already painted most of Franklin's body so that he looked like he had fallen into a vat of dirty grease, but now the blackness reached out, covering the span of ten inches to Jojin's nearest thigh. It latched onto the goblin, leaving Franklin behind, and flowed over and up into the space underneath the body armor on Jojin's leg.

The goblin began convulsing, jumping around like he was practicing a ritualistic dance, all the while shrieking in pain. He tore at his armor, and with some difficulty, was able to get the leg plates off.

Juma heard his comrade's cries, saw his awkward dance, and though the larger goblin was annoyed, he walked over to see what on Dark Earth was the matter with him. But by the time he had taken the fifteen steps to get there, the lower half of Jojin's body had been devoured by the black slime, leaving only some bigger bones and a few of the more durable ligaments. Jojin, without any muscle or meat on his legs to hold him up, collapsed onto the ground. The chief goblin quickly backed away, fearful of being the next victim of the starved sludge. In his long life, he had seen the grim work of a StyJeen only twice, this time included, and wanted nothing to do with this powerful, Dark Earth entity.

Nefari continued to work his way underneath the goblin's chest armor, going up his torso, and finally seeping out from under the top of his metal body plate, right beneath the neck of what was once Jojin.

The black ooze, now finished with the festivities, flowed off from the dead guard's body and coated the ground around him. Juma came over, keeping a safe distance from the slime, and with a good-length spear he had retrieved, he poked at the body of the lower ranking guard.

"Jojin? You alive?" he asked.

In response to the poking, the dead goblin's chest armor collapsed inward, with nothing to support it except some half-ruined ribs.

Franklin lay on the ground, still unconscious. Nefari had chosen not to consume the boy when his dark essence had covered him. Not yet, anyway. Nefari slithered towards Franklin's lifeless body, once again. As he did, he slowly morphed back into his human form. Juma gave one look at the faceless man, who opened his mouth wide and hissed wickedly at him, and backed up so that he was behind the cage.

Nefari bent down to take a hold of Franklin's limp body but was interrupted by a bothersome human voice.

"Leave him alone, you freak!" Rufus had yelled at the top of his lungs.

This little misshapen human was calling him names? Nefari straightened himself back up and turned around. "Me, a freak? Aren't you the overweight boy that criessss in your bed every night as you ssssqueeze an old worn sssslipper tight, drifting off into your lonely dreamssss?" He scoffed. "You're a bald, fat, little human nobody."

Rufus looked hurt and somewhat shocked. "Hey, how did you…? I've had that slipper since I was little! And that was before I had these guys as my friends, so you keep your nasty hands off of him!"

"Rufus, knock it off," Shad mumbled quietly. "You want him to come over here, too?"

Juma, still hiding near the cage, rapped on the bars with his massive hand, slapping Rufus across the face in the process. "Shut up, meat!" he ordered.

He then went around to the other side of the cage and put his hands onto the bars again, but this time he leaned into it with all his weight and strength, and using his feet as leverage, began pushing the small jail cell, containing all three children and the dead troll, back into the confines of the slave camp.

Helpless, Shad and Rufus looked back as the StyJeen bent down to grasp their unconscious friend.

Franklin was on his own, and so were they.

"I really don't like how I think this ends," said Shad.

The cage was shoved past hundreds of slaves in the middle of their futile labor, and the boys saw the slave that Sami had tried to help, glaring at them as they passed him by, something like a smirk on his face. Rufus and Shad knew now that these slaves, who had once been human, were only shells of their former selves.

Juma guided the cage to the center of the work camp and left it to sit where the Cave Goblins, Chenoos, ZiShans, and other trolls paused in their abuse of the workers long enough to come over and taunt the three children.

As they looked in through the bars, some drooled over the tender meat they saw. They all hoped to get even just a small taste of these humans, who unlike the slaves they beat into submission all day, were still alive and had flavor. A flavor with a sweetness that they craved.

Shad leaned down to see if Sami had made any improvement yet. He felt for her breath, which was very slight, and her pulse, still slow. Slumping down against the cage bars, he thought with all of his might, racked his brain, trying to come up with any way to get out of this highly problematic situation.

CHAPTER FORTY-EIGHT
A BLEAK ENDING *BUT* A
BLACK SPECK

With the other humans gone now, as well as those brainless goblins, there was nothing to distract him anymore, and Nefari reached down and lifted Franklin up, dragging him by his armpits to the base of the dirt mound from where he had first emerged. Out in the field, he heard the sharp yelp of a dog in pain. Radulf was going to get his meal soon. He knew the boy's dog would not last long against his Dire Wolf, and that his wolf would almost certainly want to eat the dog afterward. For that reason, he would have to come back and retrieve Radulf later, after he dealt with this boy, this son of Bramfasa.

Another yelp, this time more prolonged. Probably the final death cry of the mutt.

With some effort, the lanky Nefari sat down and crossed his legs. He laid Franklin, who was still in a deep comatose state, next to him in the dirt. Then, grabbing his shoulders, the StyJeen positioned the boy so that his head rested up on Nefari's own lap. He ran his creaseless, pale fingers through Franklin's hair. "Oh Franklin, Franklin. We both knew thissss time would come," he said arrogantly. "But I have waited far too long. I need to do thissss now."

Saying that, Nefari took his hand from atop Franklin's head and gently ran two of his fingers down the smooth cheek of the boy. He brought them back up his cheek, past his mouth, along the side of his nose, and then raised his palm, keeping his fingers poised on Franklin's face. With a gleeful cry, he violently twisted his fingers downwards, directly under Franklin's eye, into the soft tissue. In his sleep, the boy whimpered, then moaned at the intense pain. His head jerked back and forth in spastic movements. But he did not wake up, so he did not resist.

Nefari dug deep down, then curved his fingers upward, like he was scooping peanut butter from a jar, and plucked the beautiful lavender-tinted eyeball from its socket. Franklin's twitching and cries of pain lessened and moments later, stopped altogether.

The monster held up the eyeball like a trophy, and the edges of his mouth turned upward into a horrific smile. He threw the gumball-sized sphere into the air, and before it had time to even start its plummet to the ground, his black tongue darted from his mouth, snatched the eye in midair, and slurped it down. He hadn't eaten it but was merely keeping it in a safe place.

Then he held his pointer finger over the sizable wound now gaping on Franklin's face. He steadied it there until bits of black ooze dribbled out from under his fingernail and fell into the open socket. Franklin's skin started smoldering, and again he cried out in his sleep. The smell of sizzling human flesh brought Nefari's mind back to happier times, back to when he had free reign on Mortal Earth, before Bramfasa had been Lord.

As the sludge burned Franklin's flesh, it seared the wound shut and stopped any further bleeding.

Nefari waited patiently for the boy to wake up from the state of oblivion he had been cast into. He wanted Franklin to be fully aware of his present condition and circumstances. Finally, the boy's remaining eye fluttered open and shut, open and shut, until it finally remained wide open.

Looking up at the orange sky above him, Franklin immediately noticed something was off about his vision. His right eye! He couldn't open it! Was it swollen shut? He was suddenly aware of an acute ache originating from this closed eye; a dull, but harassing pain. He had a very faint memory of a nightmare, an agonizing nightmare, where his eye had been... been what?

Before he had a chance to reach up and see what might be wrong with his eye, he saw the sickening countenance of Nefari's face looking down upon him. His head was resting on this demon's lap! He sat up in a flash and scooted away.

Franklin's face, as deformed as Nefari had made it, became even more distorted as he spoke, "Where are my friends? What have you done with them you sick, twisted, slimeball? Where's my dog?" His voice had a combination of anger, sadness, and fear about it.

"Well," Nefari put his hand to his chin and pretended to think, then he pointed into their air four times as he said, "Hmmm, oh, I know. Dead, dead, dead and dead. All dead."

Somehow, seeing this awful creature mock him brought to Franklin's mind a childhood holiday special on television, called *How the Grinch Stole Christmas,* right after the creepy character in the show had stolen a whole town's worth of presents. Crazy things run through your head in the most desperate of situations.

"You murdered them?" Franklin screamed at him.

"Oh, I didn't have to. Thosssse hungry goblinsss, ogresss, and trollsssss in the work fieldsss behind ussssss did that for me."

Nefari was enjoying the moment. It was his victory. Not only was Franklin missing one of his eyes, the source of his power, but the boy was also beyond despondent and close to completely breaking.

Franklin sank his forehead down into his palms, ready to sob. But when his fingers spread out to support his head, one of them brushed by the rough, still-tender crater of where his eye used to be.

No!

What Franklin had thought was only a nightmare, or an appalling hallucination, was as real as the monster in front of him.

It wasn't just swollen shut; his right eye was gone.

Open socket.

Burned flesh.

Nefari had carried through with what he had said he would do.

Seeing that Franklin had just discovered what happened while he slept, Nefari said, "Don't worry. I'll take your other eye later ssssso that they match, but for now, we need to leave."

He spoke coldly, matter-of-factly. There would be an army coming after him soon, so there was no more time to enjoy this moment. No more time to ridicule this wholesome, pure, and disgustingly good boy. He could do that later too, before he ripped his soul from him.

"I'll kill you!" Franklin screamed at the top of his lungs. He glared at the creature with one empty crater and one eye that had lost the sparkle it once had. Despite his threat, Franklin didn't attempt to attack the StyJeen again. It had brought too much pain to him the last time.

Nefari laughed at this threat, and his body shook with his emphatic cackles. His mocking laughter didn't stop, and soon he was in such stitches that his whole frame trembled violently, so violently that it splintered and crumbled into a million tiny pieces of Darkness. Somehow the shrieks of laughter continued; his wicked chortles hanging in the air even after his human form had completely wasted away.

No sooner had these shards scattered over the earth around Franklin, then they started to wiggle and writhe and then split down the middle, allowing a black fly to escape from inside each one. Some of the bigger fragments had been holding two of the black winged vermin, and they burst forth as a duo from their cell. The flies, upon their release, took no time at all to converge together as a single, great, dancing swarm. The swarm began to arrange itself in such a way that it seemed to Franklin like each fly had memorized a blueprint of whatever form it was they were creating.

This display sickened Franklin, and he had to look away. But even looking away, he could not avoid the swarm, for the army of flies had blocked the sun and cast a nefarious shadow next to him. The shadow took on a life of its own, in the manifestation of a coiled serpent, which loomed before and above him. As the hooded head of the serpent swayed back and forth, preparing to strike, something changed in Franklin.

He gave up. It was over.

He opened his arms wide and looked up to the sky, not to Nefari's flies, but to the wicked sun, and cried out in despair, "I surrender!"

A thin wisp of a tongue flicked from the serpent-shadow's mouth. It saw his anguish and took advantage of the moment, striking with quickness and precision. As the serpent struck, the league of black flies swarmed once again over Franklin.

This time he had no will to defend himself or offer up any struggle at all. Even the idea of using his remaining eye to call upon powers didn't enter his thoughts, so distraught was his soul. Darkness was consuming both his mind and spirit.

As they converged on him this time, some of the flying vermin formed themselves into long bands, which wrapped around his wrists like handcuffs, and although they were individual insects, they seemed to solidify into a solid, connected state, much like a rubberized material.

He watched as the remaining flies, like trained animals in a flea circus, assembled themselves into two colossal, black wings, spanning at least six feet in either direction. These expansive wings at first flailed and flopped in the air as the insects adjusted their timing with each other, but after a while, they flapped in concert, creating a steady rhythm, a constant, fluid motion.

Nothing was strange to Franklin anymore, and this turn of events certainly didn't surprise or even scare him, for it seemed to him that just about everything on Dark Earth had wings, anyway.

Almost in a state of craze, he hollered at the wings, "Real creative, you freak! Wings? Couldn't you have thought of something a little more sinister than this?"

In response, the wings flapped with more intensity and finally lifted Franklin into the air. He hung helplessly by the black shackles that cuffed his wrists. The featherless and far-stretching wings ascended into the sweltering midday sky.

Franklin let his head swing down; his one eye remained open, staring blankly at the ground. The mangled socket still ached horribly.

It didn't matter anymore, though.

As he dangled from his shackles, Franklin's wrists and shoulders began to ache severely from supporting the entirety of his weight. He struggled to breathe; inhaling was painful in the position he was in. His lungs were collapsing, and the air was thin up here, anyway. If he was carried in this manner for long,

He was a failure. His three friends would be dead as soon as those beasts guarding the camp became hungry. He would never be able to help his mom now, and his dog had died trying to protect him.

But something was pestering him, harassing his brain....

What? He opened his eye again, and he looked down.

Yes. The fleck of black was smaller now, as the wings had carried him farther away, but he could still see it.

There was something different about the speck in the field, the one which was pursuing them. As it moved, Franklin could see that surrounding it was a faint, pink glow.

Because of the pure evil from which the Dire Wolf had been formed, only a black shine, if any, would ever surround its body.

That meant one thing… somehow his dog had done it! The speck chasing after them was Nellie! The other black mass, the one lying motionless in the field, was the demon wolf that Nefari had called Radulf. Nellie had gone against a larger, stronger, more ferocious opponent, and she had taken it down.

At that moment, the Darkness that had almost completely engulfed Franklin's soul stopped just short of ruining him forever.

It had been blocked by a formidable adversary; Hope.

Darkness was not able to defile anything with even the smallest amount of hope remaining, and his dog had just given him a good-sized dose of it. Nellie had somehow defeated pure evil. Which meant he had to try, too.

He wasn't finished. Not yet, anyway.

Then, behind Franklin's only eye, he felt the steady thump of a pulse, which soon changed into a familiar tingle. And where his other eye had been, beneath the blistered flesh, there, too, stirred a peculiar prickle.

Hope can do funny things.

To Be Continued...

his bones would either snap or he would suffocate. What did it matter? It was over.

The Darkness in him was overwhelming. This must have been what Nefari meant by taking his soul. Was he going to be like one of those slaves in the field he'd seen?

He couldn't fight this hopeless feeling, it was easier to just let Darkness have its way.

The wings found a current to hang onto, and they carried him off in a northerly direction, traveling slowly, staying no more than twenty feet above the ground.

Not because he was looking, but because the slave camp below him was so large that it entered his fixed gaze, he could see tens of thousands of slaves digging meaningless holes. His curiosity caused him to lift his head a bit so that he could take in more. The camp stretched much farther than he had thought, covering at least a square mile. From the look of it, the slaves had been divided into four separate camps, with a wall between each of them. This was probably to help control them more effectively if they ever decided to fight back. From what he had seen from the slave that Sami tried to help earlier, though, he couldn't imagine that these walking corpses would ever resist their masters.

He and his friends had only seen a very small section of the camp, and that section was directly beneath him now. It was from here that he heard the sound of creatures yelling, some sort of commotion taking place. Franklin wanted to see what was happening; he felt that it somehow held importance to him.

There seemed to be something going on right in the center of the camp. Then he noticed a cage, which many of the slave masters were gathered around. Some were banging on the bars, others just laughing. He saw one throwing a fistful of dirt at the prisoners it held.

This caused one of the bigger guards to turn towards the creature who had done this and scream, "We want them clean, you moron! Are we scavengers? Now you need to wash them before we feast!"

A fight broke out between the two, and many of the burly overseers decided to move several paces away and watch the brawl.

He didn't need to see them. Franklin knew who was in the cage and how scared they must be. He knew it was his fault. It was *all* his fault, and now he couldn't do anything to help them. They weren't dead yet, but they would be soon.

As he continued to be carried away, the heartbreaking scene of the cage became smaller and smaller, and in a very quiet whisper, he said, "Goodbye, Sami. Goodbye Shad and Rufus."

Breathing was becoming increasingly harder for him.

He finally turned away and looked toward the field on the other side of him. There was the hill. Cast Maker Canyon. Where he had first entered this awful parallel Earth. He could see the rocks jutting out from the sloped ground, and he could identify the boulder that he had been leaning against with his broken leg, when Nefari had almost succeeded in killing him. It had only been several days ago, but it seemed like a lifetime away. Thinking back, he wished he had just died then. He wished he had just given up.

That's when he noticed a black speck, motionless in the field. When he tried to look closer at it, he saw that there was a second black speck, this one moving. Running! It acted like it was trying to keep up with the wings that were carrying him away.

His heart sank even lower if that was possible. This confirmed what Nefari had said. His dog Nellie was also dead. She was the unmoving black speck lying in the field. And Nefari's wolf was following them.

Franklin closed his remaining eye, but that couldn't stop the flood of tears that rushed down his cheek and fell to the field below.

He was a failure. His three friends would be dead as soon as those beasts guarding the camp became hungry. He would never be able to help his mom now, and his dog had died trying to protect him.

But something was pestering him, harassing his brain….

What? He opened his eye again, and he looked down.

Yes. The fleck of black was smaller now, as the wings had carried him farther away, but he could still see it.

There was something different about the speck in the field, the one which was pursuing them. As it moved, Franklin could see that surrounding it was a faint, pink glow.

Because of the pure evil from which the Dire Wolf had been formed, only a black shine, if any, would ever surround its body.

That meant one thing… somehow his dog had done it! The speck chasing after them was Nellie! The other black mass, the one lying motionless in the field, was the demon wolf that Nefari had called Radulf. Nellie had gone against a larger, stronger, more ferocious opponent, and she had taken it down.

At that moment, the Darkness that had almost completely engulfed Franklin's soul stopped just short of ruining him forever.

It had been blocked by a formidable adversary; Hope.

Darkness was not able to defile anything with even the smallest amount of hope remaining, and his dog had just given him a good-sized dose of it. Nellie had somehow defeated pure evil. Which meant he had to try, too.

He wasn't finished. Not yet, anyway.

Then, behind Franklin's only eye, he felt the steady thump of a pulse, which soon changed into a familiar tingle. And where his other eye had been, beneath the blistered flesh, there, too, stirred a peculiar prickle.

Hope can do funny things.

To Be Continued…